KATHRIN TORDASI

BRAMBLE

FOX

TRANSLATED FROM THE GERMAN
BY CATHRIN WIRTZ

PUSHKIN CHILDREN'S

Pushkin Press
Somerset House, Strand,
London WC2R 1LA

Original text © 2020 Fischer Kinder- und Jugendbuchverlag GmbH,
Frankfurt am Main

English translation © Cathrin Wirtz

Bramble Fox was first published as *Brombeerfuchs. Das Geheimnis
von Weltende* by Fischer Kinder- und Jugendbuchverlag GmbH,
in Frankfurt am Main, 2020

First published by Pushkin Press in 2022

1 3 5 7 9 8 6 4 2

ISBN 13: 978-1-78269-345-1

Designed and typeset by Tetragon, London
Printed and bound by Clays Ltd, Elcograf S.p.A.

www.pushkinpress.com

For Erika Grams
& Wolfgang Gramps

Contents

Characters

HUMANS

Benjamin Rees	*Boy from Trefriw, Wales*
Portia Beale	*Girl from London, Viola's grand-niece*
Olivia Stephen, *Bramble*	*Author, Viola's partner*
Viola Evans, *Rose*	*Editor, Portia's mum's aunt*

FAIRIES

Titania	*The Fairy Queen*
Oberon	*The Fairy King*
Peaseblossom, Cobweb	*Fairies from Titania's royal household*
Pricklethorn	*Titania's Lord Chamberlain*

SHAPESHIFTERS

Robin Goodfellow	*Oberon's troublemaker*

BIRDS

(Welsh: *Adar*)

Ridik ap Mwyalchod	*Scout*
Preet, Tatap	*Scouts*

SALAMANDERS

(Welsh: *Salamandrau*)

Gwil Glumheart	*Scribe and illuminator*
Meralyn Quickly	*Head seamstress*
Tegid Greyfinger	*Librarian*

THE PALE TOWER'S INHABITANTS

Arawn	*The Grey King*
Hermia	*Arawn's Huntress*

Prologue

*L*ong, long ago, humans and fairies could pass back and forth between their worlds effortlessly. The kingdoms of mortals and immortals were as close to each other as the banks of a river, with nothing but an empty stretch of land in between. No one ever gave the Borderlands a thought. But someone sensed every person who passed. And one night he who had been sleeping for a hundred years stirred.

Red autumn leaves fell from the trees as the Grey King rose from his lair. He roamed the in-between world, shrouded in swirling fog. Anyone caught in that fog either vanished without a trace or became a Mistwalker, a creature existing without a single memory of its former self. All at once, those travelling between the worlds had to fear for their lives.

And there was more. The Grey King sent his army into the Human and Fairy Worlds. Pale riders brought the fog with them, making lakes, fields and villages disappear and dissolve into a grey ocean. Eventually, humans and fairies joined forces, and together they pushed the King and his army back into the Borderlands. The fairies put him into a deep sleep—but they could not say how long their enchantment would last.

Exhausted from the battle, humans and fairies made a grave decision. They would seal up the border between their worlds, in the hope that the Grey King would never be able to leave his

Borderlands ever again. And that was what came to pass. The human folk turned to their druids. Those wise women and men used rune magic to close all the doorways to the Fairy World, or Faerie as some call it. From that day onwards, they were locked, and only a handful of chosen ones possessed a key. Those Key Bearers were bound by one rule: if they opened a door leading to the other realm, they must close it as soon as they had crossed over. However, centuries went by, and the memory of the story of the Grey King began to fade into oblivion.

When we came into possession of one of those keys, no one remembered about the rule, or the Grey King for that matter. Unknowingly, we crossed over to Faerie, and for a while, we lived in blissful ignorance.

We left the door open behind us, since no one had told us why it must be closed. When the Grey King returned, no one saw the signs, no one raised an alarm. That morning, when the fog surged from the woods like a storm flood, it was already too late.

OLIVIA STEPHEN,
Stories from the Otherworld (1965)

A Holiday in Wales

The town of Conwy nestled against the coast like a blob of jam inside the curve of a croissant. The houses of the old section stood on a hillside, overlooking the blue bay. Its narrow alleyways lay in the shadow of a castle with the Welsh flag fluttering from its turrets: a red dragon on a green and white base.

At the foot of the castle, a short distance from the ramparts, was the train station. It had two sets of tracks, and a platform so narrow that two adults were barely able to walk down it side by side. Behind the station was a car park, which was as empty as the station itself—except for a brown seagull rooting through the rubbish bins in the hope of finding some lunch.

Portia Beale stood at the entrance to the car park, occasionally glancing down at the note in her hand. Her mother had written down her aunts' address and phone number on a piece of squared paper. "Just in case," she had said. "They'll come and pick you up, so you won't need the number; at least not for now."

Well, Mum, you thought wrong.

She pulled her phone from her pocket, trying to ignore the lump in her throat. No reason to panic. She had taken the train from London to Wales all by herself, so why would she be scared of making a simple phone call? After all, her mother had warned her that the aunts were a tad scatter-brained—perhaps they had simply forgotten that their guest was arriving today.

Portia had already typed in the first three digits when a Nissan car came barrelling noisily into the car park, brakes screeching and exhaust popping, and halted in front of her. The door flew open, and a stocky woman with a short grey plait heaved herself out. Portia's thumb was still hovering over the screen when the woman came stomping towards her, in clumpy green wellington boots.

"Damn and blast it!" she said by way of a greeting. "I really thought I was going to make it in time."

That was Portia's first impression of Aunt Bramble.

Initially Portia and her mother had been planning to spend their summer holidays in Andalusia—but a week before their scheduled departure, her mum had cancelled the trip. Portia had been disappointed, but not particularly surprised. Her mother had been feeling unwell all month. Signs that the holiday wouldn't happen had gathered like storm clouds on the horizon.

Gwendolyn Beale had broken the news to her daughter three days ago. Andalusia was off. Instead, she said, Portia would be spending a fortnight with some relatives in North Wales. Rose was Gwendolyn's aunt and Bramble her partner. They lived in a cottage in the countryside, but had been travelling on and off for years, so Portia hadn't seen them since she was very little. Still, they were really looking forward to her visit. At least that's what Portia's mum had said. Now that Bramble was right in front of her, large as life, Portia wasn't so sure.

"Where on earth is my blasted watch?" said Bramble in a voice as thorny as her namesake, rummaging through her trouser and coat pockets. Portia had no idea how to greet the older woman, so in the end she simply stuck out a hand. "Hello, I'm Portia."

She felt foolish as soon as the words left her mouth, but Bramble paused for the first time since she had jumped out of the car. She looked Portia up and down with a smile on her face, before taking her hand in a firm grip. "I know who you are, girl. Even though I've got to say, you've grown an awful lot since I last saw you."

She produced a battered wristwatch from the depths of a pocket. "Shall we?"

Without waiting for a response, Bramble grabbed Portia's bag and headed back towards her dented grey Nissan. Portia followed, adjusting the straps on her backpack.

"That train's always, always late," Bramble grumbled. "And then today of all days it's on time. Have you been waiting long?"

"No, not really," said Portia, but Bramble didn't seem to be listening anyway. She opened the boot, swore again and pushed aside a big bag of bark mulch to make space for Portia's suitcase.

"Go ahead and get in! Rose is waiting with the tea, and if I don't deliver you on time, she'll do her eyebrow thingy."

"Her what thingy?" Portia asked as she opened the passenger door.

Bramble snorted. "Oh, you'll see, you'll see."

The boot closed with a bang, and before she knew it they were on their way.

The Nissan rattled and clattered so much during the ride that Portia was worried the old rust bucket would fall apart at any moment. Bramble on the other hand didn't seem to be bothered at all. She sped along the narrow streets at a speed that must surely have been over the limit. Portia clasped the backpack on her lap with both hands and nervously watched the stone houses swoosh by outside.

She would have liked to ask Bramble to slow down but didn't dare. In her half-moon glasses, she reminded Portia of the headmistress at her school, even though the tousled grey plait didn't quite fit the image of a strict teacher. Her clothes were what you might charitably call practical: a flowery blouse, a washed-out green cardigan and a faded pair of jeans tucked into her wellies. Portia wondered what Bramble had been up to before she had left the house to pick her up at the train station.

"When we last saw you, you were three years old," Bramble said, hurtling through a roundabout without even touching the brakes. A little gnome dangling from the rear-view mirror bounced frantically up and down. "You probably don't remember, do you?"

"No, I don't, actually," Portia replied. *That gnome must be sick to his stomach*, she thought.

"Well, it would be quite unusual if you did, actually." Bramble rattled over a speed bump. "But I remember you used to love hiding things." She laughed. "Once, you put Rose's shoes in the oven. It must have taken her an hour to find them."

"Um. I'm sorry, I suppose?" Portia stuttered, thrown off guard.

"Not at all!" said Bramble. "I discovered your little hiding place after about ten minutes, but it was simply too much fun to watch Rose searching high and low. We could do it again, but I reckon you're too old for such shenanigans by now, aren't you?"

Portia couldn't help but smile. "I suppose I am."

"What a shame," Bramble sighed. "Music?"

Without waiting for Portia's reply, she turned the radio on. Abba's 'Waterloo' blared from the speakers, and Bramble immediately began humming along. Portia glanced over and noticed that her glasses had slid down to the tip of her nose. In fact, she didn't look like a teacher at all, Portia decided. She was more like an archaeologist who dug up buried treasures or explored pyramids.

The only thing missing is an old leather hat, Portia thought. As if she had read her mind, Bramble glanced over at her and winked—perhaps she wasn't as thorny as Portia had feared after all.

A Thief in the Night

Driving inland from Conwy, the road took them along the edge of the Snowdonia National Park, home to Wales's highest mountains, most beautiful lakes and most of its sheep too. At least that's what Portia's mother had told her. The River Conwy meandered across green meadows like a blue ribbon, and it was true: there was barely a patch of grass not occupied by a grazing sheep. Twenty minutes later, Bramble had steered the old car to a place called Trefriw. Portia tried several times to pronounce the name, but couldn't manage it.

"Trair-vruew," Bramble corrected her. "And if you're having trouble with that, you just wait until we take you to *Llanfairpwllgwyngyllgogerychwyrndrobwllllantysiliogogogoch*."

"Come again?" Portia spluttered.

Bramble repeated the name.

"It's actually the longest place name in the world," she explained. "It roughly translates to *Mary's church resting in a hollow of white hazels near a fierce whirlpool and the church of Thysilio of the red cave*. The Welsh are quite particular when it comes to their names."

"Aren't you from Wales?" Portia asked.

18

Bramble shook her head. "Migrated here from Shropshire. But don't tell anyone." She honked the horn vigorously and waved at a man walking along the side of the road.

"We're almost there now," she promised, before glancing at her watch and stepping on the accelerator even harder. The Nissan roared out of Trefriw, over a stone bridge and past a lush green meadow before entering a little wood of gnarled oaks that pressed up against the road from either side. Then they emerged from the trees, and Portia caught her breath.

The view was stunning—to their right, a beautiful little valley, with a stream running along its bottom, bordered by dark-hued willows; ahead, forest-clad foothills rising to distant, craggy mountaintops.

"Wow," Portia gasped.

Bramble grinned. "Beautiful, but remote," she said. "Don't worry, though. If you take my bike, you'll be in town in no time at all. And Llanrwst isn't far, either."

"Hlun...?" Portia gave it a try.

"Hlan-roost," Bramble repeated. "They've got a little cinema and a bookshop and what have you. So you won't have to be cooped up in the house with us two old bags all the time. Aha, speak of the devil."

Portia peered ahead through the windscreen. An apple orchard appeared at the end of the road, and beyond that, a grey stone house.

"Home sweet home," Bramble proclaimed as she parked under an apple tree. With another glance at her watch, she climbed out of the car. Portia did the same, all the while staring at her aunts' house. She hadn't expected anything as beautiful as this! There was even a conservatory, and a hammock tied between two trees. The aunts must have plenty of green fingers between them, she thought. Flowers flourished all over the garden and along the windowsills. A dog rose climbed up the front wall of the house, and the purple flowers of a clematis cascaded from the porch like a waterfall. Portia wouldn't have been surprised to see Peter Rabbit himself hopping around the garden.

"Are you afraid of dogs?" Bramble asked as she hoisted Portia's luggage from the boot.

"No... Why?" She had barely uttered her question when a black-and-white bullet came shooting towards them.

"Marlowe!" Bramble yelled sharply, but the dog was already jumping around Portia, panting excitedly. He trod on her feet with his paws, pressed his flank against her knees and wagged his tail as if they were the dearest of best friends.

Portia squatted down to scratch Marlowe between his ears. Judging by the way he rested his head on her thighs he liked that.

Bramble shook her head in mock disapproval. "Quite the fierce guard dog, aren't you?"

"Love at first sight, I see."

Portia turned around and looked up to see a woman of about Bramble's age walking towards them with a broad smile on her face, drying her hands on a tea towel. This had to be Rose. She wore glasses too, but unlike Bramble, Rose had short, curly hair, and was quite smartly turned out, in a red blouse and a poppy-patterned skirt. Portia wiped her hands on her jeans, anticipating a handshake. But Rose didn't waste any time with that. Still smiling, she placed both of her hands on Portia's shoulders.

"Portia, my dear," she said. "Just look at you. And look at how much you've grown! We haven't seen each other in far too long. How old were you when we came to visit the last time? Maybe two?"

"Three," Bramble cut in. "And yes, girls usually do a fair bit of growing up over nine years."

"You're late," Rose shot back in reply.

"You should have seen the traffic," Bramble retorted.

"The traffic?" Rose's right eyebrow arched in obvious disbelief. Bramble flashed Portia a meaningful glance.

Ah, Portia thought. *The eyebrow thingy!*

"Terrible traffic," Bramble confirmed without even batting an eye. "All because of those new traffic lights in Tal-y-Cafn. Why they built those things in the first place is beyond me, really." She carried Portia's suitcase towards the garden gate as Marlowe dashed past her and into the house. "On top of which, I had to drive sensibly. After all," she added, "one should never speed when travelling with young passengers, you know."

By now, Portia's red face could have given a ripe tomato a run for its money. She'd never heard anyone lie so smoothly.

"No less than I would expect from a driver as conscientious as you are," Rose said drily. She threw the tea towel over her shoulder and stretched out her hand. To her surprise, Portia glimpsed a tattoo on her wrist: a row of zigzag lines—like the traces of little birds' tracks.

21

"Come along, dear," said Rose. "You can help me set the table."

The house's name was written on a slate above the doorbell: *Afallon*. Portia stepped in through the open door and stopped dead.

The entrance hall was crammed full of stuff: a coat rack, a basket filled with umbrellas and a knee-high elephant made of bronze. A vase filled with lilies and hortensia stood on an old telephone table with a gold-framed mirror hanging on the wall above it.

Portia had never seen that much stuff in one place—other than in a museum. Except that it didn't smell like freshly baked cakes in a museum. She sniffed the sweet air. *Vanilla*, she thought. *And lemon.* She walked slowly into the house and saw the open doors on each side of the hallway.

Perhaps this was the kind of house with secret passages? Great big oil paintings that swung open to reveal hidden doors? Portia's heart was racing. She would have loved to begin exploring all the rooms right away. She stared about her, taking in the walls, ceiling and the dark-brown wooden staircase with ornate banisters that climbed up towards the first floor.

"So, what do you think?" Rose was leaning against the door frame with folded arms. "Can you bear to spend a few weeks with us?"

"Definitely!" Portia blurted out. "Thank you so much for having me."

"Ah, nonsense, we've been looking forward to your visit.

In fact," she continued in a raised voice, "that tea has been looking forward to meeting you for more than an hour."

"You just can't help yourself, can you," Bramble harrumphed, as she edged past Rose and set off up the stairs with Portia's suitcase.

"Your room is upstairs," Rose explained. "But let's have some tea and cake first, shall we?"

"Cake sounds lovely," Portia said immediately.

Rose laughed. "I thought it would!" She pointed to a door to her right. "The living room is through there. Why don't you go ahead while I fetch us some tea from the kitchen?"

Portia shrugged off her backpack, feeling a pleasant tingle under her skin as the weight was lifted, and pushed open the living-room door.

"Amazing," she whispered.

The room was like a magical hollow dug beneath the roots of a tree. The low ceiling was held up by oak rafters and the walls were painted a pastel green. A crimson Persian rug lay on the wooden floorboards between three wing-backed chairs facing a fireplace. But the best part was the books. Shelves crammed full of them, stood against every wall. An open glass door led out to the conservatory. Even out there, Portia could see books piled up on a chaise longue, surrounded by buckets overflowing with greenery, and beautiful plants trailing from hanging baskets above.

Portia was so impressed by all the books that she was unable to take in anything else for a moment. Only on reaching the middle of the room did she realize that she was not alone.

A fox was sitting in the doorway between the living room and the conservatory. The animal looked straight at her, its fur gleaming like copper in the afternoon sun. Portia held her breath, but the fox stayed where it was, watching her with pricked ears and golden, inquisitive eyes. Fascinated, she held its gaze, until she heard a whimpering behind her. She turned around to find Marlowe crouching in the living-room doorway, his head tucked between his paws.

He clearly wasn't a hunting dog, judging by how frightened he looked. The fox, on the other hand, didn't seem to be scared at all. Quite the contrary—it was calmly sizing Marlowe up. Portia even thought she saw it give a cheeky smirk, although of course that wasn't possible.

"Marlowe, old chap," Bramble called from the hallway. "Are you begging for treats again?" A second later she came through the doorway and spotted the fox. "You!" she thundered, the sound of her voice making the fox flinch. "I can't believe it! Get out of here!"

The fox cowered, hesitated, and finally dashed back into the conservatory and out into the garden.

"Don't let me catch you in here again, or I'll make gloves out of you!" Bramble yelled from the open doorway. "Honestly, it's enough to drive a person mad," she said, turning back towards Portia.

"A fox!" Portia said, still in shock, as Bramble came back into the living room.

"Yes. Well, more or less," said Bramble evasively. Her gaze wandered to a closed door next to one of the bookshelves. Marlowe trotted over to her, and she scratched him between his ears, still shaking her head in disbelief. "You got a bit of a fright there, didn't you, boy?"

"What's going on in here?" Rose asked as she came into the living room, carrying a teapot and cups on a tray.

"A fox!" Portia cried. "Right here! In the living room!" It was unbelievable. She had never seen a fox so close up before. "Does that happen often?"

The aunts' house was becoming more exciting by the minute, but Rose didn't seem pleased by the fox's visit either. She flashed Bramble a worried look, but her partner merely tightened her mouth into a thin line in response.

"Welcome to the countryside," Bramble said curtly, pushing Marlowe to one side and taking the tray from Rose's hands.

By the evening, Portia could no longer say which part of the house she loved most. For a while, it was a neck-and-neck race between the kitchen, the conservatory and the living room. In the end, however, she decided it had to be her own room. "We're just down the hall, in case you need anything," said Rose when it was time to go to bed. She gave Portia a hug. "We're so happy you're here."

"So am I," said Portia. The aunts had welcomed her so kindly—now she understood why her mum had always loved spending her summers here in Afallon.

"Sweet dreams," said Rose, turning to go.

"Don't let the dog in!" thundered Bramble from the other end of the hall.

Rose rolled her eyes, yet couldn't help but smile. "Good-night," she said, and Portia wished her the same. When Rose closed the door, Portia finally got to take a good look at her new room.

The guest bedroom wasn't big. In fact it was rather cosy. A reading lamp shaped like a bellflower sat on a table beside her bed, and there was a white wooden chest of drawers for her to put her clothes in. The room was at the rear of the house, and Portia was certain that she'd be able to see the river from her window in the morning.

She turned on the lamp and opened her suitcase. Her pyjamas were right on top. She picked them up, and then stopped short—underneath them lay her mum's favourite poncho. Staring at the carefully folded material, Portia suddenly felt a bit of a lump in her throat. She remembered the last time her mum had worn it.

It was the morning she cancelled their holiday. Portia had been tiptoeing around the flat for the past fortnight, bringing her mum breakfast in the morning and tea in the evening. This routine was nothing new to her. Most of the time Gwen was a cheerful, positive person, but every now and then she would be hit by a wave of sadness. If they were lucky the emotional storm would pass after a few days, but often it would loom overhead for weeks—and that's how it was this time around.

When Portia had walked into the living room that Monday before they were supposed to leave for their trip, Gwen was sitting on the windowsill. She was wearing the poncho, a big purple woollen one. Portia sat down and snuggled up against her mum, who put an arm around her daughter's shoulder. The poncho felt warm and soft against Portia's cheek.

Andalusia isn't happening, I'm afraid, her mother had said quietly.

Disappointment burned in Portia's throat, but she wouldn't let it show. *Never mind*, she had replied. *We'll just go next year.*

Her mum had pulled her into a hug and kissed the top of her head. *My brave Lion-Girl.*

Portia had been sure she'd managed to hide her disappointment from her mum. But now it seemed as if Gwen must have felt it and packed the poncho for her as consolation.

Oh, Mum, thought Portia. She slipped into her pyjamas and wrapped the poncho around her shoulders. The wool smelt faintly of Gwen's perfume. Portia pressed it to her nose and took a deep breath, trying to imagine what her mother was doing right at that moment. She hoped she was feeling better. That she was remembering to make herself breakfast, and perhaps to leave the house every now and then to get some fresh air.

Not for the first time that day, she wondered whether she should've stayed in London. But her mother had insisted that she should have a fun summer holiday. Portia ran her hand over the poncho and trusted that her mum wouldn't miss it too much.

She sighed, turned off the main light and climbed into bed. Kneeling on the duvet, she looked out of the window. Outside, it was already getting dark—too dark to make out anything in the back garden. The stars were hiding behind clouds, and the willows were no more than vague shapes lining the river. But there was something strange, too.

Portia squinted. A shadowy shape was moving across the grass down below. She leant forward. The fox flitted through the beam of light falling from her window, and then disappeared into the shrubbery. Portia frowned. It really was persistent! Could its den be nearby?

Anyway, her feet were getting cold. Portia huddled under the duvet, and fished out of her backpack the book she had started reading on the train. The down crackled softly as she nestled against her pillow, the poncho still wrapped around her shoulders.

Portia had no idea what had woken her up. All she knew was that she was suddenly sitting bolt upright in her bed. It was still pitch black outside. She frowned. So strange! Had she had a nightmare?

She rubbed her eyes. Now that she was awake, she might just as well go to the loo. She had probably overdone it with the third cup of tea, but it had been so satisfying pouring milk into the china cups. Barefoot, she stepped out of her room onto the dark landing and groped blindly along the wall next to the door, but couldn't find the light switch. She was drowsily making her way down the landing when she heard a noise downstairs. She froze. There it was again—the low creaking of a door.

Her eyes had adjusted to the dark by now, and she could make out the outline of the banister. She crept over to the top of the stairs and stood, listening intently. But the house was still. She had just decided that the noise must have been old Marlowe lolloping about, when a shadow flitted past the bottom of the stairs. The fox!

All at once, Portia was wide awake. For a second she considered waking her aunts, but her curiosity won out. She tiptoed down the steps. When she got to the bottom, she could hear noises coming from the living room: a scratching sound at first, followed by the thud of a book hitting the floor. What on earth was that fox up to in there?

Sneaking to the open living-room door, she peeked inside. Blueish moonlight was filtering in through the windows at the other end of the room, but even so Portia could barely make out a thing. All she could see were the dark shapes of the armchairs. The noises were coming from the next room now—the one she hadn't been into yet. She padded across the thick carpet and gave the door next to the bookshelf a gentle push.

She heard the sound of rustling paper. Something was moving in the shadows, rooting around the top of a wooden table—something with a bushy tail.

Portia was still peering into the darkness when she heard paws scrabbling on the floorboards behind her. Then Marlowe bolted past her into the room, barking. The next thing she knew, someone had reached over her shoulder and switched on the lights. Portia's heart skipped a beat—but that was nothing in comparison to the fox's reaction: the instant the lights clicked on, the animal froze, its tail bristling like a bottlebrush. It was standing in the middle of a desk, surrounded by a mess of crumpled paper and open drawers.

"Oh, no, you don't," growled Bramble, who seemed to have appeared from nowhere. She barged past Portia and charged into the study like a warhorse. The fox crouched down, flattened his ears and hissed, but Bramble wasn't fazed. She lunged forward and almost managed to grab the intruder, but the fox was quick. At the very last second it ducked under her arm and shot out of the study as if the devil himself was after it.

Bramble swore. Then they heard a scream coming from the hall. The lights in the living room came on to reveal Rose, her hand on the switch.

"For heaven's sake, what is going on here?" she asked, tying the belt of her dressing gown.

The fox, Portia was about to say, but Bramble beat her to it. "*Crwydriadgoch,*" she blustered in Welsh.

It didn't mean anything to Portia, but Rose looked shocked and did her eyebrow thingy.

"What in the world did he want?" she wondered aloud, clearly astonished.

"To steal something, as usual," snorted Bramble. "That scoundrel will give me a heart attack one day."

"Bramble," Rose said soothingly, but Bramble wouldn't calm down.

"I've had it. The next time he dares to show his face here, I'll get the shotgun from the attic. You know what, actually, give me the phone."

"Who do you want to call at this hour?"

"Pest control? A hunter? How should I know?" roared Bramble.

Marlowe nuzzled his angry mistress's leg, and Rose rubbed her back, making shushing noises until Bramble closed her eyes and took a slow, deep breath.

"I'm too old for this nonsense," she muttered, before starting to clear up the chaos on the desk.

Rose checked her watch. "I'll make some tea. The sun will be up in half an hour, and I'd say we won't be getting any more sleep tonight anyway."

"How did the fox get in, by the way?" asked Portia.

"Oh, I must have forgotten to lock the kitchen door," Rose said breezily. Portia frowned. She distinctly remembered Rose locking the door. And now that she thought about it, she felt certain that the door to the study had been closed as well. Could foxes turn door handles?

Rose went out into the hall, but Portia hung back. Something was going on here, and she needed to ask Bramble about it. But as she came to the study doorway again, she stopped short. Unaware she was being watched, Bramble was bent over the desk, feeling carefully along its edge with her fingertips. What was she up to? Then Portia saw the edge of the desk come away in Bramble's hand. A secret drawer slid out from its hiding place. Bramble took something out, and for a moment Portia saw a silvery object twinkling between her fingers, before she sighed with relief and put the shiny object back in its place.

Curious. Very curious, Portia thought. She tiptoed away before Bramble slid the drawer back into place, but she had memorized the exact spot she needed to push to open it.

Pendragon Books

Ben Rees stood on a ladder, arranging cookbooks on the top shelf of a rather crowded bookcase. The ladder was a bit wobbly, but he was used to it. Steadying himself against the bookcase, he pushed a book into a narrow gap with his free hand.

A few years earlier, his parents had taken over Pendragon Books from his grandfather, painted the shopfront blue and hung a string of lights in the window.

Like his mother, Megan, before him, Ben had grown up in that bookshop. He had learnt to read in the armchair in the back corner. Megan loved to talk about how he had spent hours sitting there, poring over picture books. At first, his legs had been so short they dangled over the seat of the chair.

Ben had been helping in the shop since he was six years old, sorting donated books and dusting shelves. He also drew pictures for the signs on the shelves: little pots for cookbook corner, bloody knives for the crime section, hearts for romance novels and dragons for the fantasy collection.

He didn't exactly *have* to help, but he loved that bookshop, and he could hardly wait to get there after school. The smell of paper, the cracked book spines and the sea of printed words made him feel at home.

The shop wasn't very busy today—no customers apart from the red-haired man, who stopped by from time to time, standing flicking through a novel. Ben was just stepping off the ladder when the bell above the door jingled and his mother called out "*Croeso!*" which means "Welcome" in Welsh.

Ben went over to a pile of boxes filled with books to fetch a few more to add to the shelves. When he came back to cookbook corner, he noticed a girl he'd never seen before in the crime section. Kids didn't wander into the shop all that often. Most of them got their books from the school library, if they read at all. This girl didn't look like she was planning on returning home empty-handed, though. She was about Ben's age, in trainers, jeans and a blue T-shirt with a pink flamingo on the front. Her black hair danced around her freckly face in wild curls.

Ben carried on shelving books, watching the new girl out of the corner of his eye. *What sort of books was she interested in?* he wondered. He got his answer when she pulled a Miss Marple mystery from the shelf. Not his thing. Just then, she glanced over and saw him looking at her. She lowered the book and raised an eyebrow.

Ben spun around as fast as lightning and knelt over one of the boxes. His heart was racing, and he felt angry with himself. *Serves you right*, he thought. *You shouldn't have been staring like that.* He fished a tattered copy of *All My Chickens* from the box but stayed crouched down in his corner, rummaging through the books, hoping that the girl would forget all about him. He was relieved when a few minutes had passed without anyone speaking to him. But then he heard his mum's voice.

"Ben? Come over here, would you?"

Ben turned around, and his heart sank into his trainers. His mother was behind the counter and the curly-haired girl was waiting in front of it.

Great. Ben knew exactly what would happen next. He went over to the counter, hoping his nervousness didn't show on his face.

"This is my son, Ben," said Megan, beaming from ear to ear. "Ben, this is Portia. She's spending her summer holiday at Afallon."

The girl smiled at him. He could feel his face turning red, his cheeks burning. He hated these moments.

Megan was constantly trying to set him up with other children. She meant well, of course—she was just worried that Ben spent too much time by himself. He didn't play football or go to birthday parties. It wasn't even that the other kids were deliberately excluding him—they just never even thought of him when making plans. And as far as Ben was concerned, that was fine by him.

At school, he kept a low profile. During class, he never spoke if he didn't have to, and at break, he would sneak off to the library where he would sit and read, write or draw.

"Is there really no one at school you might want to be friends with?" his mother often prodded. "They can't all be that bad, can they? Why don't you just give it a shot?"

Ben promised her every time to do just that. What he didn't tell his mother was that he had a hard time looking the kids at school in the face—he always felt they were expecting something from him, waiting for him to say some secret code word that he didn't know. Or perhaps they were just waiting for him to say something stupid and make a fool of himself.

Books were easier—when he was reading, he had loads of amazing friends. He journeyed to Mount Doom with Frodo and Sam, discovered Hogwarts's secret passageways with Harry Potter and rode to Bolvangar on an armoured polar bear's back. His life wasn't boring at all, but somehow it was impossible to convince his mum of that. She might have given up pestering him to join the football team, but she still never missed an opportunity to set him up with a potential friend. Which was mortifying for Ben, and must also have been awkward for... what was her name again? Portia. She surely had better things to do than make a conversation with a perfect stranger. But apparently, she was too polite to let on.

"Hi," said Portia.

Ben managed to mumble a quiet "Hello". Brilliant. Now her smile did look a little forced. If only he could go back to his box of books.

Megan seemed completely unaware of the awkwardness of the situation. "How long will you be staying in Afallon?" she asked.

Portia turned towards her. "Two weeks."

"Ah, how lovely," Megan said. "Then you've got enough time to explore the area. Have you already made plans?"

"We're going to Conwy today, actually."

"Ah! To the pier?"

"To the castle."

Megan was still holding Portia's book in her hands, and Ben was hoping that she'd finally ring it up and wrap it—but no such luck.

"That should be exciting," she continued chatting. "Are you interested in Welsh history?"

"I don't know much about it yet. But my mum says some of the oldest places in all of Britain are here in Wales," Portia replied.

"That's true," said Megan. "Did you know that there's a stone circle nearby? It's even older than Conwy Castle, isn't it, Ben?"

Ben cast his mum a pleading look. It was painfully obvious what she had in mind: trying to get him and this girl to go off somewhere together. And if that didn't work, she'd send him to Afallon on some made-up pretext. He would go along with it, for her sake, but his heart sank as he realized that his visits to the cottage weren't going to be much fun for a while.

Ben really liked the Afallon women. He had read all of Bramble's books, and he had even shown her some of his drawings. Bramble had asked to keep one of them—a Nazgûl dragon from Middle Earth—and Ben had taken that as huge praise. In return, she had gifted him a book filled with pictures of dragons, knights and castles for his birthday.

"A stone circle?" Portia asked.

"Oh, yes, up by the lake. Why don't you head out there with Ben some time—he knows the area quite well."

36

Bingo, thought Ben.

Portia hesitated for a split second, and then she smiled at him. "Sounds good. If you're up for it?"

Megan nodded encouragingly.

"Okay," he said, resigned to his fate. He would spend a morning taking Portia up the lake. They'd chat a load of nonsense on the way. Ben would show her the five knee-high stones his mum had so generously called a "stone circle". She would be disappointed, having expected something like Stonehenge. And then Ben would finally have his peace and quiet again.

Unless, of course, Portia found a last-minute excuse to not hang out with him—arguably the ideal scenario.

"If you're interested in the real Wales, you really must see that stone circle," Megan said as she punched the book's price into the cash register. "That castle is really a foreign imposition, built by the English to keep us Welsh in check."

Ben bent down to pick up a box of books next to the counter, and as he straightened up, he noticed something peculiar: the red-haired man, half hidden by the shelves, was watching the counter closely. No, wait, that wasn't quite right. He was watching Portia.

"Hey, Ben?" his mum called. Ben winced. The red-haired man dropped his gaze and disappeared between the shelves. "Why don't you two make a plan right away?"

All right, Mum, Ben thought. Best to jump in at the deep end. "Are you busy tomorrow morning?" he asked Portia.

"No, that's cool, tomorrow morning is great." Portia raised an eyebrow. "Eleven o'clock okay?"

Ben nodded.

"Fabulous," Megan exclaimed, clearly satisfied. "Ben can come pick you up from Afallon." She handed Portia the wrapped book. "Have lots of fun in Conwy then. And tell Rose and Bramble I said hi, okay?"

"Will do." Portia turned to Ben one last time. "See you tomorrow, then?"

"Okay," he said, feeling incredibly stupid. Portia waved goodbye before stepping outside. The bell rang, the door swung shut, and she was gone. Ben sighed.

"Well?" Megan said, smiling. "That wasn't so bad, was it?" Ben frowned in disagreement. The bell rang again as the red-haired man left the shop too.

"Now, don't look so glum. You'll see—once you're out and about, I'm sure you'll have fun. Portia seems really nice."

"Mmm," he replied. It was hard to stop himself contradicting his mum, but he knew if they got into an argument, she'd just end up lecturing him about how it wasn't healthy to be a loner. How he needed friends his age. How he'd miss out on all sorts of important experiences if all he did was sit there with his head in a book.

Ben knew his mum wished he was more like other kids, and for her sake he wished he was different too. But every time he tried to behave the way she thought he should, his stomach tied itself in knots.

Dad had never tried to push him into making friends with other kids. Ben knew his mother was only acting out of love for him, and yet... at moments like these, Ben wished his dad were still around. Dad had always understood him.

38

Sadness settled on his shoulders like a heavy blanket, as it so often did since his father had passed away.

"Ben..." Megan began, but just then something smacked against the shop window with a thump. They both spun around.

"What on earth was that?" Megan wondered aloud, while Ben was already on his way over to the door. Stepping outside, he immediately saw what had happened: a dishevelled blackbird was lying on the pavement, right in front of the shop. It must have smashed into the window at full speed.

Ben ran over to the bird and squatted down to discover that it was still alive. The blackbird was trying to flutter away, but one of its wings was sticking out at a funny angle.

His chest tightened in pain. That poor bird! Where had it been flying to? He looked up and noticed a sparkle in the windowpane—and then the reflection of the red-haired man, watching him from the other side of the street.

Megan appeared next to Ben. "Goodness me! The poor thing."

Ben was only half listening. He turned around just in time to see the red-haired man disappear around the street corner. For a moment it seemed as if a cloud of golden dust was hanging in the air in his wake. Then Ben blinked, and the cloud was gone. He must have been mistaken.

Peculiar Events

Later that afternoon, Portia sat in the living room at Afallon, drumming her fingers on the arm of her wing-backed chair. She had just got off the phone with her mum, and it had been nice to hear her voice—most of all because Gwen had sounded like she was in good spirits again, up for anything. Portia had told her all about the trip to Conwy: the old town filled with the smell of sea salt and spindrift, the giant seagulls, the narrow lanes and the fish and chips she and the aunts had enjoyed on the harbourside.

The day had been a busy one, and Portia hadn't had much time to ponder the events of the previous night, but now her gaze wandered to the closed door of Bramble's study.

Thoughts of the fox had been flitting through her mind all day. The aunts had dodged all her questions about the incident, which obviously piqued her curiosity even more.

Portia got up from her chair and went over to the study door. She was alone in the house—Rose had retreated to her writing shed in the garden to work on an editing project, and Bramble was walking Marlowe—so no one would know if she went into the study now.

Forget it. It's a stupid idea, Portia told herself. But then again, it wasn't like Bramble and Rose had explicitly forbidden her to go into the room. And hadn't Rose told her to make herself at home? So, what harm could it possibly do if she took a quick look?

Portia peeked through the open conservatory door to make sure that neither aunt was around, and then she stepped into Bramble's study.

Bramble had an old-fashioned desk: a bureau with a front that folded down to give a writing surface, revealing lots of compartments and drawers behind it. Unlike her car, her workspace was neat and tidy. Notebooks were lined up along the open compartments, a fountain pen and pencils had been tucked into two mugs, and a Welsh dictionary sat at the edge of the desktop. An empty vase stood on top of the bureau next to a shoebox.

Portia placed both hands on the desktop. That's where the fox had been, and that's where Bramble had been poking around right after chasing it away. *Curiosity killed the cat*, said the voice of reason in her head, but she ignored it. The mystery surrounding the fox in the study was just too intriguing.

She felt along the desktop edge with her fingertips until she found a thin join in the polished wood. A smile crept over her face. Bingo. She pushed lightly against it and heard a clicking noise. When she pulled back her hand, the secret compartment slid out from the desktop.

"Abracadabra," Portia whispered. In the secret drawer, she found a flat metal box. Her heart beating with excitement, she opened the lid—and raised her eyebrows in surprise. Inside the box lay an antique, ornately decorated key, with a tatty green silk ribbon tied to it. The wide bit at the end didn't look like it would fit any modern lock. Portia picked up the key and ran her thumb over the knot in the ribbon. Why was Bramble hiding a key? And more importantly, had the fox been looking for it? No way. Impossible.

Portia ran her fingers along the metal. Would Bramble tell her what it was for? Probably not, she decided. Especially since Portia would have to confess to snooping around her desk before she asked. But perhaps there were more clues to be found elsewhere in the study?

She put the key down, letting her eyes wander around the room and over the drawers and compartments, before picking up the shoebox sitting next to the vase. Inside was a wild jumble of odds and ends. On top sat a pincushion with a single needle stuck in it, and next to it a small jewellery box made of blue velvet that Portia opened to discover a silver locket. Inside it, instead of a photograph, there was a flower pressed under the glass. Portia held it up against the light. Unless she was mistaken, they were the faded white petals of a dog rose. Portia put the locket back in its case and continued to search through the shoebox.

Underneath the pincushion were two postcards from a Greek island, and a photograph showing Bramble and Rose at a beach. She put them aside and flipped through a pile of old newspaper clippings. Bramble had kept a book review, and a magazine article with pictures of Afallon's garden.

And there was an older cutting with the headline, *Search for Missing Students Continues*.

Deeper down, she found a photo of Marlowe as a puppy, and another of a group of seven friends in hippie clothes, posing in front of a theatre. And a more serious scene, too: six students in long, black gowns, wearing mortar-board caps as if at a graduation.

Portia turned the group pictures over. Something was scribbled on the back of each one: *The Order of the Needle*, 1963 on the first and *The Order of the Needle*, 1966 on the second. She frowned. What was The Order of the Needle? She inspected the photos more closely. The group of students consisted of five women and one man. Portia stopped short. The woman in the middle looked just like her mother—she had Gwen's pitch-black hair and the same heart-shaped face. But the young woman in the photo was arching her right eyebrow in a way that reminded Portia of somebody else. Then she realized—it had to be Rose on her graduation day. She was just about to put the photo aside when she saw another familiar face: Bramble! She was standing next to Rose in the picture, but Portia hadn't recognized her right away. This Bramble was all smiles, with her hair down, wearing an embroidered cap instead of a mortar board.

Portia saw that she had come to the bottom of the box. She contemplated the keepsakes spread out on the desk in front of her. There was no explanation for the secret key to be found here. Portia picked it up again and weighed it in her hand. Did she dare to keep on trawling through the desk?

The sensible thing would be to tidy up all this mess. *Before* she got caught. Then again, another five minutes of searching might just unearth the clue she was looking for.

She was already reaching for one of the notebooks when she heard the soft jingle of the wind chimes in the conservatory. Portia turned around and then froze. The fox was sitting in the study doorway, looking up at her with pricked ears. No, not at her... He was staring at the key in her hand.

"Portia," Rose called from the conservatory. "Is that you?"

Portia felt a jolt of cold fear shooting through her body. What if Rose found her here? Fox or no fox: she spun around, collected Bramble's keepsakes, returned them to the shoebox and hurried to place it back on top of the desk. She was about to put away the key as well, when she heard footsteps in the living room.

"Portia?"

She turned around, quickly stuffing the key into the pocket of her jeans. The fox had disappeared once more, and instead Rose appeared in the doorway.

"Ah, *there* you are. What are you doing in here?"

"I was looking for a pen," Portia improvised. She prayed that her body was concealing the still-open secret drawer behind her. "I'm sorry."

"No problem. Take whatever you need." Rose was carrying a bunch of freshly cut roses, hydrangea and euphorbia, and now absent-mindedly sucked one of her thumbs, which must have been pricked by a thorn. Portia saw her chance and groped behind her back for the edge of the desk and closed the drawer.

"What do you think?" Rose asked. "Time for dinner?"

"Sounds great." Portia's heart was in her mouth, but luckily, Rose didn't seem to notice anything.

"Wonderful." She pointed at the desk with her elbow. "Could you bring along that vase, please?"

Portia was hoping Rose would go ahead, but she waited in the doorway for Portia to leave the study before shutting the door behind her. The key felt as heavy as lead in her pocket.

✎ BEN ✎

Ben and Megan lived in Trefriw, in a narrow terraced house on the hillside above the church. The entire row had been whitewashed, but the Reeses' house alone had blue window frames and a blue front door.

With their bags of takeaway food from the pub in one hand, Megan used the other to unlock the door. Ben slipped past her, holding the cage containing the injured blackbird carefully so as not to shake it.

In the hallway, Megan set the food down on the telephone table: chicken tikka for herself, and fish and chips for Ben. She threw the keys in a little wicker basket and peeled off her denim jacket.

"Dinner in five minutes?" she asked.

"Let me just take the blackbird upstairs," said Ben.

"All right, but hurry up. Otherwise your chips will get soggy, and you know there's a No Returns policy."

Ben grinned and went upstairs with the cage. His room faced the street. It wasn't exactly big to begin with, and the piles of books on the floor, as well as on the shelves and the desk by the window, made it seem even smaller. There were posters on the door and above his desk, but the wall next to his bed was still covered by the forest his parents had painted for him when he was little.

Ben placed the blackbird on his desk and pulled away the cloth he had used to cover the cage. The bird immediately started hopping from one perch to the other, trying to flap its wings.

"Easy," Ben said softly. "No one here is going to hurt you." He stood still and waited a moment until the bird had calmed down. The vet, Dr Davies, had splinted its broken wing.

"It's a miracle that it's still alive," he had said. "Most birds that fly into windows get a concussion and die."

His mother had shot the vet a sharp look, and Dr Davies had instantly turned bright red. "This little fellow is look-ing quite tough, though," he had hastened to add. "He'll be flying again in no time, easy-peasy!"

That kind of exchange between his mum and Dr Davies was nothing new to Ben. Since his dad had passed away the previous year, grown-ups seemed to think they had to handle him with kid gloves. Ben wasn't exactly annoyed by it—he simply didn't like all the attention.

He took off his backpack, pulled out the bag of birdseed he'd just purchased and dug around for the small plastic bowl and water bottle that Dr Davies had given him. On the wall next to him, shaggy, round-eyed monsters peered out from between the trunks of red- and green-leaved trees. *Where the Wild Things Are* had been his favourite book when he was little. He had asked his dad, Tom, to read it aloud to him so many times that one day, Tom had looked Ben in the eyes and said: "If you want to spend that much time in a story, boy, you've got no choice but to learn how to read yourself." Three months later, Ben was reading the book aloud to his dad. Every now and then, Tom had to help him with longer words, but from then on they worked their way through dozens of books together, taking turns to read aloud. Tom's well-worn copy of *The Hobbit* still lay under Ben's pillow. Even though he had not opened it for a while, he could still hear his dad's voice as he read Bilbo's adventures to him: *In a hole in the ground there lived a hobbit.*

Ben put the plastic bowl on the desk and filled the bottle on the side of the cage with fresh water. The blackbird nervously scuttled back and forth on his perch, but it didn't seem too panicky any more.

"You'll feel better soon, I promise," Ben assured the bird.

"Ben!" his mother called from downstairs. "Soggy chips in T-minus ten seconds."

Ben ripped open the bag of birdseed, poured a generous amount into the little bowl and carefully placed it in the cage.

"Enjoy," he said, and headed downstairs.

INTERLUDE

Night had fallen on Trefriw like a cloak of black velvet. Around midnight, the clouds parted to reveal the full moon, which bathed the town in an unearthly, milky shimmering light. The moonlight flooded into Ben's room, wandering over the sleeping boy's body and along his blanket, grazing the palm trees on the wall and illuminating the birdcage on his desk.

The blackbird was awake. It sat on its perch looking out through the window. Down there, in the street, a shadowy figure was moving about. Someone walked along the row of parked cars: a tall figure, striding with soundless ease. Below Ben's window, the figure paused, and glanced up.

The blackbird's neck feathers bristled. Moonlight sparkled on its head, and silvery rays ran down its plumage like rivulets of rain. A shiver went through the bird. It ruffled its feathers, puffing them out in all directions. Then, in the blink of an eye, a tiny man stood on the perch instead of the blackbird. His hair was as dark and shiny as the blackbird's feathers of which his robe was made. His legs and feet were bare and he held his splinted broken arm tightly to his chest.

Ridik ap Mwyalchod stepped closer to the cage bars. On the street below, the night wanderer put a cigarette between his lips. A moment later, the flame of a lighter and then the glow of the cigarette lit up the man's narrow, pointy face and head of red hair. He visibly relished taking a deep puff before tucking his free hand into his trouser pocket.

"Robin Goodfellow," Ridik whispered. "What are you up to?"

The man sent a smile towards the window above, as if he had heard the question. He raised the hand holding the cigarette and drew the shape of a key in the air in front of him.

"No." Ridik clutched the cage bars.

The cigarette held between two fingers, the man sauntered away down the street. The shadow that followed him was far too small for a man his size.

The Human Door

Portia sat on the wall by Afallon and checked her watch for the fifth time. It was ten past eleven, and Ben had not made an appearance yet.

Portia's backpack sat by her feet—she had packed it the evening before: a map, a few plastic bags for collected leaves and flowers and her journal, of course. That morning, she had added two sandwiches, a thermos filled with tea and a cloth to use as a picnic blanket. It would be such a shame if all that effort had been for nothing.

She tilted her face towards the sun. Perhaps she could just take off on her own? Rose was out shopping in Llanrwst, and Bramble was at her desk, working on her newest book. All morning, Portia had been nervously waiting for her to notice the key was missing, but so far luck seemed to be on her side. She was gambling on Bramble taking Marlowe for his walk again later that day. She would put the key back then. And in the meantime, there was no point in her sitting about twiddling her thumbs.

Portia let her legs dangle over the wall. The morning sky was bright blue, not a single cloud in sight. In the meadow over the lane, a few early butterflies were flitting about, while a bluish haze of morning mist still lingered at the edge of the woods. Portia took a deep breath. It was too beautiful a day to waste indoors. There were meadows and paths waiting to be explored.

She was just getting up when she noticed the fox crouching at the northern end of the wall, underneath a bramble hedge. This time she was not surprised by its appearance.

"You just can't stay away, can you?" Portia expected him to bolt at the sound of her voice, but far from it. He just sat there, his bushy tail neatly curled around his legs. Portia couldn't help but smile. Would he let her come closer?

She slid cautiously off the wall. Suddenly, the fox began to move. But it didn't run off. Instead it started trotting casually towards Portia. She stopped in her tracks. Such a strange animal! Was it tame, perhaps? Otherwise, there was no explanation for how it was behaving.

The fox stopped right in front of her. Portia hesitated briefly, but then squatted and held out a hand. It retreated at first, but then came forward and nudged her jeans pocket with its muzzle. She raised her eyebrows. Did it know that she had the key in her pocket?

The fox backed away, staring her in the eyes.

"Are you really after Bramble's key?" she asked.

The fox's right ear twitched.

Portia rose, glanced back towards the house over her shoulder, and then fished the key from her pocket. The fox stayed calm, but Portia could see it was pressing his paws into the grass just a little deeper. Portia let the key dangle from her finger on its green ribbon. The fox took a step closer.

"Blimey," she whispered. But if she had thought this fox couldn't behave any weirder, she had thought wrong. It sidled past her and peeked through the gate up towards the house. Having made sure they weren't being watched, he came back, brushed past her legs, crossed the lane to the edge of the meadow and looked back at her expectantly.

Portia watched all this with increasing fascination. What was happening here was basically impossible. A tickle stirred underneath her breastbone, and the desire to follow the fox pulled at her like the wind tugging a sail. But she mustn't give in to that wish. That would be absolutely ridiculous, perhaps even dangerous.

Then again, what was the worst thing that could happen if she did follow him? Just a little way, just to see what he would do next. Bramble and Rose didn't have to find out. They would think she was out and about with Ben.

I'll just follow it a little way, she thought. The voice of reason in her mind was about to protest, but Portia had made her decision and silenced it. She looked back to the house one last time, then picked up her backpack. Was it her imagination or did the fox curl its lips into a smile?

"Go on, then. Show me where you want to go," she muttered.

The fox crossed the meadow, slipped underneath a fence and went on into the woods. The further they went, the faster it trotted. Every time Portia dropped behind, it paused and waited: it clearly wanted her to keep up, and it was obviously leading her somewhere. They left the shelter of the forest, went down a broom-covered slope, then skirted the shore of a lake before diving back into the woods. From there on, the going got steadily steeper, and Portia worked up a sweat. The fox ran up the hillside ahead of her, slipping nimbly between rocks and tree trunks. There was no path, but Portia wasn't worried about losing her way. Down below, the lake glittered like a mirror between the trees. She was confident she would be able to find her way back again at any time.

In fact, she was feeling more and more at ease, walking through the beautiful, unfamiliar landscape. Aside from herself and the fox, the hillside was deserted. No hikers in colourful jackets, no groups of students out for an excursion. The only sound was the faint whine of a chainsaw coming from the other side of the hill, but soon that faded away too.

Portia and the fox climbed still further up the hillside. The tree trunks were covered in thick, shaggy moss now. Ferns sprawled between rocks, and the ground was a soft carpet of dead leaves.

Glancing down to the side, Portia realized the lake had disappeared, hidden by a mass of rocks and ferns. She stopped, but then heard the fox yapping a little further ahead. Portia set off again, following the sound of its call. Scrambling up the slope, she skirted round a large rock, and then at last she saw it.

In a clearing fringed by oak trees and dense undergrowth loomed the remnants of a grey stone wall. Portia stepped closer. A pair of oak trees had grown up against the wall, framing an old door like two columns.

The fox was pacing back and forth in the doorway. As Portia approached, it stopped and stood still, with only its bushy tail twitching to and fro.

Portia ran her fingers over the door. The wood was rough and worm-eaten, covered with a wrought-iron pattern of leaves. From the centre of the door hung an iron ring, with a rusty lock below it. She touched the lock with her fingertips and glanced down at the fox.

"Let me guess," she said. "That's what the key is for."

The fox's ears twitched. Portia pulled the key from her pocket. Walls like these often ran around the grounds of old manor houses. But why would Bramble hide the key to a remote country estate in her desk? And what was hidden behind the door? Portia took a step back and tried to see whether there was another way to get around the wall—but a mass of brambles formed an impenetrable natural barrier. The only way to the other side was through that door.

Portia weighed the key in her hand. Now that she was here, she might as well see if it fit. She put the key in the lock and looked at the fox. It didn't move, but its eyes seemed to shine. Portia turned the key, pulled at the iron ring and opened the door.

She was hit by a gust of cold air that filled her nose with the scent of damp grass. Goosebumps ran down her neck, and the hair on her forearms stood on end. Was this how an archaeologist felt when they prised open the door to a pharaoh's sealed tomb?

She had barely got the door open when the fox dashed past her, leaping across the threshold in a flash of red fur.

Portia hesitated. She could feel her heart beating against her ribs as another gust of cold air came rushing through the doorway. She felt as if she were standing in the middle of a hurricane, and if she let go she would be whirled away by the wind.

What if there was a magical place waiting on the other side? A secret place, that she would be the first to discover? That was nonsense of course, but her heart still raced faster at the idea. She spared a brief thought for Bramble and Rose, and for her mum who would be worried sick if she got lost somewhere in the Welsh wilderness. She should really go back. But every centimetre of her body was longing for an adventure, however small.

The fox barked on the other side of the wall. It was strange, but despite all her worries, Portia had the feeling that she was in the right place at the right time. She pulled the key from the lock and stepped through the arched doorway to the other side. She didn't bother closing the door behind her.

✍ BEN ✍

Ben stood at the counter of the chemist in Llanrwst, waiting for Mr Duke, the pharmacist, to come back from his storage room. In front of him on the countertop stood the carefully covered blackbird's cage. The bird seemed calm just now, but Ben expected it to start fluttering again at any moment.

When he had come back into his room that morning after breakfast, the bird had been hopping about so frantically that Ben was worried it might hurt itself. Megan was already on her way to the bookshop, and Ben had been planning to cycle to Afallon—but the bird just wouldn't settle down. Flapping its healthy wing, it had bashed its body against the cage bars again and again. In the end, Ben couldn't take it any more. Throwing on a jacket, he took the cage and headed into Llanrwst.

As he arrived at the chemist, he realized he should have called Afallon. Was Portia waiting for him? Probably. If he hadn't made a terrible impression yesterday, he must have done now. He told himself he didn't care, but that wasn't entirely true.

Behind the counter, Mr Duke's trainee was sorting pill packages on the shelves while humming a tune. Ben caught himself tapping his fingers to it. Then Mr Duke returned, a little bottle in his hand.

"Here you go," he said. "That's much better than what young Davies prescribed."

Ben had stopped by the vet's office first. Dr Davies had told him there was nothing more he could do, but sent Ben to the chemist to pick up a sedative for the bird.

Ben looked sceptically at the little bottle in Mr Duke's hand.

"What?" Mr Duke snapped. "It's valerian. Works just as well as that chemical brew that whippersnapper of a vet recommended. And it's far less harmful."

Ben was already familiar with Mr Duke's tirades—he had a habit of complaining about both doctors and vets.

"Amateurs, the lot of them." Mr Duke pulled the cloth off the birdcage. The bird sat staring at them from its perch.

"Now, just you be reasonable and let us help you," he said, pouring a few drops of valerian into the bird's drinking water. Then he covered the cage with the cloth again, and Ben felt himself relax.

"You can keep the bottle. But it's for the bird only, got it? Don't even think about taking a little sip."

"No, absolutely not," Ben assured him. Then he pocketed the little bottle and made a bolt for it.

Outside the chemist, Ben strapped the cage to his bike rack. The bird stayed calm. Perhaps the valerian was already working? He tucked the cloth in place and set off home.

Pushing his bike down the street, he wondered how he was going to confess to his mum that he had flaked on Portia. He knew exactly how she would react: she'd make him go and apologize.

Ben was already imagining that ordeal in excruciating detail when he saw a solution to his problem further down the hillside. The Afallon women's old Nissan was sitting in the supermarket car park, and Rose was just stepping out of the shop, a carrier bag in each hand. Ben's heart leapt. He would explain to Rose why he hadn't been able to make it to Afallon today, and she would pass on his apology to Portia. Perhaps Mum would be satisfied with that?

Yeah, right, thought Ben. Still, he couldn't miss this opportunity. He hopped on his bike, pushed off on the pavement and sped down the steep road. Down in the car park, Rose had finished packing her shopping in the boot and was walking to the driver's side. She was going to leave before he could get there! Ben bit his lower lip, plucked up some courage and began frantically ringing his bike bell.

He had just called Rose's name when the bird started panicking. It chirped and flapped about so fiercely that its cage started to shake and rattle behind Ben's back. Startled, Ben twisted around to look, but as he did so he jerked the handlebar, causing the bike to fishtail. The back wheel skidded out to one side, sending the bike, Ben and the cage hurtling to the ground.

Someone called out to him, but Ben didn't care. He got back to his feet, ignoring the stinging pain in his arm.

The cage had landed on its side next to the bike, still covered by the cloth. Ben's fear at what might have happened to the bird clutched like a cold fist at his insides.

"Ben!"

He turned around to see Rose running towards him, her skirt flapping around her legs. Still slightly dazed from his fall, he stepped over the bike and squatted down next to the battered cage. The fluttering sounds had stopped. His heart pounding, he pulled the cloth aside, expecting to find the bird lying there with a broken neck. Tears blurred his eyes, but he quickly wiped them away. When he lowered his hand, what he saw made him freeze: instead of the bird, a tiny man was kneeling inside the overturned cage.

The ground seemed to shift beneath Ben's feet.

"Oh, Ben, are you all right?" Rose crouched down next to him, putting her hands on his shoulders. "Ben, what..."

she began again, but then fell silent. Ben knew why. She had seen the man in the cage too. The tiny, impossible man, who raised his head at the sound of her voice, then struggled to his feet. He was wearing a robe as black as the blackbird's plumage. He held his right arm—*his wing*, Ben thought—pressed protectively against his chest.

I must be concussed, thought Ben. He was clearly hallucinating. That was the only possible explanation.

The man in the cage turned towards Rose and gave a dignified bow. "Viola Rosethorn," he said in a voice surprisingly deep for a man his size. "It pains me that we meet again under such circumstances, but I am the bearer of terrible news." He stepped nimbly across the grid at the bottom of the cage until he was holding the bars in his tiny fists. "And time is short."

The birdman can talk, Ben thought. *Of course he can*. He wasn't even surprised to hear him call Rose "Viola". Even stranger was Rose's reaction.

Her hands slid off his shoulders. She reached out to touch the cage with her fingertips.

"Ridik ap Mwyalchod, my old friend," she said in a hoarse voice. "What happened?"

The birdman leant forward and placed his uninjured hand against Rose's finger. "It's Goodfellow," he said. "He has opened the door."

Between Worlds

Rose raced along the winding lane. Ben sat in the Nissan passenger seat, pressing his feet into the bottom of the footwell as if he might be able to brake himself if he pushed hard enough. His hands were cupped in his lap, where Ridik ap Mwyalchod sat on his upturned palms. The tiny man felt warm against his skin, and his robe was as soft as a bird's feathers. His mere existence was so incredible that Ben could hardly tear his eyes away. The boy's left forearm was badly grazed, but he barely felt the burning pain.

He stared and stared at Ridik. He was holding a magical creature in his very hands! A living, breathing magical creature! He hadn't felt such a tingle of excitement in his stomach in a long while.

When he was little, his parents had always prepared a surprise for his birthday. A bunch of colourful balloons, a dragon carved from a cucumber. Mum and Dad had always had the best ideas. On his fifth birthday he'd gone out fishing with his grandfather and discovered a forest on his bedroom wall when he got home. His parents had been standing in the doorway, his dad with a splash of paint on his cheek.

When he looked at Ridik, he felt the same excitement as he had that day when he had stepped into his room to see the Wild Things romping among exotic palm trees on his wall.

"You must be mistaken," said Rose from the driver's seat.

"I'm afraid not," Ridik replied. "I can feel the shift in the air."

"He can't have opened the door," Rose insisted. "There's no key."

Ben looked down at the tiny man who gave no reply.

"Ridik?" Rose pressed.

"Goodfellow always said he didn't believe you really got rid of the key."

"But we did!" Rose exclaimed. "Dear Lord, we'd have been foolish to keep it."

"And you took care of it yourself?" Ridik asked, a hint of hope in his voice.

"Bramble did," Rose said. "She threw it into the lake."

"Did you see her do it, Mistress Rosethorn?"

"Well, no, I..." Rose broke off. She stared straight ahead through the windscreen, a realization visibly dawning on her. Then she sank down slightly into her seat as if someone had placed a heavy weight on her shoulders. "No."

She turned the Nissan off the road and onto a dirt track leading into the woods. It was an access path that only foresters were allowed to use, but Rose didn't seem to care.

"Rose?" asked Ben. "Can I ask you a question?"

Rose chuckled drily. "I'm sure you have plenty of questions, Ben," she said. "But even if I could answer all of them, you probably wouldn't believe me."

Ben looked back to Ridik. "I'm not sure about that."

Rose shook her head. "Where should I begin? With the Door Between Worlds? The key? The Grey King?"

"Perhaps we might begin with me?" Ridik asked softly. He turned around and looked up at Ben. "Allow me to introduce myself. My name is Ridik ap Mwyalchod. The Blackbird's son. Scout of the Adar."

"The Adar?" Ben repeated. He knew enough Welsh to understand the word. "Scout of the birds?"

"Indeed."

Ben was about to ask more questions when suddenly he remembered something. He had seen Ridik before! There was a drawing of a tiny man in one of Bramble's books who looked just like him!

"*In the Forest of Talking Birds!*" he exclaimed. "The blackbird scout Bramble wrote about... That was you, Ridik... I mean, that was you, Mr ap Mwyalchod, wasn't it?"

Ridik smiled. "It was an honour to serve as inspiration for one of Mistress Brambleblossom's characters."

"But then..." Ben's thoughts turned somersaults in his head. "Everything else in that book, the flying frogs, the fairies, that's all real as well? Bramble didn't just make it up?"

"Oh, she does have a very vivid imagination, I will say that," Ridik smirked. "But she's also well versed in the art of describing things she's seen with her own eyes. She has the heart and talent of a true bard, no doubt."

"That's true enough," Rose said darkly. "She's always been a good storyteller."

Ridik flashed her a glance. "I'm certain she had a good reason for not telling you about the key, my lady."

"You mean a good reason for lying to me," said Rose. The crease between her brows deepened. "That's why Robin has been trying to break into our house all this time. That's why he stole from us. *Damio*, Bramble! How could anyone be so foolish!" She pounded the steering wheel with the heel of her hand and stepped on the accelerator, making the engine roar. "If Robin leaves the door open..."

"... then all of our struggles have been in vain," Ridik finished her sentence. Then he doubled over, his face contorted in a grimace of pain.

Ben moved his thumb a bit so Ridik could lean against it. Then he looked over at Rose. "What door?"

∾ PORTIA ∾

Portia followed the fox through a meadow of wildflowers, then a grove of oaks, going further and further into the hills. *I'll keep going until I can see the next road.* That's what she'd told herself when they went through the door, but by now they'd been walking for ages without a road in sight. At first, the thrill of excitement had drowned out everything else, but now she was conscious of a small but growing feeling of unease in her belly.

Perhaps it was because the weather was beginning to turn. Dark clouds were gathering overhead, there was a chilly edge to the wind, and Portia thought she could smell a hint of rain in the air. They'd also been traipsing up and down hillsides for what seem like for ever without stopping for a rest. Portia had no idea how long they had been walking for. When she checked her phone she saw the display was pitch black. The battery must have died. If only she'd remembered to charge it last night.

She really wished she knew what time it was.

The hillside they were walking up now was getting more and more wet underfoot. The grass was giving way to clumps of wild heather, with large boggy puddles in between. The mountains lay beyond the treetops like sleeping giants. They had definitely inched closer now.

Portia looked up at the sky. The clouds were blocking out the sun, so it was impossible to tell how low it had sunk. Had Rose and Bramble realized by now that she had set off on her own?

She stopped, gnawing nervously at a fingernail. For the first time, she was really aware of the stillness surrounding her. There was no birdsong, no revving of distant engines. Nothing but the sound of heather quietly rustling in the wind. Goosebumps crept across her skin, making her wish she had brought a jacket. She looked around her, trying to see which direction they had come from, but the oak grove was nowhere to be seen, and she had left no footprints on the soft ground between the clumps of heather. Had they been walking across the marshy hillside in a straight line or in an arc?

She would have loved to turn around now, to follow her tracks all the way back to that strange door, and to Afallon beyond. But she was long past the point where she could still have found her way home.

✤ BEN ✤

"Damn it, Robin." Rose stared at the open door in the crumbling wall, with clenched fists. Ridik, still standing on Ben's palm, gasped with shock.

Ben looked around him. He knew these woods. His parents had brought him here to forage for mushrooms a few times. He'd never seen that door on any of their trips, though. It wasn't that surprising—there were no walking trails leading to the clearing where it stood.

"How long has the door been open?" Rose asked.

"Hard to say," Ridik replied. "But I wouldn't be surprised if Goodfellow is nearly at the second door."

Doors leading to other worlds. Kingdoms full of fairies and other magical creatures. It all sounded like something from a book to Ben, not like real life. But he had witnessed Ridik transform from bird to man with his own eyes—that sight had shifted the boundaries between *impossible* and *possible* in his head. It was an amazing feeling, even though Rose was clearly very worried about the open door, and Ben realized that he should be too.

And yet—when he looked through the door, he felt a warm thrill of anticipation deep inside.

Rose whipped out her mobile phone and began writing a text message.

"The second door," Ben began. "Does it really lead to Faerie?"

"Oh, yes," Ridik said. "The door in front of you was built by Druids, wise women and men in ancient times. It leads from the Human World into the Borderlands. The second door awaits at the border of my world. My home. Faerie, as you call it."

Ben was eager to ask more questions, but Ridik peered over the edge of his palm, down at the forest floor. "Could you please put me down?" he asked.

Ben squatted and let the tiny man walk from his hand to the ground. Ridik walked back and forth through the carpet of long-dead leaves. He seemed to be searching for something. Ben stepped closer to the door and lightly brushed it with his fingertips. The door frame was twined about with brambles. Beyond it, the forest gave way to a meadow. High grass swayed gently in the wind. Above a pair of white butterflies tumbled in the air.

The Nissan boot slammed shut. Ben flinched guiltily, pulling his hand back from the door. He hadn't seen Rose go back to the car. Now she came back across the clearing with a rake in her hand and a face as dark and menacing as a storm cloud. Ben's gaze had wandered back to the door when he felt a tugging at this trouser leg.

He looked down to see Ridik clutching the hem of his jeans in one tiny hand. He stared up at the boy, a solemn look on his face.

"Better keep your distance, young Ben."

"But are the worlds beyond the door dangerous?" Ben asked.

"Every world has its own danger," Ridik said. "But in the Borderlands between the worlds anything could happen. There the Grey King awaits, and who can tell what else might emerge from the cracks between the Here and There."

These words made Ben's blood run cold. "Why is this Goodfellow opening these doors?"

"Because he wants to go home," Ridik said simply.

Ben frowned. He had assumed that Robin Goodfellow was the villain of this story—but it almost sounded as if Ridik had some sympathy for the key thief.

"Why did he leave the Humans' Door open, though?" Ben wondered.

"Because he's angry," said Rose. "He has been for forty years."

She had pulled the metal head from the wooden shaft and began to carve something into the wood with a pocketknife.

"If Goodfellow's going to get to the second door soon, shouldn't we hurry?" Ben asked.

"We?" repeated Rose. "No chance. You're going home now, Ben." She blew a few wood shavings off the shaft and put her knife away before resting her hand on Ben's shoulder. "It's bad enough me dragging you all the way out here into the woods after the fall you've had. I'm certainly not going to take you any deeper into this whole mess."

Ben opened his mouth to argue, but she shook her head. "No. The only foolish human passing through this door today is me."

Ben felt a wave of disappointment rolling through him. Then Ridik cleared his throat.

"That's not quite true, Mistress Rosethorn," he said.

Rose stared down at him. "What are you saying?"

"Goodfellow was not alone," replied Ridik. "I found human footprints."

"Bramble?" Rose's hand tightened on Ben's shoulder.

"No, these footprints are too small. They belong to a child."

"Portia," groaned Rose, screwing her eyes up and raking her fingers through her hair. Alarmed, Ben looked back towards the door. How had Portia fallen in with such questionable company?

"Who is this Portia?" asked Ridik.

"My great-niece," explained Rose. "She must have found the key among Bramble's things. I wondered what she was up to in that office!"

"Do you think Goodfellow has persuaded her to help him?"

"My guess is that he tricked her. That would be just like him." She swore again. "Ben is right—we have to hurry. Perhaps we can reach them before he rouses the Grey King from his sleep."

With each word Rose spoke, Ben's disappointment grew. How often had he dreamt of climbing into one of his books? Of exploring foreign lands, riding a dragon or swimming with mermaids? And, just when he found out that those fantastic worlds were real, he was supposed to just turn round and go home? To the dog-eared old copy of *The Hobbit* tucked underneath his pillow? To his dad's favourite mug gathering dust on a shelf in the kitchen?

Something snapped inside of him. Suddenly, the idea of walking away from all this seemed unbearable. He clenched his fists and screwed up all his courage.

"I'm coming with you."

"What did you say?" asked Rose distractedly.

Ben thrust out his chin, determined. "I'm coming with you," he repeated.

"Ben, we don't have time for—"

"If you won't take me with you, I'll just follow you," he cut in.

Ben had never argued with a grown-up like this before. He could feel himself going red, and a prickly sweat broke out on his brow. But he forced himself to look Rose in the eye.

"This day just gets better and better," murmured Rose. "Ah well." She beckoned Ben over and rested her hand on his shoulder once more.

"When we are on the other side of the door, you do everything I say, okay? No hesitating, no questions. Understood?"

The relief made Ben's knees feel as wobbly as jelly. He nodded.

Rose gave his shoulder a quick squeeze. "Good. Stay close to me," she said, her voice softer now. Then she looked down at Ridik. "Think you can catch up with Goodfellow?"

"I can try," he replied. "Young Ben, kindly pick me up so that I can sit on your shoulder."

Ben did as he was told. "Are you going to shapeshift again?"

Ridik smiled. "I will have wings, yes. And so will you."

Rose took Ben's hand in hers. "The scouts of the Adar possess the gift of swiftflight," she explained. "As soon as we pass through the door, Ridik will grant us magical speed. It will be as if we were wearing Seven-League Boots." She turned to Ridik again. "Will you be able to cope with your broken arm?"

"I'll manage," he said.

"Then let's go." Rose gripped the rake shaft in one hand and Ben's hand in the other. Together they walked towards the door. Rose went through the archway first. Ben felt a shiver of excitement as he stepped through in turn. He heard Ridik whispering words in an unknown language, followed by what sounded like the beating of an enormous wing. Then a current of air sucked him forward through the doorway.

The Faerie Door

The clouds were so low that the mountaintops in the distance had disappeared behind a shroud of mist. The wind was whistling more fiercely across the heather now, carrying the smell of brackish water to Portia's nose.

Her feet were hurting, but she kept on walking. She still hadn't given up hope of coming across a road or a house. Portia stepped over a tuft of heather and up onto one of the grassy tussocks that stuck out of the marsh.

She caught sight of the fox up ahead, and then for the first time she saw where it must be taking her. Beyond the high moor a long, low rocky slope rose out of the heather like a sea monster's scaly back. And standing right in the middle of the slope was... Portia felt as if the ground was giving way beneath her feet. Cut into the rocky hillside was a second door.

She marched on mechanically, until she fell to her knees in front of the door. There was no crumbling wall this time. Instead, two rough-hewn stone pillars protruding from the ground, with a third pillar resting on top as a lintel. The wooden door itself was inlaid with carved, knotted patterns. On either side of the doorway grew a rowan tree,

71

their intertwined branches forming an archway above the stone pillars.

The fox was sitting underneath the left-hand tree, watching Portia expectantly. Portia stared right back.

She felt sick with exhaustion and fear. She had no way of getting her bearings and finding her way back home to Afallon. Another door was all there was. A spark of fury flickered in her chest. Fury at herself for not turning around when there was still time. For being foolish enough to follow the fox in the first place. And at the fox too, who didn't seem to care about her suffering, and who was probably even taking pleasure in having tricked her.

Portia scowled down at the fox. "I don't know what's going on here," she said, "but I've had enough. I'm going back." As she spoke, her resolve strengthened. The fox narrowed its eyes to mere slits.

Portia struggled to her feet. "I'm going back," she repeated, turning to leave. She'd go back to the cottage and make herself a big mug of tea. Then she'd snuggle up in Rose's reading chair, and for the rest of her holiday she'd only look for adventures between the pages of a book.

"Please don't do that." Portia flinched so violently at the sound of the voice that she almost fell to her knees again. She jerked around, her heart hammering in her chest.

The fox was nowhere to be seen. Instead, a man stood by the door. He was tall and slender, wearing a white shirt and sandy trousers with blades of grass sticking to them. His hair was the same shade of coppery red as the fox's fur.

Portia's mouth was suddenly bone dry. *No. What you're thinking is impossible. It can't be real.*

The man took a step towards her and she backed away.

"Hey, there," said the stranger and smiled. "We've been such good friends up until now, haven't we?"

Portia's head was spinning. She wanted to run but her legs felt heavy as lead.

"I won't stop you going home," the man assured her in a voice like honey, "I won't keep you. We just need to unlock this door." He squatted down in front of Portia and held out his hand. His eyes were the colour of dark amber.

Fox eyes, thought Portia, and shuddered.

"The key," he said. "Please."

With trembling fingers, she produced the key from her pocket. The man snatched it from her hand, pressed it to his lips and briefly closed his eyes. Then he rose and walked back to the door.

"Do me a favour, Portia," he said without turning around. "Go back to the women in Afallon and tell them the key is truly gone now. They no longer need to lie about it." He pushed the key into the lock and placed the palm of his hand on the door.

"What?" Portia croaked.

"They won't have much time for regrets," he said. "Before the fog rolls in."

He turned the key in the lock and opened the door. A gust of wind hit Portia in the face. The red-haired man glanced up to the sky. He hesitated for a moment, then took the key out of the lock and stepped through the doorway.

73

Travelling with Ridik was the most peculiar thing Ben had ever experienced. In one sense, he felt as if he were standing still while the landscape rushed past him. In another, it was as if he were striding into a strong wind that parted and flowed around him like water.

There was one last wingbeat, then suddenly Ben was standing by Rose's side on a wide-open moor. He staggered, unsteady on his feet, as if he had just stepped off a ship onto solid ground—although this particular ground didn't feel very solid. Were those tufts of grass and heather really moving under his feet, or was it just his wobbly legs?

A small hand grabbed Ben's shoulder. "Here we are!" said Ridik, panting.

Ben jerked up his head. Right ahead of them, on the edge of the moor, a rocky ridge rose from the ground. In it stood a door framed by two trees. And in front of the door stood a man who looked as if he was just about to push it open.

"Quick!" Ridik's voice sounded like a rasping caw. Rose started running, and Ben stumbled after her. Then he noticed the small figure with a head of black curls standing stiffly to one side of the Faerie Door. *Portia!*

The man stepped through the doorway and made to pull it shut behind him.

"Robin!" Rose yelled. "Don't do it!"

Portia spun around, staring first at Rose then Ben. She looked exhausted, pale and dishevelled. Ben stopped at her side, panting heavily. Portia gently touched his arm, as if she couldn't quite believe that he was really there.

"He's got the key!" Ridik shouted.

Rose rushed towards the archway and seized the edge of the door with both hands. The man on the other side let out an angry howl and fiercely tried to yank the door shut, but Rose dug her heels into the ground.

"Robin, please," she pleaded, "give me the key!"

For a moment, there was silence. Then they heard a voice so deep it sounded like a growl: "The key. So that's why you're here."

"Robin..."

"All these years," the man said. "All these years you swore there was no way back."

"But I didn't know!" Rose exclaimed. Her left foot was being dragged across the ground now, but she didn't let go of the door. "Robin, I really didn't know."

"So she lied to you too? Well, well. A fine companion you picked."

Rose would not be deterred. "I'm begging you," she pleaded. "You know very well what will happen if the door to our world remains open."

All of a sudden the door flew open, sending Rose tumbling backwards. She scrambled back to her feet. Robin Goodfellow stood in the doorway: a tall, slender man who towered over Rose by at least a head. His hands were raised in front of him, his fists clenched. A memory flashed through Ben's mind. It was the man from the bookshop! The man who had been watching Portia, right before Ridik had crashed into the window.

"Perhaps that's exactly what I want," Robin hissed. "Perhaps it would only be fair for you to realize what it feels like to lose your world."

Rose stood tall. She was silent now, watching Robin intently. He stared back, his chest rising and falling, as if his rage was billowing inside him like a storm. Was he going to attack Rose? Ben found he was clenching his own fists, his fingernails digging into the palms of his hands.

"Come on now," whispered Ridik, and then Robin finally dropped his hands to his side. Without a word, Rose held out her own hand for the key.

"Hmmm," Robin bristled, as if disgusted by the whole situation. Then he curled his lips into a smile that was entirely devoid of friendliness.

"Portia!" he called. "Thank you for your help." He threw the key towards her, and it landed right by her feet. Then he turned to face Rose one last time. "Don't ever come back here."

"We won't—" Rose began, but Robin cut her short.

"But of course I'm well aware how much your word is worth. *We're not leaving anyone behind.* I wonder whether Hermia believed you, too?"

Rose flinched as if he had slapped her. Then Robin stepped backwards through the archway and pulled the door shut with a bang.

For a moment, Ben and the others stood in silence. Then Rose came alive with a jolt, marched over to Portia and picked up the key that lay on the ground in front of her. She pushed it into the keyhole and turned it twice, before pulling it free and stuffing it into her skirt pocket.

Ben looked about him, taking in their surroundings properly for the first time. The moor lay in a saddle-shaped depression between two ridges. Their tops were shrouded in clouds. The wind had dropped and the air felt damp. If he was reading weather correctly, they would soon be immersed in a grey soup of fog.

Portia was the first to move. She sat down on a flat rock, curled up with her head resting on her knees, as if she was refusing to acknowledge the whole crazy situation. Ben felt as if he should go over and comfort her, but what could he do really? Give her a pat on the back and tell her to cheer up?

Rose beat him to it anyway. She knelt down in front of Portia and cupped the girl's head in her hands, gently brushing the hair from her face. "Oh, Portia," she said softly. "Girl, what on earth are you doing here?"

Portia mumbled something that Ben couldn't make out. She raised her head and opened her mouth as if she was about to tell Rose everything—but then her gaze wandered back to Ridik. She shook her head in disbelief and buried her face in her palms. "It's all a bad joke, isn't it? It must be."

Rose gave her a quick hug. "I promise I'll explain everything as soon as we're back home," she said. "Okay?" Then she looked at Ridik.

He nodded. "We shouldn't waste any more time."

While Ridik got to his feet, Rose held out a hand and pulled Portia back to her feet. "Now, this may feel a little strange," she warned.

Portia shot Ben a questioning, almost desperate glance, but he had barely opened his mouth to reply when the strong winds of the swiftflight surged about them.

The Grey Riders

The world dissolved into a swirl of wind and flowing colours. Portia held her breath as she was yanked over the shifting landscape below like a fish on a hook. Only a few seconds later, with a wingbeat as loud as thunderclap, the world snapped into place again. Portia stared about her, wide-eyed. The moor had disappeared. She was standing in a grove of gnarled oak trees.

A wave of nausea rose in her stomach, making her gasp. She held on to the straps of her backpack, closed her eyes and took deep breaths. In, out... In, out...

"Are you okay?" someone asked.

Portia opened her eyes to see Ben's concerned face. "Yeah, fine. Aside from the fact that I've lost my mind."

Ben ventured a cautious grin. Portia smiled back, and the urge to throw up finally went away. She took a breath of cool air, brushing the curls from her forehead with a trembling hand. She recognized the oak grove they were standing in. Just past it was the meadow, and beyond that, the first door that she had opened for the fox. The fox who had turned out to be a man.

She turned to face Ben. "I'm not imagining this, am I? This is all really happening."

Ben nodded, and then glanced down at the tiny man crouching on his shoulder.

"I am very sorry," the man croaked weakly.

Rose joined them and held out her hand. "No reason to apologize, Ridik. You've taken us far enough. Thank you."

The tiny man briefly pressed his forehead against the back of her hand and gave her an exhausted smile. Rose smiled back before marching towards the edge of the forest at a brisk pace. "Let's go."

Ben followed her without hesitation, and Portia followed in his wake. She still didn't understand how the others had found her, or what was going on. Why was Rose accepting everything so calmly? Yes, she seemed tense, but otherwise completely unimpressed by all the miniature humans and the foxes turning into people. It even looked like she was friends with the tiny person sitting on Ben's shoulder. And then there was that broomstick-like staff that Rose was carrying like a samurai sword. Who *was* Rose, really?

At the forest's edge, Rose came to a halt and raised her hand. Ben stopped immediately, but Portia passed him to stand by Rose's side. Wisps of grey fog were drifting across the meadow like soap bubbles on bathwater.

Rose bit her lower lip and drummed her fingers on the staff, lost in thought. On the other side of the meadow, no more than fifty metres way, the door in the wall was waiting for them.

"We're not going to make it," the tiny man said. What had Rose called him? Ridik?

Rose came to life again. "We have to." She turned to Portia and Ben. "Stay close behind me."

Portia shot Ben a questioning glance, but he just shrugged. He obviously didn't understand what was going on any more than she did.

One by one, they stepped out of the safety of the woods.

They began to walk across the foggy field, cleaving through curtains of mist. With every step, the haze grew denser, until they could barely make out the door on the other side of the meadow. Then, about halfway across, Rose stopped.

"They're here," she murmured.

To their right, from somewhere in the swirling mist, came a whinnying sound, followed by the muted drumming of hooves. Portia was instantly covered in icy goosebumps.

Ridik straightened up and stared intently in the direction of the sounds.

"What on earth?" Portia said in a low voice. She reached out and took Ben's hand. He jumped in surprise before giving her fingers a reassuring squeeze.

Rose raised her staff to her lips and seemed to whisper to it. As she spoke, a web of glowing blue veins appeared on the wood, like the veins of a leaf.

Ben gasped. Portia just stared, wide-eyed. This couldn't be happening!

"Rose—" she began, in a small, frightened voice, but the older woman cut her off.

"Keep calm," she said, stepping in front of Portia and Ben, holding the staff ready at her side. Portia noticed blue lines glowing on the inside of her wrist as well. *Her tattoo,* Portia thought, but then all thoughts were washed away like a sandcastle by the tide.

Just a few metres away from Rose, a horse emerged from the mist, snorting and pawing at the ground with its grey hooves.

"Nazgûl," mumbled Ben.

Portia shuddered. The rider was wearing a hooded robe. Both man and horse looked as if they were made of fog, their outlines fraying at the edges like skeins of smoke.

Just then a dog appeared at the horse's side. Portia backed away automatically. It was a big, wiry beast with a long snout, a white coat and ears as red as if they had been dipped in blood. Its eyes blazed like headlights on a foggy night.

Ben flinched at the sight of the animal too, and Portia heard Ridik breathing heavily on his shoulder.

"To the door," Rose said calmly. "Now."

She had barely finished speaking when the rider raised a hand, and the dog bolted forward across the meadow towards them. Ben was squeezing Portia's hand so hard it almost hurt. They both stumbled backwards and froze, unable to run.

Rose stood stock-still, not moving an inch. Only when the dog was almost upon them, about to spring, did she spin around, whipping her staff through the air and hitting the beast in its flank. The pattern on the staff glowed brightly, glittered—and then, suddenly, the dog was gone.

"Watch out!" Ridik yelled.

While Rose was fending off the dog's attack, the rider had spurred his horse towards the door. Rose ran across the meadow to block his path. The rider pulled hard on his reins, making the horse rear up, its hooves beating the air. Rose swayed backwards and struck out with her staff, hitting the horse on the leg. The blue pattern glowed brightly once more, and a fizzing sound rent the air. The rider grabbed at Rose, but she ducked underneath his arm, caught hold of his robe and pulled him from his saddle. As he fell, Rose swung her staff again, and this time the horse burst apart in an explosion of fog and smoke. Then, before the rider could get to his feet, she spun around, raised the staff over her head and thrust it down. There was a flash of blue light and the rider vanished, as if he had never been there at all.

Portia stood in silence, open-mouthed. Ben let go of her hand and took a few dazed steps towards Rose. Fog surged and broke around her, like waves against a rock.

"Rose?" Ben had hardly uttered her name, when from the depths of the fog came a thundering sound of hoof beats, growing louder and louder. *That's not just one horse. That's a lot of horses*, Portia thought. *And they're all galloping our way!*

"Too late!" Ridik said, his voice a warning. "Too late!"

Just then a rider burst out of the fog, tearing towards the open door. He was too fast and too far away for Rose to stop him. Roaring with frustration, she spun around. "Ridik!"

The tiny man stood up on Ben's shoulder, holding his arms out straight from his body. His cloak of feathers seemed to puff up for a moment before he leapt into the air and shifted into his blackbird shape in the blink of an eye. Portia could hardly believe what she was seeing. Swift as an arrow, the blackbird man shot towards the Grey Rider. Rose was running too, her staff held firmly in one hand and the other thrust into her skirt pocket.

The key, Portia remembered, and that thought finally jolted her back into action. She grabbed Ben's sleeve. "Come on! Quickly!"

For a moment he stared at her, frozen, but then he too seemed to come to his senses. They set off running across the meadow towards the door. Portia's backpack banged awkwardly against her back as she ran, but the straps were done up too tightly for her to just drop it.

In the meantime, the blackbird had caught up with the rider. It flew a tight circle around the horse's head, making it shy up, before diving towards the rider's face, its tiny claws outstretched.

"Ridik!" Ben stumbled, but Portia grabbed his arm and pulled him to his feet again. Another dog appeared, tearing past them so close that Portia felt a buffet of air as it barrelled by. It wasn't after them, this time. It was making straight for—

"Rose!" Portia yelled. Up ahead, Rose had reached the wall and slammed the door shut. She spun around just as the dog leapt. This time the beast caught her staff in its fangs, splintering the wood, but Rose swung her weapon in a wide arc, flinging the dog away from her. Barely had it landed when it scrambled to its feet and leapt again, but this time Rose was ready. She thrust the staff into the dog's body and it vanished in a blaze of blue light.

At the same moment, Ben cried out in alarm. Portia whirled around to see a second horse rearing wildly as the blackbird kept up its darting attacks on its rider. Struggling with the reins, he lashed out frantically until finally one of his blows hit home, knocking the bird from the air.

"No!" Ben yelled, and started to run towards the fallen bird.

Rose swore and pulled the key from her pocket. Before Portia had time to realize what was happening, Rose had locked the door and was sprinting over to Ben who was kneeling over the blackbird. The grey horse was still agitated, and Ben would have been crushed under its hooves had Rose not arrived in the nick of time to snatch the reins and drag it aside.

As she did so, the rider sent a long streak of fog lashing towards her like a whip. Rose cried out in pain as the grey tendril coiled around her forearm. She pulled herself away, tearing free of the foggy rope just as the rider prepared to attack again.

Portia ran over to Ben too, even though the further away she got from the door the louder the alarm bells rang in her head. *This is bad. This is very bad*, she thought despairingly. They needed to get away from here and back through the door before more of those riders showed up.

Ben was crouching in the grass, bent over Ridik's body. As Portia reached him, she saw that he was holding the blackbird in his hands. Portia felt a stab in her heart when she noticed his twisted wing, but there was no time for sorrow now. She grabbed Ben's arm and pulled, but he didn't budge.

"Come on!" she hissed. But Ben didn't even lift his head. Frantically, she looked over to Rose for help, but she had her hands full. The rider was sending whip after foggy whip towards her, like a knife thrower at a circus. Rose was managing to dodge his attacks, but in doing so she was retreating further and further from the door. Panic rose in Portia's throat, but then she understood that Rose was deliberately steering the rider away from her and Ben. As soon as she had drawn him far enough, she caught one of the nasty fog whips on the tip of her staff. The rider tried to retreat when he realized what was happening, but his own weapon would be his undoing. Portia could see now that those swirls of fog were a part of the rider, attached to him like an octopus's tentacles. And one of those tentacles was tightly coiled around Rose's staff.

Rose smiled, grim and determined. She clutched the staff more tightly, and the wood started to glow. The rider squirmed, but it was too late. A pulse of blue light shot along the fog tendril, then Rose tore the staff free and leapt forward. While still in mid-air, she struck out with her staff, swinging it in a glittering arc through horse and rider. Both dissolved in a puff of mist, but in the distance yet another bank of fog was already building, threatening to cut off their escape in no time.

"Ben!" Portia pleaded desperately. "Ben! We have to get away from here!" She might just as well have been shouting at a rock. He didn't move an inch.

Then, suddenly, Rose was by her side. As she squatted down in front of Ben, she noticed the lifeless blackbird in his hands. Shining tears welled up in her eyes, but she wiped them away.

"We have to leave. Now!" she told Portia, who managed to nod in reply.

"Ben," she urged. "Ben, come on!"

Finally, Ben raised his head. He was crying, and Portia felt his sorrow like a weight on her own heart. Rose held his face with both hands and looked him straight in the eyes. "No hesitation, no questions," she said.

Ben let out a long, shaky breath. Then he got to his feet.

Portia looked back towards the door—but where the wall had stood before, there was now only a swirling bank of grey fog. Portia could make out ghostly shapes stirring deep within the murk, and hear a terrible scratching sound, like claws scraping on a wooden door. Her blood ran cold.

"We can't go back now," Rose sighed. She took Portia by the hand and pulled her towards the oak grove, gently pushing Ben ahead of her. "We have to get to the Faerie Door. That's our only chance."

"But..." Portia began.

"It's no good, my dear," she said, and this time her voice cracked. "There are too many of them."

They reached the edge of the oak grove, and Rose gave Ben a gentle shove into the safety of the trees. Portia glanced back one final time before she followed, and what she saw made the blood curdle in her veins. Out in the meadow, more and more shadowy figures were emerging from the fog. There were no horses now. Instead, the creatures were on foot: grey ghosts in tattered robes, all swarming towards the closed door like moths to a flame. And then, from somewhere beyond the meadow, came the long, drawn-out call of a hunting horn.

Dead End

The journey back to the Faerie Door seemed never-ending. Ridik had sped Ben on his way earlier, but now his lifeless body weighed heavy as a rock in the boy's hands.

Rose led the way, striding determinedly ahead. Portia looked exhausted and was trailing behind.

They had long left the oak grove behind and the lush meadows were giving way to rockier ground as they drew closer to the mountains. After a while, Rose shot Portia a worried glance. "We're taking a break," she announced.

A withered rowan tree rose from the grass nearby. It seemed a good spot to rest.

Portia dropped to the ground in front of the tree. Rose sat on a flat rock nearby and Ben did likewise, carefully balancing Ridik on his thigh. Rose raised one hand, hesitated briefly, and then touched his plumage with her fingertips. She swallowed, as if fighting back tears. "*Swirne saff*," she said softly.

Safe travels, Ben translated. Tears welled up in his eyes, but he didn't make a sound. He had to pull himself together, he told himself. He had only just met Ridik, after all. But the sight of the blackbird's lifeless body was rattling a door hidden deep inside him, one he'd kept tightly locked since his father passed away. Rose put an arm around his shoulder, but he stiffened at her touch. It reminded him of all the other hugs he'd had to put up with. There had been a seemingly endless line of aunts and cousins at his dad's funeral, all squeezing and patting him. He had wanted nothing more than to run out of the brightly lit living room and into the safety and solitude of the forest on his wall.

Rose took her arm away. She didn't ask him to put Ridik down and Ben was grateful for that. Portia gave him a look full of compassion, but he avoided meeting her eyes.

Rose rubbed her face with both hands and ran her fingers through her hair. Her forearm bore a narrow grey mark where the rider's whip had caught her. When Rose caught sight of it, she snorted dismissively, as if it were a trifling annoyance.

"Does it hurt?" asked Portia.

"No."

Portia frowned, incredulous. "How did you know how to do all that stuff?" she asked. "The fighting I mean. And..." She swept her hand through the air. "What *is* all this?"

"It's a very long story," Rose sighed. "But I should at least tell you the most important part." She rubbed her face again, then folded her hands in her lap.

"Bramble and I were in our last term at university," she began. "The plan was to go on a trip after our gradu-ation, but we didn't have any money. So we and a group of friends decided to earn some by helping to clear out a big country estate near here. I remember, when we walked into that house, the great hall with its enormous fireplace and beautiful wainscoting—it was as if we had travelled back in time."

A faint smile stole over her face. "We were absolutely fascinated by all the bric-a-brac that had piled up in those old rooms. Chests, porcelain figurines, antique weapons, tapestries..." She paused for a moment, as if summoning up the courage to tell the next chapter of the story. "On the second day, our friend Hermia came across a little casket," she continued eventually. "In it, we found a diary, a hand-drawn map of the area around Trefriw and a very old key."

Portia gasped.

Rose nodded grimly. "Yes, exactly. *That* key." She brought it out it of her pocket and turned it around in her fingers. "The diary belonged to a certain W.H.," she went on. "He was a folklore collector. You know, one of those people who go around collecting and recording myths and fairy tales. Apparently he had come to Wales because of all the stories about fairies who were said to inhabit these parts. It seems he had brought the key along himself," Rose went on, "although the diary didn't reveal who gave it to him or where he got it from. Anyway, W.H. came to these parts because he had heard there was a magical door somewhere around here, which could be opened by that key. And behind that door was the Fairy World. The *Otherworld*, as we call it in Wales. At first, he was convinced that those stories were mere fairy tales. But then, about ten pages into his diary, he changed his mind."

"He found the door," Ben said.

"Precisely. He found one door leading out of the Human World, and then another leading to the Otherworld. And the map supposedly showed the location of the first door."

Portia gave a faint snort of disbelief, as if to say that this all sounded rather unlikely to her.

Rose just smiled. "Well, we didn't believe it at first either. But we also thought it would be fun to try and find the door using the map, so we took the key and set off."

She fell silent, gazing off into the distance. "It was all true," she said. "Every bit of it. Fairy Queen Titania's underground palace, the magical lanterns in the trees, the Pale Tower."

Rose closed her eyes, as if recalling the beauty of the Otherworld. Portia flashed Ben a sceptical glance, but he just shrugged. He believed Rose.

Portia leant forward. "So, if the first door leads out of the Human World, and the second into the Fairy World, where are we now?"

"In the Borderlands between the worlds," Rose replied. "And we should not be here."

"The Grey King..." Ben began. Ridik had mentioned his name during the journey through the woods, but hadn't said much more.

"Errm, who?" Portia asked, a hint of desperation in her voice.

"The Grey King," Rose repeated. "The ruler of the Borderlands. Those riders at the door to the Human World? They were his hunters."

Portia fell silent again, a tense look on her face.

Hunters, Ben thought, feeling the flesh on his neck crawl. "And who are they hunting?"

Rose held up the key meaningfully. "The King senses it whenever anyone opens one of the doors," she explained. "Like a wolf getting the scent of a wounded animal. For him, the Borderlands are like a prison. The King wants to get out: into the Human World or the Fairy World. And wherever he goes, he brings with him the fog of forgetfulness. Once released, the fog will devour any trace of life it comes across, until all lands are empty and silent."

She gazed over their heads as she spoke these last words. Ben turned around to see wisps of fog rising through the canopy of the oak wood they had just come through. Was that the fog of forgetfulness Rose was talking about?

"We saw it happening back then," Rose went on. "We left the doors open, and the King led his army into the Otherworld."

"But why didn't you just shut the doors behind you?" Portia asked.

"Because we were fools," said Rose mournfully. "Careless. We didn't have the faintest idea about anything. And some of us obviously haven't changed." She stuffed the key back into her skirt pocket. "Bramble was supposed to throw the key into a lake, so we would never again be tempted to open the doors. And I thought that she had done it. All these years..." Rose paused for a moment, then carried on in a strained voice. "We tried to make up for our mistake. Ridik fought the Grey King's ghostly army alongside us back then. So did Robin Goodfellow. In the end, both were stranded in the Human World. Robin wanted to go back, but we decided it was too risky, so we destroyed the key. Or at least I thought we did. Robin never forgave us for that."

Portia was biting her lower lip, still seemingly wrestling with her doubts. Ben believed everything Rose had told them, but his excitement at the discovery of these new worlds was fading. Now that he held Ridik's lifeless body in his hands, he knew: no matter how many worlds existed, death had a place in every single one.

Portia stood up. She picked up her backpack, rummaged around in it and brought out a blue cloth.

"Here you go," she said. "For Ridik."

Surprised, Ben accepted the gift, and gently folded Ridik in the soft fabric. It felt right, covering him like that. Respectful somehow.

Rose waited for him to finish, then she got up as well. "We have to get moving."

Portia looked up at her. "What's your plan?"

Rose was just about to respond when they heard the long, drawn-out howling of a pack of dogs from across the plain below.

Rose pressed her lips together, determined. "First of all, we have to get to the Faerie Door."

∾ PORTIA ∾

When they reached the moor, the ridges on both sides were already smothered in fog. Scraps of white mist drifted like smoke over the heather. Portia tripped over a grassy tuft and fell to her knees in a boggy puddle.

Rose was by her side in seconds and helped her to her feet. "Are you okay?"

What Portia really wanted was to burst into tears, sink to her knees again and never get up—but she nodded anyway. Even though nothing was okay. Her mind was a muddle and she couldn't think clearly. She didn't know how she'd manage to take a single step more, and her throat was aching from all the sobs she was fighting so hard to hold back. Without another word, Rose drew her into a hug.

Portia's first reaction was to try to squirm free of the embrace, but Rose held her tight. "There, there," she said softly.

For a few seconds, Portia felt protected from everything that was happening. She leant her forehead against Rose's shoulder and closed her eyes. *Don't panic*, she told herself over and over again. *Don't panic*. Rose was here, and she knew what to do.

Behind them the fog hounds' howling swelled only to fade once more. Rose gently eased out of their embrace, and pressed the key into Portia's hand. "Take this," she said. "Now run to the Faerie Door and make sure you get through. I'll lead the pack away from your trail."

"What? No!" Portia tried to give the key back, but Rose grabbed her hand and closed her fingers around it.

"Take it," Rose insisted. "Seek shelter in the Otherworld. And look for Robin Goodfellow. I realize he made a rather poor first impression, but I know he'll help you."

Portia opened her mouth to speak, but Rose had already turned to Ben. "Take Ridik back to his world. And remember to close and lock the door behind you."

"But what about you?" Portia insisted. Panic was roaring like a storm in her ears now.

Rose wouldn't look her in the eye. "I'll catch up with you as soon as I can."

"But if we lock the door behind us..." Ben began.

Rose shook her head vehemently. "You have to lock that door." Her lips curled into a sad, thin smile. "We have no choice now," she said. "Tell Robin... Tell him I'll fix everything."

The baying of the hounds seemed terrifyingly close now, and once more the call of the hunting horn rang out across the moor. Every single hair on Portia's neck stood on end.

"You have to go now," Rose urged. Ben just stared at her, but Portia looked over Rose's shoulder and saw a flood of fog surging towards them. How many hunters were hidden within the mist? A dozen? A hundred?

"Portia!" Rose's voice cut through the air. Portia squared her shoulders and fought down the panic raging inside of her. Her stomach was twisted into a painful knot, but she grabbed Ben's hand and pulled him along with her.

Portia had no idea how, but they made it to the door. Panting and sweaty, she and Ben found themselves between the two rowan trees at the portal to the Fairy World. With a trembling hand, Portia put the key into the lock and turned it. The door opened easily, but rather than walking through it right away, they both turned around.

A delicate mist had fallen on the moor like a veil. Rocks, heather and grass had all vanished in the haze, while to the west a fog bank cut off their view entirely. It seemed as if the moor was surrounded by a white wall of nothingness—but the nothingness was moving.

"Come on, come on," Portia muttered under her breath as she stared at the approaching white wall, willing Rose to come running out of the fog. At least they could no longer hear any sounds of the hunt. Maybe her aunt's foolhardy plan had actually worked?

"Portia?" Ben sounded nervous.

Portia didn't dare taking her eyes off the fog bank. "She'll make it," she said. She *had* to make it.

Ben rested his hand gently on her arm, and just then Portia saw what she had been hoping so much to see. A shadow was moving deep inside the rolling mist! Someone was coming towards them, a single figure cutting through the grey-white soup. She felt a wave of relief wash over her... only for it to evaporate a moment later.

The figure that emerged from the fog was not Rose. It wasn't riding a horse either, though it was as grey as the hunters that had attacked them at the door to the Human World. Whatever it was, it was tall. Taller than a normal human. Its body was shrouded in a long coat, and where its face should have been was a gleaming white stag skull, which peered out from underneath the edge of a hood, with black antlers branching out to either side. When it was less than a hundred metres away, the creature paused. Some of the fog swirling around it solidified into the shape of a dog.

A second hound quickly materialized in turn, and then a third.

Where was Rose?

"Portia!"

She whirled round to see a stunned Ben staring at the ground. Thin tendrils of fog were rising from the grass and curling around their ankles.

"The door!" Ben shouted in warning. A few white fingers were already snaking their way towards the archway.

Portia hurriedly pulled her foot away from the groping fog, glancing nervously back at the moor. The hounds were already edging closer.

Ben grabbed her arm. "We... We have to go."

"No! Have you lost your mind? Rose is in there somewhere!" Portia clenched her fists stubbornly, but Ben tugged at her sleeve.

"Portia, please," he pleaded. Just then, as if they had been waiting for a signal, the dogs set off towards them.

Portia gasped in fright, stumbling backwards against the archway. She felt Ben's fingers gripping her arm as they fell through the doorway together and he tore the key from her hand. Behind them, the dogs were getting closer and closer as the fog thundered towards them like a tidal wave.

"Rose," Portia whispered, just as Ben slammed the door and turned the key in the lock.

Ridik's Final Journey

The door to the Fairy World opened into a dark tunnel that burrowed into the ridge before emerging onto a bracken-smothered plain. A few wisps of fog that had drifted through the tunnel after them disappeared into the ferns, but Portia immediately charged after them, kicking and scuffing at the ground until every trace was gone.

Ben had turned around to discover two stone columns covered with an ornate pattern of knots and ribbons flanking the entrance to the Fairy Tunnel. But all he could really see in his mind was Rose, walking alone towards the fog.

We left her behind. The thought made him numb. How had everything turned into such a terrible mess so quickly?

Ben turned his back on the tunnel once more and forced himself to take a closer look at their surroundings.

A circle of half a dozen standing stones protruded from the mass of ferns. Portia was standing in the middle of it, in front of a mossy pile of rocks, but she didn't seem to be paying the stone circle any heed. Instead, she had taken off her backpack and was rummaging around inside. As Ben arrived at her side, she pulled out a map, which she proceeded to unfold and study intently. Ben was baffled.

Did she really think the Otherworld would be on an ordinary map?

As he thought about it, he realized how serious their situation was. Not only had they lost Rose, but now the way home was blocked too! And while Ben was stranded here... and while the Grey Riders were roaming the Borderlands between the worlds... his mother must be waiting and waiting for him to come home. He felt a lump in this throat at the thought of her watching for him through the bookshop window.

Then he glanced down at the little bundle in his hands and swallowed a sob. Rose had asked him to take Ridik back to his world. He had no idea what awaited them here, but honouring her wish and paying his last respects to Ridik was the least he could do.

Ben walked to the pile of rocks and touched the soft green cushion of moss covering it. It gave way under his fingers, warm to the touch as if it had been storing sunlight all day long. He knelt and placed Ridik on top of a rock, carefully folding back the cloth so his head was resting on the moss. *You're home now*, he thought. Ben felt tears pricking at his eyes, but this time he held them back. Then he rose and went over to Portia.

She was still studying the footpaths and forests on her map. "Do you know your way around here?" she asked. "Is there a path leading from this side of the moor back down to Trefriw?"

Ben raised his eyebrows. "I don't think that's how it works," he said. "We have to go back through the doors to get home."

Portia huffed defiantly. "No thanks," she muttered, clenching the map tighter in her hands. "We'll have to find shelter before it gets dark," she continued without looking up. "Do you know what time it is? My phone died."

Ben glanced at his watch. It had stopped. Did the Otherworld stop all human technology working?

Portia looked around then, not waiting for his reply. "If we head west, we should come to Lake Crafnant. There's a hikers' hostel there, I think." She stared at the map, seemingly not even interested in what he might have to say. "We'll have to walk cross-country, but we should be fine if we use my compass."

Ben didn't know what to say. How could he make her understand that she was wasting her time? Then again, he had no idea what to do or where to go either. He was just about to ask Portia whether she understood that they were no longer in the Human World when he heard a fluttering overhead. Looking up, he saw a pair of chaffinches had settled on one of the standing stones.

Portia had jammed the folded map under her arm and was rummaging around in her backpack again. Meanwhile, more and more birds were arriving to perch on the rocks: blackbirds, finches, tits and even a spotted woodpecker. Their shiny, beady eyes were all focused on Portia and Ben. Meanwhile, oblivious to what was happening around them, Portia had found the compass. She held it up for a moment, then shook it despairingly.

"Come on! Work!" she hissed.

"Portia?" Ben said softly.

But Portia was intent on the compass, and only looked up when Ben touched her arm. He gestured at the stones around them, and Portia's eyes widened in surprise.

Just then, a female blackbird dropped from her perch and swooped towards them. Ben and Portia broke apart and backed off as the bird glided between them towards the mossy pile of rocks. Just before she reached the rocks, she gave a quick flap of her wings and changed shape. There was a blur of brown feathers before a tiny barefoot woman landed lightly on the moss next to Ridik's body. As if that had been a signal, the other birds shed their feathers too. Within moments, there were tiny people sitting or kneeling on top of all of the standing stones.

Portia stood dumbstruck, the compass still in her hand. Ben gazed around him at the wonderful gathering. "*Yr Adar*," he said under his breath. The Bird People had arrived.

The Blackbird Woman slowly circled Ridik's body. Then she crouched, touched his wing and whispered something Ben couldn't make out. A ripple passed through Ridik's black plumage, then the feathers receded into his body with a rustling noise. The scout of the Adar lay on the moss in his human form, clad only in his coat of black feathers, his skin white as snow. A murmur passed through the audience seated on the rocks.

"What happened?"

"Preet, what is the meaning of this?"

"Where did he come from?"

"How did he die?"

Ben cleared his throat and stepped forward. "Ridik fell in battle with the Grey Riders," he said in a thick voice. As soon as the words left his mouth, he felt foolish and theatrical. The Adar stared at him as if they were surprised he could speak at all.

"The Grey Riders," a podgy little man in a robe made of yellow and blue feathers repeated. The others whispered nervously among themselves.

"The Grey King's riders!" a woman cried, and then another called out: "So the Grey King has returned?"

"No," a third voice cut in. "That can't be. He is sleeping!"

Then the Blackbird Woman addressed Ben directly. "Is the door closed?"

Ben nodded quickly. "Yes. We locked it behind us." He turned to Portia. "Didn't we?"

Portia, still looking stunned, nodded as well.

Two of the Adar shifted back into bird shape and flew off. Those who remained began to yell and argue among themselves. The Blackbird Woman ignored the uproar. "Do you have the key?" she asked.

Ben and Portia exchanged another look. Portia pulled the key from her pocket, and the Adar fell silent.

"Little Humans," the Blackbird Woman said. "You had better come with us."

The Grove of the Adar lay within an oak forest just a few miles from the border of the Otherworld. The trees did not grow tightly there, but their crowns spread out to form a thick, dark-green canopy.

Up high in the trees the Adar had built their homes. Round nest-like dwellings, tiny huts and open platforms nestled in the crooks of branches. Since their world was hidden from the sky by the forest canopy, it was filled with gloom and shadow, and the Adar had hung lanterns all about, so the treetops were filled with tiny glowing lights.

There was a Guest Hall for visitors, too. A dome made of braided willow branches, standing by the bank of a broad stream; it reminded Ben of an igloo. The walls and roof were covered in silvery leaves, and a curtain of twigs hung over the round entrance hole. Inside, the floor was a mossy hollow. There were roots to lean against here and there, and several blue and red cushions scattered in between, some of which already looked a bit rumpled. Carved wooden lanterns hanging from the roof bathed the hall in a milky light.

Ben climbed on a root, standing on tiptoes to try and get a better look at one of the lanterns. Where was the light coming from? No flame he knew of burned with that strange colour. He peered inside, and saw no candle or oil wick. Instead, he discovered a cluster of moths with wings that gleamed as if they had been dipped in moonlight.

He gently touched the lantern window and marvelled at how one of the moths landed directly on the other side of the glass from his fingertip. Ben wished he had brought along his sketch pad and pencils. He would have loved to draw this place and its inhabitants. The Adar had led him and Portia to the Tree Town after their encounter at the stone circle. Preet ferch Mwyalchod, the Blackbird Woman, had shown them to the Guest Hall, and suggested they rest for a while. News of the two Human visitors to the Otherworld must have reached the grove ahead of them. When they had stepped into the Willow Dome, two bowls awaited each of them: one filled with blackberries, the other with grilled mushrooms. There were also two wooden cups, which sat next to a spring that splashed gently in the middle of the mossy hollow. While Ben was exploring the dome, Portia stood by the entrance, peering out through the curtain of twigs. Once Ben had finished examining the lantern, they sat down on the mossy floor together.

"Animals that turn into people. Tiny houses in trees. It definitely can't get any weirder," she said in weak voice.

"The lanterns are full of glowing moths," Ben added.

"Of course they are. What else would be in there?" Portia sighed. She rested a hand on her backpack. "That map really isn't any use, is it? The only way back is through the doors."

"I think so, yes." Ben glanced nervously across at Portia. He was expecting her to get angry again, or maybe burst into tears. But instead she was staring blankly into space. Ben carried on, before he could change his mind. "Look on the bright side, though. At least they're doors and not a wardrobe. You know, like in Narnia."

To his surprise, Portia laughed weakly. "Or a rabbit hole, like in *Alice's Adventures in Wonderland*."

She shook her head, as if trying to clear her thoughts. Then she opened her backpack and brought out not only a thermos, but two wrapped sandwiches as well.

"I prepared these for our little trip to the stone circle." She shrugged. "I suppose we did see a stone circle in the end. But I'm guessing it was a bit different from the one you were planning to show me?"

"Oh, yeah. Just a bit." Despite everything, Ben couldn't help but grin.

"Here you go." She handed him a sandwich. "I'm pretty sure that'll fill you up better than a handful of berries."

Ben took the sandwich, so surprised that he forgot to say thank you. He had assumed Portia had only agreed to go to the stone circle with him to be polite. Now it seemed she had actually been looking forward to it, and had even packed a picnic. For both of them. He definitely hadn't expected that. Lifting a corner of the sandwich, he found ham, cheese, salad and mayonnaise inside—his favourite.

He remembered the blue cloth. The one she had given him for Ridik's body. It must have been meant for a picnic blanket.

Portia unscrewed the thermos and poured peppermint tea into the wooden cups left for them by the Adar. The scent of mint curled towards the ceiling of the dome with the steam rising from the cups. "You're right," she said. "We have to go back and through the door. If only to find Rose."

"Do you think she's all right?"

"Well, you saw how she dealt with those ghost riders. Obi-Wan Kenobi's got nothing on her."

Ben took a bite of his sandwich. Somehow, Portia's confidence that they would be able to find Rose and get back home made him hopeful, too. Of course they would go back for her.

He was just taking a sip from his mug when a blackbird came fluttering into the dome through the twig curtain, landed on a root and took Preet's human-like form. A plump wren followed close behind, landed at her side and transformed into a stocky, bald man who only came up to the Blackbird Woman's shoulder.

"Little Humans," Preet said. "I hope you've replenished your energy and strength."

"Oh, yes," Portia replied, quickly grabbing a blackberry. "Thank you so much for your hospitality."

"Yes, thank you," Ben hurried to add.

Preet smiled. The Blackbird Woman had thick brown hair that hung down to her hips, elegantly shot through with streaks of silver. She wore a sleeveless brown tunic, and a shawl made of mottled brown feathers, fastened at her right shoulder by a silver brooch. A tattooed pattern of knots and spirals flowed up her arms and neck all the way to her temples. A similar pattern covered the plump wren's bald head.

"This is Tatap ap Drywod, son of the Wrens," Preet introduced her companion. "He's a scout, as am I."

"Like Ridik?" Ben asked.

Preet nodded. "Ridik was my uncle," she explained. "When he disappeared, I had only just earned my scout badge." She bowed her head, clearly upset. Tatap rested a comforting hand on her shoulder.

"Now, kindly tell us how you came to be here," Preet said, when she had regained her composure. "How did you find yourselves in the Borderlands?"

Portia and Ben looked at each other before beginning to tell their story. Ben told the Adar of Ridik's accident, about his transformation the next morning, and how they had followed Robin Goodfellow and Portia to the first door. But when he got to the part where he had to describe the Grey Riders, he clammed up. Portia took over.

"If it hadn't been for Ridik, the rider would've made it through the first door... the door to the Human World," she said. "Ridik slowed him down. And the rider killed him for that."

Ben clutched his cup with both hands, avoiding the Adar's eyes. Portia glanced his way, but thankfully she carried on talking.

"We hurried back to the other door, the one on the moor, but those fog creatures caught up with us. Rose stayed behind to distract them, so we could escape."

"This Rose," Preet interrupted. "Does she know her way around the Borderlands?"

Ben nodded. "Yes, she's been there before. And here as well, actually. Many, many years ago. With Bramble and a few other friends."

"Oh," Tatap said. And then, more excitedly: "Oh! You speak of Viola Rosethorn and the other Humans!" He whistled. "I didn't think we'd ever see them again."

"We didn't even know she'd survived the battle against the Grey King," Preet added.

"We knew only that they had driven him into the Borderlands and locked the door behind them." Tatap shook his head in amazement. "Feather and fluff, what news this is!"

"Those were terrible times, when the Grey King came to our world," Preet said gravely. "The fog overran the Curlews' dwelling place."

"My grandmother saw it in her nightmares until the day she died," Tatap said. "She witnessed the fog rushing in across the ocean. It was as if the world was dissolving and devouring itself at the same time—that's how she always described it. And now the Grey King has awoken again." He shuddered. "Are you absolutely sure that the door is locked?" he asked.

"Yes," Ben confirmed. "Both the Fairy and Human doors."

"How long do we have to wait until we can open the doors?" Portia asked. "Until the... you know, until those fog things are asleep again?"

"Open the doors?" Preet repeated.

"Yes, how long do we have to wait until—" Portia began, but Tatap cut her off.

"No, no," he said firmly. "The doors must remain locked."

"The risk is too great," agreed Preet. "If the Grey King has awoken, then the Borderlands must be swarming with his riders."

"They may even be waiting on the other side of the door," Tatap said darkly.

Preet nodded.

"But we have to go back," said Portia. Her voice sounded calm, but her tensely clenched fists told a different story. Ben felt ice-cold fear creeping through his body too. He couldn't bear the idea that they might be stranded in this place for ever.

"There must be another way," he said. "Perhaps a different door, or maybe a secret path?"

Preet and Tatap exchanged a look. "We're very sorry," Preet said.

Portia fumbled in her pocket, as if to make sure that the key was still there. "What about that fox? Robin Goodfellow?" she wondered. "Rose said he would help us."

"Goodfellow?" Tatap seemed surprised. "Robin Goodfellow has returned?"

"Oh, but of course!" Preet exclaimed. "That makes sense. He disappeared at the same time as Ridik. We thought he'd become lost in the fog, remember?"

"That's right," Tatap agreed. "Stranded in the Human World, the both of them. My goodness. You can't help but wonder who else might show up around here one of these days."

"And Mistress Rosethorn really said you should ask Goodfellow for help?" Preet asked, sounding sceptical.

"Yes," Portia insisted.

"Well now," Preet said, still sounding doubtful. "They do say he had a soft spot for Viola Rosethorn. Perhaps asking him for help might not be the worst idea."

"Whether he will grant it to you, that's a whole other question," Tatap said drily.

"Why? What's wrong with him?" Ben asked.

"He was... or rather, he *is* a trickster. He's a troublemaker in the service of Oberon, the Fairy King," Tatap explained. "I for one wouldn't trust him. Presumably we can thank him for the fact that the doors were opened again?"

"Yes," Ben confirmed. "Ridik thought he must have wanted to get home."

"That sounds just like Uncle Ridik," Preet sighed. "He always did believe that there was something good in everyone."

A solemn moment of silence followed. "So many years," Preet said at length, dabbing at her eyes. "Ah, my heart is breaking just thinking about how he couldn't come home for so long. He must've been so lonely."

Tatap took her hand. "At least he's returned home now."

Preet patted his hand and turned to Ben. "Thank you for bringing him back to us. From here, his soul can embark on its next journey. That would mean a lot to him."

Ben nodded, a lump in his throat.

From outside in the forest came the blaring of a horn. Preet and Tatap stiffened. "The time has come to bid Ridik farewell," Preet said. She turned to Portia. "If you really want to try your luck asking Goodfellow for help, Tatap and I would be happy to take you to him. We can leave tomorrow morning."

Portia managed a strained smile. "Thank you."

"And until then, you're our guests, of course," Tatap said. "Eat well, rest well." He smiled. "You look as if you need it."

INTERLUDE

The stone circle beyond the Faerie Door lay deserted. The Adar and the Human children were long gone. Now the sun had set, and fog began to rise amidst the bracken. At first just a few gossamer wisps snaked upward between the ferns, but then the mist thickened until the ground inside the stone circle resembled a round white pond. For a moment, the fog was still, then its surface began to ripple and churn. From the centre of the maelstrom, a shape materialized, like the prow of a ghost-ship emerging from the sea.

The clouds parted, and the moon cast its silvery glow on the circle. The woman standing in its centre was shrouded in a long black veil that covered her face like a delicate cobweb. A crown braided of bare winter branches rested on her head, and a horn carved from a giant boar's tusk hung from her shoulder. Her hands were hidden by gloves. Fog surged about her, and when it cleared, two pale, growling hounds stood at her side.

The woman turned to gaze towards the tunnel leading to the Faerie Door. She could sense that this passageway was closed, but there was still a faint silver-bright trace of the World Key lingering in the air. She turned to face the woods, towards the path leading to the Tree Town of the Adar. She raised a hand, and the dogs trotted forwards. The Grey King's Huntress followed in their wake.

Gwil Glumheart

At dawn the next day, Ben and Portia were waiting at the outskirts of the Adar's dwelling place. A shallow brook meandered by their feet. The water gave off an earthy woodland scent as it gurgled between the rocks.

The graze on Ben's arm was itching. He automatically reached for it with his hand, before stopping himself at the last moment. The night before, an Adar healer had smeared a red salve onto the wound and urged him not to scratch it while it healed.

Portia was carrying her backpack again. She looked a bit pale, but was holding on to the straps tightly and looked eager to get walking. Ben's muscles were sore, but it seemed all of yesterday's exertion had hardly affected Portia at all.

Ben sighed wistfully. He had read so many books about adventures in magical worlds—but in those stories people never seemed to get blisters while they were on quests.

Nearby, a small flock of young birds were splashing around in the shallow water near the bank. They chirped and laughed while effortlessly shifting shape: one moment fluffy little birds, the next looking like tiny children.

"Well, welcome to Wonderland," Portia said.

The corners of Ben's mouth twitched into a smile, just as a blackbird and a wren came flying towards them.

Preet and Tatap landed on a rock next to Portia and transformed into human shape. "First the good news. We know where Goodfellow is."

Portia pursed her lips. "And the bad news?"

"He's at the Fairy Queen's court," Tatap said. "And Titania bears no great love for humans."

Ben and Portia exchanged a worried look, but Preet raised her hand reassuringly. "Don't worry. We have a plan." She glanced over at Tatap, who grinned.

"We're taking you to meet a salamander."

Apparently, all the Adar's scouts had mastered the art of swiftflight. This time Ben took the journey through swirling winds and colours much better. When Preet ended their magical flight in a distant part of the forest, he was able to stand upright without staggering and he hardly felt dizzy either. Ben was still taking in his new surroundings while Preet gave him her instructions. "Gwil is down by the clay ponds," she said. "You keep back for now. I'll fly ahead and prepare him for your visit."

With that, she transformed into her feathery form and flew off ahead. Tatap stayed on Portia's shoulder as they slowly followed on foot.

"It's been some time since we saw Humans on our side of the door," Tatap explained. "And Gwil Glumheart... well, he's a rather skittish salamander."

114

"Magical creatures who are scared of us?" Portia said. "Shouldn't it be the other way around?"

Tatap laughed. "Don't be so surprised! You're as wondrous to us as we are to you. But have no fear, Gwil is a decent fellow. He works as a scribe at Fairy Hill. There's no one better to take you to Goodfellow." Tatap pointed to a boulder up ahead. "Here we are!" At his bidding, Portia and Ben hid behind the rock and cautiously peered around it.

Beyond the boulder, the forest opened into a clearing. The ground was thick with plants with fan-like leaves, and pale yellow blossoms that seemed to float around their stems like little stars. Amid the plants stood a strange figure, gazing at the ground in concentration. Gwil Glumheart was a thin, hunched little man, the size of a human, if a rather short one. He had his back to them, but Ben could see that he was bald. Gwil wore a long robe of faded black cloth and fingerless gloves. In one hand he held a basket filled to the brim with the fan-like leaves, and in the other a small sickle.

Preet had landed on a rock rising from the plants and shifted back into her human shape.

"Gwil Glumheart!"

At the sound of his name, Gwil turned around, surprised. "Scout Preet!" he cried. "What a pleasure!"

He went over to her and they both bowed. Then Gwil set his basket aside and sat down in front of Preet. Only when he was at eye level with the scout, did they begin to talk.

Ben leant forward, straining to hear their conversation, but Gwil and Preet were too far away for him to catch more than a few snippets.

"What are they saying?" asked Portia. Ben just shook his head, but Tatap squared his shoulders.

"Get ready," he whispered.

Just then, Preet turned towards them and chirped loudly.

"Come on now, let's go," Tatap urged.

One by one, they stepped out from behind the boulder and into the clearing. Gwil Glumheart looked over at them, confused. Then his eyes widened in shock. He leapt to his feet, stumbled backwards, fell over his basket and sprawled headlong in the plants.

Portia, Ben, the two Adar and Gwil sat in a circle in the clearing. Preet was telling Gwil all that had happened, with some help from Ben and Portia, while Gwil dabbed at his forehead with a handkerchief. They saw now that he wasn't just bald. His eyebrows were missing too, and his skin was waxy and pale.

"So there's a key again," said Gwil, after Preet had finished speaking. She looked over at Portia, who reached for her pocket, but Gwil held up his hand. A black tattooed line encircled his wrist like a bracelet.

"No need, I believe you!" he said. "Oh, dear. I fear this is not good news. The Grey King? Oh, dear, oh, dear." He dabbed his lips with his kerchief.

Preet tried to get to the point. "Gwil, these Humans would like to return home."

Gwil's eyes widened again. "Yes. Of course. Yes. But I'm afraid that won't be possible."

"Viola Rosethorn advised them to seek Robin Goodfellow's help," Tatap added.

"Goodfellow?" Gwil repeated incredulously. "What was she thinking?"

"We don't know," Preet said. "But we must help these two in some way or other. Could you guide them to Fairy Hill, perhaps?"

"Oh, Titania won't like that one bit."

Gwil blinked, and it took Ben a moment to realize that he didn't have human eyelids. Instead, a sort of filmy membrane flicked quickly up over his eyes from below—like a salamander's eyes.

"Why doesn't Titania like humans anyway?" asked Portia.

"Actually, there was a time when she was quite fond of visitors from the Human World," Tatap said. "She would sometimes even send out her fairies to lure mortal musicians and poets to Fairy Hill."

"But that has changed," Preet added.

"Yes," Gwil nodded gravely. "Since the Humans left open the doors and let the Grey Riders into our world."

An uneasy silence descended upon the group, until Ben spoke up. "Do you mean Rose and her friends? I think she was really sorry about it all. And she did everything she could to stop it from happening again."

"Totally," Portia agreed. "If she hadn't been so determined to stop those ghost riders, she'd be here with us."

"I did like Viola Rosethorn and the others," Gwil said. "All their stories from the other side... I could've listened to them for hours and hours."

"And they loved our world," Preet added. "Do you remember the stories that Mistress Brambleblossom used to tell about it?"

"Oh, yes," Gwil said. "She's a true poet!"

"Indeed, I am surprised she didn't accompany Viola Rosethorn to the Borderlands," Preet said. "Please don't tell me her soul has travelled on?"

It took Ben a moment to understand that Preet was talking about Bramble. Rosethorn and Brambleblossom. Rose and Bramble. The Afallon Ladies' nicknames came from the Otherworld.

Portia had apparently come to the same conclusion. "No, no," she hastened to say. "Bramble... I mean, Olivia, is fine. But I'm sure she's very worried about us." She looked around the circle pleadingly. "Please! We really must go back. If only to find Rose."

"And we have to hurry," Ben added. "We need to get to her before those Grey Riders do."

Gwil looked at Preet, but she ignored him. "You're right," she agreed. "We can't let her down."

Gwil seemed hesitant, but then he nodded in agreement. "All right." He crumpled his handkerchief and stuffed it into the depths of his robe. "We'd better be on our way then I suppose."

The Hollow Hill

P reet gave Ben a feather from Ridik's coat as a parting gift, a token of the Adar's gratitude for bringing him home. While Gwil was helping him attach the feather to the collar of his T-shirt, Portia sat cross-legged on the ground with her hand clutching the key in her jeans pocket.

"I'd stop doing that if I were you."

She guiltily pulled her hand from her pocket and looked down to see Tatap standing next to her knee, gazing up at her solemnly.

"Fairy Hill is no place for humans," he warned. "Especially not now Titania regards them as a threat." He placed a small hand on her knee. "Don't tell anyone about that key."

Tatap's warning echoed in Portia's head as Gwil led them deeper into the woods. The forest was dense now, and barely any light filtered through the thick canopy of leaves above their heads. There were no paths to follow, no maps, and their compass didn't work either. On top of that, every step took them further away from the door, and Rose. Portia chewed on her lower lip as Gwil explained his plan.

"Fairy Hill—we call it *Bryngolau*—has several minor entrances," he said. "For servants and such. If we keep our wits about us, we may be able to get in without the fairies even noticing."

"Aren't there any guards?" Ben asked.

Gwil shrugged. "Well, it's been a while since there's been anything to guard against. Not since..." He stopped himself.

"Not since the Grey King's last attack," Portia finished his sentence.

Gwil nodded, a pained look on his face. "Yes, and since that attack Titania has distrusted all Humans." He shook himself like a dog trying to scare away a wasp. "Maybe we'll be able to smuggle you past her. Perhaps we'll get lucky!" He sounded anything but confident.

Portia had a picture of Titania in her mind by now, and it was anything but encouraging. She imagined her a bit like Maleficent, the evil fairy from *Sleeping Beauty*: tall and severe, with sharp cheekbones and a bluish tint to her skin.

What kind of a place had she ended up in? Portia stopped in her tracks. She tried to take another step but all of a sudden the thick green undergrowth seemed to be pressing in on her. Her chest felt tight, and she could barely breathe.

"Portia?" Ben turned around, looking surprised.

"Just a minute." Without waiting for a reply, she pushed off the path and into a clearing of waist-high bracken. She had to get out of there, if only for a moment, before Gwil and Ben noticed that she was losing it. She trampled a path through the ferns to a rock, then sat down with her back to it. She closed her eyes and breathed shakily in and out. She thought of her mother, sitting at the kitchen table, her face pale, turning an empty cup round and round in her hands. Was this how it felt to be caught in one of her mum's grey moods?

Breathe. Just breathe.

A mosquito buzzed next to her ear. She shooed it away, then reached into her pocket, pulled out the key and pressed it against her chest. There was a way out. As long as she had the key, there was a way out.

Breathe. She exhaled slowly and felt herself begin to relax. More bugs buzzed around her head. Portia sighed, swatted at the mosquitoes and opened her eyes again. Then she returned the key to her pocket and went back over to Gwil and Ben on wobbly legs. The two of them had been resting on the ground, but when Portia stepped out from the bracken, Gwil jumped to his feet, a worried look on his face.

Portia frowned. Another one of those annoying insects landed on her shoulder, and she swatted it away without even looking. "What happened?" she asked. "Is something wrong?"

"Good question," said a voice like a tinkling bell.

Ben's jaw dropped, and Portia spun around. Behind her stood a dainty girl with a head of wild silver hair. She was a few centimetres shorter than Portia, and her short green dress was as delicate as a dragonfly's wing. Her eyes were the same shade of green and gleamed like two candle flames behind coloured glass.

Portia stumbled backwards, bumping into Gwil.

"What is that?" she said under her breath.

"A fairy," he whispered.

Something whirred past Portia's ear. She stared in disbelief as another tiny creature with dragonfly wings landed on a frond of bracken. A plume of blue smoke rose into the air, before falling to the ground like a waterfall. In the dragonfly creature's place now stood another girl, this one with sky-blue hair.

"Peaseblossom," said Gwil, greeting the blue fairy in a husky voice, before turning to her companion. "Cobweb. Allow me to introduce you to Portia and Ben, from the Human World."

The blue fairy smiled, revealing a set of sharp pearl-white teeth. "Guests for Queen Titania! She'll be so pleased to hear it."

Peaseblossom skipped ahead of them with a feather-light step, while Cobweb brought up the rear. When Portia risked a glance behind, the fairy glared at her, so she quickened her pace until she caught up with Ben.

"Is this how you imagined fairies would be?" she asked under her breath.

Ben looked over his shoulder. "I thought they'd be nicer."

"What are we going to tell them if they ask what happened in the Borderlands?" she whispered.

"No idea," he replied quietly. "But we'd better not mention the key. Preet warned me. Titania still blames Humans for endangering the Fairy World."

"Tatap told me the same thing." Portia felt Cobweb's gaze burning into her back like a laser beam. She had to fight the urge to reach for the key again. Suddenly, she remembered how she had pulled it from her pocket when she had stepped off the path earlier. Those bugs buzzing around her head—those had actually been fairies, hadn't they? What had they seen?

Portia walked on in silence. She didn't tell Ben that the fairies might already know about the key. What would they do if they found out she had awoken the Grey King? At least they had locked the door leading to the Fairy World, so Titania wouldn't be able to use that against them. Even so, Portia was beginning to feel queasy.

After some time, the forest gave way to a wide clearing. A glade of foxgloves lay ahead of them. From the midst of the purple flowers rose a rocky, moss-covered hill. On top of the hill a leafless tree stretched its bare branches to the sky.

Peaseblossom spun around. "Welcome to Titania's court," she exclaimed excitedly.

"Where is this palace supposed to be?" Portia asked Ben.

"Inside the hill, I suppose?" he replied. "Fairies always live inside hollow hills in fairy tales."

"Less talking, more walking," said Cobweb, chivvying them along, and she gave Ben a little shove between the shoulder blades.

They marched through the foxglove glade in single file. As soon as they passed into the shadow of the hill, the air grew chillier and Portia got goosebumps all over. The closer they got, the sharper and more jagged the rocky hillside looked. Portia nervously wet her lips with the tip of her tongue, but kept walking until she saw the archway in a rocky crevice up ahead. Beyond the archway was an inky black void, as if night itself awaited them in the hill. The sight hit her like a blow in the chest, and the next moment Cobweb gave her a dig in the back for good measure.

"Keep moving," she hissed, and before Portia could brace herself, the shadows beneath the archway had devoured them.

The Audience

The darkness was so impenetrable that even the air itself felt heavy. Portia groped along a damp rock wall with her fingertips. She was afraid of losing her bearings, but then she saw a weak light up ahead. Shortly after that, they emerged from the tunnel onto a balcony. Ben, Gwil and Portia went up to the balustrade and gazed around. The hill really was hollow—high above them, roots snaked across the roof of a great cave, covered in white and gold glowing moths, like fairy lights. The light of their fluttering wings pulsed in ripples over the rough rock walls.

It's like we're underwater, Portia thought. Then she looked down and gulped.

The balcony loomed over an abyss. Here and there the light of a moon-moth drifted down into the dismal depths, but the bottom remained shrouded in darkness.

"Oh, man," she groaned, trying to catch Ben's eye. She saw his face in the flickering moth light. His eyes were wide and his pupils looked pitch black. But was it out of fear or amazement? Just then Cobweb cleared her throat impatiently, and they began their descent.

A spiral staircase wound down the rock wall, leading them deeper and deeper into the earth. As they walked, they passed moss-covered pillars that lined the stairs like a cloister in a monastery.

Portia's nerves were all on edge. Until now, she'd never been afraid of the dark. But Fairy Hill's darkness felt different, menacing somehow, as if the rocks themselves were whispering to her.

Several bends later, they finally reached the bottom. As Peaseblossom hopped off the last step and onto the ground, a labyrinthine pattern of quartz-crystal veins began to glow beneath her feet.

Portia looked all around her. Several doorways were cut into the rock walls. She could make out groups of shadowy shapes moving about beneath the archways. Then one of the shapes came out of the darkness towards them.

Portia's whole body stiffened. The woman—if that's what she was—seemed to flow across the floor. Her silk dress billowed around her like the wind made visible. Her long hair drifted in coils about her head as if she was underwater. And her face... her face was too long and thin to be human. She passed by Portia and the others without sparing them a glance. Portia's blood ran cold.

Only when Ben gave a little moan of fear did Portia tear her eyes away from the mysterious figure. More figures had stepped forward out of the shadows, and several pairs of glittering eyes were examining the newcomers.

Peaseblossom seemed about to run to one of the groups, but Cobweb grabbed her by the collar of her dress. "Find Titania and tell her who we've brought."

"But..."

"Now!"

Peaseblossom pouted but shifted into her miniature shape with a *Puff!* before flying away. Portia remembered how she had swatted the tiny bright-eyed fairy with her hand and it made her feel sick again.

"You stay here," Cobweb commanded, before marching over to a group of fairies.

Portia watched her with growing unease. "I think they saw the key."

"What?" Ben spun around. "Are you sure?"

"No, I'm not." Portia bit her lip and made a decision. "You take it."

"What?"

"If they saw me with the key, they're bound to ask me about it. So you take it."

Ben looked like a rabbit in the headlights, but when Portia subtly passed him the key behind her back, he closed his fingers around it.

"They'll take you to Titania," Gwil said in a high-pitched voice. "Oh, dear!"

Portia wished his fear wasn't as obvious as it seemed to her. Her stomach felt as if it was filled with cement.

"What are we going to do?" Ben asked.

Before Gwil could reply, Cobweb came back. "Don't you have anything else to do, Glumheart?" she snapped.

Gwil cowered, staring at his feet. "Well, I thought..." he began, trailed off. Ben swiftly went over to his side, took his hand and squeezed it firmly.

"Thank you, Gwil," he said. Gwil winced and opened his mouth as if about to reply.

"Chop, chop! We don't have all day!" Cobweb growled, cutting him off.

With one last glance at Ben and Portia, Gwil went off towards one of the archways, clutching his basket of leaves.

Ben stared after him anxiously. Portia felt her heart begin to beat faster too. Gwil had wanted to help them, but she was pretty sure Cobweb had the opposite in mind.

Cobweb led them hurriedly along a dimly lit tunnel until they came to another archway. Portia frowned. There was an unusual scent in the air—sweet and flowery and somehow... strange.

Before she could work out what it was, Cobweb shooed them through the arch.

They had barely passed through when Peaseblossom came running towards them from the opposite direction. "She's expecting you," she panted, out of breath.

Before Portia knew it the fairies had seized her and Ben and marched them forwards into a great vaulted room.

No sooner had Portia passed through the doorway than a flower-shaped lamp began to glow overhead. Moon-moths flew up in all directions from its glass petals, illuminating bushes of irises and white chalice-shaped lilies.

They were in an underground greenhouse! Giant plant pots lined a winding path of pale stone slabs. Wild vines with beautiful flowers tumbled from the ceiling, while everywhere delicate flower lamps glowed amid the tangled foliage.

Portia was no gardening expert, but she was pretty sure plants didn't normally grow so lushly underground. She could hear water burbling somewhere and a dragonfly buzzed past the tip of her nose.

Soon, they left the plants behind and found themselves at the centre of the room. In the middle of the floor was a round pond. More dragonflies buzzed over the large lilies growing along the water's edge. The fish that swam below the green lily leaves glowed pink, blue and purple, like underwater shooting stars. Thick Irish moss grew all around the pond and carpeted the wide steps rising on the far side. On the steps a group of fairies were lounging on pillows, talking in whispers. They all turned to look at Ben and Portia, but their blank dolls' faces showed neither curiosity nor surprise.

"This is definitely not weird," Portia muttered under her breath. Ben could only manage a wordless whimper. Then somewhere beyond the steps a little bell chimed, and the fairies went back to their conversations as if nothing had happened. Portia felt the soft hair on the back of her neck standing on end.

Cobweb led them past the pond and up the steps to a raised gallery. There they found a chaise longue upholstered in fabric the colour of magnolia flowers, and lying on it a fairy dressed all in white.

"Titania," Ben whispered.

Portia couldn't help but stare.

Titania—for it could be none other than the Fairy Queen—rose from her bed. She was only inches taller than Portia, and her face was that of a child. Her long chestnut hair hung in pretty curls behind her little pointy ears. Portia had expected a woman clothed in the kind of splendour befitting a queen, but instead Titania wore a plain, straight-cut white dress under a robe of the same colour. Only when she stepped closer did Portia realize that the garments weren't so simple after all: The sleeves of the robe were embroidered with hundreds of tiny pearls, while the dress underneath seemed to be woven from shimmering flowers.

Cobweb and Peaseblossom curtsied before their Queen, and Ben and Portia did their best to imitate them. Portia felt very silly doing so, but Titania gave them a warm smile.

"So it is true then," she said. "We do have visitors from the Human World." Her eyes wandered from one to the other of them. "Portia. And Ben?"

"Yes, Your Majesty," Ben said in a quiet voice and lowered his gaze.

Titania laughed, clearly pleased. "Such good manners. Please be seated."

They sat down on two cushions made of blue silk, while Titania lowered herself onto the edge of her chaise longue. She wore no shoes, and her bare feet dangled just inches above the ground. As far as Portia could see the only blemish on her pristine appearance was her fingertips, which were as black as if she'd dipped them in ink.

Peaseblossom joined them, sitting on a cushion in front of the chaise longue. Titania raised a hand, and a servant came forward. The girl appeared to be a salamander, like Gwil. She had no eyebrows, and her head was wrapped in a sky-blue scarf. She carried a silver tray of glasses filled with a red liquid. Titania took a glass from the tray before it was offered to Portia and Ben. As the girl held out the tray, Portia caught a glimpse of a tattoo on her wrist. It was the same as Gwil's. Perhaps all salamanders had the same tattoo?

As the guests reached for their glasses, Titania beckoned Cobweb over and whispered something in her ear. Cobweb bowed her head and rushed away. Shortly after, the melody of a lute filled the air.

Titania watched Ben and Portia in silence. She seemed to be waiting for them to drink, but Ben simply held his glass in his hand, and for some reason Portia also hesitated to sip the red liquid.

"Well," Titania said after a while. "Do you want to tell me how you were able to cross the border to my kingdom?"

Ben and Portia exchanged glances before recounting their story for the third time. This time, though, they held some details back. They told Titania that they had stumbled into the Borderlands unwittingly, that Rose had made sure the doors were closed behind them, but that the Grey King's servants had somehow become aware of their presence.

Titania listened with a friendly and attentive expression. When they mentioned the Grey Riders, the salamander servant girl began to tremble so violently that the glasses on her tray rattled and clunked. Titania, on the other hand, remained unmoved. Ben was recounting their flight across the moor after the first battle, when he faltered. Portia quickly took the story up.

"We made it to the Faerie Door, but the riders were right behind us." She forced herself to hold Titania's gaze. "Rose wanted to be sure we would escape, so she sent us through the door and stayed behind." As she spoke, Cobweb came back and sat down behind her. Portia fought the urge to move away from her. "She held off the Grey Riders. Didn't she, Ben?"

"Yes," Ben confirmed. "She... she wanted to make sure the fog couldn't get into the Fairy Kingdom."

Portia looked at him out of the corner of her eye. He was telling the story in a way that suggested Rose had been trying to protect the fairies rather than just her and Ben. It was a good idea, but would Titania buy it?

"'Viola Rosethorn," Titania said pensively. "I thought she would already have departed on her next journey. Humans don't live very long, do they?"

"No," Cobweb replied. "Not particularly." Was it her imagination or did Portia detect a note of satisfaction in her voice?

Titania took a sip of her drink, a soft silver glow in her eyes. "What about the key? Where is it?"

Portia was feeling more and more uncomfortable about lying, but she could still hear Tatap's warning echoing in her ears. "I don't know," she said. "Rose probably still has it. She locked the door from her side."

Titania exchanged glances with Cobweb. A drop of sweat trickled down Portia's spine. *Don't clench your fists*, she told herself. *Stay calm.*

"Would you mind emptying your pockets?" Titania asked. Cobweb instantly took a step towards Portia, but Titania raised a hand to stop her. "I'm sure young Portia here needs no help."

Relieved that she had given the key to Ben, Portia got to her feet and turned her pockets inside out to show that they were empty. Titania seemed neither surprised nor disappointed. Portia hoped she'd forget about the key now, but instead the Queen shifted her attention to Ben.

"And how about you, young Ben? Would you mind emptying your pockets as well?"

Portia felt a hot flush of fear. Her heart beat wildly as she watched Ben get up and turn his pockets out too.

The key wasn't there.

Portia tried to hide her surprise and look unflustered as she tucked her pockets back into her jeans. Cobweb's face fell as Titania slid from her chaise longue and took Portia's hand. Portia winced in shock, but the Queen smiled. She seemed glad the interrogation was over too.

"Do accept my apologies for the inconvenience," she said. "When it comes to the Grey King, we really can't be cautious enough." She waved the servant over and set her glass down on the tray. "Awel, be a dear and bring me some tea, will you?" she said. "I need something to calm my nerves after all this excitement."

The servant bowed her head and hurried away. Titania turned back to Ben and Portia. "You've seen the Grey King's riders. You understand why I had to ask those questions, don't you?"

"Of course!" Portia managed to splutter. Titania was so different from what she had imagined. She was puzzled by her friendliness and had no idea how to deal with it. Still, the squeeze of her hand was warm and comforting, and her smile seemed sincere. For the first time since arriving in Fairy Hill, Portia began to relax.

Titania gave Portia's hand a pat before letting it go. "Now then. What do you wish to do? May I be of assistance in any way?"

Portia was speechless. In all their frantic preparations for this encounter, it had never even crossed her mind that Titania would grant them a wish. Had Tatap and the others been wrong about the Fairy Queen?

Ben cleared his throat. "We'd like to go home, Your Majesty."

"Of course you would," she said, sounding understanding. "But without the key, it won't be possible. I'm afraid you'll have to wait for Mistress Rosethorn to take you back."

That was a reasonable suggestion. Too bad it would never happen. Portia nervously plucked at the hem of her T-shirt. This was a dead end all of their own making.

"I will send two of my fairies to stand guard at the door," Titania continued. "They can welcome Mistress Rosethorn as soon as she appears and escort her here." She clapped her hands. "Until then, please make yourselves at home," she said. "It's been a while since we've had Human visitors. Peaseblossom!" The blue-haired fairy leapt to her feet.

"Take these two to Mistress Quickly. Have them clothed. Show them the guest quarters. And tomorrow, we'll have a celebration in their honour!"

Peaseblossom was far more pleasant company than Cobweb. She was much more curious too—she cheerfully quizzed them about the Human World as they walked through Fairy Hill. Ben answered all her questions, but Portia was still thinking about their audience in Titania's Water Lily Chamber. Maybe they should have told her the whole story after all. She remembered Titania's friendly words and kindly expression. Why would she deceive them?

"... very good that Mistress Rosethorn locked the door behind herself," Peaseblossom was saying. That made Portia's ears prick up. Actually, where *was* the key? She glanced her at Ben but he gave her a brief shake of the head.

"It's so very dramatic," Peaseblossom continued, "how she took on the Grey Riders—a lone figure on the great bleak moor!" She turned a corner then led them down a flight of stairs.

"Perhaps I should take you to our scribes," Peaseblossom said. "They could immortalize Mistress Rosethorn's sacrifice in verse. Turn it into an epic poem. What do you think?"

Portia was just about to tell her what exactly she thought, when Gwil appeared at the bottom of the stairs. Ben's face lit up, and Portia felt relieved too.

Peaseblossom frowned, but then skipped towards the salamander with a few quick steps. "Gwil! What are you doing here?"

Gwil was out of breath and dabbing his forehead with his handkerchief again. "The guest quarters for the Humans are ready," he panted.

"What do you mean?" Peaseblossom asked, clearly confused.

"But that was Her Majesty's order, wasn't it?"

Peaseblossom glanced over at Ben and Portia. "Yes, that's right. But I thought..."

"May I take the Humans there now?" Gwil said, looking at Peaseblossom expectantly.

The fairy was twirling a strand of her blue hair around her finger. "Well, now that's really quite perplexing. Titania wanted me to take these two to Mistress Quickly."

"Oh, that's not a problem at all," Gwil replied promptly. "The sewing room is on the way."

Peaseblossom bounced on the balls of her feet, seemingly undecided. Gwil clutched his handkerchief so tightly that his knuckles went white, but the fairy didn't notice.

"Very well," she said eventually. "I'll go and tell Pricklethorn and the others about our guests from the Human World. I bet they're bursting with curiosity." She smiled from one ear to the other. "You'll be the talk of the celebration tomorrow!"

With that she twirled around once before shifting shape in a puff of blue smoke and buzzing away.

"Oh, thank the spirits," Gwil groaned. "If Awel hadn't told me that your audience was over, I'd have missed you." Ben was still standing a few steps above Gwil so he reached down and patted the salamander's shoulder gratefully.

"Thank you, Gwil," he said. "Have you got the, errm...?"

"Oh. Yes." Gwil glanced around quickly, then pulled the key out from underneath his robe and pressed it into Ben's hand.

"What?..." Portia stared at Ben. "When did you give him the key?"

Ben smiled bashfully. "When Cobweb sent him away. I guessed nobody would expect Gwil to have it."

Portia whistled admiringly. "Great idea!"

Ben's smile grew even wider.

"Ahem." Gwil cleared his throat. "We should get going. It's quite a way to Goodfellow's quarters."

Ben tucked the key in his jeans pocket and they set off on their way.

Shapeshifters

Robin Goodfellow's quarters were located deep inside the hill, far from Titania's Water Lily Chamber. Portia walked at Ben's side, barely noticing her surroundings. She was trying to stay positive, but the further they advanced into Fairy Hill, the more she began to doubt their plan. If you could even call it that.

"Everything okay?" Ben asked.

"I'm not sure," she replied. "Are we doing the right thing?"

"What do you mean?"

"Finding Robin Goodfellow. I mean, he's the reason we're stuck here in the first place."

"But Rose said he'd help us."

"I know, but I'm still not sure." Portia remembered the cold smile on Robin's face when he spoke to Rose about finally understanding what it feels like to lose your world.

Ben fell silent for a moment. "But what else can we do?" he sighed eventually.

Portia shrugged. *We could ask Titania for help*, she thought, but kept that to herself.

"Here we are!" Gwil stopped in front of an archway and pushed aside a curtain hanging over the entrance. "Hello?" he called. When no one answered, he stepped inside.

Ben looked quizzically at Portia, but she just shrugged and went in after Gwil.

Robin's quarters looked more like a burrow than a human home. Then again, he wasn't human, was he? *Trickster. Troublemaker*—that's what Tatap had called him. *Scoundrel*—that had been Bramble's verdict.

Behind the curtain was a single room about twenty paces across. To their left, the embers of several logs were smouldering in a fireplace. The shelves along the walls were crowded with jars, colourful little glass bottles and sealed clay pots, while bunches of dried herbs were hanging from the ceiling. Despite herself, Portia was intrigued. It was like a wizard's kitchen!

"It looks as if he'd never been away," Ben observed.

Gwil shrugged. "Goodfellow was King Oberon's right hand. When he disappeared, Oberon gave orders to maintain his quarters."

"But Oberon isn't here?" asked Ben.

"Oberon is travelling. Has been for years," Gwil explained.

On the other side of the room, a narrow bed stood in an alcove. Portia went over to it, passing between the fireplace and a rough wooden table. In a nook in the wall above the bed stood a vase of wild yellow roses. Next to it lay a locket on a silver chain. Curious, Portia picked it up, but before she could open it, a voice said: "Well, well, look at that. You just couldn't resist, could you?"

Portia hastily put the locket back in its place and turned around.

Robin Goodfellow was leaning in the doorway, observing them coldly. He wore a grey waistcoat over a fresh white shirt and light-brown linen trousers. On his feet were the same dusty leather shoes he had been wearing in the Human World.

"Goodfellow!" Gwil croaked. "We... we need to talk to you."

"Do you now?" Robin said, feigning interest. He walked over to Gwil and stood so close that the salamander flinched.

The corner of Robin's mouth twitched. He turned towards Ben and Portia. "Tell Rose she can keep her self-righteous nonsense to herself. You know, all that talk of how the risk of opening the doors is too high."

He strolled over to the fireplace, squatted on his haunches, then took a steel tea kettle and hung it above the fire.

Robin appeared to be completely indifferent, as if none of this was any of his business. "Actually, we can't tell her," Portia said. "She stayed behind on the other side."

Robin froze.

"The Grey Riders attacked us," Ben cut in. "Rose stayed behind to hold them off."

Turn around, Portia thought. *Turn around and say something.*

Instead, Robin simply got to his feet and walked wordlessly to one of the shelves. Portia could sense her dislike towards him like a bitter taste on her tongue, but Ben was persistent: "She told us to look for you."

"What fantastic advice!" Robin opened a clay pot, took a mug from a shelf and threw in a pinch of herbs. Ben and Portia exchanged a look, but she didn't trust herself to speak. She knew that if she said anything now, she would end up exploding and venting all her anger. Then she remembered Preet's words: *They do say he had a soft spot for Viola Rosethorn.* Well, it seemed the Adar had got that completely wrong.

"Please," Ben said. "Rose said you'd help us. We need someone to take us back through that door."

Robin snorted dismissively. "A foolish idea. Unless you fancy serving as the Grey Riders' quarry." He turned around and headed back over to the fireplace, but Portia blocked his path.

"Then we'll go through a different door."

Robin's face darkened. "You just don't get it, do you?" he asked in a menacingly calm voice. "There's nothing I can do to help. And Rose can't be saved."

"That's not true!" Ben protested. He stood shoulder to shoulder with Portia. "If the Grey Riders haven't caught her, she might be waiting right on the other side of the door."

"And if they did catch Rose," Portia added, "then she'll need someone to rescue her! We have to do something!"

Robin snorted dismissively. "It doesn't matter how fast or how slow you are. Rose is long gone. Whoever is taken by the fog either disappears—or is doomed to lead a miserable existence as a Mistwalker. Hasn't Gwil explained to you what that means?"

Portia pressed her lips together. *He's lying,* she thought.

Robin's eyes glittered with anger. "The fog devours all the memories and thoughts that make you the person you are. What remains looks like the person you once were—but a Mistwalker is nothing but a shell, a mere shadow. They breathe and move around, but no one who's become a Mistwalker will ever recognize you again. You can't help Rose. Rose is dead. One way or the other."

"No!" Ben cried.

Robin gave him a look that was somewhere between disgust and sympathy, then turned and squatted down by the fireplace again. "Rose has long owed a debt to the Grey King. And now she's had to pay it."

Ben's breathing was so heavy that his whole body shook. Portia finally boiled over with rage. "This is your fault!" she yelled. "You woke up that grey whoever-he-is on purpose."

"Portia," Ben warned. But she wasn't listening.

She slapped Robin's shoulder.

"If it wasn't for you, none of this would've happened!"

Robin laughed bitterly. "Oh, but I think perhaps you're forgetting one little detail. Without *you*, I wouldn't have got my hands on the key."

Portia flinched as if she had been struck. "I had no idea what was going to happen."

"True," Robin said. "And yet still off you went, carefree as a little lamb, opening doors and not thinking about the consequences. Who does that remind me of, I wonder?"

A knot of frustration burned in Portia's chest. *No crying,* she told herself. No way was she going to cry in front of this scoundrel. "But we have to get home!" she exclaimed.

"This is your home now," Robin snapped. "You'd better get used to it. I'm sure Titania will put you to work in the scullery."

Robin was clearly finished with the conversation. He turned his back and stared down at the smouldering embers in the fireplace. Portia's eyes burned with tears. She had to admit that he was right. She was just as much to blame for the situation as he was. Even so, she felt like shoving him into the mantelpiece. Gwil placed a hand on her shoulder and stepped between her and Robin. "Let's all calm down," he said. "I'm sure we'll find a solution."

"If I were you, I'd keep my mouth shut," Robin snarled.

Gwil stiffened, but he persisted. He took another step closer to the fireplace as Robin poured steaming hot water into a mug.

"None of us wants to let the Grey King cause trouble here again," he said soothingly, "but I'm sure we could still help Mistress Rosethorn, if only you would..."

In a flash, Robin spun around and threw the boiling water in Gwil's face. Portia and Ben screamed. There was a hiss, and a cloud of steam filled the air. When it had cleared, a little salamander was sitting on the ground, just where Gwil had been standing.

The Salamanders
of Bryngolau

Ben carried Gwil around Fairy Hill on the palm of his
hand. In his salamander shape, Gwil had black skin with
yellow spots, a long tail and tiny feet.

"Why doesn't he shift back into his human shape?"
Portia wondered.

"Perhaps he doesn't feel like it?" Ben suggested. "Or
maybe he just can't?"

Judging by the glum way the salamander hung his head,
the second guess was right. Nevertheless, he guided them
through the warren of tunnels, halls and servant quarters
like a little living compass. At every turning, he pointed
his head in one direction or the other, until they reached a
brightly lit cave with a pair of brass scissors hanging above
its entrance.

"Is that the sewing room?" Ben asked. Gwil nodded,
white eyelids twitching over his eyes.

They stepped inside and found themselves in a cave
that looked more like a bazaar. Rolls of fabric in all colours
of the rainbow were piled up next to the entrance. There
were shelves filled with folded cloth, and two half-finished

dresses draped on mannequins. Dozens of lanterns hung from the ceiling.

Two women stood next to one of the mannequins. The shorter of the two—young, with a bushy red plait—was holding a basket filled with flowers made out of cloth, while the second, somewhat older woman attached a flower to the shoulder of the dress. When Ben and Portia approached, the redhead gasped, and the other woman spun around to face them.

"Sweet spirits!" she exclaimed. "So it is true! Humans!"

Portia guessed this was Mistress Quickly, the head seamstress. She seemed to be a salamander as well—at least she didn't have any eyebrows, just like Gwil. Mistress Quickly was wearing an elegant turban made of purple fabric. She had rolled up the sleeves of her dress, and a pincushion was strapped around her wrist.

"Hello," said Portia, and the two women looked at her as if horns had just sprouted from her forehead.

Ben cleared his throat. "Mistress Quickly?" he asked. "I believe Gwil Glumheart wanted us to come and find you."

"Gwil?" the older seamstress repeated. Then she noticed the salamander sitting on Ben's hand. "Oh, not again!" She threw the cloth flower back into the basket. "Sian, dear, would you fetch a jar of spring water, please?"

"Yes, Mistress Quickly, of course." The younger woman set her basket down and hurried over to a table.

Meanwhile, Mistress Quickly plucked Gwil from Ben's hand.

"Why doesn't he shift back?" Portia asked.

"Because he's a salamander. We need help to shapeshift," she replied. "Ah, thank you, Sian."

The girl had returned and handed a jar to Mistress Quickly, who gently placed Gwil on the ground. "Heat makes us shift into our animal shape," she explained. "And to shift back into our human shape, we need something cold." With those words, she emptied the contents of the jar over Gwil.

Again, there was a hiss, and a cloud of steam, and then Gwil was sitting on the ground—in his human shape.

"Gwil Glumheart." Mistress Quickly put her hands on her hips and sighed. "What kind of a mess have you got yourself into now?"

Shortly afterwards, Portia and Ben were sitting in Meralyn Quickly's living room telling her everything that had happened. Meralyn and Gwil sat in two flowery armchairs while Portia and Ben shared a sofa. On a round table between them stood a porcelain teapot decorated with a pink peony pattern. The teacups were made of porcelain as well, but were all patterned differently. There were oatcakes with clotted cream and bramble jam, and thick slices of toasted bread. They were also offered butter, salt and pickled parsley to go with it, which was surprisingly tasty.

After all the excitement of their ordeal, Portia had worked up quite an appetite. As she devoured the last crumbs of an oatcake, she took a closer look at Meralyn Quickly. The head seamstress was taking a sip of tea, and Portia noticed the stamp of a famous porcelain brand on the bottom of her cup. She started.

"Is something the matter?" Meralyn asked.

"No, not at all," Portia said hurriedly. "I was just wondering... Is the crockery from the Human World?"

Meralyn smiled. "It is indeed! You wouldn't think it today, but once upon a time there was plenty of exchange between your world and ours, even though most people on your side had no idea."

She put her cup back down, her pearl bracelet gleaming in the light of the table lamp.

"Some of the things humans introduced us to are now being made here as well," she went on. "Obviously not by the fairies. But many shapeshifter families do good business with human inventions. Especially since the doors have been closed."

Gwil was still stirring his tea even though the sugar must have dissolved long ago. "It is safer that way," he said.

"Yes, because of the Grey King," Meralyn agreed. "But this closing-the-borders thing doesn't seem to be working, after all. And now the Grey King has awoken again, and poor Mistress Rosethorn is stuck in the middle of all that chaos." She shook her head. "What a tragedy."

Portia put the biscuit she was just about to bite into back on the plate. "Was Robin telling the truth?" she asked. "Is Rose gone for good?"

"Oh, I wouldn't give up hope so easily," Meralyn replied. "I'm sure we'll think of something."

"You'd help us?" Ben was surprised.

"But of course," Meralyn shot back.

"But won't Titania be angry?"

"Salamandrau help when others hesitate," the older woman said proudly. "And no matter what Titania thinks, we don't always have to dance to her tune."

Gwil cleared his throat, and Meralyn put her hand on his. "If we're careful, of course," she said reassuringly. She let go of his hand and reached for her teacup again. "It'll be a challenge, admittedly. We know very little about the Grey King, his fog and its effects." Meralyn looked at Gwil, and he nodded.

"When the Grey King last attacked, a party of hare merchants were on their way to the Night Market," Gwil recalled. "The fog must have surprised them during their journey, and they never arrived at their destination. Their families looked for them, but there was no trace of any of the missing ones. But then one of them showed up again after all. Branys was his name. Two of his cousins found him wandering in the woods and took him home." Gwil was trying to hold Portia's gaze, and she forced herself to look him in the eye as he spoke.

"He did not remember his family. He did not speak," Gwil continued. "He did not react when they asked him questions, and whenever they took their eyes off him, he began to wander off and drift away, westwards."

"Like a cloud of fog," Meralyn said sadly.

"What happened to him?" asked Ben.

The salamanders faltered. "Well, one morning he disappeared," Gwil said eventually. "His grandson had been sitting on a chair in front of the house all night. He swore he hadn't opened the door, yet his grandfather was gone, and there was nothing but cold dew on his bed."

"So Robin is right, after all," Portia said flatly.

Ben wanted to reach out and take her hand, but thought better of it.

"Perhaps," Meralyn said, "but perhaps, there's still hope. Branys was missing for a whole moon before they found him. Rose has only been lost for a short time. And she's smart. It's quite possible that the fog hasn't overpowered her yet."

"But what if it has?" Portia asked.

Gwil shrugged. "There are stories of Mistwalkers who have been saved, even after falling victim to the hold of the fog."

"Every child knows the story of Ifor and Nerys," Meralyn confirmed. "It took place in the times of the Grey King's first attack on our world. A young warrior by the name of Ifor was swallowed up by the fog and disappeared. His sweetheart, Nerys, went after him and brought him back. They were missing in that fog for a whole moon, but when they finally returned, both were unharmed."

"How did they manage it?"

"The story goes that Nerys placed her own heart in Ifor's hand, so his memories of her came back."

Portia snorted. "Well, if that's all we have to do!"

Meralyn smiled. "The part with the heart is probably a metaphor. You know, a flowery description of what actually happened. Bards love things like that. Whatever Nerys really did... well, we'd have to look into that."

Gwil's eyes widened. "Oh, but of course!" he exclaimed. "World's End!"

"World's End?" Portia repeated incredulously.

Gwil nodded. "When humans were still travelling between the worlds, they and the Salamandrau elders created a place where all knowledge from both worlds was gathered," he explained. "It's a library, and its name is World's End. If there's a solution to your problems, that's where you'll find it."

Meralyn nodded eagerly. "Yes, that's a great idea. Actually, I know someone who might be able to help you—Tegid, the librarian there. Gwil, you'll take the children to the library, won't you?"

"Me?" Gwil turned pale.

"That's all well and good," Portia interjected. "But even if we do find some kind of miracle cure for the fog in this library, how will we make it through the Faerie Door? Titania has sent guards to watch over it."

The confident glow quickly disappeared from Meralyn's face. "I hate to say it, but Titania's right—the Faerie Door must remain closed. If the Grey Riders are roaming the Borderlands, their bloodhounds are surely lurking near the door."

Portia was about to object, but this time Meralyn beat her to it. "There's actually another door," she said. "In fact, Mistress Rosethorn and her friends used it all those years ago. She may have found her way back there again."

Ben sat up straight. "Where is this door?"

"It's inside the Pale Tower," Meralyn replied.

"How lovely," Portia sighed.

"The Pale Tower is where the Grey King sleeps." Gwil nervously cleared his throat. "Well, rather, where he was sleeping."

"You said Mistress Rosethorn intended to set things right, didn't you?" Meralyn asked.

Ben nodded.

"Which could mean that she is trying to put the Grey King back to sleep. And what better place to try that than the place where she succeeded once before?" Meralyn drummed on the table with her fingertips. "The Pale Tower would be well within reach of World's End."

Portia stared at the salamander. "Just to be clear— are you suggesting that we go through a door leading straight into the Grey King's living room?"

"He won't be expecting that," Meralyn said.

Portia clenched her fists. "Well, a lion wouldn't expect me to just go wandering into its den either," she replied. "He'd still eat me though."

Ben made a noise somewhere between a cough and a nervous laugh.

Gwil ran a hand across his bald head. "You're right. Of course you are." He looked at Meralyn, who gave him an encouraging smile. "It's the best path for you to take right now. Unless you've got a better idea?"

"Titania!" Portia said immediately. "We'll tell her the truth and ask for her help."

The salamanders remained silent, but they looked doubtful.

"She seemed quite reasonable earlier," Portia insisted.

Meralyn sighed. "Well, she is... as long she's hoping to get something from you."

Gwil turned to Ben. "What do you think?"

Ben frowned. "I don't know..."

"You all said it: if we want to save Rose, we have to be quick," Portia said. "Otherwise, we'll lose our best chance of finding her."

"But don't we need to know the best way first?" argued Ben. "Or what we should do if the fog has already stolen her memories?"

"But maybe that hasn't happened yet! What if she's waiting for us? If every second counts?" Portia was on the edge of her seat, gripping the table. Libraries, faraway fortresses—all that would take way too long. She wanted to do something right now, to go back to that door, and undo everything that had happened. Robin had been right: if it wasn't for her, Rose would be safe. She had stolen the key. She had opened the door to the Borderlands. Just to satisfy her bloody curiosity. And if Rose never came home, it would be her fault.

She felt as if her stomach was turning into a tight fist. She would put everything right. She just *had to*.

Ben stared at the table.

"Ben?" Portia asked desperately.

"I like Gwil's idea."

Gwil gave him a shaky smile. Portia could barely believe what she was hearing.

"Portia?" Meralyn asked.

Portia stared at their faces. She remembered saying goodbye to Rose, remembered the warmth of her hug, and the cold when Rose had turned around and marched towards the wall of fog all by herself. She could feel that they were running out of time, could practically hear the ticking of a clock in her head. "No," she said eventually. "There are too many 'maybes' for me." She avoided the salamanders' disappointed looks, cleared her throat and tried to sound confident. "I'm sorry. I just think we have a better chance if we ask Titania for help."

An uncomfortable silence descended.

"If we find a cure for the Mistwalkers at the library, couldn't we send a message to Fairy Hill?" Ben asked suddenly.

"Yes, certainly," Gwil said. "Tegid has a few carrier pigeons. They could be back here in no time."

"That way, we could try to help Rose in two different ways," Ben suggested, turning to Portia. "You ask Titania for help. Then if you find Rose and she's all right, everything is fine. But if not, we can send you the instructions for the cure."

Portia bit her lip. She disliked the idea of splitting up from Ben just as much as the idea of going further away from the Faerie Door and Rose. But if that was the only compromise Ben was willing to agree on...

"I just don't know," Meralyn cut in. "I really wouldn't trust Titania, if I were you. Portia, are you sure you want to try asking her for help?"

She was not. But panic was gnawing and pulling at her, and the idea of fairy warriors confronting the Grey Riders seemed somehow more reassuring than her wandering into the unknown. "Yes," she replied eventually.

Meralyn sighed. "Okay. Then I'll help you prepare for the audience, and Gwil will go with Ben."

"There's just one problem," Gwil said. "If Portia wants to go through the Faerie Door and we want to go through the one at the Pale Tower..."

"... then we'll need two keys," Meralyn finished his sentence.

"Oh," Ben said. "I didn't think of that."

Meralyn smiled. "Don't you worry. That's one problem we can solve right away."

Merron Pathfinder

Meralyn disappeared to an adjoining room and returned a few minutes later with a bottle, two glasses and a small leather-bound book. She pressed the book protectively against her chest until she had set down the bottle and the glasses and taken a seat. Then she brushed some crumbs off the tabletop, cautiously put down the book and opened it at the first page.

"This is my great-grandfather's journal." She touched the dense handwriting with her fingertips, tracing each line, a bitter smile on her face. "Merron Pathfinder was his name. Although the fairies had a different name for him."

"Merron the Reckless," said Gwil glumly.

"He was given that name after he took on the fairies—and then lost in spectacular fashion." Meralyn uncorked the bottle, and the sweet scent of bramble wine tickled Portia's nose.

"What happened?" she asked. Next to her, Ben leant forward to get a closer look at the book.

Meralyn raised just one shoulder. "Well, there are many stories, but they agree on one thing. Merron crossed the border between the worlds without permission."

155

She poured wine into the two glasses and pushed one over to Gwil, who took a generous sip. "Since the first doors were created, the fairies have decided who should be allowed to pass through them," he explained.

"Merron wasn't happy with the fairies' reign," Meralyn said. "He wanted to decide for himself where he should travel, whom he should meet. He had a dream that all Salamandrau might one day be able to wander between the worlds, gathering knowledge from beyond our borders."

"Of course the fairies didn't care much for that dream," Gwil said.

Meralyn nodded sadly. "So he decided to make his own key."

"And did he manage it?" asked Ben.

"Yes, and he wrote the secret down in here." Meralyn closed the book and handed it to Gwil. "It seems we are in luck—according to Merron, a key can only be crafted by the dwellers of two different worlds working together."

Gwil let out a sad whimper. "Apologies," he mumbled and took another sip of wine.

Meralyn smiled, but her features now looked strangely hard, like marble. "If Titania knew of this book's existence, she'd throw all of us into the deepest of the Fairy Hill's dungeons."

Should she really be asking Titania for help? Portia wasn't sure, but she ignored the doubts she felt stirring in her gut.

"Is that why you don't make keys any more?" she asked.

Meralyn snorted. "If the fairies didn't have such control over us Salamandrau folk, one of us would surely have made another key." She sounded as if she would have liked to be that rebellious salamander herself. "But our hands are tied, in the truest sense of the word."

"After Merron... After he..." Gwil began, but he couldn't finish the sentence.

"The fairies caught and punished him," Meralyn said tersely. "And with him, all the Salamandrau."

She loosened her wristband to reveal a tattoo like those Portia had seen on Gwil and Titania's servant: a black ring around the wrist.

"This is the mark of our servitude," she explained. "It means we have to serve and obey Titania, and we are not allowed to leave Bryngolau without her, or her permission."

Portia frowned. "You really can't leave?"

"No," Meralyn said. "If we tried, the mark would stop us."

Handcuffs, Portia thought, horrified. *The tattoos are handcuffs.*

"Which brings us to another problem." Meralyn nodded towards Gwil.

Gwil placed a hand on his tattoo. "If I'm to take Ben to World's End, then I'll need a spell that stops the mark working, temporarily at least."

"I think Pricklethorn could cast a spell like that." Meralyn turned to Ben and Portia. "He's Titania's Lord Chamberlain."

"He could," Gwil agreed. "But he won't. Not without a good reason."

"Or a good bribe." Meralyn smiled again, then got up and opened the trunk next to the sofa. She carefully removed some layers of tissue paper before bringing out a bundle of cloth that she let unfurl in her hands into what looked like a woven starry sky. A sheet of dark blue silk ran down Meralyn's arm, shimmering all over with tiny rhinestones—or were they diamonds? The sight of it left Portia breathless, and she wasn't the only one.

"Pricklethorn has long coveted a garment to rival our Queen's attire. I'd say this would fit the bill." Meralyn smiled mischievously, her eyes twinkling. "Provided that he helps us, of course."

Later that evening, Portia lay in bed staring at the ceiling. The guest bedroom Meralyn had shown her to was near the sewing room. She could hear the muffled voices of the seamstresses, still at work. A glass filled with moon-moths stood by the door, glowing softly.

Portia was thinking over her conversation with the salamanders, turning her decision round and round in her head.

I'm making the right choice, she kept telling herself. But then why were there so many doubts gnawing at her?

Portia turned over. Ben's bed was just a few inches away, but a silence as vast as an ocean had grown between them. He hadn't said a word to her since the salamanders bid them goodnight. Was it just because he was tired—or because he was upset that Portia was going to leave him on his own?

She wished she could explain, and tell Ben how guilty she felt. She didn't want to put any more distance between herself and Rose, but at the same time she felt she was letting down Ben as well.

After a while, she just couldn't take it any more. "I wish we could do this together."

Her voice was fading away into the darkened room when at last Ben quietly replied, "Me too."

Portia sat up in her bed. "Then stay! Help me convince Titania!"

Ben lay still for a moment. "Are you a hundred per cent sure that she'll help us?" he asked.

She could have lied. Perhaps Ben would have stayed with her then, so she wouldn't have had to confront Titania by herself. But she didn't have the heart. With a deep sigh, she lay down again. "No," she admitted. "No, I'm not."

The silence grew between them again. "If you get home before me, could you please tell my mum that I'm okay?" asked Ben.

The question felt like a little stab in the heart. "Of course," she said. "And if you make it there first, will you do the same for me?"

"I will. I promise."

Ben stared at the ceiling. Portia chewed her lip, filled with indecision. She wished she could tell him about her doubts—but if she did that he might convince her to come along with him after all. And that would be a mistake. Or would it?

"Portia?" said Ben. "Be careful when it comes to Titania."

"I will," she said.

"I'm serious." He rolled over to face her. "In stories, humans always end up losing when they make deals with fairies."

"I'll watch out," she promised. "But you be careful too. Stay away from those creepy grey knights. Making yourself invisible should do the trick."

Ben laughed softly. "Well, I've got some experience there. I'm mostly worried that we'll have to walk for hours again tomorrow. I'm so sore. I'm aching in places I didn't even know I had muscles."

Portia couldn't help but grin, despite everything. Ben smiled too. It suited him, Portia thought.

"You can do it," she said, then turned to look up at the ceiling again. She could hear Ben arranging his pillow. She really liked him. He was cautious, but at the same time nothing seemed to really faze him. She was glad he was with her.

For now, at least.

Her smile faded. Sometimes Portia wished she could shut the mouth of her inner voice with a piece of tape.

Departure

After waking the next morning, Ben lay in bed with his eyes closed for a little while. His pillow was marvellously soft and smelt of hay. *I'm in Faerie*, he thought. *At Queen Titania's court.*

When he finally opened his eyes, a moon-moth was tumbling across the dark room. He reached out, and the feather-light moth settled on his hand. Its little feet tickled his skin, and it glowed more brightly. It was like a light bulb you could dim with a switch—just way more amazing. Ben softly blew on its wings, and it fluttered away. He sat up and threw off his blanket. As he moved, the other moon-moths in a jar by the wall woke up, casting their milky light over the walls and ceiling. Ben looked anxiously at Portia's bed. If she was still asleep, the light would surely wake her up.

He was surprised to see her bed was empty. Ben frowned and got up. He had no idea what time it was, but he felt well rested. More and more moon-moths fluttered about the room until Ben felt he was standing in a cloud of glowing pollen. Portia's backpack was sitting on the stool by his bed. She had attached a note to the safety pin holding Ridik's feather. Ben tore it off and began to read:

*For your journey. You can ask Meralyn to refill
the thermos. Blister plasters are in the mesh pocket
inside. Good luck!*

Ben took a moment to process the message. Then he understood. This was Portia's goodbye. And she was leaving him her backpack. He felt a warm glow spread through his chest like sunlight.

Curious, he opened the backpack, and found the thermos, Portia's map, the promised blister plasters, as well as a slim red notebook. Ben opened the notebook and found that it was empty—except for the very first page. With a black felt pen, Portia had written *Summer Holiday in Wales* at the top of the page. Underneath, she had glued in a section of a map of North Wales, and a Welsh flag. In the lower corner, she had pasted in the ticket for Conwy Castle with sticky tape, and next to it she had written *Conwy, 10th August*. It was a travel diary!

Ben flipped through the blank pages, thinking how he would have liked to find out what else Portia was going to add to her diary. He could have helped her, could have shown her some exciting places or helped her cut out pictures. Perhaps she would have let him add a few small drawings of his own.

Suddenly, he wished he'd had a chance to say a proper goodbye. Or rather, he wished there had been no need for a goodbye. It was a strange feeling for Ben. He never wanted to spend time with his classmates, but he would have liked to get to know Portia better.

The dye works were in a big cave in the eastern wing of the palace, where daylight streamed in through gaping cracks in the ceiling.

The cracks provided natural ventilation, which was fortunate, because the cave smelt absolutely disgusting. Large tubs of coloured water lined the walls, and the air was thick with the stink of vinegar and urine. The dye workers didn't seem to pay the smell any mind, though. They hustled and bustled everywhere, dipping fabric into the tubs or stirring plants and other ingredients in steaming water. No one paid any attention to Gwil and his companion.

Meralyn had dressed Ben in Fairy World clothes: a pair of comfortable boots, brown wool trousers, a plain shirt and a scuffed leather jacket that was a few sizes too big. Last but not least, he wore fingerless gloves, just like Gwil's. The only mismatched detail was Portia's green backpack.

Gwil's face wore a determined expression, but his hands revealed how tense he really was. He laced and unlaced his fingers again and again. It was strange, but somehow Gwil's nervousness made Ben feel braver. He was on the brink of an adventure. And he had come well prepared.

"Ah," Gwil sighed suddenly. "There she is."

Ben followed his gaze, and saw Meralyn making her way through the dye workers, easily clearing a path with her long stride. In her hand, she held a folded piece of parchment.

"Has he..." Gwil asked when Meralyn had reached them.

"He has indeed." Meralyn grinned and handed the parchment to Gwil. "One look at that fabric, and he immediately agreed to allow you some travel time."

"Good, good." Gwil's hand was trembling. Meralyn's expression was serious again. She took his hand and squeezed it gently.

"Good," Gwil repeated. He opened the note and read the foreign-sounding words it contained aloud. A shiver passed through his whole body, and then he sighed, clearly relieved.

"Are you okay?" Ben asked.

"Yes." Gwil smiled faintly and raised his wrist. His tattoo had paled to a grey band.

"It feels as if an iron manacle has been removed from my wrist."

"Five days," Meralyn said. "That's as long as I could get."

"Pricklethorn believed the story?" Gwil asked.

Meralyn nodded. "I told him you're going to look for a recipe for cerulean ink at the library. Five days," she said again, and now Ben thought he heard some doubt in her voice. "Long enough for a journey to World's End."

"And for everything else as well. Now," Gwil looked at Ben, "shall we be on our way?"

Ben was still staring at Gwil's wrist. "What happens if Titania finds out that you took me with you? Won't she activate the mark again?" he asked, concerned.

"She can't," Meralyn said. "For Titania to do that, the bearer of the mark must be there to hear her words."

"And if she does realize that you've come along, we'll be miles away by then," Gwil added.

"Okay," Ben said. "Thank you, Meralyn."

"Oh, don't mention it." She smiled, and then turned to Gwil again. "Weather permitting, you'll make it to World's

End by tomorrow evening. Here." She pulled a little pouch from a pocket of her robe and held it out to Gwil. "Take these with you."

Gwil accepted the pouch and opened it. His eyes widened. "Oh. Oh, no. That's not a good idea, Meralyn."

Curious, Ben peeked inside the pouch, but all he saw were a few smooth grey pebbles. "What are they?"

"Ember pebbles," Meralyn replied. "One touch and they grow as hot as if they've been sitting in a blazing fire."

"No, no," Gwil repeated and handed the pouch back to Meralyn, closing her hand around it. "I can't have these on me. I... I wouldn't be able to restrain myself."

"But you'll need them. Maybe. If you're running out of time."

"What's so bad about a few hot pebbles?" Ben asked.

"If I take one in my hand, I'll shapeshift immediately," Gwil explained. "And I won't be of any use or help to you in my animal shape."

"Well, I'm not suggesting you use them right away," Meralyn said. "But five days isn't such a long time. And if the mark is reactivated..."

"Meralyn!" Gwil protested.

"... then the pain will return," she finished her sentence.

"Pain?" asked Ben, aghast.

Meralyn nodded gravely. "The mark spell inflicts terrible pain if Titania discovers we have disobeyed her, or if we stray from the hill without permission. Only when we shapeshift do we lose the pain. That's the choice she has given us. Either we submit to her rule completely, or we spend our lives in our animal shape." Her expression softened. "Gwil, take the pebbles."

Gwil blushed. "All right. But Ben should look after them for me." He turned to Ben. "Please don't give them to me until it's absolutely necessary."

Ben took the pouch and put it in his jacket pocket. "Why would you want them earlier?"

Gwil gave a shamefaced smile. "Because we salamanders love fire, and everything that gives off heat. It's in our nature. And sometimes that is, let's say, rather disadvantageous."

Meralyn shot him an amused glance. "Gwil likes the heat just a little too much." Gwil's face was still glowing, but he was smiling too.

"Now then," she said. "That's that." She looked from Ben to Gwil and back to Ben. "Be careful, both of you."

Ben felt a tingling sensation crawling across his skin. They were setting off on a journey. A journey into the Otherworld, where even more wondrous places and creatures must await. This hill of fairies and shapeshifters was just the beginning.

INTERLUDE

A dense blanket of clouds darkened the skies above Bryngolau as the boy and the salamander set off on their journey. They left Fairy Hill by a side entrance, and began trudging westwards.

From the shadow of a rowan tree, the Grey King's Huntress watched the pair depart. The fog that followed her everywhere clung to the hem of her robe. Behind her, where the shadows grew darker and the undergrowth wilder, the fog was thicker, and ghostly shapes flitted back and forth in its depths.

She hesitated. Two Human children had come from the Borderlands to the Fairy World. But only one was travelling onward to the mountains. What should she do? She took a deep breath, drawing her black veil close to her face. Then she jerked her head up and sniffed the air. There it was. The faint silvery scent of the World Key. It stuck to the boy and left behind a trace like floating pollen. Her hand reached for her hunting horn, but no—it was still too early to call for her Master.

She waited until the boy and the salamander were nearly out of sight, and then beckoned her hounds. A pair of them stepped out of the shadows and strode past her, soundlessly, heads lowered and eyes dimly glowing. The Huntress waited a little longer, until the dogs had picked up their scent, and then followed in their wake.

Titania

✌ PORTIA ✌

All day long, curious shapeshifters had been seeking out Portia's company, quizzing her about her world, doing her hair and making her try on different garments as if she was one of Meralyn's mannequins. Now she sat on a bench in the corner of the sewing room, waiting for someone to take her to Titania's celebration. Everyone seemed to have left her alone for a while, and Portia was glad of it—she was so nervous by now that she wouldn't have been able to talk about anything. She was relieved when Peaseblossom finally burst into the room. At least she wouldn't be getting pushed around by Cobweb again.

"Look at you!" Peaseblossom said cheerfully. "All spruced up. With, hmm, trousers! Interesting choice."

Portia raised an eyebrow. Rather trousers than the flimsy, flowy sequined nightgown Peaseblossom was wearing. The fairy's hairdo was even weirder than the day before—piled up high, and braided with a jumble of twigs, feathers, velvet ribbons and borage blossoms. It looked as if she was wearing a bird's nest on her head.

Portia's outfit was quite simple in comparison: the brown leggings Meralyn had found for her reached just below her knees. She had also given her a white shirt and a cobalt-blue waistcoat with a cornflower pattern to go with it. The shirt was a bit longer than the waistcoat, hanging down to her hips.

Portia resisted the urge to smooth her clothes. She had hidden the key in the inside pocket of the waistcoat, and was hoping its shape didn't show through the fabric. She had decided she wouldn't play her trump card until she had made her deal with the Fairy Queen. She dried her damp hands on the leggings and trusted that no one would notice how nervous she really was.

Peaseblossom twirled around once before offering Portia her hand. "Shall we?"

Outside Fairy Hill, it was already dark, but the clearing was bathed in silvery moonlight. Peaseblossom led Portia across the foxglove field to a cluster of oak trees. A flight of stairs made of roots led down into a brightly lit hollow, where a lake awaited them, flat and clear as a mirror. Oak trees lined the shore, lanterns hanging from their branches. More lights had been placed on moss-covered rocks, and bowls filled with whirling moon-moths floated on the lake's surface.

Titania's royal household had gathered by the shore. Portia saw fairies in shimmering garments, with pinned-up hair and floral corsages. Among them, small groups of shapeshifters gathered here and there: fluffy-eared squirrels and short, stocky men with black stripes on their faces. As she descended the stairs to the hollow, Portia passed a young man with a pair of antlers growing from his head.

The delicate sound of little bells and harps was coming from somewhere, but the crowd's murmur almost drowned out the music completely.

Peaseblossom guided her straight to Moon Lake. Wooden platforms drifted close to the shore, like big lily pads. More fairies were standing on the platforms, and pale ivory-haired girls swam in the water below.

All eyes were on Portia. She felt as if she were on display. At the same time, she couldn't help but stare back—the Assembly of Otherworldly Creatures was just too beautiful and peculiar. As she reached the lake shore, a fat toad with iridescent dragonfly wings buzzed right past her face.

No one will ever believe any of this, she thought.

A narrow footbridge led straight out over the lake to a crescent-shaped platform, in front of the dark hillock of an island, where Titania was holding court.

Portia slowed but Peaseblossom waved her eagerly onwards. "Chop, chop! Let's not keep Her Majesty waiting!"

Her Majesty, Portia thought, her blood running cold.

Titania sat on a throne of woven branches. Leaves, mushrooms and frilly ferns all sprouted from the tangled wood. The branches of an oak tree growing on the island formed a canopy above the Fairy Queen.

Titania looked nothing like the harmless young woman Portia had met the day before. She sat bolt upright on her throne, staring at Portia with her silver eyes. The bodice of her dress clung to her upper body, and a cascade of shimmering flowers flowed from her shoulder to her feet. A stripe of cobalt-blue paint stretched from temple to temple across Titania's face, highlighting the unnatural glow of her eyes. On her head sat a crown of peeled willow-tree branches, and her long hair hung down to her shoulders. Instead of flowers, glittering dewdrops decorated her hair and crown.

Portia approached the platform with trembling knees. What had she got herself into?

Cobweb stood at Titania's left side. On her other side was a rotund fairy man in a long robe dyed in shades of blue—presumably this was Pricklethorn, the Lord Chamberlain.

"Curtsy!" Peaseblossom hissed in a low voice.

"What?"

"Curtsy!" she repeated, before bobbing respectfully before the Queen. Portia tried her best to copy her.

"Portia Humanchild." Titania's voice echoed across the lake. She raised her hand and beckoned Portia to come closer. Her fingertips had been dipped in silver-blue paint.

Portia walked up to the throne, trying hard to ignore Cobweb's stony expression. Titania was smiling at least, although her smile seemed a bit cold and formal. "Welcome to the Dance of the Fairies. Do you like it?"

At first Portia couldn't speak. She swallowed before managing to choke out a few words. "Yes, very much. Your Majesty."

"If I remember correctly, there were two of you. Where's your companion?" asked Titania.

There was no turning back now. Portia could only hope that Ben and Gwil had put some distance between themselves and Fairy Hill by now.

"Ben is on his way to the World's End," she said. "He wants to help Rose, so he's gone to find out whether it's possible to bring someone back from the fog."

Portia stood stiffly, feeling her heartbeat pounding in her throat. Any moment now, Titania would surely explode in anger and have her thrown into the dungeons. But instead, the Fairy Queen raised her hand and let a moon-moth land on a fingertip.

"Surely the boy has not gone all by himself," she said. "Who's showing him the way?"

"It's Gwil Glumheart," Cobweb cut in. "It was he who brought the Humans to your court in the first place."

"Is that true?" Titania asked.

Portia nodded. There was no sense in denying it, but she felt a wave of heat rising from her neck to her face. Far too late, she was realizing that she had underestimated the danger to Gwil and Meralyn. Even if Titania never found out about Merron's book, the salamanders had still acted without permission. What would Titania do? Punish Meralyn and Gwil for treason?

"So Glumheart has left the Hill." Titania turned to the Lord Chamberlain. "Did you grant permission?"

Pricklethorn lowered his head, his face bright red. "Yes, my Queen."

"Interesting." Titania flicked the moon-moth from her fingertip. She gazed thoughtfully at Portia. "You and the boy are clearly rather fond of Viola Rosethorn."

Her tone was friendly, but still Portia felt a bead of sweat running down her back. "She's my aunt," she replied. "And she saved our lives. Please, Your Majesty. I know everyone's saying we can't help her. But we've got to try at least."

Titania settled back on her throne. "I do understand, child," she said. "Everyone who remembers the Grey King's last attack knows what it feels like to lose someone to the fog. And if there's an answer to your questions anywhere, then it's at World's End. There's one thing I don't understand, though. How do you plan on reaching Rose, since the key is with her, in the Borderlands?"

It felt as if the key was burning a hole in Portia's pocket. She really did want to tell the truth, but now that she had the chance she didn't dare.

"Are you hoping that Rose is still herself enough to be able to open the door to our world?"

"No, Your Majesty."

"Could it be that you haven't told me the whole truth?" Titania asked. "Perhaps my Cobweb was not mistaken, after all, and she did see the key in your hand?"

Portia looked up, her face ablaze with fear, but Titania was smiling, and this time her smile seemed warm. "I thought as much," she said. "And I understand that you wanted to be careful. You didn't know me and couldn't have known how I would treat you. As I remember, Humans are fond of telling stories about cunning fairies and their tricks."

Portia lowered her head, and at long last the knot in her chest loosened. "We shouldn't have lied, Your Majesty. I'm sorry."

Titania nodded. "I do hope you understand me as well," she said. "My folk have suffered greatly at the hands of the

Grey King's army. And the World Key poses a great risk. Especially if it is used several times in a short period. But I also understand that you want to help Rose. And I'm sure you want to go home."

It seemed as if all Portia's worries had been for nothing. "Yes," she said, feeling so grateful she would have liked to hug Titania.

"How would you feel about a deal?" Titania asked. "I'll agree to help you. And when you have the key again, you'll hand it over to me, and I'll keep it safe."

Did Titania think the key was still hidden somewhere? That would have been a good idea, actually. She could hear Ben's warning in her head: *In stories, humans always end up losing when they make deals with fairies.* Titania's offer sounded straightforward, but it was better to play it safe. She tried to sound as confident as possible: "If I agree, will you allow Gwil and Ben to finish their mission? And there won't be any punishment, either?"

Titania raised an eyebrow. "Punishment," she repeated, glancing at Pricklethorn, who looked increasingly pale. "Very well. I agree. I'll allow them to do what they need to do. You have my word."

Portia hesitated for a moment, but then she took a step forward, holding her head high. "Then I accept the deal."

Titania clapped her hands. "Wonderful," she said. "Then let's set the seal on our agreement. Pricklethorn?"

The Lord Chamberlain reached inside his robe and handed Titania a silver bracelet. "This bracelet shall be my pledge," she said solemnly. "I hereby swear to get you home safely." She leant forward and held the bracelet out to Portia. Portia took it, and Pricklethorn gestured for her to put it on her wrist.

Titania smiled again. "Your turn now. Will you reveal where you're hiding the key?"

Portia pulled the key out of her waistcoat pocket. Pricklethorn drew in a sharp breath, but Titania remained calm.

"As promised." Portia held the key up, and Titania took it nonchalantly. Then with a thin smile, she leant back in her throne, twirling the key between her sparkling blue fingertips. "Such a tiny thing," she mused, "and yet it does so much harm. Cobweb!"

"Your Majesty."

"Make sure that the Humanchild is taken home."

Portia frowned. "Right away?" she asked, taken aback.

"But of course," said Titania, in a friendly voice.

"Don't we need to get ready first?" Portia asked. "I don't know... gather provisions? Get together a troop of warriors, or something?"

"You'll hardly need provisions. It's not far to the servants' quarters."

"What?" Portia stared blankly at Titania. "I thought you were going to take me home."

"And that's exactly what I intend to do." Titania smiled again, but this time there was no warmth in her expression. "Bryngolau is your home now, Humanchild."

Portia felt an icy chill run through her. "You promised to help me!"

"Oh, yes," Titania agreed. "I'll help you find your place in my world. I'll help you survive here. Instead of imprisoning you in a cloven oak tree, as anyone who is a threat to my people deserves." She leant forward. "Did you truly believe I'd let you open the doors?" she hissed. "Never again will I allow any Human to put my people in danger."

"But... I didn't mean to..." Portia stammered.

"You didn't mean to what? Lead the Grey King right to my door? Lie to me?" She sat bolt upright on her throne, glaring down at Portia. "You did well to ask for forgiveness for your human friend and the salamander. I wasn't expecting that. Too bad you didn't ask the same for yourself."

Portia backed away, but Cobweb was standing close behind her and grabbed her by the arm, holding her with an iron grip. Portia stared about her wildly, desperately looking for someone to help her. She saw Peaseblossom gaping at her, wide-eyed, her hands pressed to her mouth.

"You tried to betray me, and thereby you broke my laws," Titania roared. "From now on, you'll work off your debt as my servant in my service. *Caethiwa!*" The final word rang out like a bird's cry.

The last syllable had barely left Titania's lips when a blazing pain burned into Portia's wrist. She screamed in shock and jerked her arm up. The bracelet that Titania had given her began to smoke, and then melt on her skin like mercury. It burned. Oh, it burned so much! Portia watched aghast as the silver sank into her skin, leaving behind a smoking band around her wrist. Her eyes filled with tears, and she fell to her knees. She clasped her wrist with the other hand, but the mark that the bracelet had burnt into her skin couldn't be wiped away.

Titania slipped from her throne and strode past her to the edge of the platform. Through the blur of her tears, Portia saw she was holding the key between her fingertips.

"No!" she croaked.

"Get used to kneeling before your Queen," Titania said, and threw the key into the lake.

The Library

Ben was grateful for Portia's blister plasters. He and Gwil had been wandering the mountains beyond Fairy Hill since the previous afternoon, sleeping only for a few hours before climbing another mountain pass at dawn. They walked on narrow trails, cut across scree-covered slopes and barren plains and followed mountain streams through deserted groves of oak trees.

Soon they left the mountains behind and trudged across wild grassland, heading towards the coast. As evening fell, a drizzling rain swept in from the west, and soon enough their clothes were dripping wet.

At first, Ben had bombarded Gwil with questions about the Fairy World but now he was too tired talk. He was as filthy as a sheep, and smelt like one too. Ben longed for Ridik's magical swiftflight, and cursed himself for having the fabulous idea of walking to World's End with Gwil. Walking to the end of the world—that's exactly what it felt like.

"Not long now," Gwil assured him. "Look."

He pointed forward. In the waning light, Ben could make out a dimly gleaming strip of sea and a hill rising above a bay like the shell of a tortoise.

"World's End," Gwil said.

Ben could only manage a weary nod. The last stretch of their journey seemed to drag on agonizingly. When they finally reached the shore, the last rays of sunlight were dying, and the tortoise-shell hill was blending into the grey twilight.

Gwil headed towards a clump of dark trees at the bottom of the hill. Amid the trees stood a low dwelling with a conical thatched roof. As they drew closer, Ben could make out a vegetable garden behind a wall, and a rough stone hut. As they passed he saw through the gaps in the walls goats moving around inside.

"Almost there," Gwil mumbled.

As they approached the house, the door swung open and a figure stepped out with a lantern in his hand.

"Who's there?" a voice called.

"Ho, Tegid!" Gwil replied. "It's me, Gwil." He and Ben kept walking as Tegid came towards them. They met at the edge of the vegetable garden.

"Gwil Glumheart!" The librarian of World's End grasped Gwil's hand and smiled broadly. "So good to see you, my friend."

"Likewise," Gwil replied. "It's been far too long since I paid you a visit."

"Very true," Tegid said. Then he turned back towards his house and beckoned them to follow. "Come in, come in. I just put my supper on the stove. Looks like I should throw some more carrots into the stew!"

Ben had never been happier to walk into a house. A house with a roof to keep out the rain, and with a fire crackling in a fireplace.

It seemed as if Tegid had made himself quite comfortable at World's End. The ceilings were low and the stone floor was covered with thick rugs. A ladder led up to the attic, where Tegid had his bed as well as a space for visitors.

When Ben was settled in a chair by the fireplace, snug in a set of dry clothes provided by their host, it seemed as if all was right with the world, at least for now. Tegid handed him a bowl of stew, and he let out a satisfied sigh.

Tegid grinned. "Long journey, eh?"

Ben nodded, already enjoying his first spoonful of stew. Tegid chuckled and brought Gwil a bowl too, before settling in the last free chair in front of the fireplace.

The librarian was a good head shorter than Gwil, and somewhat plumper too. His figure seemed even rounder thanks to the thick swaddling of clothes he wore: leather slippers, linen leggings, a dark-brown gown and a chunky grey woollen jumper. The whole outfit was topped off with a green woolly hat.

Ben took another spoonful of the stew and felt his whole body warming up. Tegid was a good cook: there were turnips, carrots, onions, parsley and garlic in the stew, with a handful of dried plums that added a sweetness to the broth, and a good pinch of pepper—enough to make Ben's eyes water.

Gwil told Tegid their story while they ate. When they had finished, he nodded.

"So the Grey King is awake again then. Well, I've always thought it was just a matter of time."

"The door is closed now," Gwil said.

Tegid tutted. "Yes, and poor Mistress Rosethorn is stuck on the wrong side of it."

"Do you know Rose?" Ben asked.

"A little. I knew her friends better. Three of them came to visit World's End, all those years ago."

Ben swallowed a mouthful of stew. "Ridik told me that Bramble and Rose fought the Grey King back then."

"Oh, yes, indeed they did," Gwil confirmed. "Side by side with the badgers and Titania's fairy warriors. Until a messenger from the Adar arrived to announce that their friends had figured out a way to kill the Grey King here in World's End. Then they rode to the Pale Tower to attack him at the heart of his power."

"That's not quite true, actually," Tegid cut in. "We didn't know how to kill the Grey King back then, either. Or even whether it was possible to do so. We did figure out how to stop him, though."

"Really?" Ben said. "How?"

"By stitching a rune charm into a cloth and throwing it over him. In this way a spell was cast that put him into a deep sleep. But you need one piece of crucial knowledge for the spell to work: the Grey King's real name."

"And what is it?" Ben asked.

Tegid leant back. "In the stories we tell our children, the Grey King came out of nowhere. He's a creature of the in-between, we say: a being made of fog and dark thoughts." He paused and smiled sadly. "But that's not true. The Grey King's real name is Arawn. And Arawn is the ruler of Annwn."

Ben flinched.

"So the human folk still speak of Annwn?" Tegid asked, seeing the boy's reaction.

Ben gulped. "Where I'm from they do."

"And what do they say?"

"They say it's the land of ghosts. The... the Underworld." Ben remembered the day he had read about Annwn for the first time. He was ten years old and had found a book of Welsh mythology in the library.

Tegid nodded. "It's *one* of the Underworlds, yes. The one that's closest to us."

Gwil set down his bowl. "Arawn is the ruler of Annwn, just as Titania and Oberon are the rulers of our world. But he left his kingdom a long time ago."

Tegid rubbed his chin. "I have no idea why he turned his back on Annwn, but something must be driving him to cross the borders into other worlds."

"He doesn't just cross over—every world he sets foot in is wiped away by the fog if nobody stops him."

There was an uncomfortable silence. There was still some stew at the bottom of Ben's bowl, but he had lost his appetite.

"May I see Merron's book?" Tegid said eventually.

"Of course." Gwil pulled the book from inside his robe, and passed it to Tegid with a trembling hand.

Tegid leafed through the yellowed pages, examining them with curiosity. "Instructions for crafting a World Key," he read. "Well, that should help you to get into the Pale Tower. Are you planning on banishing him again?"

"No," Gwil replied. "We think Rose has become a Mistwalker, and we want to bring her back."

"Not an easy task," Tegid said. "But I'm sure there's a solution hidden away somewhere in my library."

The research appeared to be a welcome challenge for him. Meanwhile, Ben was still pondering Tegid's suggestion of banishing the Grey King again.

"Why doesn't Titania get rid of the Grey King?" he asked. "If anyone could do it, surely she could?"

"Titania has no interest in confronting Arawn these days," Tegid said. "As long as the doors to the Fairy World are closed, she doesn't care what he does."

Every shapeshifter Ben spoke to seemed to agree that they could expect no help from Titania, and yet Portia was pinning all her hopes on the Fairy Queen. Worry wormed its way into his mind. *How did her negotiations go*, he wondered. *Is she getting the help she was hoping for?*

"As for your plan," Tegid said, "I don't suppose I need to tell you how dangerous it is?"

"We know," Ben said quietly.

"And yet, you still want to try. For Rose's sake." A grin spread across Tegid's round face. "That, my friends, is the stuff that great heroes' stories are made of."

Gwil snorted. "But this isn't a story."

Tegid winked. "Are you quite sure about that?" He got to his feet, scurried to a shelf and returned with a clay bottle and three little mugs.

"This is what we need right now!" He poured some liquid into the mugs, and the scent of honey reached Ben's nose. "I'll help you two as much as I can." He handed each of them a mug and raised his in a toast. "I know just where to find the books we consulted the last time the Grey King attacked. We'll surely find answers to your questions there."

Ben took a sip and coughed. Tegid's brew tasted sweet, but it burned his lips. "When are we going to the library?" he asked.

Tegid beamed. "A real bookworm, eh?" he chuckled. "Tomorrow. My Lady looks her best in daylight."

INTERLUDE

At dawn, a soft white mist rolled in from the sea. Thick fog swept across the shore to coil around the hills of World's End, smothering all sound.

No one yet stirred in Tegid's house, but a white dog slunk along the wall outside. It moved as lightly as a breath of air, on long, sinewy legs. It paused in front of the door and listened. Grey clouds swirled within its eyes—as if someone had filled two glass orbs with a thunderstorm.

Far away, the sun was rising over the sea, and the mist on the waves began to clear. A bird sang from a nearby tree. The dog flinched, turned and ran back across the meadow in front of Tegid's house. There, amidst the high grass, stood the Grey King's Huntress. The second hunting dog waited by her side.

When both dogs were near, she touched their heads, and they dissolved into fog. She looked at the house. A lantern was burning in one of the windows. The Huntress turned and disappeared into the mist.

Her time had not yet come.

The Fairy Curse

Outside dawn was breaking, but not a single ray of sunlight penetrated the depths of Fairy Hill. Portia flattened herself against a wall and peeked around a corner. At the bottom of a broad stairway, a group of young salamanders had gathered to report for service. Those who were to work in the kitchens tied their aprons while those who were to serve breakfast to the fairies smoothed out the wrinkles in their headscarves or turbans. Titania couldn't stand her servants looking dishevelled.

I hope she chokes on her breakfast, said Portia to herself bitterly.

Awel, the salamander girl Portia had seen in the Water Lily Chamber, glanced about, looking for Portia. She quickly drew her head back and hid behind the wall. Awel had taken her under her wing after the "celebration" by Moon Lake, found a sleeping place in the servants' quarters for her and explained all the jobs that would be hers from now on. But her words and everything else that had happened since that evening by the lake were just a blur for Portia. She kept touching her wrist, again and again. Despite the burn mark, the skin was still smooth. She couldn't really feel the manacle, but every time she looked down at it, her stomach twisted into a painful knot.

Bryngolau is your home now.

The memory of the gleeful glitter in Titania's eyes left a sour taste in Portia's mouth. She would never give up, and there was no way she was staying here!

She threw a last glance at the salamanders before setting off to make her escape.

Portia didn't know the way out of the Hill, so she chose her route more or less at random, going up staircases when she could, turning and hurrying off into deserted side tunnels when she heard voices up ahead. She forced herself not to run. There had to be a way out. Several even, as Gwil had said: forgotten gates, secret servants' doors... She'd keep looking until she found an unguarded exit. A whole choir of doubts were singing inside her head, but she blocked them out.

Away from the main thoroughfares, pathways through Fairy Hill were simply tunnels drilling through black rock. The one Portia was walking down at the moment was gloomy and cave-like, with an uneven floor and rough walls dripping with lime. Whole colonies of shimmering blue mushrooms grew on the rock, bathing the passageway in a watery light. The air felt cooler and more humid, too.

The further she walked, the narrower the passage became—until she had to hold her arms tight to her body to avoid touching the glowing mushrooms. She was about to turn around and go back when she noticed a flight of stairs up ahead.

Portia started with excitement, and accidentally touched a clump of mushrooms with her elbow. To her horror, the little round heads shuddered, and a hissing noise surged through the passage. Portia clamped her arms to her sides and made a run for the stairs, only to trip over her feet and tumble to the floor when she heard a choir of faint voices whisper: "Don't go."

Portia felt goosebumps creeping up her neck. The voices seemed to be coming from nowhere. Or perhaps they were coming from the walls?

"Don't go," the choir murmured once more.

Portia got to her feet and began to run again, but in her haste she brushed against the soft, cool mushrooms once more. This time the whole wall of mushrooms began to tremble and sway, like the tentacles of a sea anemone, searching for a tiny fish to ensnare.

"Turn back!"

"You're putting yourself in danger!"

Fear clawed at Portia's stomach, but she kept running, her eyes fixed on the stairs. The noise of the voices swelled to a terrible groan, but by then she was hurrying up the staircase.

After a while, the passage became so narrow again that Portia could feel damp moss brushing against her arms. She had left the stairs behind long ago, but still the shaft was climbing steeply. Portia scrambled upwards, on hands and knees now, and shuddered each time her elbow scraped against the wall. What if the tunnel got too narrow? What if she got stuck and couldn't turn around? She could feel the fear in her chest, like a trembling rabbit, but she forced herself to focus on the way ahead. She could see a circle of light in the distance now, and slowly but surely it was growing bigger.

Almost there, she told herself. *Almost. There.*

When she saw some green fronds of bracken against a slice of blue sky at the end of the tunnel, her heart nearly leapt out of her chest. She scrambled the final few metres to the way out, which was no more than a hole in the rock, squeezed herself through into the daylight and slid down a slippery rock face to tumble into a tangle of brambles and bracken. Finally, she had solid ground beneath her feet again! Portia almost sank to her knees with relief. She lifted her face to the sky and sucked in a deep lungful of fresh air. A ray of sunlight fell on her grubby, sweaty features.

She stood there for a few seconds, just breathing in and out. She'd made it. She'd really made it. Once she was sure that her legs would carry her, she began to explore the area. Ahead of her lay a narrow clearing amid the scrub. Beyond that, the woods began. How far would she be able to get before Titania realized that she had escaped? *Far enough,* she told herself.

She'd follow Gwil and Ben to World's End, then they would find Rose together. She knew the library lay to the west—all she had to do was to make it to the coast, then she should be able to find her way.

But Portia had barely taken a step towards the clearing when a searing pain shot from her wrist to her shoulder. She looked down at Titania's mark, and saw to her horror that the edges of the tattoo were glowing golden-red. It felt as if stinging nettles were flowing through her veins.

Portia clenched her fists and forced herself to keep putting one foot in front of the other. She would *not* be stopped. She *would* catch up with Ben. She *would*... The next wave of pain made her scream out loud. She staggered forward, but the clearing began to blur before her eyes. *Keep going,* she told herself. *Keep going!* A burst of pain struck her in the chest like a bolt of lightning. Her knees buckled, she pitched forward into the bracken, and the world turned black.

Rune Magic

After a breakfast of porridge and berry jam, Ben and Gwil followed Tegid outside. He led them through the little wood around his house and up onto the hill behind, with the thunderous rumble of waves breaking on the shore accompanying them all the way.

World's End library stood at the top of the hill, next to the edge of a cliff that plunged a hundred metres or so to the waves below. Like Tegid's house, it was a low, round stone building with a thatched dome for a roof. As they climbed towards it, Ben was buffeted by the sea wind. When they drew near, a scattering of jackdaws took off from the roof to soar on the breeze.

At the entrance, Tegid turned to face them, his eyes sparkling.

"Ready?" he asked. And then he opened the door to World's End.

Ben was so excited as he stepped inside that his nails were digging into the palms of his hands, but he was immediately disappointed with what he saw. The library consisted of only one room, with two circular rows of shelves, one nestled inside the other like a tree's rings.

There were certainly plenty of books on the shelves, but not a remarkable number.

Was this really the great library of the druids and salamanders? After everything Gwil and Meralyn had told him, Ben had expected piles of scrolls, folios and precious old books.

Tegid watched Ben's reaction with a broad smile. "Still not impressed?" he asked. "Then watch this."

He walked to the middle of the room. Dead in the centre of the shelf rings was an empty white circle. Tegid stopped at the edge of the circle, and stepped on a rune that had been burnt into the floor. He had barely touched the rune with his foot when a gritty scraping sound filled the room. The white circle sank down and split into two halves, which slid apart to leave a perfectly round hole in the floor. Tegid beckoned Ben over. Ben went to his side and peered cautiously into the hole. Floor after floor stretched out below them. Dozens and dozens of levels of shelves filled with books. They were standing on the top floor of a tower that stretched down into the ground! Light shone dimly into the tower at each level, as if sunlight were streaming in at the sides.

"Welcome to World's End," Tegid said, clearly in good spirits. "Let's see what we can find."

The salamander had not been exaggerating. World's End was a miraculous place. The outer wall of the upside-down library tower seemed to protrude from the cliff face, and on the second floor down, a huge curved window let in plenty of light. There was no glass in it; instead, runes carved into the walls created an invisible shield, protecting the tower against wind, rain and cold. It looked as if you could step right out of the tower into the sky.

Tegid set to trawling through the library's shelves right away, but Ben stood awestruck, tracing the rune shapes on the wall with his finger.

"Most of us can use runes," said Gwil, standing at Ben's side with his hands clasped behind his back. "Fairies, humans, shapeshifters... But making the runes powerful—that takes a lot of practice. You don't only have to see the word the runes are spelling in your mind's eye—you have to see the meaning and purpose too."

"The meaning?" Ben repeated.

Gwil reached out and touched one of the runes. "Let's say you scratch runes into a young tree and speak the rune word: *Grow.* If it's done correctly, the rune speaker should see an image of a sprouting sapling in their mind. They are not only imagining the tree growing; they can sense it too. If they aren't careful the sapling might only grow a few leaves... or a whole forest might shoot up instead." Gwil smiled. "Everyone knows some rune magic, but some have a special gift for it. Take Rose, for example—she's got a talent for combat and defence runes."

Ben looked up at the lintel of the window, which was entirely covered in runes. "How about you? Can you write runes?"

"Yes," Gwil said. "But I don't really have a talent for magic."

"Hooray!" Tegid's voice came from behind the shelves.

Gwil and Ben exchanged a smile and went over to a worktable by the window.

Tegid emerged carrying a pile of books. "Here you go," he said, enthusiastically plonking the pile down on the table. "These should keep us busy, for starters. And look what else I've found." He reached inside his cardigan and pulled out a slim red notebook with a worn linen binding.

"This was Rose and Bramble's notebook," Tegid explained. "It's one of the rune books they practised spells and magic with."

Ben was itching to get his hands on the notebook. Tegid noticed his impatience and pushed the book across the table to him.

Ben accepted it gratefully. "Is the rune spell to banish the Grey King in here?"

"No," Tegid replied immediately. "One of the humans stitched that on a cloth."

"A cloth?" Ben asked.

"A charm cloth. She and the others took it to the Pale Tower. Rose must have awakened the runes in the tower to banish the Grey King."

"Do you know which rune spell they used?" Gwil asked.

Tegid plucked a book from the pile and tapped its cover. "*Taliesin's Evening Blessing*."

"Could the thing with the charm cloth work a second time?" Ben asked.

"It could," Tegid said, "but it's too dangerous for you two to try it."

"I know," Ben agreed. "But if we bring Rose back here, she can do it, can't she?"

Tegid rested his chin on his folded hands. "Maybe. But that's just it, isn't it? *If* we bring Rose back here."

Ben lowered his gaze and felt along the edge of the red notebook with his thumb. Yes. If.

Tegid briefly placed his hand on Ben's. "Don't be disheartened!" he said. "We'll find a way to snatch her from the fog's claws. These few books are just a start, and if we don't find what we need here, we'll keep on searching. There's an answer to everything buried somewhere in this tower."

"Buried?" Gwil asked, worried.

Tegid beamed at him. "Indeed. We may have to go deeper than I've ever been so far to find it."

He didn't sound remotely worried at the prospect.

That afternoon, the salamanders went back to Tegid's house for some tea and a bite to eat. Ben stayed at the desk at the window all by himself. They had pored through three piles of books by now, with no luck.

Ben leafed through Rose and Bramble's notebook. They had copied paragraphs from books about runes and elemental magic, both making notes in the margins commenting on each other's writings. There was even a sketch of a standing stone covered in runes.

Ben flicked ahead until he got to a page that had a number of runes and their respective translations listed in three neat lines. That morning he had made sure to bring Portia's travel diary with him, so he could take notes in it himself. He took it out of his pocket now, snapped off the rubber band keeping it shut and, using the pen clipped to the front, began sketching one of the runes. Ben liked its shape: one vertical line, and two diagonal lines that jutted out of its side like branches. For some reason, the runes reminded him of the forest on his bedroom wall, where the Wild Things hid. So many times, he had imagined stepping through the painted trees to another world. And that's where he was right now, wasn't he? In another world.

Ben kept browsing, copying combinations of runes at random without giving it much thought. Rose's and Bramble's translations were in Welsh, and he understood most of them. With every rune he copied, his desire to say them out loud increased. He felt silly, but excited at the same time. Ben placed a finger on the last line of runes he had drawn, wet his lips with the tip of his tongue, and then spoke the rune's name.

"Darganfydda." *Find.*

Ben held his breath for one tense moment, but nothing happened. Disappointed, he breathed out, shaking his head. What had he expected? A tingling in his fingers? For the runes on the page to glow blue, like the ones on Rose's staff?

Ben sighed and returned to Portia's notebook. He was about to sketch a small pile of books when something fluttered into his field of vision from the right. He lifted his head to see a moon-moth tumbling towards him. It landed on the open diary, right on the drawing of the rune he had just read aloud.

Ben didn't dare to take his hand off the page. He didn't even dare to breathe. As he watched, the moon-moth began to glow a deep blue. Its antennae quivered, then it took flight again and fluttered to the middle of the room. It stopped above the stairs leading down, deeper into the tower, hovering in place as if waiting for something. Or someone.

Ben stared, frozen for a few moments, then jumped to his feet and followed the moth as it began to descend the tower staircase. The light coming through the window faded as he went further and further down. The moon-moth flew ahead of him like a particularly keen guiding star. Or perhaps a will-o'-the-wisp, set to lead him astray? At that moment, however, his curiosity was stronger than his fear. Where had the moth come from? Had he summoned it? And what did it want to show him? Trying to solve the puzzle was irresistible. Finally, Ben understood why Portia had followed a fox into the wilderness.

With every step, Ben descended further, and the deeper he got, the gloomier his surroundings became. The scent of old leather grew stronger, and Ben noticed that the air wasn't musty or damp. No dust, low humidity: the perfect conditions for a library. His dad would have loved this place.

Ben imagined what it would be like to tell him about the library, and how he would have set out for World's End right away. As always, he felt a twinge of pain when it struck him that he would never talk to his dad again.

He was still lost in thought when they reached a new level and the moon-moth finally came to a halt. Ben stopped, too. It was utterly silent and still down here. He could make out the vague shape of shelves nearby, which ran off and disappeared into darkness.

It wasn't cold, but Ben's forearms were covered in goosebumps. The moth didn't stay still for long, soon fluttering off up one of the aisles that ran between the shelves like the spokes of a wheel. Ben glanced back one last time at the stairs, and then followed it.

As they left one wall of shelves after another behind, Ben felt increasingly ill at ease. How far was the moth leading him? And was it his imagination or did the tower seem much wider down here than the entrance room on the top? Up there, Ben had seen only two rings of shelves, but down here he had already passed through four of them. He was just thinking of turning back when the moth seemed to reach its destination. In the middle of the aisle, a few feet away from Ben, stood a desk. On it lay a single book. The moth was dancing above it like a tiny star. With his heart pounding, Ben approached the table.

The book's binding was so ancient that the leather looked black. It was scuffed from the touch of many hands—or perhaps the hands had belonged to just one person, who had taken the book from the shelf time and time again. Ben placed his own hand on the cover and felt a gust of air behind his back. He spun around with his heart in his mouth. It had felt as if someone was running up the aisle behind him, but there was no one there. He was alone.

Reluctantly, he turned back to the book and opened it. A loose slip of paper fell out from between the pages, and Ben picked it up. There were only two words on it: *Codex Reditus*. They meant nothing to him. Cautiously, he began to turn the pages. The scuffed binding was misleading: the book was old, but not ancient. The pages were made of thick cream-coloured paper covered in handwritten text—yet another notebook, apparently. One page seemed to have a date written in the corner, but the ink was so smeared that Ben couldn't decipher it. The writing was crammed tightly on the pages, as if the author had been trying to save space. Here and there the lines of text were interrupted by strangely contorted faces.

The author probably just hadn't been very good at drawing faces, but still those uncannily long heads and black misshapen eyes sent shivers down Ben's spine. As he leafed through the book, Ben found ripped-out pages from other books that the author had collected and added to their own notes. One showed a woodcut of a man sitting on a rock, holding a lute. He was surrounded by animals, who appeared to be crying. Another page was decorated with a colourful image that reminded Ben of illuminated Bibles from the Middle Ages. There were no praying monks or angels here, though. Instead, there was a slim man, his head downcast and shoulders hunched, walking towards the left margin of the page. Ben shivered. Another figure, a human-like creature wearing a robe, was following the man. Or were they chasing him? Ben gulped, turned another page, and then caught his breath. He recognized the Black Door in this drawing. The paper was grooved, as if the artist had scratched the page violently with a quill, many times over. The door looked like a gaping black maw, like an abyss leading through the book to who knows where. As he stared at the page, the moth fluttered over to Ben and landed at the edge of the page. Ben's hands were trembling.

Underneath the Black Door was just one word. *Annwn.*

Shards

✿ PORTIA ✿

The Fairy Queen was posing on a pedestal in the Water Lily Chamber, trying on the latest creation from Mistress Quickly's sewing room. Around her, a dozen fairies lay or sat on cushions and pillows. A harpist gently strummed at his instrument.

Portia stood next to the pedestal, holding a tray bearing a silver plate filled with pralines. The sweets were covered in white chocolate and decorated with little candied violets. She was tight-lipped with frustration, fighting the desire to hurl the tray across the room.

She had tried to escape three times now. Each time the pain radiating from the mark on her wrist had almost made her lose her mind before she passed out. Then Titania sent Peaseblossom or Cobweb to fetch her, and as soon as she woke up back inside Fairy Hill, the pain was gone. But the more often she opened her eyes below ground, the more the walls of Bryngolau seemed to be closing in around her.

Up on the pedestal, two of Meralyn's seamstresses were scurrying around the Queen, adjusting and pinning a sky-blue gown strewn with tiny pearls. Meralyn Quickly stood to one side, observing their work.

When the girls were done, Meralyn sifted through the pile of fabrics she had brought along, and chose a long sash made of dark-blue velvet. Then she approached Titania and draped the sash over her shoulder, so that it hung down to her waist.

"I think this would make a lovely addition to the gown, Your Majesty," she said.

"Fine, fine, whatever you think is right," the Queen said impatiently.

Meralyn lowered her head in a bow.

Portia wished she could have at least stayed with Meralyn as she had on her first night in Fairy Hill, but now, she was denied even that safe haven—Titania had forbidden any contact with the head seamstress.

After the fitting, the seamstresses gathered their material, curtsied and left the salon. Portia forced herself not to follow them with her eyes.

Titania stepped off her pedestal and lay down on her divan. She was wearing the simple white dress that she had on when she first received Ben and Portia. It had all been a trick, Portia realized now. Her harmless appearance was nothing but a mask. Anger simmered in her stomach—at Titania, and at herself for having been foolish enough to trust her. Titania had completely outsmarted her. But if she thought she had Portia under her power, then she was wrong.

She would never give up. She was going to escape and find Ben and Gwil. Together, they would find a way out of this glittering hellhole. And Titania could burst with rage, for all she cared.

"Humangirl!" Titania cried in her most commanding voice. She had stopped calling Portia by her name a long while ago. "Have you grown roots over there or something?"

Portia forced herself to hide her emotions as she went over to the Queen. She curtsied silently, offering her the tray. Titania didn't say anything, but Portia couldn't help but notice the amused twitching at the corners of her mouth.

She thinks she has won. Portia's anger left a sour taste on her tongue.

Titania picked a praline, and bit into it with visible pleasure. Then she snapped her fingers, and the harpist switched from a rather cheerful melody to something slow and sweet. Portia was about to back away when Titania addressed her once more.

"Humangirl," she said. "What instrument do you play?"

Portia swore inwardly. "None," she replied loudly, before reluctantly adding, "Your Majesty."

"None?" Titania repeated, feigning surprise. "Then you must come up with something else to entertain us. Let me think. You must be able to sing or dance, mustn't you? No? Such a shame."

She daintily brushed a crumb from the corner of her mouth, cocked her head and looked Portia over. "Are you sure you're really a girl?" she asked, before turning to the assembled fairies. "Humans simply aren't particularly gifted," she explained. "There are some exceptions, of course, but most of them are quite clumsy and ordinary." She examined Portia again. "Rather oafish too, though it's no fault of their own." She beckoned Portia, who reluctantly approached the Fairy Queen.

Titania sighed. "You see?" she said. "That square chin, those eyebrows. No natural beauty, inside or out. We could dress this creature in one of Quickly's most beautiful garments, and it wouldn't make any difference."

Portia's face was hot and aglow with anger. She knew Titania was just trying to provoke her, and yet the Queen's words still got under her skin like tiny thorns.

Titania smiled in mock sympathy and placed a hand on her cheek. Portia flinched.

"Humangirl," Titania said. "Has no one ever told you that you're not beautiful? I feel I must, since your family obviously couldn't bring themselves to. They must have been trying to spare your feelings, but it's no kindness in the long run. Better to face up to the truth."

Because you're such an expert when it comes to the truth, aren't you? Portia thought bitterly.

Titania turned to her fairies again. "You can always rely on Quickly's judgement. See how she's dressed this creature in trousers. She's just not pretty enough for a dress."

Portia was struck dumb with anger and frustration, but didn't understand why. Why did she care what that harpy thought?

Titania raised an eyebrow and smirked. "Yes, Portia?" she asked. "Did you want to say something?"

Portia ran the tip of her tongue along her lips. "No, Your Majesty." She would have loved to spit all the bitterness she was feeling right in her face.

The corners of Titania's mouth curled into a triumphant little smile. "Well then, don't just stand there gaping. Go and clear the crockery."

Portia left the Water Lily Chamber on shaky legs. She had piled all the teacups, plates and the silver teapot on her small tray, and it was now so heavy that she was barely able to carry it. The fairies had giggled as they watched her go, waiting for her to drop the wobbly load. She hadn't given them the satisfaction, but her composed façade was crumbling, and her fury dwindling under the massive weight of her own helplessness. She couldn't understand how anyone could be so spiteful. Tears burned in her eyes, but she couldn't wipe them away.

She managed to carry the tray all the way to the tunnel outside the scullery, but then one cup skittered off and smashed on the ground. Portia tried to keep the rest of the pile steady, but it was too late: it all came down onto the mosaic tiles with an almighty crash. Portia swore, knelt amid the debris and began to gather up the broken crockery. By now, tears were streaming down her cheeks.

"That's not going to work," someone said above her.

Portia looked up. It was Robin Goodfellow, his hands casually tucked into his trouser pockets. It was too much for Portia. She wiped the tears from her face. "Mind your own business," she snapped. "Ouch!" Portia had cut her hand on a shard of china. Of course she had, what else should she expect? She put the bleeding finger in her mouth and defiantly began picking through the debris with the other.

Robin crouched down next to her. "Is it a Human quirk to always do exactly what you shouldn't? Careful!"

Portia jumped to her feet and glared at him. "I wouldn't even be in this horrible situation if it wasn't for you!"

"Careful, dammit!" Robin darted up from his crouched position and kicked a broken cup away from Portia's bare feet. He reached out a hand, but she slapped it aside.

"Don't you dare touch me!" She put her finger in her mouth again and glared at him. "Bramble was right. She should have made gloves out of you."

"Are you sure you're not related to *her*?" Robin asked sharply. "You've got a big mouth anyway, that's for sure."

"I'd rather have a big mouth than a heart of stone."

They stared at each other for a few seconds, like two gunslingers in a Western. Then Robin sighed and raised his hands as if in surrender. "Come with me and we'll get that bandaged up."

For a brief moment, Portia had a vision of the fox sitting under the bramble hedge. "Ha! Like I'd ever follow you anywhere ever again."

"Oh, come on..." He took a step towards her. She backed away, but he grabbed her arm.

"Do you want to save Rose or not?" he hissed. Portia froze. "Meralyn told me about your genius plan," he said quietly. "Using the World Door at the Pale Tower? I've never heard such a foolish idea. If you really want to go through with it, you'll need all the help you can get." He let go of her arm and raked his fingers through his hair. "And I can't believe I'm really saying this, but I'll help you."

Portia tried to read his expression. She couldn't believe she was even listening to him, after what he had done to her. "Why should I trust a single word you say?"

Robin sighed again. "Spirits, give me strength. For the last time: do you want to save Rose or not?"

Portia hesitated. Then she nodded.

"Great." Robin turned on his heel. "Then come along."

The Book of Return

"*Codex Reditus*," Tegid read aloud. "The Book of Return."

Gwil leant forward. "That sounds promising."

Ben sat by the picture window and watched as the salamanders examined the black notebook. There was tea and ginger biscuits on the table, so far untouched.

"And the moth really led you straight to this notebook?" Gwil asked a second time.

Ben nodded.

"After you spoke the rune?"

Ben nodded again.

Gwil looked him over thoughtfully. Then he smiled. "It was a Discovery Rune. Who knows, perhaps you have a talent for rune speaking too."

Ben felt his face getting hot, but he was pleased. A Rune Speaker! Wouldn't that be something.

In the meantime, Tegid was mumbling to himself as he marvelled at a particularly chaotic page. "Interesting. Most interesting."

"Have you found something?" Gwil asked. "Something helpful?"

"I'm afraid not." Tegid tapped the book cover. "It's not about the Return of Mistwalkers. This book deals with the question of whether a dead person can return to the realm of the living. Look!"

He pulled out one of the loose pages. "This illustration is from the story of Orpheus. According to the myth, he descended into Hades to bring back his dead wife."

"So we're still no closer," Gwil said, sounding discouraged.

Tegid smiled. "Don't give up, old friend. We're only just scratching the surface."

Gwil nodded, but he still looked glum. He absent-mindedly rubbed his wrist with Titania's faded, yet still-visible mark.

Meanwhile Ben stared at the picture that Tegid had laid on the table. It showed a man walking with head bowed, a woman in a white dress following behind. A hot, tight knot had settled in his chest, and Tegid's words echoed in his head. Was there really a way to bring the dead back to the realm of the living?

"Why that moth would have led Ben to this book in particular is a mystery to me," Tegid said.

Ben wet his dry lips with the tip of his tongue. "The door in that drawing—is that another World Door?"

Tegid creased his pale forehead and flipped back through the book until he reached the picture of the Black Door. "Yes," he confirmed. "Yes, I think so."

Gwil bent over the book. "Annwn..." he read. "Tegid... do you think that's Arawn's door?"

Tegid tapped a finger on the page. "It's possible." His face brightened. "Perhaps that's why the moth wanted you to find the book! You must have been thinking of our destination. It is said that there are two doors in the Pale Tower. One leads to Faerie, and the other to Annwn."

"You said Annwn is one of the Underworlds. Is there really more than one?" asked Ben.

"Oh, yes, dozens!" he replied. "Our Orpheus here, for instance—he wouldn't have been looking for his wife in Annwn. He'd have descended to Hades. Wait!"

Tegid jumped up and hurried over to the rows of shelves, obviously in his element. Ben felt as if he was standing on a thin sheet of ice that was beginning to crack under his feet.

"Is everything all right, Ben?" Gwil asked.

Before Ben had a chance to reply, Tegid came bustling back to the desk carrying a giant book.

"Brace yourselves, friends," he wheezed, and dropped it on the table, where it landed with a thud. "That," he said, "is an atlas of the worlds. One of the good ones."

Ben forgot his stress of only a moment ago as Tegid opened the atlas and spread out its wonderful pages. The map before them was immensely detailed, drawn in black and blue ink. The cartographer had drawn rivers, mountain ranges, and even waves breaking along the coasts. The page they were looking at showed the region of Faerie they were in. The shape of the land and contours of the coast looked like North Wales, but the fantastical place names were different from those he knew: Bryngolau, Llywernog, Gwaunygog... The map was also criss-crossed by a veiny network of dotted lines that Ben couldn't quite make sense of.

"We are here," Tegid explained, tapping a peninsula marked "World's End" with his fingertip. Tegid lifted a corner of the map, and Ben realized it was drawn on tracing paper. He hadn't noticed at first that there was a page of thicker card underneath the map itself. In fact, the whole atlas seemed to be made of alternating layers of card and tracing paper.

"And now, pay attention my friends." Tegid smoothed the map of Faerie back onto its card underlayer, before carefully pulling out a second map from the pages of the atlas and placing it on top of the first.

The outlines of both maps aligned perfectly. The dotted lines were identical as well, but now Ben could recognize place names on the top map. Harlech. Caernarfon. Those were the names of castles the English had built in North Wales in the thirteenth century.

Ben bent over the map to get a closer look. It looked like a map of Wales in the Middle Ages!

"Wow," he muttered.

Tegid beamed. "Impressive, isn't it. And look at this." He lifted the remaining pages and card dividers in his hand.

As far as Ben could tell, the atlas must contain more than a dozen maps. Were they all maps of Other Worlds, he wondered?

"Are those all the worlds that exist?" he asked, in awe.

"Sweet spirits, absolutely not!" Tegid said. "This is just a selection from our little corner of the macrocosm. Here we have the Human World, for example," he said, tapping the upper map, "and Faerie is below."

"And Annwn?" Ben asked.

Tegid cocked his head. "Yes, I suppose one could insert a map of Annwn. Arawn's realm is one of the Underworlds of our region, after all."

"But?" Gwil prompted.

"But no map of Annwn exists," Tegid explained. "Or of any other Underworld, for that matter."

"How curious," Gwil commented.

Tegid shrugged. "Not really. Some worlds cannot be drawn on a map. Which must be why so many are fascinated by them. In any case, this author seems to have been obsessed with the rules governing the passageways between the middle and outer worlds."

"What kind of rules?" Ben asked.

"All worlds have their own laws of nature," Tegid explained. "Their own time, their own moon phases, sources of magical energy and so on. But they do have a few things in common. For one thing, in every world there are places where the boundaries with other worlds are thin. Some call these places Ley Lines. Or Spirit Paths. Or World Seams."

He traced a dotted line with his fingertip until he came to a point above a lake, where a five-pointed star had been drawn. Ben frowned, but then realized what he was looking at. He knew that lake! It was right above Trefriw.

"The Human Door!" he called out. "The star marks the Human Door."

Tegid smiled and nodded. "Correct. What you see here is a World Seam, and a gate to cross from one world to the other."

Ben's gaze drifted back to the *Book of Return.* "So the door to Annwn must be on a seam too, right?"

"Indeed," Tegid replied. "And you'd need a key for that door, too."

Ben swallowed hard. "But if you had one..."

"Then you could cross over to Annwn, yes," Tegid finished Ben's sentence. "But I wouldn't recommend it."

"Why not?" Ben's voice came out in a rasp, but Tegid didn't seem to notice.

"The passageway from the Worlds of the Living to the Worlds of the Dead has its own set of rules." Tegid pointed at the loose illustrated page. "Take our good Orpheus here. According to the legend, he did find a way to get into his Underworld, and he convinced Hades's ruler to give him his wife back. But on one condition: that he didn't turn around to look at her until they got back to their own world. And what do you think happened?"

"He turned around," Gwil said.

"He turned around," Tegid confirmed. "He heard her footsteps behind him, turned around, and she disappeared into the Underworld again."

Ben was looking at the illustration and imagined that it started moving, how Orpheus was walking ahead as the woman in white followed him, her gaze full of longing. *Don't turn around*, Ben thought. *Just keep looking straight ahead.*

Tegid closed the atlas with a loud thud, making Ben flinch. "I'll go and fetch us a few more books."

"Wonderful," Gwil sighed, and Tegid gave a determined nod. Then he hoisted the atlas off the table and tottered off to the back shelves. Meanwhile, Gwil gathered up the loose pages from the codex to make space for the next book. Ben should have given him a hand, but was finding it hard to concentrate.

His thoughts turned to his father. He couldn't help it. He remembered a trip to the seaside. His parents had never had the money for a big holiday, but whenever possible Tom had loaded the family into the car to drive to the coast for the day.

On that day, the sky had been clear and light blue, like a pane of tinted glass. The wind had whistled across the beach blowing tiny grains of sand against Ben's calves. His parents had taken off their shoes and rolled up their trouser legs before wading into the water to paddle in the shallows. They tried to convince Ben to join them, but he was too nervous, so his dad started clucking like a chicken, making him laugh. Ben stuck his tongue out, and the next moment Tom came running towards him.

Ben ran away, laughing, but Tom caught up with him, and grabbed and swung him up onto his shoulders.

"Now, my boy. Let's see how big a splash you make."

"Noooo! Nooo!"

Ben laughed and squealed as his dad carried him towards the water. Tom pretended he was going to throw him in the sea for real, but Ben knew that he wouldn't do that. He was holding him tightly and safely in his arms.

The memory was fading, but Ben could still hear the waves, and his father's laughter.

He wasn't here any more. That was what he had told himself again and again after the funeral. The grown-ups all kept assuring him that his father was now in a better place, but Ben had never been able to believe that. Some part of him was convinced that after they died, humans simply... stopped. The empty space they left behind was just too vast, too bottomless to imagine they could just be in another room.

But now he realized that everything he had believed was wrong. There *were* other places. And doorways you could pass through to reach them.

Ben's gaze kept drifting back to the codex that Gwil had pushed to the edge of the table. *No distractions*, he told himself. But in his mind's eye he saw the Black Door leading to Annwn.

A Fateful Sandwich

Back in his quarters, Robin cleaned Portia's wound. He spread a thin layer of an unpleasant, stinging salve on the cut before wrapping a bandage around her finger. Portia's gaze wandered to the myriad of pots, bottles and wooden boxes lining Robin's shelves. She suspected they held more than just tea.

"What have you got in all those?" she asked, nodding at the shelves.

Robin put the bandages and salve back in a cupboard. "Medicine," he replied. "Shapeshifting potions, sleeping powder, dream seeds." When he saw the doubtful look on her face, he only shrugged. "Fairies have their elemental magic, Druids have their runes. But we shapeshifters know there are plenty more kinds of enchantment besides."

He took another clay jar from a shelf and went over to a small table, where he had placed two teacups and a teapot. The kettle that had been Gwil's undoing during their first visit simmered over the fire in the hearth.

Portia followed Robin to the table, and warily sat down. She was determined not to forget how unpredictable he could be. He seemed friendly now, but who knew what tricks he might have up his sleeve?

"I thought you said there was no way to help Rose."

Robin put three spoons of tea leaves into the pot. "Well, maybe that's not entirely true," he admitted.

"What a surprise."

Robin snorted dismissively, but a smile tugged at the corners of his mouth. He opened a box of biscuits and offered them to Portia. When she refused to take one, he sighed, put the box on the table and went to fetch the kettle from the fireplace.

Portia waited until he had returned. "You also said you wished Rose would suffer the same way you had."

"Wouldn't be the first wish I've regretted." Robin poured steaming water into the teapot. He had dark circles underneath his eyes, as if he had been sleeping badly.

"So you think we can save Rose?" Portia asked.

"We might have a chance. A small chance." He put the kettle on the floor and settled in the chair opposite Portia. When he held out the biscuit box again, Portia took one this time. It tasted spicy, like a gingernut with a hint of orange.

"There's a story," Robin began. "Well, actually it's just a legend. It is said there was once a couple who managed to find each other in the fog."

"Yes, Ifor and Nerys," Portia said. "Meralyn told us about them. In the story, Nerys gives Ifor her heart."

"A romantic story, nothing more," Robin said. "However, I've heard elsewhere that a memory can actually bring back a Mistwalker. But not just any memory. You have to remind the Mistwalker of something that's worth staying alive for."

Portia placed her half-eaten biscuit on the saucer. "You've known that this whole time? And yet, you refused to help us?"

Robin shook his head. "Even if I'd told you, what memory would you have used to bring back Rose? Do you know her that well?"

The question snuffed out Portia's last spark of hope. "Then there's no way to help her after all."

"Probably not," Robin admitted. "But that doesn't mean that we shouldn't try."

Portia had a lump in her throat again. "Why didn't you tell us before?" she repeated. "Why did you send us away?" *If you had helped us, I wouldn't have made a deal with Titania.*

She didn't say the last sentence out loud, but it hung in the air unspoken.

For the first time, she thought she saw something resembling regret in Robin's face. "If you carry around anger like that for long enough, it blocks out everything else," he said. "Rose... Rose was a good friend before she imprisoned me in her world. A part of me can't forgive her for that. But the thought of her being lost in the fog for good? She doesn't deserve that, no matter what happened between us."

Portia felt those words had been hard for him to say. But could she trust her feelings?

"Show me your wrist," Robin said.

Portia pressed her lips together and held out her right arm. Robin examined the mark. "Ah. That complicates things."

"You don't say." Was it her imagination, or was there an amused glint in Robin's eye at that?

"Well, yes. But as it happens, I'm pretty good at solving complicated problems."

"I see. And what do you have in mind for this problem? As long as I have that magical mark on my wrist, I can't leave Fairy Hill without permission. And Titania is hardly going to grant me that."

A foxy smile spread across Robin's face. He took down an empty jam jar from the shelf. "Oh, that's easy," he said. "We'll use Titania's own favourite method. Trickery."

It was almost midnight when Titania called for Portia again. Dutifully, she set out for the kitchen and then the Water Lily Chamber. This time, she was carrying sandwiches and a glass with elderflower cordial on a tray. Robin's empty jam jar was also on the tray, now serving as vase for a bunch of buttercups. Robin himself trotted along at her side in his fox shape.

"I really hope your plan works," she said under her breath. "Otherwise, we're both done for." The fox shot Portia a pointed look, then scampered on ahead of her into the Water Lily Chamber, and disappeared between the flowerpots.

Portia was relieved to see that there were no other fairies in the chamber. The lanterns had been put out, so that the only light in the darkness came from the colourful fish swimming in glowing circles in the pond and a few moon-moths dancing in the air above the gallery where the Queen lay.

Titania was reclining on her chaise longue, reading a book. She lazily acknowledged Portia's arrival. "Put the tray down," she said in a bored voice. "No, not there. On the table."

Portia did as she had been told and stepped back. Titania marked her place with a bookmark, and glared up at Portia. "Why are you standing around like a cow chewing its cud?" she hissed. "Get lost!"

Portia bit her lip. "Yes, Your Majesty," she replied, and was turning to go when Titania called her back.

"No, wait."

Titania stared at her thoughtfully. Portia forced herself to appear calm. *She has no idea what we are planning*, she thought. *There's no way she could know.*

Over tea in his quarters, Robin had taken a small glass vial from his shelf of wonders. *A very special seasoning, for the next time you bring her a snack.* Three drops of the clear liquid had been sprinkled on each of the sandwiches she had just served Titania.

She has no idea, Portia repeated to herself. And she could only hope that mind reading was not among the Fairy Queen's skills.

Titania was still looking at her with that alarming scrutinizing look.

"I was expecting you to whimper and whine more."

You'd like that, wouldn't you? Portia thought grimly. Instead she said: "Would it make any difference if I did?"

Titania raised an eyebrow. "Well, well. I thought your new position would have taught you some humility and respect. But apparently you haven't learnt your lesson yet."

Portia crossed her hands behind her back to hide her clenched fists. "Whatever you say, Your Majesty." Were her eyes playing tricks on her, or was there a shadow moving behind the lily bushes lining the edge of the chamber?

"Stubborn girl," Titania scoffed. "This won't make your life around here any easier." She opened her book again and reached for a sandwich. Portia could not help herself—mesmerized, she watched as Titania lifted the sandwich to her mouth.

"You're probably trying to work out how to get your revenge on me," Titania said, alarmingly close to hitting the mark. "Feel free to try. I could use some entertainment."

With those words, she took a bite of the sandwich.

Portia held her breath. Titania chewed, swallowed and took another bite." Still here?" she asked without looking up. "Honestly, if you keep annoying me like this there are plenty of... of..." She broke off in the middle of her tirade. The book slipped from her hand and tumbled to the ground with a thud.

"What...?"

A shudder rippled through Titania's body, followed by a wave of glimmering light that shot over her skin up to her face. Portia gasped in shock. Titania whirled around to glare at her, wide-eyed. She looked down at the sandwich in her hand and then back at Portia.

"You!" she yelled, jumping to her feet, but another shudder of light passed through her, and she fell back on her chaise longue. There was a sizzling noise, like sparking electrical wires. Titania clutched the chaise-longue's armrests tightly, still glaring at Portia. The Queen's eyes were now shining with such a bright silvery light that it made her blood run cold.

Titania dug her fingers into the armrest. "I will..." But that was as far as she got. Silvery smoke rose from her skin and swirled around her slender shape, turning faster and faster until she was caught in a spinning cocoon pulled tighter by the second... Finally, there was a loud bang, and where Titania had been sitting a moment ago, there was now only a tiny figure, fluttering on firefly wings.

Portia snatched the flowers from the jam jar and stumbled backwards. In the same moment, Robin leapt out from the lily bushes in his human shape. Grabbing the jar, he swiftly trapped the Fairy Queen inside and screwed on the lid. He muttered a few words under his breath, and ribbons of blue runes glowed on the walls of Titania's glass prison. It was all over in moments.

"Oh, man," Portia managed to croak. Her throat was bone dry.

"Not bad, eh?" crowed Robin, holding the jar aloft. It was filled with smoke, and glittery silver swirls as Titania tried to break out. But the glass, fortified by Robin's magic, held firm.

"What is she doing?" Portia asked, stepping closer.

"She's trying to shift back into her old shape." Robin brought the jar close to his face. "I'm afraid that won't work, Your Majesty."

The whirling smoke cleared to reveal a tiny Titania, stomping her foot on the bottom of the jar.

"Let me out! Let me out!" she shouted, her shrill voice audible through the air holes Robin had pierced in the jar's lid.

"No, I don't think we will actually," said Robin, unperturbed.

She buzzed against the glass like an angry hornet. "LET. ME. OUT."

Robin and Portia exchanged glances.

"What if someone hears her?" Portia said nervously. At that, Titania screamed even louder, hammering her fists against the glass. Robin sighed, and went down the steps to the edge of the pond. He squatted on his haunches and held the glass above the water's surface. Titania fell silent at once.

"What do you think, Your Majesty?" he asked pleasantly. "With a dozen holes in its lid, how long will it take for a jam jar like this to fill up with water?"

Titania remained silent, but Portia could see that she was trembling with rage. Robin held her suspended in the air for another moment, then set the jar down at the edge of the pond. He sat down next to it, and Portia did the same on the other side.

When Titania spoke again, she sounded more composed, but no less furious. "What do you want? I assume there's a purpose to this betrayal?"

"Indeed. And you can make it easy on yourself," Robin said.

Portia held her wrist next to the jar. "The spell on my mark. Lift it."

Titania crossed her arms. "Absolutely not."

Robin placed a finger on the lid and tilted the jar towards the water. Titania cried out. Robin tipped it back. "Would you like to rethink your answer?"

But if he believed that he had intimidated her enough, he was wrong.

"Oh, please," she snorted. "You know as well as I do that drowning me won't break the spell."

Portia glanced over at Robin, who nodded regretfully.

"Better luck next time," Titania sneered. "Now, if you set me free right now, I won't punish you too harshly. The Humanchild can keep serving me. And you, Robin, you can go into exile for a few moons."

Robin gave one of his finest foxy smiles, then got to his feet and picked up the jar. "What a generous offer, Your Majesty. But I'm afraid we're going to pass. As I said, you could have made it easy on yourself. But now it seems you'll have to come with us."

Farewell to World's End

At dusk the sky outside the great window had turned a deep violet. A seagull flew by, so close that Ben felt he could lean out and touch it. He stifled a yawn and was reaching for his mug of cold tea when Tegid came bouncing up the stairs, gathering up the skirts of his robe. "Finally!" he cried. "I knew the books wouldn't let us down!"

Ben and Gwil turned around in surprise, but Tegid was already at their side, excitedly tapping at the open book he held in his hands.

"Olwen Sevenbright!" he said breathlessly.

Ben rubbed his tired eyes. "Olwen who?"

"A salamander folklore expert," Tegid explained. "She found out what the legend of Nerys and Ifor was really about. Look!" He held out the open book. "She writes about the fog that follows Arawn wherever he goes. She says the fog is a part of him—a part of his original world that he can't leave behind. In Annwn, the fog absorbed the memories and emotions of the souls that had passed on. All their longing, fear, sorrow, anger... It was all sucked into the fog, relieving the souls of their burdens." He held the book up and read aloud: "'Outside of Annwn, however, any living being overtaken by

224

the fog will be drained of all its memories, leaving behind nothing but an empty shell, which will eventually dissolve into the fog entirely.'"

"But..." Ben began.

Tegid raised his hand and continued reading. "'As long as the Mistwalker in question has not yet dissolved, they may be called back by means of a memento. It must be something of great emotional value to the person.'" Tegid broke off. "That's where the fairy tale about Nerys's heart comes from. Instead of her actual heart, she must have given Ifor something that reminded him of who he once had been."

"Her love," Gwil murmured. "She reminded him that he loved her."

Tegid winked. "You old romantic. Yes, perhaps that's what it was." He looked from Gwil to Ben. "Do you have a memento we could use for Rose?"

Gwil buried his head in his hands. "Oh, dear, it's never easy, is it?" he groaned.

Ben, however, had an idea. A memento... He bent down and picked up Portia's backpack. Ridik's feather was still attached to the outside, fastened with the bird scout pin.

"Ben?" Tegid asked.

Carefully, Ben detached the feather from the backpack. "This was Ridik's feather. He and Rose were good friends. They fought side by side." He handed the feather to Tegid. "Do you think that counts as a memento?"

Tegid twirled the feather between his fingertips. "Hard to say. But, why not? Perhaps the bond of their friendship is strong enough to show Rose the path back to herself?"

"She did love Faerie," Gwil said. "If she associates Ridik with her time here, then it might work."

But they didn't sound fully convinced, and Ben had his doubts too.

"Well then," Tegid said, folding his arms. "It's better than nothing."

Ben and Gwil spent another night at Tegid's house. Ben lay awake for a long time, while the salamanders sat up downstairs carving attack and defence runes into a broken chair leg and a broomstick.

Ben had quickly got used to being at World's End. He liked Tegid's house, and the sound of the waves crashing against the cliffs. He would have liked to stay longer, but time was running out. Not only was Rose in need of their help, but soon the spell on Gwil's mark would be activated again.

Even so, as Ben stood in front of Tegid's house the next morning, he hoped that he would get to return one day.

"Here you go," Tegid said, handing Ben his backpack, now stuffed with provisions for the road. "I put the map of the route to the Pale Tower in the side pocket. And don't forget this!" He presented Ben with the rune-carved chair leg. It wasn't exactly an impressive-looking weapon.

"Don't go playing the hero," Tegid advised. "Find Rose, awaken her memories, and then get out of the Borderlands as fast as you can."

"That's the plan," Gwil said with a crooked smile.

Tegid placed a hand on Ben's shoulder. "Take good care of yourself."

"I'll try my best," Ben said.

"And if you happen to pass through here on your way back, don't you dare go by without knocking on my door," Tegid said, his voice full of warmth.

"I promise."

Tegid nodded. "Off you go, then! On your way! Time to put your daring plan into action!"

He was still standing in the doorway when Ben turned around for one final look, then they went around a bend in the path and the house disappeared from view.

INTERLUDE

Morning had broken, but in the depths of World's End, it was still dark. Tegid had set his moon-moth lantern on a table as he cleared away the traces of their work. Humming contentedly, he returned the last book to its place. Ben and Gwil had all they needed to know. It had been proven once again that you could find the answer to almost any problem by looking in the right book.

Tegid smoothed the leather spines of the books with his fingertips, smiled and went back to his desk. He picked up the lantern and was about to leave when he suddenly froze. In the moon-moths' shimmering light, he could see wisps of grey smoke rising through the floorboards.

Tegid stared at the smoke in disbelief. It was impossible. There was no risk of a fire at World's End—the runes protected against that. Then he understood. This was no smoke. It was fog.

"Oh, no," he whispered, and as he did so he felt all the warmth leave his body.

He raised his lantern. Ahead of him, the corridor between the shelves lay in darkness, but the floorboards were creaking.

As if in a trance, Tegid opened the lantern door. The moon-moths fluttered out towards the black chasm between the shelves, revealing the figure that was waiting for him there.

Motionless, the Grey King's Huntress stood between the walls of books. Her black veil trembled with each breath. She did not move, but behind her, the fog gathered and reared up to form a giant hand. No sooner had the moths flown into the cloud than they were snuffed out like candles. In the fading light, Tegid saw fog pouring down from the shelves like a waterfall. He did not move. The time to escape was long past.

Traces of Fog

✢ PORTIA ✢

On the second morning of their journey, Robin and Portia left the mountains behind. They were following the shore of a lake, heading towards the coast. Rain blew in from the west, turning the ground beneath their feet into a quagmire. Portia pulled up the hood of her leather jacket.

Robin had stowed Titania inside his backpack at first, but she had kicked up such a fuss that he had relented and attached the jar to the outside. Since then the Fairy Queen had merely sulked, hissing insults under her breath as they walked.

They were resting beneath a waterfall when she spoke up for the first time in hours. "What exactly are you hoping to achieve with this foolishness?" she asked. "Do you really think you'll be able to hide anywhere in my realm? No matter where you go, my subjects will find you."

"There are other worlds besides yours," Robin said curtly. He took a sip from a waterskin before passing it to Portia.

The Worlds of the Dead, for example, Portia thought. Robin had told her who the Grey King truly was. Arawn, King of the Underworld, who had abandoned the world of shadows and ghosts. Did that make him any less scary? Not really.

"Nonsense," Titania said scornfully. "Without the key, there's only this one world, and my power reaches every corner of it."

Neither Robin nor Portia replied to that, which clearly puzzled Titania. She frowned and looked from one to the other. Portia tried hard to keep a poker face, but something must have given her away.

"You've got a key," said Titania. "Either you've got one, or that boy and the salamander do." She stepped closer to the glass wall of her prison. "That's it, isn't it? That's why they left Bryngolau. They have a dratted key!"

Robin didn't say a word. He silently took the waterskin back from Portia and began stowing the rest of their provisions in the backpack. Titania stared up at them in disbelief. "Why are you doing this? Why are you putting my people in danger?"

"We're not putting anyone in danger," Portia shot back. She got to her feet and shook her tired limbs. "All we want to do is save Rose."

That afternoon it stopped raining, and mist began to rise from the sodden ground. Portia ran a hand over her face—it was dripping wet, and when she ran her tongue over her lips, she tasted a hint of salt. From somewhere in the fog came a seagull's cry. They had reached the coast. Finally.

Portia quickened her pace. Maybe Ben and Gwil had already moved on. That would actually be a good sign, as it would mean they had found a way to help Rose. Still, Portia was hoping to catch up with Ben before he left for the Pale Tower. It worried her to think of him going there with only Gwil for support. Then again, if it came to a fight she'd probably be no more help than the timid salamander.

At least we've got Robin on our side now, she told herself. Her new ally had shifted into his fox shape some time ago and was trotting lightly ahead of her along the narrow sandy path while Portia carried his backpack. Now and then bushes of yellow broom emerged from the fog only to disappear again just as quickly.

It couldn't be far to World's End now. The air was thick with the smell of seaweed, and soon Portia could hear the boom of crashing waves. She followed the path up a hill, until it ended on a grassy clifftop. Robin was nowhere to be seen.

"Brilliant," she muttered. She considered risking a whistle, but decided against it. There was a light wind blowing up here and the fog was getting a bit thinner. Portia followed the sound of the waves until she reached the cliff edge. It looked as if the land had broken off and fallen into the sea long ago, leaving behind a sharp drop to the jagged rocks below.

The cliff edge was strangely sickle-shaped, as if a giant sea monster had taken a bite out of it.

Portia brushed the curls from her face and took a step back from the brink. Fog billowed past her, and when she turned around, the path had already disappeared behind a grey wall.

She felt goosebumps prickling her arms. *It's just normal fog*, she told herself. *No need to panic.*

It was strange, though. Hadn't the wind been blowing just a moment ago? Now it was perfectly still, and the sound of the waves below was oddly muted too. Portia gulped and walked back towards where she thought the path should be. Damn it! Where was Robin? She was just about to whistle when she saw something moving in the fog.

"Oh, no," she whispered. Suddenly, she was ice-cold. A few metres ahead of her, tendrils of thick fog emerged from the grey mist and began to grope along the ground like tentacles. Then they drew back, only to grow into a dense, seething brew of fog. And it was moving towards Portia.

Arawn's fog, she thought, aghast. *Oh, God, it's the fog that wipes memories!*

She stumbled backwards, but it was too late. The swirling wall of fog was surging towards her. She just had time to fall to her knees and bury her face in her hands before it engulfed her.

I don't want to forget. Oh, please, no. Portia squeezed her eyes shut tight, waiting to feel the fog seep into her head, but nothing happened.

When Portia cautiously opened her eyes and looked around, she found herself in the middle of a grey cloud. Then she gasped with shock. She was not alone: barely an arm's length away stood a young woman. A woman... or a ghost? Everything about her was pale: her skin, her hair, her skirt, her blouse. She was staring off to her left into the fog, and didn't seem to notice Portia.

Portia was utterly bewildered and hardly dared to breathe. Suddenly, a jolt went through the pale woman's body, and her eyes snapped open. Portia turned her head just in time to see an enormous figure in a black hooded cloak, taller than a full-grown man, come rushing out of the fog, brushing past her so close that Portia fell to the ground. The creature swooshed towards the woman, cloak blowing. The woman stumbled backwards, but whatever it was had already grabbed hold of her.

"No!" Portia cried, scrambling to her feet. She didn't know what was going on, but the black-clad stranger was surely up to no good. He was holding the woman's face in both hands now, and suddenly glittering symbols began to glow on her cheeks. She squirmed and pulled at her attacker's wrists, but he wouldn't be shaken off.

Sympathy struck Portia like a bolt of lightning. She leapt towards the pair without a second thought and grabbed the attacker's sleeve, but to her surprise her fingers closed on thin air. With a gasp, she pulled her hand away.

The cloaked figure's arm dissolved into dark smoke, and wisps of fog began to rise from the fighters' bodies. Their silhouettes were already blurring when the black-clad figure finally let go of the young woman. No sooner had his spindly fingers loosed their grip than he collapsed like a puppet when its strings are cut. The woman still stood as stiff as a post, however; her eyes rolled upwards, her mouth contorted in a silent scream. Her figure grew ever more transparent, but the symbols on her face burned as bright as white-hot iron. Portia stared at her, dumbfounded. Then she heard someone call her name, and in the same instant the two figures disappeared entirely. Their bodies vanished, leaving nothing but a cloud of swirling fog.

"Portia?" Robin grabbed her arm and anxiously looked her up and down.

Portia just shook her head, staring at the spot where the pale woman had just been.

"What was that?" she asked hoarsely.

"A memory." Robin's hand was still on her arm, and she was grateful for it. His grip was firm—at least that wouldn't dissolve into the fog.

"A memory?" she repeated.

"That must have been Arawn's enchanted fog," Robin explained. "That's how Mistwalkers are born. Arawn's fog steals your memories, but neither the memories nor the emotions they evoke disappear. Those memories leave the person, but then they become one with the fog." Robin let go of her arm and looked around, clearly worried. "The fog holds on to everything, and sometimes lost memories reappear as so-called chimera—moving images that others can see as well."

Portia tried to focus on his words, but her thoughts clung to his first sentence like a cat's claws. "You mean it really was Arawn's fog?" she asked, hugging herself.

"Only a wisp of it," Robin said. "Not enough to do us any harm." He fell silent and looked around them nervously once more.

She should have been relieved, but instead her head was filled with swirling questions. "If that was a memory we saw, whose was it?" she asked.

"It belonged to the woman."

Portia's hands fell to her side. "How do you know that?"

"I was there when it happened."

"You were *there*?"

Robin nodded. "The woman you saw—her name was Hermia. She was one of Rose's friends."

The group photograph from Bramble's shoebox flashed up in her mind's eye. One man and five women. Which one had been Hermia?

"What you saw was a memory of the end of our final battle, when Rose and the others were trying to put the Grey King to sleep," Robin continued. "The black-cloaked figure—that was Arawn's Hunting Master. It is said Arawn forced him into his service long ago. Hermia was preparing our trap for the Grey King. I wanted to help, but the Hunting Master got to her before me. There was nothing I could have done. He put a spell on her and made her Arawn's Huntress in his place, releasing him from his servitude." He faltered. "I've never told Rose. She's always believed that Hermia died in battle."

Portia's gaze wandered back to the fog. She still had a nervous feeling in the pit of her stomach. "I don't understand," she said. "When you told me about Arawn earlier, you said that the enchanted fog follows him wherever he goes. So what's it doing here? We locked Arawn in the Borderlands!"

"I'm asking myself the same thing," Robin muttered.

The fog was lifting now, and soon they could make out the cliff edge through the haze. Robin frowned, then turned suddenly pale.

"May the spirits be with us," he whispered. "If we can see Hermia's memories, then it means she must be weaving the fog."

"What?" Portia asked, confused.

"As Arawn's Huntress, she has the ability to control the fog too. That's why he sends her ahead of his army, so she can dissolve as many foes as possible." He spun around. "Portia, did anyone follow you into Faerie?"

Portia was startled. "No. No, of course not. We closed the door, just like Rose told us to."

"Before any fog had made it through?"

Portia was about to say yes, but then she remembered the thin threads of fog that had floated through ahead of them. "There was some fog..." she admitted. "It came through the Faerie Door with us." Panic fluttered in her throat. "But no one came through with it, I'm sure. We were alone, so..." She fell silent when she saw the fear on his face.

"As Huntress, Hermia can take on the fog's form. She can dissolve and reform at will."

Robin ran his hand over his mouth and stared at the fog surrounding them. "We've let the Huntress into Faerie."

"She wants the key." Titania's voice was low and bitter. Portia looked down at the jar on the backpack. "That's why she's come slinking into my realm. She wants to open the doors for Arawn."

Portia looked up at Robin. "Does that mean she's going after Ben? And Gwil?"

Robin didn't say a word, and nor did the Fairy Queen. Why had she been silent for so long anyway?

"Robin!" Portia grabbed his arm. "We have to get to World's End! Right now!" What if it was already too late? Why had she let Ben head off without her in the first place?

"Tell her," Titania snapped.

Portia frowned. Tell her *what*?

Robin looked at her, and her hand slid off his arm. In the gloom of the fog, his face looked as forlorn and grey as the doomed Hermia's.

"We are at World's End."

"What?..." Portia just stared at him. Then her gaze wandered back to the shreds of fog drifting above the empty clifftop, with the crescent-shaped bite taken out of its edge.

Once released, the fog will devour any trace of life it comes across, until all lands are empty and silent.

Rose's words echoed in her head like a muffled bell. Finally, she understood. World's End, the great library of the Salamandrau, had disappeared. An icy cold crept into her heart. Where were Ben and Gwil?

Metamorphoses

❧ PORTIA ❧

Portia crouched on the deserted clifftop, her hands clasped so tightly in her lap that her knuckles were white. Robin was gone. He had shifted into his fox shape again and was searching the fog for a trail. Any tracks, any sign that might suggest Ben and Gwil were still alive.

Portia's thoughts were going round in circles. If she had been here, if she had gone along with Ben's plan from the beginning, could she have helped? Again and again in her mind's eye, she saw herself leaving her backpack by his bed as he slept. If only she had talked him into staying with her.

"We're wasting our time!" cried Titania suddenly. The jar was sitting next to Portia on the ground, but she refused to look at it. That didn't stop the Queen from ranting, though.

"While we're sitting around doing nothing, that fog's spreading throughout my realm," she said. "And if those damned traitors really did have a second key, Arawn's fog witch will have it now. She'll open the doors! Don't you get it?"

"Ben and Gwil are alive," Portia retorted firmly. She was drowning in guilt, but couldn't let Titania see that. She had to stay in control.

"Oh, wake up, you silly goose! Your human friend and the salamander are history!"

"No, they are not!" Portia grabbed the jar and leapt to her feet. So much for staying in control. Titania let out a startled scream.

Portia was about to hurl the jar to the ground when the fox emerged from the fog and shifted back to his human shape mid-trot.

Portia ran to meet him.

"And?" She felt sick with tension.

"They're alive."

Portia almost hugged him. "Where are they?"

He glanced at Titania. "On their way to the World Door in the Pale Tower."

Titania swore and slammed her hand against the glass.

Portia ignored her. "What about Hermia?"

"Following close behind."

That meant there was still a chance to save Ben and Gwil. A chance that was growing smaller by the minute.

Stay in control, she told herself, and squared her shoulders.

"Then we have to hurry."

The fox trotted ahead, through wet grass and wild sprawling hedges. Portia ran behind him for mile after mile, her hands tightly clutching the straps of the backpack. She was doing her best to keep up with him, but no matter how hard she tried her legs just wouldn't go any faster. On the contrary, in fact—her legs didn't want to run at all. Her lungs were burning, and she had a nasty stitch as well.

Think of Ben. Think of Gwil.

Portia squeezed through a gap in a hawthorn hedge and slipped down a rocky slope on the other side, crashing down hard on her bottom. The jar in the backpack rattled, and a volley of curses rang out behind her. Portia tried to get back to her feet, but her right leg buckled beneath her and she sank back to the ground. For a moment she just sat there, eyes closed and panting.

Robin returned to her side in his human shape. "Are you all right?"

Portia nodded. She wiped her muddy hands on her trousers and winced. Robin took her hand in his and turned it upside down. She had grazed the skin on her palm.

He tutted. "Hand me the backpack, will you?"

Portia did as she was told, and Robin opened it. Titania was kneeling inside her jar, her whole body trembling. Portia couldn't tell whether it was from fear or anger, but then again she didn't really care.

Meanwhile, Robin rummaged about inside and pulled out a leather bag, which he opened and laid on the ground in front of him. A dozen vials were tucked in small loops attached to the inside of the bag, which also held two clay pots and several wax-paper sachets. Robin took out a pot.

"More magic potions?" she asked.

Robin pointed at the vials. "Those are, yes. The rest are just things that can come in handy on a long hike." He opened the pot. "This one is iodine salve."

Titania snorted dismissively. "Amateur."

Ignoring her, Robin applied the red salve to the scrape on Portia's hand. Portia winced again. Her hand stung, but the exhaustion that was weighing down the rest of her body down was worse.

"You don't happen to have a magic potion to make me super-fast and super-strong, do you?" She meant it as a joke, but Robin raised an eyebrow.

"Do you?" Portia asked again, suddenly hopeful.

Robin looked at her thoughtfully, then plucked a vial from the bag and held it up. A clear golden fluid sloshed inside the cut-glass container.

"A metamorphosis charm," he explained.

Portia's heart skipped a beat. "Metamorphosis," she said. "What... what would I be turning into?"

"Into your spirit animal. The one that matches your soul," Robin replied. Portia's mouth was suddenly bone dry.

"Great!" Titania snarled. "Then she'll turn into a tortoise, and what good will that do?"

"Would it last for ever?" Portia asked.

Robin shook his head. "No, the effect wears off after a while." He looked her in the eye. "You don't have to do it. I can keep running on my own and try to close in on Hermia."

Portia thought about it for one, maybe two seconds. She could stay behind, yes. But would she be able to live with it if she gave up now? The answer was clear.

She set her jaw and took the vial from Robin. "Hopefully, my spirit animal is faster than I am. How much do I have to take?"

"One drop will do, for now," Robin said.

Titania pressed both hands against the glass jar. "It's a stupid idea. She'll panic. She won't be able to handle it."

Portia pulled the cork from the vial and stared at the golden potion. *I'm not afraid,* she repeated. Then she raised the vial to her lips and trickled a drop onto her tongue.

The Pale Tower

The Pale Tower was a ruin of black stone, rising from the earth and into the sky like a broken tooth. It stood in the bend of a bay on an island that seemed to consist entirely of craggy rocks. About a mile of sea separated the Grey King's fortress from the shore.

Ben stood above the bay, looking down at the waves. "I'm not a strong swimmer," he admitted.

Gwil pulled a piece of paper from his pocket and unfolded it. "According to Tegid's map, there should be a causeway," he said. "Perhaps we can't see it right now because the tide is high. Let's wait until it goes out, then we should be able to walk over."

Ben glanced at Gwil. "The suspension of your spell ends tonight, doesn't it?"

Gwil sighed and returned the map to his pocket. "Ah, it won't be the first time I've been outside Fairy Hill past curfew. It'll be fine."

Ben could feel doubt gripping his stomach like a cold fist, but Gwil smiled.

"What do you say we find a sheltered spot and have a bite to eat?"

As dusk fell, they were sitting on the beach, protected from the wind by the surrounding slopes. Bramble and honeysuckle grew above their heads, while grey pebbles stretched down to the sea in front of them. The water came and went in soft waves over the flat stones.

Tegid had packed plenty of provisions, and eating was more than welcome. Ben chewed on a piece of dried apple and looked out towards the Pale Tower. The black castle stood out even more distinctly now against the pink evening sky.

"If there's a guard up there, he'll be able to see us, won't he?" he asked. The rune-carved broomstick was lying at Gwil's side, and the chair leg was sticking out of Ben's backpack. He still had a hard time believing that their "weapons" would be of any use.

"The castle in our world is deserted," answered Gwil. "Only once we open the World Door will we enter the Borderlands."

"So the castle on the other side of the door isn't deserted?"

"It wasn't as long as Arawn was sleeping there. But now he's awake. He has long since left the fortress behind to search for an open door." He put his half-eaten roll back in his food bag. "Are you full?"

Ben nodded. Gwil stowed what was left of their provisions in his backpack, then stretched himself out on the pebbles, stuffed his cap under his head like a pillow and closed his eyes. After a few seconds, he placed his left hand over the mark on his right wrist.

As quietly as he could, Ben reached into Portia's backpack, checked that the ember pebbles were still in their place and pulled out the travel diary and a pen. Then he leant back against the slope, rested the diary on his thighs, and began sketching the Pale Tower. The reassuring weight of a pen in his hand was always comforting when he was afraid.

"You draw?"

Ben looked up in surprise. Gwil was still lying down, but his eyes were open and fixed on Ben.

Ben shrugged. "Sometimes."

Gwil sat up. "May I see?"

Ben hesitated for a moment, but then handed Gwil the notebook. The salamander looked at the sketch of the Pale Tower and nodded approvingly.

"This is very good," he said as he flicked through the pages.

Ben knew what Gwil was going to find, but he didn't dare ask him to give the diary back. He had drawn a few sketches while they were at World's End: a seagull in flight, Tegid carrying a stack of books and the moon-moth fluttering between the shelves...

Ben felt his face burning. He waited for Gwil to scold him for having spent his time doodling rather than poring over books.

Instead, Gwil smiled. "You have a gift," he said.

Ben's cheeks burned all the more at these words, but he also felt as if a ray of sunlight had burst through the clouds to hit him in the chest. He plucked up his courage and said: "There's a drawing of you on the next page, actually."

Gwil turned the page and his smile grew broader. "Very good indeed. Perhaps you should stay in this world and become my apprentice."

That made Ben smile in return. "My mum's waiting for me," he said. But just for a moment he imagined what it would be like to stay with Gwil in this world. A scribe's apprentice. What would he learn? How to make ink? How to write runes and make them come alive?

"Of course, you have to go back," Gwil said hurriedly. "No one should take a child away from their parents."

"It's just Mum. My dad died last year." Ben had no idea why he was telling Gwil this. Normally, he avoided drawing attention to his dad. Or to the empty space where his dad had once been.

Gwil looked at Ben thoughtfully, then handed the diary back with a solemn nod. "I am very sorry to hear that."

To his surprise, Ben realized that Gwil's sympathy didn't bother him. And he was even more surprised by how good it felt to confide in him. He remembered the funeral, all those people in their black suits and dresses, asking him how he was holding up, the concern on their faces... When he couldn't take it any more, he had gone and sat at the top of the stairs, watching from above as the mourners came and went from his home. And all the while, he had felt the closed bedroom door behind him. He was afraid to go in there, knowing that his dad would never sit on the edge of his bed and read to him again. He knew it, but a part of him just didn't want to believe it.

The truth was, he still didn't want to believe it.

Ben took the pen and looked out to sea at the castle again. A fortress that existed in two worlds at the same time. No, in three: Faerie, the Borderlands and—if Tegid was right—the Underworld, Annwn. Ben drew the castle's broken tower and filled the outline with dark-blue shadows. He thought of the *Book of Return*, and of Orpheus who had tried to bring his wife back from the Underworld. *Don't think about it*, he told himself. But as he drew, he kept seeing the Black Door leading to the Underworld.

Tegid said he had never heard a story of anyone being successfully rescued from the Underworld. But did that really mean it was impossible to come back from Annwn?

The tide began to fall in the early morning, exposing the causeway. A walled walkway led from the beach to the island, where it ended at the foot of a flight of steps cut into the rock. From there it was just a short climb to the fortress wall.

Rain clouds were gathering overhead as Gwil and Ben entered the courtyard of the ruined fortress. The wall behind them was half collapsed, and the ground was strewn with rubble from the collapsing turrets. Only the keep stood unscathed at the centre of the castle.

Ben stared up at its dark walls. In the middle of the keep was a closed door. He could sense immediately that it was a World Door. Perhaps his senses were sharpened now that he had crossed two world borders. Whatever the reason, the door had a magnetic pull on him.

Gwil stared long and hard at the door before setting down his backpack to find all that they would need for the key spell.

"Ready?" he asked when he had done so. Ben nodded.

They squatted down, and Gwil set a wooden bowl on the ground between them. It was carved all over with runes, as was the little knife that Gwil handed to Ben.

Ben, who had memorized Merron's instructions, took the knife, scraped a bit of soil from between the cobblestones at his feet and dropped it in the bowl. Gwil took the knife back, shaved a few slivers of wood from the door and dropped them on top of the soil. Then he cleaned the blade with some of Tegid's honey brandy before pricking his and Ben's thumbs, and finally letting a drop of blood from each fall into the bowl too.

Gwil whispered the rune spell, as if hoping that this way, no one in this world or any other would notice what they were up to. As he spoke, the runes on the inside of the bowl began to glow, and the mixture of soil, wood shavings and blood started to spin and soon formed a vortex. The little whirlpool turned faster and faster, whispering like the sea wind blowing over a beach.

A faint tremor passed through the door making the old wood groan and creak. A gust of wind ripped through the ruined castle. Gwil shuddered but carried on speaking the rune spell. Ben felt as if he could hear each of the elements in the bowl. There was another gust of wind—and then silence.

Ben leant forward.

"It worked!" Gwil said, clearly stunned. He was right. At the bottom of the bowl lay a key, moist and glistening, as if it had been washed up by the sea. Ben's heart was thumping in his chest as he took the key, got to his feet and, with a trembling hand, pushed it into the lock of the World Door. He held his breath as he turned the key—and then heard the lock click open.

The World Door swung open, and Ben was hit by a wave of musty air. He was about to pass through the doorway when Gwil grabbed his shoulder.

"I'll go first." Fear was written all over Gwil's face. Nevertheless, he clutched his broomstick and went ahead through the door. Ben clenched his fist around the key and took a firm grip on his chair leg before following Gwil across the border between the worlds.

In the Borderlands the castle was as much of a ruin as it was in Faerie. The entrance hall beyond the door was bare and deserted. The torch holders on the walls were empty, and the flagstone floor was riddled with cracks and potholes where the rainwater had been pooling for what must have been ages.

Three paths led out of the hall. A passageway was in the left corner of the room, while a staircase led upwards from an archway opposite the World Door. The third way out was through a gaping hole in the floor, beneath which a flight of stairs descended into the darkness.

Gwil stood with his broomstick raised, as if expecting a horde of Grey Riders to storm into the hall at any moment. Ben hurried to his side and waited, holding his breath in anticipation, but when a few seconds had passed without any attack, he let out a sigh of relief.

Gwil lowered the broomstick. "We'd better lock that door," he said.

Ben nodded and turned around before recoiling, aghast.

In the doorway stood a woman of night and shadow, her whole body wrapped from head to toe in a black veil, and a crown of spindly branches on her head. As if in slow motion, she lifted her head and sniffed, like a hound catching a scent.

Ben gave a stifled scream and stumbled backwards into Gwil. The key slipped from his hand to the floor, and the woman *hissed*. It was the ugliest sound Ben had ever heard.

Gwil grabbed his shoulder and pulled him back. Stepping in front of him, he raised his staff again, holding it diagonally at chest level. Ben raised his own weapon with a trembling hand. He tried to speak the spell to activate the runes on the chair leg, but the words caught in his throat. Gwil succeeded, but the runes on his staff glowed only dimly.

The Woman in Black stared at them. Clouds of fog billowed up from beneath the hem of her dress before collapsing once more. She held out her hands, and the fog curled up to swirl about her fingers. As they watched, the swirls of smoke grew thicker and thicker before transforming into three pale dogs with pointy ears and long snouts. No sooner had they taken shape than they moved forward, silently baring their teeth.

Gwil's whole body was shaking, but he stood his ground. Ben ran a hand over his mouth, whispering the rune spell.

Please, he begged. But the chair leg in his hand remained...
a chair leg.

The dogs were moving closer.

They're trying to surround us, Ben realized with horror.
Gwil took a step back and turned his staff so he was holding it like a spear. The dimly glowing runes were flickering
now, but at least it seemed as if that was keeping the dogs
from attacking them.

Ben's glanced down at the key, now a foot away from
him. "Gwil."

"Down the stairs," Gwil commanded.

Ben glanced over at the hole in the floor. It was the closest
way out, and yet it seemed like it was miles away. "Gwil,"
he tried again. "The key!"

"The stairs!" Gwil spat.

The Woman in Black whispered something, and the
dogs crouched and flattened their ears. Their eyes glowed
menacingly.

"Now!" Gwil shouted, and as if on command, the dogs
leapt forward. Gwil backed off, swinging his broomstick as
he went. The runes lit up, burning bright white, and two of
the dogs shied off to the side, but the third came straight on
and the next moment it was clutching the staff in its jaws.

"Run!" Gwil screamed. Then he dropped the staff, spun
around—and fell.

"Gwil!" Ben's blood froze. A tendril of fog had caught
Gwil by the ankle and brought him down. Now three more
tentacles had emerged from the haze to grope towards him.
Without thinking, Ben grabbed his chair leg, leapt forward,

fell on his knees and thrust the wooden staff into the tendril that was holding on to Gwil's leg. As he did so, he called out the rune spell. This time the runes on his chair leg glowed brightly, and the fog tentacle disappeared in a puff.

Ben was gripping his staff so tightly that he could hear the wood splintering. He spoke the runes once more, but now in the sequence that stood for *protection*, and struck the flagstones with his chair leg. A flash of light pulsed from it to the ground, and for a brief moment, a pale-blue ring glowed about Ben and Gwil, pushing the fog back like a force field.

"Ben!" Gwil staggered to his feet and put his arm round Ben's shoulders. They looked on dumbstruck as the Woman in Black bent down and picked up the key. The dogs had returned to her side: two of them were looking up at her while the third watched Ben and Gwil with its gleaming eyes.

Ben's mouth was bone dry, and his heartbeat was pounding in his ears. "Why aren't they attacking us?"

"We don't matter any more," said Gwil in a hollow voice.

More and more fog poured through the doorway. The ground disappeared beneath a white carpet, and shapes began to emerge from the murk—half-formed creatures and strange, ephemeral beasts, like demons in a steaming cauldron.

The woman stood in the midst of the maelstrom, drawing runes on the back of the World Door. The wood smouldered at the touch of her fingertips. Then she reached for the hunting horn at her hip. Gwil's fingers dug into Ben's shoulder.

"She's calling the Grey King!"

Ben was transfixed, but Gwil pulled at his arm.

"Ben," he urged him. "Ben, to the staircase!"

Ben got to his feet. As soon as the chair leg left the ground, fog surged into the circle of protection.

Panic began to rise to his throat, but he let Gwil usher him through the hole in the floor. He turned around just in time to avoid falling down the steps. Gwil hobbled ahead, with Ben following him into the darkness. They had made it to the first landing when they heard the call of the horn above their heads. A long, high-pitched wailing sound.

"Sweet spirits!" That was as far as Gwil got before the castle was shaken by a thunderous crash.

The Dogs of Annwn

Robin hadn't lied, after all. The metamorphosis didn't hurt. Quite the opposite. The sweet, resinous taste of the potion was heavy on her tongue, but her body felt light. The world was a soft blur of colours that flowed around her like cool, velvety water. She could feel her body changing, but the transformation felt right, like a homecoming.

Portia opened her eyes and breathed through the nose of her spirit animal for the first time. For the first time, she saw the world with new eyes, and with a sharpness she had never before experienced. She could feel the earth beneath her four paws and taste the approaching evening on her tongue.

Meanwhile, Robin had removed everything he could from his backpack and fastened it to Portia's back like a saddle bag. Then he squatted down in front of her, took her head in his hands and stroked her fur with his thumbs.

He grinned. "You've got quite the thick coat for a tortoise." Portia nudged him with her snout, and his smile grew even broader. He stood up, rubbing his hands. "Shall we?"

Portia put one paw in front of the other, digging her claws into the soft ground. She had control over every part of her new body, and it was unbelievably easy. She could feel her leg muscles brace, and how her whole being was anticipating the run. Portia shook her limbs, and heard an indignant scream coming from the backpack. She bared her teeth in a grin.

Robin gave a little bow in front of her, and then shapeshifted himself. The fox winked, turned tail and dashed across the hillside. And the wolf that was once Portia loped after him.

They ran all through the night, but the wolf didn't mind the dark. On the contrary—it was in its element. When a strip of lemon-yellow light lit up the horizon, the scent of the air began to change. Portia could taste sea mist, salt and a bitter hint of algae. She licked her lips and kept on running.

She could keep up with Robin now, running full pelt through grassy meadows, leaping over rocks she would have had to skirt as a human. She raced through fields of nettles without feeling a thing and tore through thick hedges without receiving a scratch. Her wolf body felt amazing. It moved in bouncy strides, wholly muscles and tendons, all working in unison, never growing tired, tearing across the land like an ice-grey wind.

The wolf's senses were sharper, too: Portia experienced the world more completely, and in more colours. She could hear the grass crackle beneath her paws, the rustling of a mouse in the undergrowth and the fox panting ahead of her. She knew she could easily overtake Robin if she wanted to, and that certainty filled her with pride and excitement.

The only problem was the bundle on her back—without that extra burden, this journey would have been perfect. Now and then Portia even forgot why they were running so fast, and what dangers awaited them at the end of this wild chase.

Eventually, they arrived at their destination. Robin led her through a thicket of honeysuckle before coming to a halt at the top of a steep slope. Below them was a bay, and in the middle of the waves sat a craggy island. At first, all Portia could see on the island were black rocks, but after a while she made out the outline of a ruined castle.

When she looked around, the fox had disappeared. In its place stood Robin, in his human shape. Portia looked out to sea once more, feeling the wind blowing on her muzzle and caressing her fur. She could still smell the fox on Robin. It seemed the wild animal in him was never fully gone, not even when he was human.

Robin took the bag off Portia's back. "Well?" he asked. "Don't you want to shift back?"

Portia didn't know whether the potion had simply worn off, or whether Robin's question had triggered the change—but the wolf shape fell off her like a coat. One moment she was on four paws, and the next she was on two legs, standing at the cliff edge in her girl shape. Unlike her transformation from girl to wolf, turning back was actually unpleasant. Her stomach cramped painfully, and when she took her first breath as a human, her knees buckled beneath her. She missed being a wolf immediately. She breathed in deeply, but she could no longer notice all the subtle details of smell and scent.

Robin was still looking at her. "The first time is hard," he said. "But you'll get used to it."

Before Portia could reply, she was interrupted by Titania,

whose angry tirade could be heard even from inside the backpack.

"Get me out of here, you maggot-spawn!"

Portia sighed and took the jar out. The Fairy Queen looked as if she had put her fingers into a plug socket—her hair was standing on end, her wings were trembling, and her face had turned a bright red.

She glared at Portia and Robin, panting. "I will never ever forgive you for that."

"Cheer up, Your Majesty," Robin said. "We've arrived."

"As soon as I get out of here..."

"... you'll skin me alive, I know, I know." He picked up the backpack and threw one strap over his right shoulder. "Portia, would you mind carrying the ego-in-a-jam-jar?"

"Sure thing." Portia picked it up. The memory of being a wolf was already fading. The regret remained. *I was free*, she thought. *I was the wind.* She wished she could have kept the experience somehow, like a smooth pebble you carry in the pocket of your coat.

Focus, she told herself. *This isn't about you.*

Robin had found a path leading down to the bay, and so they began their descent. Titania had seemingly exhausted her repertoire of insults and was now kicking and throwing herself against the side of the jar. At one point it almost slipped from Portia's hands, but she just managed to hold on to it and wedged it under her arm.

"You stop that now, or..." But that was as far as Portia got when she was interrupted by the piercing sound of a hunting horn.

A shiver went down her spine. She had heard that sound before. Between the doors, when the hunt was after her and Ben.

Portia and Robin stood stock-still.

"We're too late," Titania said, her voice breaking on the last word. "The door is open."

Portia leapt off the path and onto a pebble beach. She was about to run straight to the causeway leading out to the island, but Robin grabbed her by the arm.

"Wait." He pointed out to sea. The causeway to the Pale Tower was clear, but fog was rising from the ruined walls to wreath the island in an ominous grey haze. Fear gripped Portia's heart.

Titania swore and shot Portia and Robin a venomous look. "Great," she said. "So what's your grand plan now?"

Portia looked at Robin, but he just shrugged.

"The causeway," he said. "We have no choice."

Titania snorted. "Oh, yes, what a fabulous idea! Just walk right into the enchanted fog. Then at least you'll get it over with quickly!"

"No one said it was going to be easy," Robin said. His voice sounded calm, but his face betrayed his anxiety. Portia's stomach churned.

"This is madness," Titania raged. "How do you think this will end? If you're very lucky you might be able to take out one of Arawn's riders. Maybe two. And then what? He can call upon hundreds of riders in his army. Thousands, if he wishes. Not to mention his dogs. And you're about as much of a threat to them as a flea to a pack of wolves."

Robin spun around to face her. "That's true, *Your Majesty*," he hissed. "But we'd have a good chance if you'd only stop your temper tantrum."

Titania stared at him, wide-eyed. "Excuse me?!"

"Fight with us," he said. "You hate the idea of the Grey King overrunning everything as much as we do. So buck up and fight with us!"

But if he thought he could appeal to Titania's sense of honour, he was wrong. "You pathetic little creature," she hissed. "I've defended my world against hordes of enemies worse than anything you've seen in your worst nightmares. It's thanks to me that my home still exists! I will fight. I'll have to fight, now that Arawn is on the loose again. I'll defend my world with everything I have." An eerie glimmer flitted across her skin. "I will fight," she repeated. "But I won't waste my strength on a fight that's already lost."

Her passionate tirade left Portia speechless. Was Titania right? Were they wasting their time? What would happen to Meralyn and the other inhabitants of Fairy Hill if the Grey Army reached their home?

"Listen to me, Goodfellow," Titania urged. "I must return to Bryngolau. I must warn my people, no matter the cost. We must be ready when Arawn attacks. Unless it's already too late!"

"What if we can stop him here?" Portia asked.

Titania groaned. "Spirits, give me strength. How? Do you honestly think you can defeat him? While you're prattling nonsense, my people are *dying*." She swore again and rested her forehead against the glass wall of the jar.

Portia and Robin looked each other in the eye. Portia nodded, and Robin took the jar from her hands. "Your Majesty," he said. Titania didn't acknowledge him, but he continued regardless. "I'd like to propose a new deal. You lift the spell you put on Portia." At that, Titania did look up. Robin carried on, determined, "You lift the spell, and in return I'll set you free so you can return to Bryngolau."

Titania eyed him suspiciously. "You'll set me free?"

He nodded. "Lift the spell, then we'll be on our way, and..."

"Wait," Portia interrupted. Robin frowned, but she bent down to bring her face closer to the jar. "The deal will be as Robin says, but you must also promise that you won't punish Robin, Gwil, Ben or me."

"Hah!" Titania scoffed. "As if any you will make it out of this doomed place anyway."

But Portia carried on, ignoring the Fairy Queen's words. "And you must also release the salamanders from their servitude."

Titania fell silent. Robin looked at Portia in disbelief, but she stared down at Titania defiantly.

Eventually Titania spoke, in a clear, firm voice, "No."

"You said you wanted to protect your people at any price." Portia clenched her fists. "Well, this is the price." She had made so many terrible decisions since entering Faerie. She wanted to get something right at last.

Robin was subtly shaking his head, but Portia didn't give an inch. Of course he could have concluded the deal without

261

her, since he had imprisoned Titania in the first place. But instead he waited.

"Very well," Titania said eventually. Portia was about to cheer out loud when she noticed Titania's smile. "I accept. But on one condition," the Fairy Queen went on. "If by some miracle you happen to survive this mess, you and the boy will return to the Human World, but you will give me your key."

"Agreed," Portia said, but Titania hadn't finished yet. "Neither you nor any other Human will ever be welcome in my world again," she declared. "And if anyone dares to cross the borders of my realm, I will imprison them in the split trunk of a dead tree for two lifetimes."

Portia felt goosebumps creeping up her spine. She was starting to wonder whether it had been such a great idea to make those extra demands—but it was too late now to take them back. Not if Titania was really willing to set the salamanders free. She thought of the black bands around Meralyn and Gwil's wrists. She thought of how she had suffered when trapped in Fairy Hill herself—the feeling of suffocation, the frustration and anger. And she had only worn the mark for two days.

"Agreed," she said, half expecting to hear a thunderclap.

Titania raised her chin triumphantly. Then she turned to Robin. "And the same applies to you." Portia spun around just in time to see the look of shock on his face.

"If you survive you too will be banished from my world," Titania said. "You will leave here with the Humans, and this time you won't come back."

"We agreed you wouldn't punish Robin," Portia broke in, but Titania cut her off.

"I'm already showing great leniency by letting him go," she said. "I can do no more. Take it or leave it."

Portia looked at Robin for support, but he just stared stony-faced at the jar in his hands. He would never agree to these terms! Portia could have kicked herself. Why had she got them into this mess?

"Agreed," Robin said.

"What?!" Titania looked as shocked as Portia felt. She was about to protest, but a look from Robin silenced her. He raised the jar, so Titania was at his eye level. "Well?" he prompted her.

Titania clenched her fists, but nodded in agreement. "We have a deal."

Robin didn't waste another second. He placed the jar on the ground and mumbled a few words. The invisible runes on the glass lit up briefly before it exploded with a loud bang. There was a flash of light, and then Titania stood before them in the midst of the shattered glass, back to her full size: a rumbling, sparking thunderstorm in fairy form.

Portia backed away with her heart in her mouth. Titania was *crackling*, as if she was about to send an angry pulse of electricity across the beach. There were no irises or pupils in her shining silver eyes. "I should skin you alive this moment," she growled.

"We had a deal," Robin reminded her calmly. Portia admired him for that—she was fighting the urge to make a run for it. Titania would never keep to their deal! She'd rip them to pieces, turn them into earthworms, or maybe just incinerate them with thunderbolts.

"So be it," Titania said. She made a dismissive gesture with her right hand, and the tattooed band around Portia's wrist glowed like liquid silver. Pain bit into her bones, but then the silver pooled on her skin and hardened, before shattering and falling to the ground in a rain of ashes. All that remained was a pale line.

Portia gasped in surprise and relief. The latter was short-lived, as Titania stepped swiftly forward and grabbed her by the hair. "I hope the fog gets you," she hissed. "I hope it devours you both, bones and all."

No sooner had she spat out these words than she shifted into her dragonfly shape and shot off like an arrow, away from the coast and the mist that was spreading across the bay like a cloud of pestilence.

The wall of fog was already halfway across the causeway. The closer they got to it, the faster and shallower Portia's breathing became. She forced herself not to look back. One glance at the safety of the shore and she would have turned tail and run. As the first threads of fog began to curl about her ankles, her whole body grew rigid. Robin was walking ahead of her. He didn't slow his pace, but Portia saw his shoulders tense as the fog enveloped him. She held her breath and followed him into the grey wall.

It was as if the fog had already dissolved the world beyond the causeway. Apart from their steps ringing out on the stone floor, all was completely silent. Portia was trying to focus on her feet when Robin suddenly stopped. She almost stumbled into him.

"We're not alone."

She stood at his side, her heart pounding. Now she heard it, too. The scraping of claws on stone and sand. A growl. Slinking shadows in the fog.

"Run."

Portia was transfixed by the movement in the mist. It took a few moments for Robin's command to register.

"What?" She turned towards him, wide-eyed.

Robin let the backpack slide from his shoulder to the ground. "Run to the castle as fast as you can."

"No, I—" Portia began, but broke off when she heard a guttural growling right behind her. She spun around to see the skull-white head of a hunting dog emerge from the fog. Three more shadows were creeping along the causeway.

Portia backed away and stumbled over Robin's backpack. She winced, and caught a glimpse of red smoke in the corner of her eye. When she looked around for Robin, he was already shifting shape. His eyes were glowing gold, and a blood-red sheen rippled across his skin and clothes. His mouth was curled into a wild grimace, revealing sharp teeth.

"Run," he whispered. "Now!"

A chilling howl came from the depths of the fog, then the drumming of paws on wet sand and a chorus of wild snarling as the pack surged forward.

Portia grabbed the backpack and ran.

Mistwalkers

When they were deep in the belly of the Pale Tower, Gwil came to a halt. He was out of breath, and so was Ben. They leant panting against a stone wall at the foot of the staircase. A few moon-moths fluttered about them, but otherwise there was nothing but pitch-black darkness above and below them. The passages underneath the castle must have been carved into the rock of the island.

Ben stared back up the staircase, his heart pounding, expecting at any moment to see a dog leap from the shadows. But nothing stirred.

"I think we got away," Ben croaked. "What do you reckon?"

When Gwil failed to reply, Ben took a good look at him for the first time. "Gwil?"

Gwil was bent double with his hands on his thighs. His whole body was trembling.

The spell. Amid all the chaos, Ben had completely forgotten that the time limit on the suspension of the spell had run out. Gwil sank to his knees, and Ben squatted next to him.

"It's bad, isn't it?" he asked anxiously.

Gwil briefly placed a hand on Ben's knee, only to remove it again right away. The skin around his mark was red and inflamed. "Ben, I'm so sorry..."

Ben was already removing the pouch of ember pebbles from his backpack. Gwil tried to turn away, but Ben took his left wrist in his hands and looked him in the eye. "Please."

Gwil looked back and nodded.

What do you do when all your plans have failed? Ben had no idea, but he did know that he needed to get as far away from the Woman in Black as he could. So he continued his descent into the depths of the Pale Tower. Perhaps there was another staircase somewhere in this underground warren, leading back up to the courtyard, then he could get out of the castle to... to where, actually? If he didn't get back to the World Door, he would be trapped in the Borderlands. He and Gwil, who was now sitting on his shoulder in his salamander shape.

A dozen steps later, Ben lost any hope of finding an escape route. The staircase ended in a windowless cellar without a door. The stone walls were mottled with moon-moths, which gave off a pale greenish light. The damp chill settled on Ben's skin. He ran a hand over his face and squinted into the darkness. Then he saw the door.

He knew immediately what was in front of him: the rough black wood and the ring-shaped knocker of tarnished green metal looked exactly like the door in the *Book of Return*. Ben could hear the sound of his own breathing in the stillness of the room, and everything else instantly lost its meaning. Nothing else mattered. He had found the door to Annwn.

A few moon-moths tumbled lazily through the air to land on the door knocker. The Door of the Dead stood in the middle of the room, beneath a chiselled stone archway. In just ten paces, Ben was standing in front of the portal to the World of the Dead.

He stared at the moon-moths twinkling on the door ring, and for a moment he forgot all about the danger he was in. He had found it. His mind was filled with the question of what was behind the door. How big was Annwn? If you tried to find someone there, you'd probably be wandering around for days or weeks searching for them... Or maybe not?

Gwil stirred anxiously on Ben's shoulder, but he barely noticed him. He touched the lock with his fingertips, just to know what it felt like. An icy breeze blew through the keyhole, chilling his knuckles. Ben took hold of the door ring and was about to pull it when Gwil nipped his earlobe.

"Ouch!" Ben drew his hand back as if he had been burnt. All of a sudden he was back in the cellar again. He took Gwil off his shoulder and held him in the palm of his hand.

"What is it?"

The salamander turned his head to point towards the staircase. Ben looked nervously over his shoulder. Fog was pouring down the stairs and rolling across the floor to wash over his feet.

Ben backed away until he came up against the Door of the Dead. Someone was coming down the stairs, but it wasn't the Woman in Black or one of her dogs. The woman striding through the fog was slim with short, curly hair, wearing a poppy-patterned skirt and a blouse that must once have been red. Now everything about the woman was washed-out grey, as if the fog had sucked all the colour out of her.

"Rose?" Ben asked in disbelief. The woman stepped from the staircase onto the floor of the cellar.

Ben's heart gave a little leap. It really was Rose. But even though she was looking directly at him, she didn't seem to recognize him. In fact she didn't seem to realize there was anybody other than herself in the cellar. Her eyes darted about the room, as if she was upset by what she saw. Or rather, what she didn't see. Ben placed Gwil back on his shoulder and approached her cautiously.

"Rose?" he called out. "It's me, Ben."

But Rose didn't hear him. A wave of fog broke about her legs and she let out a deep sigh. She turned even paler, and her outline flickered as if she was in an old silent film.

Why was she down here? What was she looking for? Ben put his hand on her arm but drew it back right away. She felt cold, and too soft somehow—as if his fingers would go right through her if he squeezed any harder.

Suddenly, Ben gulped and slapped a hand to his forehead. He had just remembered why he was in the castle in the first place. Ridik's feather! Gwil scuttled back and forth on Ben's shoulder while he frantically fumbled in his jacket pocket for the memento. When he found it, his hands were trembling so much that it almost slipped from his grasp. Then he looked up and gasped in shock. The spectre that had once been Rose had turned around and was gliding back towards the stairs, carried by a pale wave of fog.

Oh, no. Ben hurried after her, and bounded up the first two steps—but then he stopped short. He looked back over his shoulder at the door to Annwn. The dark gateway standing on an impossible border. Ben hesitated, until Gwil nipped his ear once more.

"I know," Ben whispered. Gripping the feather tightly, he set off after Rose.

No matter how fast Ben ran, Rose got further and further away, turning around corners and climbing ever higher into the tower. He had given up calling her name. Stopping was not an option, but he began to doubt he would ever be able to give her the feather.

It just has to work, he told himself defiantly. It just had to.

The stairwell Rose was rushing up was so narrow that Ben touched the walls on both sides as they went. Moon-moths followed him like tiny torchbearers, and whenever he left them too far behind, he was plunged into pitch darkness.

Ben gritted his teeth and kept climbing while Gwil clung to his shoulder with his tiny feet. The salamander gave him hope. He had to rescue Rose from the fog, and not just to save her, but also because it was their only chance of making it out of this castle alive. Rose would know how to deal with the Woman in Black.

Finally, he had reached the end of the staircase and found himself in a large hall, dimly lit by the light coming through two arched windows. Somehow, he had ended up on one of the keep's upper floors. There was no sign of Rose anywhere, and to make matters worse there were two ways she could have gone. On the left of the hall was a flight of stairs leading down, while on the right a staircase climbed upward.

Ben took Gwil off his shoulder and held him up at eye level. "Any ideas?" he asked.

Gwil scurried back and forth on Ben's hand but seemed to be as stumped as he was.

Ben cursed himself. If only he hadn't been so distracted by the door down there in the cellar, he could have reacted faster when Rose showed up. Ben decided to try the stairs leading up first. He put Gwil back on his shoulder and set off towards them.

It seemed the hall had once been an audience chamber. There was a podium in the middle of the room, and on it stood a high-backed chair of worm-eaten wood. It was the first piece of furniture Ben had seen in the castle and the sight of the empty chair—the *throne*, he corrected himself—made him shudder. He found himself tiptoeing past the podium.

The throne and podium were surrounded by a ring of standing stones. That was strange, Ben thought—as far as he knew, stone circles were usually found outdoors. He passed close to one stone on his way to the staircase and saw that its surface had been carved with a pattern of knots and snakes.

Ben put his foot on the first step and stopped. Gwil crawled closer to Ben's neck, and he could feel the warmth of the salamander's small body. The staircase above him was as black as the night, but Ben could hear a swishing sound in the darkness, and soon the shadows began to stir.

"Rose?" Ben called, even though he already suspected who was coming. He stumbled backwards, but it was too late. The Woman in Black emerged from the shadows and strode down the stairs, heading straight for Ben. He didn't even notice Ridik's feather slipping from his fingers.

A Glimmer of Hope

Portia sat on the steps leading up to the Pale Tower, staring back at the beach. Below her, the fog still covered the causeway, but the sounds of the battle raging inside had faded. She had heard it all—the panting and barking of the dogs, the snarling of the fog. She had seen red lightning light up the fog like an Otherworldly thunderstorm, and the sight had frozen her feet to the ground.

But now it was completely silent. The fog was rolling like a stormy sea, and an ominous stillness had settled over the causeway and the bay.

Portia's head was spinning. She felt like she was stuck in a time loop. This was how she had lost Rose. Rose, who had gone into the fog alone to give them time to escape. Had that fog and the creatures that hunted in it now devoured Robin as well?

She hugged her knees to her chest. It was just too much! A strangled sob escaped from her throat. Portia wanted to pull herself together; she wanted to be strong. But no matter how hard she tried, things spiralled further and further out of control. She really was useless. Worse than useless! Other people had put themselves in danger because of her. And now? All she wanted was to curl up somewhere and not see or hear anything any more.

Portia leant forward and pressed her forehead against her knees. *Five more breaths,* she told herself. *Come on. Five more breaths, and then...* but that was as far as she got.

Something emerged from the fog and stepped onto the causeway. The red fur had lost some of its sheen, but for Portia it was as if the clouds had parted to reveal a clear blue sky. Relief flooded her heart—for exactly one second. Then the fox collapsed to the ground and lay still.

No! Portia ran to the causeway and fell to her knees at his side. Arawn's dogs had mauled him badly. The fur on his left flank was crusted with blood, and a nasty wound gaped on his right hind leg. He was breathing but didn't shift back into his human shape.

"Robin?" Portia whispered, gently stroking his head. The fox's eyes flickered open for a split second before closing again.

Portia looked down at the injured fox, and then along the causeway to the rough steps climbing to the castle and the fog king's home. Never in her life had she felt so helpless.

Because there was nothing else she could do, she carried the fox up to the Pale Tower. She stopped in the courtyard of the ruined castle and stared at what was left of the World Door. Broken wood hung from twisted hinges. The ground was strewn with charred splinters. The doorway itself stood open and unguarded.

She needed no explanation to understand what had happened. Someone had made sure the door would never be closed again. The Grey King could come and go freely now.

The fox stirred, and she shifted his weight in her arms. Portia knew they had to keep moving, but the sight of the destroyed door had drained all her remaining energy.

"That's the door to the Borderlands, isn't it?" she asked.

The fox glanced at the archway and twitched an ear. Portia could guess what he meant.

We're done for.

No one stopped them from passing through the doorway. Portia should have been relieved, but instead the same question kept going round and round in her head. Where were Ben and Gwil?

When she had carried Robin through the door to the Borderlands, he squirmed from her arms and finally shifted back to his human form. He leant on Portia's shoulder and together they limped to the end of the hall, where Robin slid to the ground and sat with his back against the wall.

He looked no less battered in his human shape. He had a bruise on his cheek, his waistcoat and shirt were torn open at the side, and one trouser leg hung in tatters.

"Spirits of the moonless night," he groaned.

Without a word, Portia pulled the backpack from her shoulders and handed him the leather satchel holding the potions and healing salves.

"Thank you." He took a clay pot from the satchel, unscrewed the lid and rubbed some ointment onto the wound on his leg. As his fingers touched the cut, he hissed and grimaced in pain.

Portia sat down cross-legged in front of him. She could feel the sting of the wound almost as if it had been hers. She couldn't stop thinking of how Robin had fought for both of them. Her guilty conscience weighed down on her like a heavy blanket.

Meanwhile, Robin put the pot of ointment down and gingerly felt his ribs before quickly pulling his hand away. He leant back against the wall with a sigh. His forehead was beaded with sweat, but when he closed his eyes, his features seemed to relax.

"What a mess."

Portia didn't say anything. She looked around the empty hall. Aside from the splintered door and a couple of sticks lying around on the floor, there was nothing to show what might have happened there.

"Do you think Ben and Gwil are okay?" she asked after a while.

Robin gave no reply but pointed to one of the sticks. "Fetch me one of those, will you?"

Portia frowned, but did as he asked. Robin took the piece of wood and turned it over in his hands. To Portia it looked like a broken broomstick. He brought it close to his face and whispered something. Blue runes glowed faintly on the wood.

"Attack and defence runes," he said. "You've got to hand it to the salamander—he was well prepared."

"Was?" Portia repeated, a lump in her throat.

"Let's not lose hope," Robin said, tapping the stick with his hand. "This doesn't mean anything. They could have been in a fight and managed to get away. If we could, why not those two?"

Guilt welled up inside Portia like brackish water. Her gaze wandered to the wound on Robin's leg before her eyes blurred with tears. She felt a lump in her throat and looked away hurriedly. "I should've helped you," she said. "I'm so sorry."

All of a sudden she felt his hand on her cheek. Startled, she spun around. There was a new, soft expression on his face.

"You're being too hard on yourself," he said. When she only gawped at him in response, a small smile tugged at the corners of his mouth. "Anyway, you don't have to worry about me," he said, his hand falling to his side. "Takes more than that to finish me off."

You're being too hard on yourself. Robin's words dripped like liquid sunlight onto the guilt and tension that was coiled so tightly around her heart.

You're being too hard on yourself. Portia was about to ask him what he meant by that when she saw something moving in the corner of her eye. Just a few feet away from them was an archway in the wall, and out of it... Portia froze.

Robin sat bolt upright, alarmed. "What is it?"

Before she could reply, a finger of fog felt its way into the hall.

Robin leapt to his feet, brandishing the rune staff two-handed, but his injured leg gave way beneath him. Portia sat, petrified, while the fog rolled ever more thickly through the archway. Then a figure stepped out of the murk.

"Portia," Robin warned. But she didn't listen. She stared spellbound at the woman emerging from the archway. Her heart gave a little jump, as if it were about to take wing. It was Rose! She came out of the fog with her head held high, and seemingly unharmed. Portia was about to run to her aunt when she realized that something was seriously wrong. Rose's steps were oddly sluggish, and her eyes darted about her as she walked. She seemed to be looking for something, and didn't notice Robin or Portia at all. Portia felt a chill in her blood.

Robin tried to get to his feet again, only to sink back to the floor with a cry of pain. Rose turned around at the sound, but her eyes slid over Robin as if he wasn't there. She hesitated for a moment and was turning back towards the archway when Robin reached out to touch the hem of her skirt. She stopped and looked straight at him this time, but still her gaze remained blank and empty.

Robin looked up at her intently. "Rose?" he pleaded.

For a split second it seemed as if Rose might be able to break through the veil of oblivion. A look of sorrow passed briefly across her face, but then she turned and went back through the archway, the fog trailing behind her like a veil.

Robin moaned softly and fumbled at his collar. Portia was so shaken by the encounter that she barely noticed him. "Was that..." Portia tried to recall the word, "... a chimera? A memory, like at World's End?"

"No," Robin replied hoarsely. "That was Rose. It's not too late! The fog hasn't dissolved her yet." He pulled out a chain from underneath his shirt and yanked it so that the links broke. "Here. Take this," he said, holding the chain out to Portia. It had a silver locket dangling from it. Portia thought the locket looked familiar and then realized why—she had seen it in Robin's quarters back in Fairy Hill, next to a vase of yellow roses.

She raised her eyebrows. "What do you want me to...?"

"Take it to Rose," Robin urged her. "If anything can free her from the power of the fog, it's this."

"How could your locket help her?"

"It's not mine. It belongs to Rose. It was a gift." He pressed the chain into Portia's hand. "Show it to her, and she'll remember who she is. Remember what... or rather who is important to her."

Seeing that she was still hesitating, Robin gave her a gentle push. "Come on now, go. Bring Rose back. It's our very last chance." He closed his eyes and leant back against the wall again. "We'll need her help to get out of this mess."

Rosethorn and Brambleblossom

✌ PORTIA ✍

Portia climbed the staircase, higher and higher to the upper floors of the castle keep. She carried the rune staff in her hand. Rose could use it as weapon if she succeeded in bringing her back. *If.*

Portia set her jaw and climbed on. The locket was in her pocket, but she didn't really believe Robin's plan would work. Was the necklace a gift from Rose to Robin or one he'd given to her? A gift that Rose had returned? The Adar had suggested that Robin had once been in love with Rose, but had she loved him? And would that emotion still be strong enough to bring her back to herself?

She followed the wisps of fog floating ahead of her up the staircase until she came to an attic room with a ceiling of dark wooden rafters. The only light filtered through a round window.

Rose sat on the windowsill, plumes of milky mist swirling around her and pouring down onto the floor.

Portia propped the staff against the wall, slid a hand into her pocket and slowly began to walk towards Rose. When she reached the edge of the fog everything in her screamed to turn back, but still she went on. It felt weird inside the fog—as if a creature with a dozen soft hands were caressing her.

With every step, she felt more and more strange. What was she doing here? How had she ever thought she could stand up to a King of the Underworld? She would be lost in the fog. She was lost already. Every memory of anyone who had ever meant anything to her would trickle away like sand between her fingers. She frowned. A guilty conscience was nothing new to her, and neither was fear, but this... this feeling was unfamiliar. It was as if an antenna in her heart were picking up radio waves from other people's emotional worlds. She felt deep grief and sorrow, and a yearning to see her loved ones again. Portia shook her head, but couldn't dispel those unfamiliar feelings. Instead, she felt a wave of fear rising within her.

Bubbles of guilt rose to the surface of her consciousness. Her recklessness had not only put Rose and Ben in danger, but a whole world too. And her mother? What about her? Portia imagined her mum hearing that her daughter had gone missing in the Welsh mountains. In her mind's eye she saw the shadow of despair fall on Gwen's face, and felt her anguish as if it were her own.

You're being too hard on yourself. Robin's words were still fresh in her memory, and so was the warmth of his hand against her cheek. Portia took a deep breath and clenched her fists so tightly that her fingernails dug into her palms. *Keep walking*, she told herself.

"Aunt Rose," Portia said, when she was finally standing in front of her. The blank look on Rose's face made her want to run away. Instead Portia reached out and took her hand. She was afraid that Rose would dissolve at her touch, but although the hand was cold and damp, it was still solid and real.

"Rose, please, you have to remember!" Portia pressed Robin's locket into the palm of her hand. Nothing happened. Not even the slightest flicker of emotion showed on Rose's blank, doll-like face.

Tears pricked Portia's eyes. "Please," she pleaded. Desperately, she fumbled at the locket until she found the clasp. She opened it, expecting to find a photograph inside. Instead, she found a flower pressed under glass. Suddenly she remembered the box of odds and ends in Bramble's room. The locket she had seen there was almost identical—except that rather than a dog rose, this one held the white flower of a bramble bush.

Portia also remembered the night Robin had tried to steal the key. Bramble had complained that the fox kept stealing things from the house. Of course! It was all so obvious now. The locket *had* been a gift. From Bramble to Rose.

The fog had filled the whole room now, and the tower's walls were disappearing behind the grey haze. Portia gulped and held the open locket out to Rose.

"Do you remember Bramble?" she asked. Rose's empty eyes seemed to look right through her, but she refused to give up.

Rose frowned. Then she leant forward and looked at the locket. Portia's heart was beating wildly. It was working! It had to work!

Rose placed a fingertip on the glass. Portia was watching Rose's face so closely that she didn't notice the voices at first. Only when she heard someone laugh did she start and spin round. She saw nothing but fog and thought she must have been mistaken—until she saw a sudden movement in the murk. A light flickered and danced through the fog. The swirling vapours parted like a curtain to reveal a courtyard. Two young women were running across the cobblestones, laughing with their long black graduation gowns gathered in their hands. Portia backed away in alarm, but just as the women were about to reach her, the scene dissolved. The show wasn't finished, though. The women's images had barely faded away when another scene appeared in a different corner of the room. *Memories*, Portia thought. *These must be Rose's memories!*

This time, a living room appeared in the fog, with a fireplace, armchairs and a sofa. A group of young people had made themselves comfortable in the room. One woman was slouched in a chair, puffing on a cigar, while another lay on the thick carpet, and two more were sitting on the sofa. In the armchairs either side of the fireplace sat a man and a woman. This time, Portia recognized the group. They were Rose's friends from her student days. Portia didn't know the others' names, but the women sitting on the sofa had to be Rose and Bramble. The young woman with the cigar was telling a story, while the others laughed along heartily. Then the scene began to fade, but not before Portia had noticed Rose reaching for Bramble's hand.

Behind Portia's back, another scene flickered into life. She turned around to see white rocks, the deep blue sea and a small island emerging from the ocean like a turtle's shell. In this memory, Rose and Bramble were both older. They stood side by side, looking right at Portia and smiling. Then a gust of wind blew Rose's hat off.

Portia was spellbound. Something strange was happening to the fog. Where before disappointment and despair had lurked in it like cold spots in a deep lake, now Portia could feel relief, happiness and a deep confidence that everything would be okay. She had no idea whether they were her own feelings or Rose's memories hanging in the fog like dewdrops and clinging to her skin, but she smiled anyway.

And then a very simple image appeared. It was Bramble, looking as she did now, with her grey hair and half-moon glasses. She was sitting in her armchair in Afallon, a book in her lap and Marlowe asleep at her feet.

The fog rippled, collapsed then surged quickly past Portia. She turned around once more. Rose had got to her feet and was standing in the centre of the fog. It wasn't flowing past her now but back to her, or rather back *through* her, swirling around her, hugging close to her and seeping into her skin. Flickering images wandered over her arms and face, like a film projected on a wall. And then the fog evaporated entirely, the walls of the room were visible again—and Rose was back. The real Rose, awake and alive, with her bright red poppy-patterned skirt and her curly, grey-streaked hair.

She took a deep breath.

"Rose?" Portia felt as if she had just stepped off a swaying deck and onto solid ground.

Without a word, Rose walked over, sank to her knees and pulled Portia into a hug.

The New Hunting Master

When Ben came to he was lying on a stone floor. He gingerly felt the back of his head and winced as his fingers touched a lump. Had he fallen? He sat up clumsily. The backpack's twisted straps cut into his shoulders. He freed himself of the extra weight and then started with fright. Gwil was gone!

Suddenly, Ben was wide awake. Frantically, he searched the floor around him. Where was the salamander? What had happened? A rumbling snort interrupted the panic-fuelled swirl of thoughts in his head, and he froze. Bit by bit, his memories came back. The throne hall. Looking for Rose and instead finding... Ben shivered. He lifted his head and saw the stone circle, the throne, and behind it—the Woman in Black.

The sight of her hit him like a punch in the chest. She was looking towards the window, but the fog hound sitting by her side was staring directly at Ben.

Without taking his eyes off the woman, he lifted himself into a crouching position. He was just about to stand up when a second dog materialized so close to him that he fell backwards in shock. Ben crawled away on his hands and knees until he bumped into one of the giant standing stones. The dog watched him with its strange eyes but did not attack.

The Woman in Black stood there, bolt upright, until a hunting horn called outside, somewhere in the distance. She lowered her head at the sound, and the tension seemed to leave her body. Her voice was like the rustling of dead leaves.

"He is coming."

Arawn! Arawn was coming! Ben felt the fear course through him like fire. He had to get away!

He slid up along the stone, but had barely got to his feet when one of the dogs bared its sharp teeth and he fell to the ground once more. He scrabbled backwards and pushed his back against the stone. The dog came closer until he was right in front of Ben, so close that he could hear the growling deep in its throat. It snarled, and then dissolved in a swirl of fog. Ben gasped, and then saw the Woman in Black approaching, her veils streaming behind her. The next thing he knew she had grabbed him by the shoulder.

"No!" He tried to struggle free, but she pulled him to his feet and pinned him against the stone.

Ben squirmed and craned his head to avoid looking at her. Everything in him was screaming *No*, but he could no longer utter a sound. The woman leant in ever closer, and he felt her breath on his skin, cold and biting, like the air on a white-frosted winter morning.

When she spoke, her voice was barely more than a whisper. "I'm tired." A sigh, a rustling of the veil. "So tired."

Ben sobbed and squeezed his eyes tight shut. Bony fingers dug into his shoulders. Rough fabric grazed his cheek, and then the Woman in Black blew gently on the standing stone at his back. The stone shook, then there was a grinding sound, and dust began to trickle to the floor. Ben's eyes snapped open when he felt something thick and rough coiling around his arms. The scream stuck in his throat.

The woman was standing so close that her forehead was almost touching his. Behind the veil, where her eyes should have been, there were only two black holes. Then she glided away from him, like a spider leaving the prey caught in its web.

Ben looked down and realized with horror that two thick grey-stone snakes were now wrapped around his upper arms, and as hard as he tried, he couldn't get free. He could only watch as the woman removed her gloves. Her hands were thin, pale and covered in a pattern of tiny runes. When she raised them in front of her, the pattern lit up, sending shimmering blue runes and knots swarming across her skin.

The sight sent Ben into a state of blind panic. He struggled desperately, throwing himself from side to side, but to no avail. The woman held her glowing hands out towards him. Ben wrenched his head away, but she seized his face in both hands and held it steady.

"Please," Ben sobbed. "Please don't!" His breath came in short, choppy gasps, and stopped entirely when he felt the runes touch his skin. It felt as if tiny maggots were crawling across his cheeks. He closed his eyes again and wished with every fibre of his being that either he or the ties that bound him would disappear. But there was no escaping that grip, or the runes taking possession of him.

The Grey King's Huntress

Portia hugged Rose tight, breathing in the scent of mint and lavender clinging to her clothes. After a while, Rose gently let go. She brushed the curls from her great-niece's face and smiled.

"Brave girl." She looked down at the locket in her hand and brushed the bramble flower with her thumb before closing it and putting it into her skirt pocket. "Is Robin with you?" she asked.

"Yes," Portia replied. "I would never have got this far without him."

Rose nodded and got to her feet. Portia did the same and felt a wave of confidence surge through her. Everything would be all right now.

"Let's go and find him," Rose said. "You have to tell me everything."

"It's a long story."

Portia took the rune staff from where it stood propped against the wall and handed it to Rose, who raised an eyebrow.

"Combat runes?"

"Ben and Gwil must have used it," Portia explained. "At least that's what we think, but..." She paused and stared at the doorway. A small black-and-yellow salamander had just appeared at the top of the staircase.

"Oh, no!" Portia hurried over and placed the salamander on the palm of her hand.

Rose rushed to her side. "What's the matter?"

"It's Gwil," Portia cried. "He's shapeshifted." She held him at eye level, but, of course, in his current shape, Gwil couldn't tell her what had happened. Portia looked expectantly down the staircase, willing Ben to appear. But no one came. Her face fell.

Rose put a hand on her shoulder. "Portia," she said gently. "Where's Ben?"

Portia ran down the staircase holding the salamander like a compass, with Ben's name ringing in her head like an alarm bell.

"Portia," Rose called after her, but she didn't listen. She jumped off the final step and charged into the hall. What she found there made her stop in her tracks. Ben! Ben with his back to a stone and Arawn's Huntress looming over him.

"No!" Portia felt as if her insides were turning into water. Light flashed from the Huntress's fingers and ran over Ben's face. It was exactly like the scene she had seen in the fog at World's End. The memory of when the former Hunting Master had forced Hermia to take his place!

"STOP!" The cry cut through the air above Portia's head like a whip. The next moment, Rose pushed her aside as she ran past her.

෴

The Huntress spun around, just in time to evade Rose's attack. Ben collapsed, the glow on his face dimming. Portia was jolted out of her state of shock. She put Gwil on her shoulder and ran as fast as she could to Ben's side, skirting the fighting women.

The Woman in Black swirled towards the middle of the room with Rose hot on her heels, rune staff in hand. With every swing of the staff, the runes glowed and blue light shot from its tip like a sickle blade. Portia leapt between two of the standing stones and came skidding to a halt in front of Ben.

"Ben!" Then she saw the stone bands holding his arms. "Rats. What the heck are they?"

Ben opened his mouth to speak but couldn't utter a word. Fear squeezed Portia's heart like a fist. She looked into his eyes and saw they were dark with pain and shock. Then she put herself between him and the fighting women, clenching her fists. She had no idea how, but she was going to protect Ben whatever it took.

The fight between Rose and the Woman in Black raged across the hall. Grey hounds joined the fray, but Rose quickly cut them into foggy swirls with movements so fast that Portia couldn't follow them. With each of Rose's blows, rune light flashed across the hall. Arawn's Huntress whipped her many black veils through the air to parry the attacks. It looked as if she had grown half a dozen tentacles.

Rose dodged one of the lashing veils, taking cover behind a standing stone. The Huntress didn't hesitate for a second. She reached out her arms, sending the tentacles of her robes swishing around the stone. Rose dove headlong to the floor, then jumped to her feet and ran straight towards the Huntress, sweeping the veils to one side and slamming her shoulder into her opponent's midriff.

Both fighters went down, and the Woman in Black let out a shrill scream. Her veils billowed about her, and she clawed at Rose's face with her fingers, but Rose broke free and pinned the Huntress to the ground with her knees. The black fabric of her dress rose up in the air to form a giant claw, but before it could snap shut, Rose grabbed the rune staff in both hands, held it up like a dagger and brought it down on the veiled woman's chest. A deafening crash rang out in the hall, like a shattering wall of glass, accompanied by a blaze of blinding blue light.

When Portia dared to look again, the Huntress and Rose remained frozen in the middle of the hall like statues. The black veils hung in the air for a moment and then fell to the floor. Once again, time stopped. Then at last Rose took a rattling breath.

"Thank God," Portia croaked.

Behind her, Ben moaned. Portia spun around to see the stone bands holding his arms crumble to dust. He slumped forward, and she leapt to catch him. Together, they sank to the ground. She put her arm around him and he rested his head on her shoulder. As soon as he did so, Gwil scuttled over to nuzzle his snout into the boy's cheek. Ben's smile was weak, but he was *smiling*.

"It's all right," Portia said. "It's all right, we're okay." She still couldn't really believe that it was true.

Ben tried to stand up, and Portia helped him to his feet. Her relief was so immense that she felt like planting a kiss on his cheek. Ben seemed to be about to ask her something, but before he could even open his mouth to speak, a piercing scream rang out.

Portia spun around. At the other end of the hall, Rose was kneeling next to the fallen Huntress. She held the black veil in one hand while the other was pressed to her mouth.

"Oh, no," Rose groaned. She hadn't realized who she had been fighting. Until now.

"What?..." Ben began, but Portia was already on her way over to Rose.

"I'll explain later," she called over her shoulder. In just a few steps, she was by Rose's side. She had already removed the crown of branches from Hermia's head, and pulled the veils aside from her face. The woman underneath the black fabric was old. Very old. She had dark circles under her eyes, her cheeks were sunken, her lips bloodless and chapped, and her skin was almost completely covered in a web of runes. She blinked once, staring up at Rose with dull eyes.

Rose stared back, stunned. "Hermia," she whispered.

"Who?" Ben asked in a weak voice. Portia hadn't realized he had followed her.

She touched his hand. "Later," she promised.

Rose's eyes filled with tears, and she pressed a hand to her mouth once more. She shook her head, as if refusing to accept what was happening. Hermia sighed heavily and raised a hand. Ben stiffened, but she only gently touched Rose's wrist and slowly shook her head with great effort.

Rose grimaced in pain and grief and took her friend's hand. Hermia squeezed her fingers in return, and then closed her eyes.

"Tired." The word was barely a whisper. Then the former Huntress's hand went limp. It was over. Rose sobbed and stroked Hermia's ruined face.

Portia took a step towards the two women. What could she do to comfort Rose? Every word, every gesture seemed ridiculous and inadequate.

A thin, colourless strand of hair had settled on Hermia's face. Rose tenderly brushed it aside and kissed her forehead. "*Swirne saff*," she murmured.

"She's got the key," said Ben. Rose looked up at him in surprise. "Gwil and I made a second World Key," he explained. "And she took it from us."

Rose's gaze drifted back to her fallen friend's body but she made no attempt to search her dress. Instead, Gwil scuttled down Ben's arm and between the folds of the garment, before reappearing with the key in his mouth. Ben took it and put it safely in his pocket.

Rose looked him in the eye. "Are you okay, Ben?" she asked in a hoarse voice.

Ben nodded, but his gaze was still fixed on Hermia's face, and the runes running over it like chains.

"Oh, what have we done," Rose groaned. Then she took the hunting horn that Hermia had carried on a strap at her hip, touched her friend's face one last time and got to her feet. She took the black veil with her.

Companions in Arms

A narrow gate led out from the rear of the Pale Tower, to where a semicircular courtyard had been carved out of the rock. It was bordered by a parapet of black stone from which a steep flight of steps led down to the sea below. Ben and his companions watched as a bank of fog rolled towards them from the horizon.

"Is that him?" Portia asked.

"Oh, yes," Rose replied. "That's Arawn. The Grey King."

"How long will it take him to get here?"

"Not long." Robin glanced at Rose. "I suppose you have a plan?"

By way of an answer, Rose held up Hermia's black veil. She whispered into the fabric, and runes unfurled on it like lightning-blue flowers.

"A charm cloth?" Robin asked.

"It worked before," Rose said curtly.

Robin sighed. "So you still want to take on Arawn. You realize we came all this way to save you from him?"

Rose eyed him coolly. "I'd have come here a long time ago if I knew we'd left a friend behind."

Robin winced and bobbed his head as if to admit his guilt. "I know."

There was a story behind their words of which Ben knew nothing. The Woman in Black must play a role in it, but her attack was still too fresh in his mind and he didn't want to hear about her just yet. Just thinking of the runes crawling on her flesh made him queasy.

"Someone has to stop Arawn," Rose said eventually. "Especially now that we can't close the door to Faerie. Titania won't be able to gather her army fast enough to push him back at the doorway."

She turned to Robin. "Could you take the children back to Bryngolau?"

"No way!" cried Ben and Portia at the same time.

Rose frowned, but before she could argue, Robin cut in. "I think it's better if we stay together." He shrugged. "They'd catch us before we got there anyway."

"Sweet spirits," Rose whispered, pressing her fingers to her forehead.

Portia gently put a hand on her arm. "So what's the plan?"

"Arawn doesn't know yet that his Huntress is dead." Rose closed her eyes briefly before placing her hand on the hunting horn slung over her shoulder. "We'll lure him up these steps with the horn. If we can distract his pack and catch him on his own, I can use the charm cloth to put a sleeping spell on him."

"I'll do the distracting," Robin said immediately. "I'll hide among the rocks by the steps and watch out for them from there."

"Will you be able to manage that with your injured leg?" Portia asked.

The corners of Robin's mouth twitched into a smile. "I told you before..."

"... it takes more than that to finish you off," Portia finished his sentence and grinned back.

The three of them were totally focused on each other—they reminded Ben of a band of heroes from one of his books. Meanwhile he felt like he was in the audience, watching them perform, but that was all right with him. He reached for Gwil, who was still sitting on his shoulder, and stroked his head with a finger.

Robin handed the rune staff to Rose with an exaggerated bow. She shook her head in mild exasperation but gave him a tired smile as well.

"The four of us against the Grey King and his horde," Robin grinned. "What could possibly go wrong?"

"Oh, I could give you a long list of things if you like," said a voice behind them. "But we're running out of time, aren't we?"

The companions spun around as one. Titania stood in the gateway to the Pale Tower. The last time Ben had seen the Fairy Queen she had been dressed to the nines in royal finery. Her current appearance could not have been more different. She was wearing a dirty, crumpled nightgown, and her hair stuck up crazily, like a bird's nest. Ben wasn't the only one left speechless at the sight.

"I thought you didn't fight unwinnable battles?" Robin said eventually.

"Oh, shut your mouth," Titania hissed as she stepped into the courtyard.

Rose bowed. "Your Majesty."

Titania looked her up and down. "So, they did bring you back then."

"I was lucky," Rose said.

"Luckier than you deserve," Titania snapped. She strode past Rose and gazed icily towards the horizon. They could hear the ominous drumming of hooves now. Titania turned back to the companions and crossed her arms. Ben saw that her fingertips were blackened with soot.

"So you plan to send Arawn back to sleep?" she asked.

Rose seemed surprised for a moment but recovered quickly. "Yes."

"And how do you plan to do that?"

Robin opened his mouth to reply but Rose nudged him with her elbow before he could do so. "We were going to use a charm cloth," she said. "But now that you're here—charm stones would increase the cloth's power."

Titania snorted derisively, but went over to the top of the flight of steps leading down to the sea. There she crouched down and placed her hands on the rocks on either side of the path. The ground beneath their feet began to shake, sending Ben stumbling against the stone parapet. A deafening rumbling and grinding of stone filled the air, and dust began to trickle down into the courtyard from the surrounding rocks.

"This can't be real," Portia gasped.

The tumult grew louder still as rock teeth sprouted from the ground around them. Shards of stone crashed down onto the steps, and the whole island rumbled as if a dragon were stirring deep inside it. In a few seconds, it was all over. Standing stones as tall as people now ran along either side of the steps like battlements. Ben stared up at them in awe.

Titania rose to her feet and spoke over her shoulder.

"Rune Speaker. Your turn."

Rose went over to the standing stone closest to her, placed both hands on its surface and began to whisper spells into the rock. Ben's heart began to beat faster. He knew what was coming, and yet the sight of it was amazing. Runes began to blossom all over the stone, before trickling down it into the island's rocky core, only to re-emerge at the base of the stone opposite. Ribbons of runes twined along the battlements like ivy tendrils. Ben could sense the air crackling with magic. It was very different from the Woman in Black's creeping, eerie enchantment. Rose's rune spell was bright and positive. Ben was tempted to touch one of the charm stones just to feel it.

Rose stepped back and spoke a final word, at which the runes faded.

"I see you're disguising the power of your runes." Titania smiled grudgingly. "Arawn won't notice how strong they are until he and his pack are standing between the charm stones. Not bad, Human. Perhaps we do stand a chance after all."

"So we have permission to fight by your side now?" Robin asked. "What an honour."

"As if you have any idea what honour means." Titania snapped her fingers and pointed at the veil that was tucked under Rose's arm. "Give the charm cloth to Goodfellow. You're a better fighter than he is."

Robin narrowed his eyes, but Rose shrugged and handed over the veil.

"What about us?" Portia asked.

Rose hesitated for a moment, before reluctantly unslinging the hunting horn from her shoulder. "Someone has to blow the horn to lure Arawn up the steps. Can you do it?"

Portia took the horn. She was very pale, apart from two deep-red blotches on her cheeks—but her voice was steady.

"Yes," she said.

Ben admired her for that.

"And what do we do if Arawn makes it all the way up here?" she asked.

"Then we die," Titania sneered.

Rose shot her an irritated glare before turning back to Portia. "If it looks as if we're going to fail, you must hide in the fortress. Wait until Arawn and his hunt have passed through to Faerie, then travel across the Borderlands by foot until you reach the door to the Human World."

Portia opened her mouth to object, but Titania beat her to it. "Excuse me?"

Rose ignored her. "Arawn will think only of the open World Door in this tower. If you hurry, you can get home before he has razed Faerie and his thoughts turn to our own world." She laid a hand on Portia's shoulder. "Remember to close the door behind you. Go to Afallon, and tell Bramble..."

"Over my dead body!" Titania cut in. She marched towards Rose, who whirled around, and raised the rune staff.

"You would give up my world to the fog?" Titania hissed angrily.

"I'll do everything I can to stop him getting through the doorway," Rose shot back. "But the children belong in their world. That's not up for negotiation."

Ben admired her determination but wondered why Titania would be willing to negotiate in the first place. Just then, Titania turned her gaze on him like a spotlight.

"You," she said. "You and the salamander. You have a key."

His hand darted automatically to the key in his pocket—he couldn't help it. Titania's silvery eyes flashed hungrily, but Rose stepped in between the Fairy Queen and Ben with the rune staff raised.

"There's no time to argue," she said. "So stop puffing yourself up like a blowfish, and let's get this done."

The insult seemed to knock Titania off balance. Ben blinked in surprise, while Robin turned away to hide his grin.

"You're pushing your luck, Rosethorn," Titania said slowly. "We shall see how much of it remains. After the battle."

"If the children are to travel to the door of the Human World, they'll need someone to guide them," Robin said with a nod towards Gwil. "Would you be so kind, Your Majesty?" he asked.

Titania stared at him. Ben was sure she would have loved to crush him to dust. Instead, a thin and entirely malicious smile appeared on her face. "Your list of debts is getting longer and longer," she said. Then she swept over to Ben and plucked Gwil from his shoulder.

"No!" Ben cried in shock, but Titania was already speaking the words of a spell. A puddle appeared out of nowhere on the cobblestone floor and Titania dropped the salamander into the water. There was a bang and a cloud of steam, then Gwil was lying on the ground in his human shape, crumpled and pale.

Titania dusted off her hands, as if she had just touched something dirty. "Happy now?"

The call of the hunting horn echoed across the bay like a drawn-out scream. Ben's blood ran cold. Next to him, Portia lowered the horn and watched the fog wall rolling across the mudflats towards them like a waterless flood. She stiffened when an answering call came from a horn deep within the fog.

Titania stood at the parapet, her long hair blowing in the wind. "So it begins," she said.

Rose turned to Portia. "You know what you have to do?" she asked for the umpteenth time.

"Keep trying to lure the Grey King up here, then wait and see if we need to hide in the fortress," she repeated.

"And then?" Rose prompted her.

"If all else fails, get to the door to the Human World as fast as we can."

"You'd better be fast," Titania sneered. "Once Arawn gets wind of that key of yours, he'll hunt you down without mercy. Who knows, he might even leave my world alone."

Ben fingered the key in his pocket once more and glanced over at Gwil. Titania had lifted the spell on his mark again, but while he said he was no longer in pain, he looked pretty worn out.

"Are you sure you're feeling okay?" Ben asked quietly.

Gwil gave him a wan smile. "Better than before."

Meanwhile, Robin folded the charm cloth into a square and went over to Portia.

"Here," he said, handing her a small glass vial. "Just in case."

"Are we ready to go now?" Titania demanded.

"But of course, Your Highness." Robin curtsied, clenched the cloth between his teeth and shapeshifted in a cloud of red smoke. The fox ran down the steps with the charm cloth in its mouth. Rose went after him, but Titania turned to look Ben up and down one last time, as if trying to pin him in her memory like a butterfly. *Later*, she mouthed silently, then went down towards the battlements.

"Sweet spirits," Gwil muttered.

"She'll snatch the key the first chance she gets," Portia predicted.

"That's if we survive this," Gwil replied miserably.

Seeing Portia's distraught expression, he hurried to correct himself. "Which of course we will!"

Portia shook her head, smiling. "I've missed your optimism, Gwil."

A dog howled in the advancing fog, and Gwil and Portia ran over to the parapet. Somewhere down below, a merciless enemy was drawing closer and closer. A decisive battle was approaching, and Ben should have been totally focused on it—and yet he was distracted. Even if the battle did go well, what then? They would return to Bryngolau, or go straight across the Borderlands to the Human Door and go home from there. Ben's hand went back to the key in his pocket. If Titania really took the key, all the World Doors would be closed. Including the door to Annwn.

Ben looked back towards the castle. He remembered the smell of the Door of the Dead, and the cold air blowing through the keyhole. His hand clenched around the key. He looked over at Gwil and Portia. They both seemed grimly focused on the coming battle. Ben's guilty conscience gnawed at him, but this was his last chance.

Ben was just an invisible boy after all. Someone people forgot about quickly. He wouldn't make any difference to the battle anyway. He took a deep breath and turned back towards the Pale Tower.

The Door of the Dead

The fog had settled around the island like a thick blanket of snow. It was dead silent. There was no clatter of hooves now, or any other sound. It was impossible to tell whether Arawn and his pack were already climbing the steps.

Portia forced herself to blow Hermia's hunting horn once again. Its screeching drone made her feel sick, like the sound of someone scraping their fingernails down a blackboard. As she took the horn from her lips, she caught Gwil looking at the scar on her wrist. His face darkened.

"Titania," he said curtly.

Portia shrugged. "You were right. You can't trust her."

Gwil clenched his fists. "Curse her."

For a second Portia thought of telling Gwil about her deal with Titania, but then she decided against it. What if Titania died before she could free the salamanders? Or what if she somehow tricked her way out of the agreement? She just didn't want to give Gwil false hope.

Below them the fog was crawling up the steps, smothering the rocky hillside as it went. Somewhere down there, Rose, Titania and Robin were hiding. Portia knew she wouldn't be of much help in the battle, but still felt as if she should be doing something more useful. She would never get used to the idea of standing around waiting while others risked their lives.

"Agreed," she said after a while. "I'm just glad that you and Ben are okay. Your plan was the better one after all."

Gwil gave a hollow laugh. "I'm not so sure about that," he said. "We should've realized we were out of our depth when we were trying to turn a chair leg into a weapon! Right, Ben?"

He turned around, and with a twinge of guilt Portia did likewise. Ben was usually so quiet that it was easy to forget to include him in a conversation. She expected to find him standing somewhere behind them, but he was nowhere to be see. Portia looked around but the courtyard was empty.

Gwil frowned. "Ben?" he called.

"Ben!" Portia shouted. No answer.

Portia swallowed against the unease clenching her chest. *Don't worry*, she told herself. *He must be somewhere nearby.* But a part of her knew that wasn't true and the worry growing inside of her made her pulse flutter.

"Where is he?" she asked.

"I have no idea," Gwil said, still frowning.

Feeling queasy, Portia looked down at the steps leading to the sea. Had Ben gone after Rose? But that made no sense! She went over to the top of the stairs to get a better look when the silence was broken by an angry cry. A sound like fizzing and crackling electricity came from somewhere inside the mist, followed by a deafening bang. A shock wave rippled through the fog, chasing clouds of vapour before it like a herd of fleeing deer. A shrill screech tore through the air, and the next moment the fog drew back out to sea—before rushing forward to break against the island like a giant tidal wave. Portia lost her feet as the rock beneath her cracked and shook with the impact. She fell on her back but picked herself up immediately. Tendrils of fog came snaking up the stairs, and the runes on the standing stones began to glow.

Another furious roar came from down below. Portia clapped her hands to her ears and backed away, bumping into Gwil. He grabbed her shoulder and spun her around.

"Ben still has the key, doesn't he?" he asked.

"Yes, but..."

Gwil's grip on her shoulder tightened as a look of horror spread across his face. "I'm afraid I know where he is!"

ᴥ BEN ᴥ

The Door of the Dead creaked like the hull of a ship on a stormy sea as Ben pulled it open. For a moment, he thought about leaving the key in the lock. But what if one of Arawn's servants found it? No, better to keep it safe. He thrust it into his pocket, before crossing the edge of the world and closing the door behind him.

The fog on the other side was thicker than any he had seen so far. He couldn't make out even a metre ahead of him. Thick white clouds of fog engulfed him, caressing his skin.

The air he breathed was cool and fresh, as if there were a lake or river nearby. Were there even such things as hills, valleys and rivers in this place? As Ben walked on, he found himself more and more fascinated by the shapeless, drifting world surrounding him. He knew somewhere back there Portia was in the courtyard with the horn, and that his friends were locked in battle with the Master of the Underworld. And yet the thought drifted away from him like a boat setting out to sea in hazy dawn light. The further it went, the easier it was for him to focus on his goal.

Ben had no idea where he was going or where to begin looking for his father. But the painful longing lodged in his chest like a fishing hook tugged him onward, deeper and deeper into the Underworld.

Ben waved his arm through the murk and watched as thin tendrils of fog twined about his forearm. For a moment it looked as if the fog was rising from his skin—it had to be some kind of optical illusion, he thought. Ben brushed the fog off and carried on his way. After a while, the clouds parted to reveal a cluster of slate houses ahead of him. He recognized it immediately. Trefriw!

Ben was standing on the bridge over the River Crafnant. It was the middle of the night, and a starry sky stretched over the rooftops of the town. An eerie silence reigned.

With a queasy feeling in his stomach, Ben set off once more, now walking up the high street. Lights were burning in some of the windows, but there were no other signs of life in any of the houses. Ben wondered if it was past midnight already, then remembered that this wasn't the real Trefriw.

He walked on, as somewhere deep in his mind an alarm bell began to ring.

Ben knew the town so well that every step he took felt like coming home. He turned a corner and went uphill, past the cemetery, until finally he was standing in front of his house. The walls glowed dimly in the moonlight, but the blue door and windows looked black. One light was on upstairs, in Ben's window.

Ben screwed up his courage and entered the house. As he stepped through the front door, it felt as if something had fallen into place. Like when a piece of a jigsaw fits neatly in its intended spot.

I'm home, he thought. *I'm home, and Dad is already here.* He got off work early today and came back with a dog-eared paperback someone had left on the bus. Tom could never bear to leave forgotten books behind.

Ben pulled the front door shut with a clunk. The house was warm and smelt of the detergent his mum used for the curtains. The lamp on the little table by the door was giving off a rosy light. Ben walked across the soft carpet to the stairs and began to climb them. He was so filled with hope and fear that he could hardly breathe. He wanted so, so much for his dad to be waiting for him upstairs. He hoped—no, he believed—it would come true, but at the same time the fear of walking into an empty bedroom was overwhelming.

His breathing grew shakier with every step until he was at the top of the stairs. His bedroom door was standing ajar, a thin sliver of light spilling out onto the landing.

Ben could hear two voices coming from the room. First, a child's voice, high and hesitant, and then, the deep, warm voice of a man.

"In a hole in the ground there lived a hobbit. Not a nasty, dirty, wet hole, filled with the ends of worms and an oozy smell, nor yet a dry, bare, sandy hole with nothing in it to sit down on or to eat: it was a hobbit-hole, and that means comfort."

Tears burned in Ben's eyes. *I'd forgotten the sound of his voice*, he thought. *I'd almost forgotten.*

He pushed the door open.

A World of Fog

Portia hurried after Gwil, running down the staircase that wound deep into the guts of the castle. "Why would Ben want to go to the Underworld?" she asked, leaping over a crumbling step.

"I think he wants to look for his father," Gwil answered.

"What?" Portia felt a stab of pain in her heart.

"He told me his father had passed away," Gwil said. They could see a faint light at the bottom of the stairs now, and Gwil quickened his pace. "And he was asking Tegid all sorts of questions about the Underworld. I think he wanted to know whether it's possible to bring someone back from there. And... Oh, no."

Gwil came up short at the bottom of the stairs. Portia pushed past him and into the cellar, desperately hoping to find Ben. But the room was empty, apart from the old, blackened door at the centre.

They were too late. Portia saw her backpack leaning against the door frame, confirming her worst fears.

"Oh, Ben," Portia groaned.

"He was so fascinated by the Door of the Dead," Gwil said ruefully. "When we came down here for the first time, he wanted to open it—I could feel it." He pressed a hand to his mouth, shaking his head. "I should've known he would try again," he lamented. "Who wouldn't want to go through a door if they knew a lost loved one was waiting on the other side?"

"Could he actually do it?" Portia asked. "Bring back his dad, I mean?"

Her heart ached in sympathy with Ben as she imagined the weight of the sorrow that had driven him through the door.

Gwil shook his head. "No. When the soul moves on, it doesn't just go to a different place; it also takes a different form. Some transformations cannot be reversed."

"So what will happen to Ben?" Portia pressed on. "When he finds his father, what then?"

"I don't know," admitted Gwil, wringing his hands. "Perhaps he'll find his way back, or perhaps he'll get lost. Or perhaps he won't even want to come back. The fogs of Annwn bring consolation, freeing the soul of all grief and regret. But they also make you forget that there's another world, and why you might want to return there."

Portia could feel icy cold trickling into her veins. "He'd become a Mistwalker," she said in a calm voice that was at odds with her feelings. "Like Rose."

Gwil nodded. He touched the lock with his fingertips. "I should've warned him."

Portia doubted that it would have made any difference at all. She understood why Ben had crossed over into the Underworld. And she didn't blame him for it, either. Gwil was right. Who wouldn't take that opportunity? At the same time, she couldn't just leave Ben. She wasn't going to let someone go into the fog alone again.

She gave the iron door ring a cautious tug, and to her surprise it moved. The door was ajar. She drew her hand back, hesitating for a moment. Out on the island, Rose and the others were fighting Arawn and his army. She had no idea how the battle was going. Had they defeated him, or had he managed to break through them to the World Door? She imagined returning to the Human World alone, knowing that Ben would be forever wandering the Underworld. She came to a decision.

"I'm going after him."

"What?" Gwil stared at her.

Portia handed him the hunting horn. "Go back and explain to Rose what happened. But only... Only once the battle is over, all right?" She reached for the door ring again. "I'm going to get Ben. I just have to."

"But it won't work," Gwil protested. "The fog..."

"I know what I'm getting myself into," she cut him off. She knew if Gwil continued, she would lose her nerve. "I won't let the fog drain me. Anyway, we don't have a choice. We can't let Ben down."

She looked Gwil straight in the eye, and he returned her gaze. Then he raised his hand, as if to hold her back, but let it fall to his side.

Portia gritted her teeth and pulled the door open. Fear burned in her chest. She had no idea what was happening outside, whether the fog had surged across the courtyard and into the fortress. Perhaps the Pale Tower had already sunk into oblivion, and this grim door in front of her was all that was left. She had to help Ben. But what if she ended up lost on the other side? Portia closed her eyes.

"Good luck," Gwil said, and with that Portia stepped through the doorway.

Portia pulled the Door of the Dead shut behind her, looked up and stumbled back against the closed door. Ahead of her lay a thick bank of fog, and it was coming closer, pale and hideous, a blind, groping mass. Everything in her shied away from touching it. There was something hungry about the white murk, which swelled and contracted like a grasping hand.

The fog will suffocate you. You will drown. You will never find your way home.

"Pull yourself together," Portia muttered to herself. Then she peeled away from the door, held her head up and walked straight into the maelstrom.

Portia took shallow breaths. The less fog made it into her lungs the better. She couldn't see her feet, but felt the soles of her boots touching water, and heard the splish-splash noise of her steps as she walked. The fog swirled all around her, clinging to her skin like damp cobwebs.

Just as it had earlier back in the castle, it felt like the fog was feeling and sensing her; its every touch sending shivers through her body. Her pulse fluttered with fear, her limbs grew heavier with every step, and she felt a knot of grief form in her stomach. Gwil had said that the fogs of Annwn relieved wandering souls of their misery. But for some reason, it was different for Portia. All the feelings of sorrow and distress that had ever been absorbed by the fog poured into her, filling her head and seeping through her skin. She felt like a sponge soaking up fear and grief. She took one step, and another, and then stopped short. Portia bent double, resting her hands on her knees, trying to make herself as small as she could, to protect herself. But she could feel her consciousness getting swept away in a torrent of strange feelings.

I don't want to leave yet, please, I don't want to leave. I wanted to tell her... I wish I had just one more...

When Portia came to her senses again, she was cowering on the ground, curled up in a ball. It was just too much. Feelings of longing, regret, guilt... They all rushed through her. She didn't want to take another step, she wanted to disappear, to dissolve. If her whole self was blown away like dandelion seeds on the wind, then at least all the pain would be over.

With her eyes tightly shut, she fumbled for her pocket and pulled out Robin's glass vial. When it was lying in her hand, she opened her eyes. What was left of the metamorphosis potion glowed like liquid amber inside.

Emotions hammered against the last of the walls protecting Portia's consciousness as she plucked the cork from the vial. She brought it to her mouth and let a drop of the smooth syrup-like substance fall onto her tongue. The taste of honey and resin exploded on her taste buds, and warmth spread through her body as if she was soaking in sunlight. It filled her completely, dissolving all her pain, every anxious thought, and turning it all into light. Her whole conscious-ness was focusing on this one sensation.

When Portia opened her eyes yet again, she saw the fog through the wolf's eyes. The strangers' emotions had receded and no longer plagued her. She shook her wolf body, and little droplets of fog flew from her coat. She sniffed the air, sorting through the smells of fog and water, until she identified a specific scent that she had already followed all the way from the mountains to the coast: *ink, human.* Ben. In her wolf shape, Portia was unable to smile, but the satisfaction of having found the trail filled her whole being. She picked up the vial with her teeth and loped onwards. The fog had no power over her now.

Where the Wild Things Are

Whlen the fog finally cleared, Portia found herself in a place that was a mirror image of Trefriw. It was the middle of the night, and an unearthly stillness lay over the town.

Portia trotted up the middle of the high street. Ben's trace was so clear that it could have been a luminous thread stretching ahead of her. It led her up a hill to where a narrow house stood at a bend in the road. A light was on in an upstairs window.

The wolf was leaving Portia as she reached the steps leading up to the front door. She could feel it going, and for a heartbeat she clung to her animal soul like a child to its mother's hand. The next moment, she was standing in front of the door as a girl, and the memory of the torrent of emotions she had experienced in the fog was churning inside her like a flash flood. She screwed her eyes shut, leant her forehead against the door, expecting to be overrun with feelings at any moment—but nothing happened. It seemed she had left the fog behind, at least for now.

Portia took a deep breath and glanced over her shoulder. The street, cemetery and church lay in darkness. For a brief moment it seemed a completely normal scene, until she spotted the first tendrils of fog creeping over the cemetery wall.

Portia reached instinctively for the little vial, but realized that only a few drops of potion were left at the bottom. Would it be enough to let her find Ben and get back to the door? She slid the bottle back into her jacket pocket. She would save the wolf's protection for the very last minute. She forced herself to turn her back on the fog and opened the door.

She entered a dimly lit hall, from which a flight of stairs led to the floor above. A clock hung on the wall, its hands frozen in time. Slowly, she climbed the stairs. The house gave her goosebumps. It seemed as if the walls might dissolve into smoke at the slightest touch. Was this just another memory? If so, it felt pretty convincing. Convincing enough to be mistaken for reality.

At the top of the stairs, she found herself facing a closed door. A strip of light was leaking out from underneath it. Portia could hear muted voices inside—a man saying something she couldn't make out, and a child laughing. Portia braced herself, and then pushed the door open a crack. Ben was right there. He was sitting on the floor with his back to the wall. Portia's heart almost stopped. He was as pale as a ghost, and the colours of his clothes were washed-out and dull. He was staring straight ahead of him.

Portia pushed the door all the way open with a trembling hand. Her mind was racing, trying to come up with a way to wake Ben from his stupor, when she noticed the other people in the room.

A bed stood against the left wall, with a man and a boy sitting on it. They were leaning against the wall too, and the man had his arm wrapped around the boy's shoulders as he read from a book in his lap.

Portia didn't need an explanation to understand what she was looking at. The man had to be Ben's father. And the little boy with the messy hair? That was Ben. A younger version of him, an illusion, a memory that had come to life. Except *life* wasn't quite the right word.

With a heavy heart, Portia stepped into the room and went over to where Ben was slumped on the floor. Without a word, she sat down next to him, close enough for their shoulders to touch.

The man and boy on the bed didn't seem to notice them at all. For each of them, only the other existed—as well as the story they were reading. A reading lamp on a shelf above the bed lit up a section of the wallpaper. Wait, no, it wasn't wallpaper. A whole forest sprawled across the bedroom wall with its slender tree trunks running behind the bed, and its branches and palm leaves reaching all the way up to the ceiling. Here and there, Portia could make out shadowy figures between trees. Were they wolves? No, these creatures were too tall and broad to be wolves. They had furry coats and pointy ears. They crept through the forest, peeking out from behind tree trunks and blinking their big lantern-like eyes.

The man pushed the book over to the boy, and the young Ben read aloud from it in a high but firm voice.

"All that the unsuspecting Bilbo saw that morning was an old man with a staff."

319

It was from *The Hobbit*, Portia realized, and couldn't help but smile.

"That was my dad's favourite book," said the Ben next to her.

His voice was so much more troubled than that of the little boy on the bed. He still wasn't looking at her. Portia took his hand in hers and hissed in shock when she saw the thin wisps of fog rising from his skin and through her fingers. He was disappearing, and she had nothing, no keepsake, to bring him back!

"Ben?" Her voice sounded much too thin. For one strange moment, she saw her mother, sitting on the windowsill with the same empty look in her eyes as Ben's. A cold blast of paralysing fear made her feel small and helpless.

For a moment, all she wanted to do was run away. Anything would be easier than facing Ben's blank face. But she couldn't do that. She couldn't leave him behind. Her heart would break and she would never be able to put it back together again.

She shifted around so she was crouching right in front of Ben. She took both of his hands in hers this time, and he flinched. It was only a weak reaction, but it was something and it gave her hope. He wasn't completely gone yet.

"Ben?" she repeated.

"He can't hear me," Ben said. He blinked, and the deep sorrow in his eyes made Portia's heart ache. "Is that really my dad?"

Portia would have given anything to say yes. Instead, unable to speak a word, she just shook her head.

Ben lowered his gaze, and then the rest of him seemed to sink down too. Something that must have kept him going for a long time had finally snapped. Portia opened her mouth to comfort him, but in the end she simply leant forward and gently pressed her forehead against Ben's. His hands were still in hers. She could sense Ben's inward struggle—how part of him wanted to disappear, but the rest of him didn't want to leave.

She risked a glance down and saw that colour was returning to Ben's skin and clothes—slowly though, like a sunrise in winter. When the first sob came she squeezed his hands, and finally—finally!—Ben responded, squeezing her fingers in return.

Ben cried silently, his whole body trembling. "He's not coming back," he sobbed, his voice breaking. Portia hugged him, holding him tight.

A Wolf's Heart

Ben followed Portia down the stairs on wobbly legs, away from the room with the forest on the wall, away from the rustling of book pages. He wouldn't have been able to do it alone, but with Portia at his side, he felt just strong enough. When he got to the bottom, he turned around—and realized that his dad hadn't followed him. A strip of light was still shining out under the door. It was strange, but somehow Ben took comfort in that sight. His dad would always be somewhere, and always be with Ben, or a part of him—even if the two people on the bed had been no more than an echo.

He wiped the tears from his face. How strange—he was exhausted, as if he had been running for miles and miles. At the same time, he felt lighter, as if a burden had been lifted. Why? He hadn't achieved what he set out to do. He wasn't going to bring his father back. He knew that now. But perhaps it was the knowledge that he had tried everything that helped him finally to let go.

Ben took a deep breath, then he turned his back to the stairs and walked to the door. Portia opened it, and Ben heard her gasp just as he reached her side.

Trefriw had been swallowed by fog. Or rather, it had disappeared as if it had never existed. Ben stared at the white-grey nothingness outside and steadied himself on the door frame. It was impossible to say whether there was solid ground waiting for them at the bottom of the stairs leading down from his front door—or an abyss.

"Do you know how to get back?" he asked weakly.

Portia pulled a small glass vial from her jacket pocket and clenched it in her fist. "I hope so." She looked at Ben and smiled, but he could see she was tense and tired. Probably exhausted from everything she had done for him. Ben hunched his shoulders. He wanted to apologize, wanted to tell her that he had never meant to put her in danger—but Portia was already pulling the cork from the vial. A golden liquid glittered at the bottom.

"Ready?" Portia asked.

Ben could only nod.

Portia brought the vial to her mouth and emptied it in one. Her eyes flashed with the same colour as the liquid in the vial, and in the next moment, she disappeared in a puff of golden-yellow smoke. When it cleared, a wolf with an ice-grey coat and black-tipped ears stood in Portia's place.

Ben stared in amazement, but the wolf didn't waste any time. It nudged Ben with its snout and then started down the steps, before stopping and turning to look at him expectantly. Ben shuddered, picked up the empty vial and followed the wolf that had once been Portia into the fog.

∾

323

Ben kept his hand firmly on the wolf's back for the entire journey. All around them, the fog swirled and danced, twisting itself into bizarre shapes, but the wolf loped determinedly onwards. Ben wished he could be as calm. On his way to the Trefriw in the fog, he had been fixated on finding his dad—but now, there was nothing to distract him from his surroundings.

The fog was as thick as ever, but now there were shadows moving in it—tall, slender silhouettes that seemed to approach before disappearing at the last minute. Ben felt as if he was being watched, but told himself it was just his imagination. That was until he noticed the face. It was floating just a few paces to his left, like a mask without a body. Startled, he stumbled into the wolf, which simply lowered its head and kept going. Ben dug his fingers into the wolf's fur and stared into the fog. The face stayed where it was, its dark, hollow eyes following him. With a great deal of effort, Ben managed to look away and fix his gaze on the fog ahead of them. Then he almost cried out. Another face emerged from the fog ahead of him, and then another behind it. Soon more and more of the shadowy figures could be seen. They were human, or at least human-like creatures, and they formed what looked like an honour guard on both sides of the pair. Their silhouettes were barely visible the fog, and yet their long, pale faces were following Ben.

He was ice-cold. Who or what were these figures? What were they waiting for? He moved closer to the wolf and felt that it was shivering. Alarmed, Ben looked down at his companion. The wolf took one more faltering step before coming to a stop and lowering its head to the ground. Ben quickly knelt at its side and put a hand on its head. The wolf gazed up at him with golden eyes, and then convulsed as if in great pain. Golden lightning flashed through its fur. Startled, Ben pulled his hand away. The wolf *glowed*, then dissolved into glittering smoke and transformed back into Portia.

No sooner had she returned to her human body than she sank to her knees. Ben caught hold of her just as the fog spirits fell on her like a swarm of furies. Portia let out a hoarse cry and curled up into a ball. Ben wrapped his arms around her protectively. The nightmare creatures glided around and over them like living shadows.

Ben thought his heart would stop from fear. He could feel Portia shaking like a leaf as she whimpered in his arms. Desperately, he looked around. There, between the wafting fog ghosts—a black shadow. *Please, let that be the door!*

More and more fog spirits surged towards them, eager to touch them. Ben gritted his teeth and got to his feet, pulling Portia up with him.

"Go away!" he yelled at the fog ghosts. They flew off, only to turn and fall on Portia again a moment later. With all her weight on his shoulder, Ben dragged them both towards where he thought the Door of the Dead should be. He forced himself to keep staring straight ahead. He could hear Portia moaning softly at his side, and that kept him going until at last he found what he was looking for. It *was* the door! Only a few steps stood between them and the way out now, and Ben almost believed that they were going to make it when one of the spirits burst out of the fog ahead and surged towards them. There was no time for caution now. Ben picked up Portia bodily and ran headlong towards the spirit. Just before they collided, he wrapped his free arm protectively about Portia's face—and jumped.

They crashed through the fog spirit like a fist through a wall of liquid cold. Ben slammed into the door with his shoulder, bursting it open, and together they tumbled through.

The Grey King

Portia and Ben landed on the floor of the cellar in a tangle of arms and legs. Portia felt a stabbing pain in her wrist as Ben fell on it, but he quickly jumped up to his feet, slammed the door shut and turned the key in the lock.

Portia stayed lying on the floor, weak and exhausted, her clothes sticking to her sweat-soaked body. When she closed her eyes, she could still feel it all—the touch of the fog, the strange emotions assaulting her mind... She buried her face in her hands.

"Portia?" She heard Ben asking in a timid voice, "Are you okay?"

All she could do was nod. *It's over*, she told herself. *It's all over.* She lowered her hands and looked at Ben. His hair was sticking up like a scarecrow's, and his face was still red and gleaming with sweat. Portia forced herself to get to her feet. "Never again," she croaked. "Never again will you catch me going anywhere near that fog."

Ben smiled sheepishly, then reached out to put a hand on her arm. "Thank you," he said. "Thank you for coming to get me."

In spite of everything, Portia smiled. "Don't worry about it."

That was as far as she got. From somewhere nearby came the sound of a stifled scream, before Gwil came rushing into the room and fell to his knees in front of them. He patted their heads and faces anxiously with his trembling hands, as if to make sure everything was in its right place, then he drew both of them into a tight hug.

"Ben!" he sobbed. Then he finally relaxed his grip, and beamed down at them with his arms about their shoulders.

"Mission accomplished," Portia joked in a weak voice. Gwil smoothed her curls. "You brave, brave girl," he said, squeezing her shoulder and glancing back towards the staircase leading up to the keep.

Portia frowned. "Gwil? What's going on?" She felt a cold hand grip her heart. "What's happening up there?"

"Arawn, he..." Gwil wiped his forehead. "He made it into the tower. The rune stones didn't stop him. He was too strong."

"What about Rose? And Robin and Titania?" Ben asked anxiously.

"Alive," Gwil replied. "They're defending the door. Or at least they were when I left them. It doesn't look good."

Portia's mouth was dry as dust. She glanced at Ben, and saw he looked almost as pale as he had in Annwn.

Gwil grimaced. "Rose told me to come down here and hide. But if the Grey King makes it into Faerie, then... then..." He clapped a hand to his mouth.

Ben grabbed Gwil's sleeve. "But we have to help them!" He twisted his fingers into Gwil's robe. "We could carve new runes—you've still got your knife, after all!"

Carve them into what? Portia thought. She desperately racked her brains for another plan. Then her gaze fell on the key, still in the lock of the Door of the Dead. She remembered something that Rose had said—that Arawn was obsessed with conquering one world after another. If he took over Faerie, what next? Wouldn't he want to move on to the next world, the Human World? But for that, he would need a key.

Portia wet her lips. *Once Arawn gets wind of that key of yours, he'll hunt you down without mercy.* That was what Titania had said. What was more important to Arawn? To seize a single open door? Or a key that could open the way to all the worlds?

"We're just not powerful enough, Ben," Gwil was saying. "If even Titania can't stop him, our runes would be as much use as throwing a handful of flower petals."

"But we've got to do something," Ben exclaimed desperately.

"I've got an idea." Portia turned around to face both of them. "Ben, do you still have the vial of metamorphosis potion?"

With a frown, he pulled it out from his jacket pocket. "But it's empty."

"I know." She took the vial from him and explained her plan.

Gwil climbed the stairs so quickly that Portia struggled to keep up. Moon-moths glowed on the walls like veins of quartz in granite.

"When Meralyn finds out I let you take a risk this big, she'll have my guts for garters," Gwil predicted. Portia remembered the combative gleam in Meralyn's eyes though. She doubted the seamstress would object to their plan. Ben had given her the key, and she had it clutched in her fist now. Robin's vial was in her jacket pocket. Her plan was as simple as it was crazy.

They had nearly reached the top of the staircase when a tremor shook the whole castle. The walls groaned, and dust trickled from the ceiling. Ben and Portia cowered, and Gwil's arms shot up to protect his head.

"Sweet spirits," he gasped.

Portia's heart hammered in her chest, but she urged the salamander on. "Keep going, Gwil!"

Gwil shook his head but kept on climbing. As they walked the sounds of battle grew louder—the clash of weapons, the crackling of rune magic, the growling and howling of a whole pack of hounds. Up above, the staircase flickered with blue light. Portia was so nervous she could hardly breathe. She could feel the teeth of the key biting into her sweaty hand.

"Oh," Gwil muttered under his breath as he raced up the last few steps. Portia followed close behind, and together they burst out into the entrance hall of the keep.

It was utter chaos. The hall was filled with thick, roiling clouds of fog that surged and broke against the walls and ceiling.

Rose stood amid the storm, assailed from all sides. There were fog hounds among her attackers of course, but other more monstrous creatures too—fog serpents with horned

dragon heads, demonic birds with cruel beaks gaping wide...
Rose's rune staff cut through them like a blade through soft
butter, but no sooner had she fought off one foe than the
next fell on her. Portia scoured the battlefield for Rose's
companions and saw Titania, conjuring a hedge of stone
thorns from the ground with one hand while she wielded
a crackling, sparking sword of light and air with the other.
Fog warriors in tattered cloaks tried desperately to get past
the thorn hedge to the World Door, but the Fairy Queen
held them off—until one of them ducked underneath her
slashing blade and thrust his curved knife into her side.

No!

Gwil cried out and Portia spun around to see what looked
like a tiny bolt of red lightning flashing low through the fog
to launch itself at Rose's attackers, its teeth bared.

Robin! Portia's heart almost stopped. The fox ripped one
of the fog hounds in two, but then a clawed hand shot out
of the fog to grab him by the throat.

"No!" Portia screamed, and then recoiled as a creature
from a nightmare stepped out of the fog. It was Arawn
himself. A bare stag's skull gleamed under the hood of his
long grey cloak. The prongs of his antlers glowed with ghostly
light. He was tall—taller than a normal human man—and
his tattered garments formed a halo of smoke and shadows
around his figure. He lifted the fox's body up in the air as if
it were weightless. Robin squirmed and kicked, but Arawn
only tightened his grip around his neck.

"HEY!" Portia was shocked by the sound of her own
voice. Panic churned in her stomach, but somehow she

managed to take a step forward, holding the key in her fingertips.

Don't drop it, she told herself. *Don't drop it.*

"ARAWN!"

The Grey King turned around to face her. Red lights glowed in the dark empty sockets of the stag's skull.

Portia had no idea where she found the courage to keep going. "Arawn!" she cried. She was sick with fear, but still she managed to raise her arm and hold the key up high. "Is this what you're looking for?"

"Portia..." She heard Gwil whisper close to her ear. Arawn was staring straight at her, his eyes glowing. He relaxed his grip and let the fox fall to the ground. Then Arawn launched himself at Portia.

Never in her life had Portia run so fast. She hurtled down the stairs to the cellar, sure she was going to trip at any moment. *Don't think, don't think*, she urged herself. If only she could have shifted to her wolf form!

Arawn was breathing down her neck. She could sense his presence like a blast of freezing air on her back. Finally—the last steps! Portia leapt down and came skidding to a halt on the stone floor of the cellar. Something soft curled around her ankle, but she tore herself away, sprinted across the room to the Door of the Dead, put the key into the lock and looked anxiously over her shoulder.

Fog came surging down the stairs and flooded across the cellar floor. Arawn wasn't far behind. As he came down the steps, it looked for a moment as if his white skull were floating in the darkness. Then he stepped into the cellar, his cloak billowing around him like steel-grey wings. Portia spun around, pulled the door open, took the key from its lock and stepped underneath the arch of the door. Her breath was coming in short, panicky gasps. She had never wanted to be this close to Annwn ever again. But she had to follow through now.

She pulled the vial from her jacket pocket, and held it in her hand next to the key, clenching her fist around both, so that only the key's silver teeth were visible above her thumb. The metal shimmered like crystal in the rippling light of the moon-moths.

Please, don't let me mess up now.

She drew her arm back, but at the same moment she felt something slap painfully against her ankle and a tendril of fog coiled around her foot like the end of a whip. The fog lasso yanked Portia's leg backwards, but she gritted her teeth and managed to stay on her feet. Then she let the key slip back into her fist. She held it tight and hurled the vial through the doorway, into the dark realm of the dead. The glass bottle glinted silver in the light of the moon-moths before it disappeared into the fog. Portia had barely let go of the fake "key", when another tendril lashed around her ankle and pulled her off her feet. She fell headlong to the cellar floor, her chin jarring on the stone, and lifted her head to see fog streaming out of the Door of the Dead, groping towards her like a giant hand. She knew what it wanted—to drag her back through the doorway to Annwn, back to that quagmire of sorrow and despair. Portia curled up with her arms over her head as the two fog whips tightened their grip on her legs and dragged her across the floor. Arawn strode past her, his cloak billowing, and through the doorway into Annwn. Two more fog tendrils curled around Portia's wrists, pinning her down as white clouds poured through the doorway and surged towards her, but she could still see Arawn. His dark cloaked form cut through the fog of his own world as he hurried after the key he so desired. Any second now he would find out what she had really thrown through the doorway. Portia opened her mouth, even though it meant breathing in the fog surrounding her.

"Now!" she yelled, and the Door of the Dead slammed shut behind Arawn with a bang. Ben leapt out from his hiding place behind the stone archway and leant against the wood with both hands.

"The key!" he called. Portia threw it towards him, sending it skittering across the floor. For one terrible moment, she thought it was going to bounce past Ben, but he stuck out a foot just in time and trapped the key under it. Then, quick as a flash, he picked it up, shoved it into the lock and turned it. The fog that had surged through the door only moments before now drew back, rushing down the wood and disappearing into the floor in an instant. The tendrils holding Portia's legs writhed and struggled, before breaking apart and evaporating.

Portia picked herself up and rushed over to Ben.

"Lock it again," she urged him. Ben turned the key once more just as something slammed against the other side of the door with the force of a battering ram. Ben and Portia leapt back, startled. The cellar was filled with the sound of splintering wood and groaning metal, and the key... the key was still in the lock!

Portia cried out in alarm, but Ben jumped forward and snatched the key from the keyhole. He had hardly done so when the door shuddered under the impact of another mighty blow. The moon-moths on the cellar walls took flight and fluttered about in alarm. Portia took Ben's hand, and together they backed slowly away. Another bang. The door was shaking in its hinges, but it was holding firm. It was holding firm! Just as Portia was letting out a sigh of relief, they heard a blood-curdling scream coming from the other side of the door. All the hair on her arms stood on end as Arawn raged against the closing of the border of his world.

"Let's get out of here," Ben croaked, but still they stood rooted to the spot, spellbound by Arawn's wordless screams. Fingers scratched and tore at the unyielding wood, then two fists pounded angrily against it. Arawn screamed and screamed. Not in anger, but despair. Portia felt a lump in her throat, and was overcome by the feeling that they had done something terrible. The fog of Annwn that had almost buried her beneath the emotions of thousands upon thousands of souls—Arawn had no escape from it now.

He's feeling all of it, Portia thought, horrified. *Just like I did.* Had that been why he'd left his world in the first place?

Another blow slammed against the door, hard enough to send tremors through the archway and the floor. Dust and mortar trickled from the walls. For one wild moment, Portia felt an urge to set Arawn free. This time, it was Ben who grabbed Portia's hand, and pulled her towards the stairs. They didn't turn their backs on the door until they reached the bottom step. Arawn's wailing followed them far up the gloomy stairwell.

◡ BEN ◡

"Damn it, damn it, damn it," Portia muttered under her breath as they climbed the stairs. Ben knew how she felt. He would have added a couple of "damn its" of his own if he hadn't been so out of breath. The sound of Arawn's desperate pounding on the door pursued them as they went, making the walls shake and chilling Ben to the marrow. When another piercing scream echoed up the stairs, Portia pressed her hands to her ears, but kept scrambling upwards. On the next landing they came across Rose rushing in the opposite direction, surrounded by a cloud of moon-moths, with her rune staff in hand. She cleared the final two steps in a single bound and grabbed Portia by the shoulders. "Where the hell have you two been?"

"I'll tell you later!" Portia pleaded, just as another scream hit their ears. Rose's eyes widened, then she nodded.

"Very well. Hurry up then," she said, waving Portia and Ben past her up the stairs.

The entrance hall was a mess. Chunks of rock had been ripped from the castle walls and lay broken on the floor. The floor itself had been torn open too, pulled up into rock splinters that loomed overhead like the walls of a stockade.

Rose's companions in arms were gathered at the back of the hall. Gwil was leaning over Robin, who was crouched on the floor in his human shape. Titania stood further off, holding a hand to her side and staring up at something. Ben followed her gaze and saw the last remnants of fog swirl along the ceiling and disappear between the ancient wooden boards. Arawn's magic had been broken.

Gwil noticed them at last, and let out a cry of joy before running to meet them.

"Did you manage to lock him in?" he asked. "Did it really work?"

"It did," Ben answered. When he saw the happiness spreading over Gwil's face, he felt prouder than he ever had before.

Rose stared at them in amazement, but before she could ask any more questions, Robin came hobbling over. He looked at Portia as if he had no doubt that the trap for Arawn had been her idea. "Crazy Humangirl," he said, but his voice was warm and full of affection. "Are you okay?"

"Yes," she replied, her voice hoarse. "But please let's get out of here now."

"With pleasure," Robin said. There was a gash running across his forehead. "Rose?"

Gwil put an arm around Ben's shoulder and nodded towards the border between the worlds.

"Shall we?"

Sunlight was streaming through the doorway. The blue skies of Faerie awaited them on the other side. Portia went over to Ben's side and nudged him gently with her elbow. They exchanged a look, and Ben felt the bond that their shared adventure had forged between them.

"Let's get out of here," he said, and smiled.

Farewell to Faerie

❧ PORTIA ❧

The fairies' feast of celebration lasted into the small hours. That was no surprise—there was a lot to celebrate after all. Titania's glorious triumph over the Grey King for a start. (She conveniently neglected to mention the part the Humans played in their victory.) The Fairy Queen had returned appearing every inch the heroic, benevolent ruler, battered but undefeated, and so touched by the courage of her salamander subjects that she had graciously decided to lift the spell on their people.

Titania's talent for self-promotion was truly impressive.

The last guests had just dragged themselves off to a quiet spot to get some rest when the first rays of sunlight lit up the horizon. A soft blue dawn stole across Moon Lake, where the celebrations had once again been held. Portia sat at the end of the jetty sticking out into the lake, her legs dangling over the edge. The wooden boards around her were strewn with burned-out lanterns, and white flower petals floated on the surface of the water below.

There were probably still a few salamanders stumbling merrily about in the woods above, but down here the hollow of the lake was dead quiet. *Not long till Peaseblossom or Cobweb shows up to take us to the Human Door*, Portia thought. The Queen had taken the key from Ben a long while ago.

Portia felt someone walking on the jetty and turned around to see Ben coming towards her with a steaming mug in each hand. He sat down next to her and offered her one. "Tea?"

"Thank you." She took the mug, breathing in the scent of summer herbs and lemon balm.

"We're going home today," she said, surprised by the lack of excitement in her voice.

"Yes," Ben said. "Have you talked to Robin?"

"No," she replied. Robin had disappeared the night before, shortly after Titania had lifted the spell on the salamanders. The celebrations must have been hard to take—the salamanders' joy rubbing salt in the wound of his own banishment. Portia had hoped their victory might convince Titania to change her mind. She should have known better. Titania had already kept her part of the bargain and released the salamanders from their servitude despite her misgivings. Now she was adamant that Robin must keep his pledge too, and submit to being banished for ever from Faerie. It was a small but spiteful consolation for the concession Portia had wrenched from her.

"Look!" Ben held up a slim package made of colourful fabric. "A gift from Meralyn." He opened it to reveal a page of parchment inside.

Portia raised an eyebrow. "Is that what I think it is?"

"Oh, yes."

Portia smiled. Now that Meralyn was free, it seemed she no longer cared a jot about Titania's orders.

"Gwil's leaving today too," Ben said after a while.

"Leaving? Where's he going?" Portia asked surprised.

"World's End. He wants to look for Tegid. He thinks that if we could bring Rose back, then there must be a chance for Tegid too."

Portia had never met Tegid, but she could tell Ben had been deeply affected by the loss of the librarian to the fog. "I'll keep my fingers crossed for him."

"Me too," whispered Ben.

The sky above was brightening as the sun rose over the valleys in the east. The leaves of the oak trees rustled in the gentle breeze. This was how Portia wanted to remember Moon Lake—still and peaceful.

Once they crossed the border, there would be no coming back. The thought filled Portia with a strange sadness. The sensible part of her was anxious to get back to their world as soon as possible. She was worried—about Bramble and her mother. And yet, somewhere deep inside, Portia couldn't help but wonder what there was left to discover in Faerie. That part of her wanted to choose a different path, wanted to return to the mountains beyond Bryngolau, or venture deeper into the woods of the birds' realm, wanted to explore the other regions of this world, and find new borders to cross. She could do it all standing on her own two feet. Or her own four paws.

Portia blew on the tea before taking a cautious sip.

"It feels weird, doesn't it," Ben said. "To be leaving, I mean."

"Yep," Portia replied as she took another sip. Ben set his mug down on the jetty, took off his boots and dangled his feet in the water. They sat side by side and looked out across the lake as flower petals bobbed about their ankles.

"It's a dangerous business, going out of your door," muttered Ben under his breath.

Portia couldn't help but smile. Perhaps she wasn't the only one in two minds about their farewell to Faerie.

"You step into the road," she said, continuing the quotation from *The Lord of the Rings*, "and if you don't keep your feet, there is no knowing where you might be swept off to."

Ben grinned. They clinked mugs and waited for the dawn to break.

✺ BEN ✺

It was already afternoon when they reached the Human Door: Ben, Portia, Rose and Robin, escorted by Peaseblossom and Cobweb. The latter had been entrusted with the key, and flashed glares of warning at anyone who dared look at it for too long. When she opened the door, Peaseblossom immediately rushed to her side and craned her neck to peer through to the other world. Cobweb sighed and yanked the other fairy back by her dress, then impatiently ushered Rose and the others through, "Come along now. Chop, chop!"

"You always did have such charm," said Robin drily as he passed.

"Enjoy your banishment," Cobweb shot back.

They were barely through the doorway before it slammed shut behind them with a bang. If a full stop could make a noise, that is what it would sound like.

Ben sighed with relief. On the other side of the forest, just a few miles away, was the real Trefriw. It was hard to believe.

"Well, that's that," Robin said calmly.

Rose shot him a sorrowful look. "I'm so sorry, Robin."

He shrugged, but still couldn't seem to stop staring at the door. Neither could Portia, who reached out her hand to rest it on the door handle once more.

"What will you do now?" she asked.

"Get a drink somewhere. Find an empty house to sleep in. It's not like I'm a total stranger in this world."

Ben tapped Portia on the shoulder. When she turned around, he pulled Meralyn's package from his pocket and raised a questioning eyebrow. Portia smiled and gave him a quick nod in return.

"Titania doesn't go around banishing just anybody. I'll simply take it as an honour," Robin said.

"Oh, don't be so dramatic," Portia said.

Robin spun around with a look of irritation on his face and Rose seemed taken aback too, until Ben unwrapped the package and produced the sheet of parchment.

"Is that...?" Rose began.

"It tells you how to make a key," Ben confirmed. "A present from Meralyn. She copied the instructions."

Rose's eyes widened, but Robin looked down blankly at the parchment.

Ben offered him the sheet. "If you like, we can make another key right away. Then you can go back to your world. Titania doesn't have to know."

Robin thought for a moment, then shook his head. "Thank you, but I think this door is closed to me for ever."

"Robin..." Rose began, but he only shrugged dismissively.

"Bryngolau didn't feel like home any more anyway," he said. "Even Oberon has left. Perhaps it was time for me to move on."

"But where will you go?" Portia asked. "You don't like the Human World, after all."

For the first time since they had returned from the Pale Tower, a smile crept over Robin's face. "There are other worlds."

"Then you'll still need the instructions," Rose said, giving Ben a pointed look. He understood and handed Robin the parchment.

Robin frowned. "Shouldn't we make another copy?"

Rose shook her head. "I'd rather not."

"Too great a temptation for your beloved?" Robin asked.

"For both of us," Rose replied.

He grinned, folded up the parchment and thrust it into his pocket.

"I think that may be wise," he said. "You were never quite right for this magic-less world either."

Rose clasped his hand in hers, but Robin lifted her hand to his lips and planted a light kiss on its back. Then he pulled a glass vial from his waistcoat pocket. Portia's ears pricked up.

344

"Valerian, lavender, twilight herb and a few other bits and pieces," Robin said.

"Oblivion powder?" Rose asked.

He nodded. "It won't work as well here as it would work in my... in Faerie. But it should be enough to make people forget the days you were gone."

"Good idea," Portia said. But had she been hoping there would be a different potion in the vial?

Robin shrugged. "It'll make life easier." He turned to Rose again, and this time, his smile seemed almost mischievous. "You might want to consider giving Bramble a dose."

Rose snorted and pocketed the vial. "Take care of yourself, you old troublemaker."

"Likewise." He turned to Portia. They looked straight into each other's eyes, and a small crease appeared between his eyebrows. He stepped closer, cocked his head thoughtfully and smiled. "It's been a pleasure."

"You could say that," Portia answered with a laugh, but Ben thought he could hear a hint of sadness in her laughter. Then Robin gave a quick bow, and Portia, her eyes sparkling with mirth, replied by performing an exaggerated but very elegant curtsy.

Robin nodded to Ben and touched two fingers to his forehead in a farewell salute. Then he put the parchment between his teeth and walked away without another word. For a moment Ben was dazzled by a ray of sunshine breaking through the trees that made him blink. When he opened his eyes again, Robin had gone. In his place there was a fox, trotting swiftly away from them. For a moment, his coat flickered like a guttering flame between the trees, then he slipped behind a rock and was gone.

The Nissan was still waiting at the end of the track where they had left it. Rose hurriedly swept the fallen leaves from the windscreen before leaping into the driver's seat and driving them all back to Afallon. No sooner had she pulled up next to the garden wall than Rose jumped out, leaving the keys in the ignition. She pushed open the gate and ran towards the house with Ben and Portia close behind. The door was unlocked, and by the time Ben had stepped into the hall, Rose was already at the bottom of the stairs.

"Bramble!" she called. No answer. She went to the kitchen while Portia checked the living room.

"Bramble?"

Ben walked down the hall, a terrible suspicion forming in his mind. What if this wasn't the real Afallon? What if they had crossed the wrong border and were now in Annwn? The World of the Dead had been deserted and still too, just like this. He imagined going home to find his mother gone, as if the earth had swallowed her up. *Rubbish*, he told himself, but still the thought gave him goosebumps.

Rose and Portia came back into the hall at the same time. "She's not here!" Portia said, clearly worried. Ben buried his face in his hands, but Rose laid a comforting hand on his shoulder. She looked towards the living-room door.

"I know where she is."

❧

346

Rose strode ahead of them, across the garden, past the hydrangea bushes and into the orchard. Beyond the apple trees they could see the white wall of the writing shed gleaming in the sunlight. Ben dearly hoped that Rose had guessed right.

The door was open, and as they drew closer, they were able to see inside. Bramble was sitting at Rose's desk, resting her head in her hands.

Rose cupped her hands round her mouth like a megaphone and shouted again. "Bramble!"

Bramble started and leapt to her feet, knocking a vase off the table that tumbled to the floor and smashed to pieces. Rose rushed towards her, but Ben didn't see her leaping up the steps and into the shed, because a bolt of dog-shaped lightning hit him in the side.

Marlowe barked joyfully and jumped up at Portia before excitedly circling the two children with his tail wagging.

"Hello there, boy," said Portia, squatting down to greet the dog, who licked her face all over in welcome.

"Gross!" Ben exclaimed, but Portia just laughed and wrapped her arms around Marlowe.

"Good boy," she said, ruffling his fur.

We're back, Ben thought, still numb with disbelief. *We really made it back!*

He turned around. Inside the writing shed, Rose and Bramble were hugging each other tightly, and Ben was pretty sure that they wouldn't be letting go any time soon.

London

ꞌ◌ PORTIA ◌ꞌ

Portia's autumn half-term began with a rain shower, but as night fell over London, the clouds cleared, leaving only the scent of wet leaves in the air. A black starry sky arched above the little park across the street from her house, and the dim yellow light from the lamp posts shone in circles on the pavement.

The fairy lights she had hung on her bedroom wall twinkled, surrounding maps of the world and Middle Earth. Piles of books sat on a sideboard below, next to a little rubber plant with drooping leaves.

Portia put a striped sweater in her suitcase. She had been packing and repacking since after dinner. There was always something missing or just too much. *Just make sure you don't forget your train ticket*, she told herself for the umpteenth time, and felt a tingle of excitement in her stomach.

Tomorrow. Tomorrow she was taking the train back to Afallon to celebrate Halloween with Ben, Rose and Bramble. She pictured the glowing pumpkin lantern that would be sitting on the garden wall to welcome her, and smiled. Then she shut the suitcase and put it on the floor.

Her red travel diary was lying open on her desk. Ben had given it to her shortly before her departure from Wales, without telling her what was inside. She had waited until she got back home before opening it and finding Ben's drawings inside. Moon-moths in flight, Gwil's face, the bookshelves in World's End, a toad with dragonfly wings, and many more. All the Otherworld was hidden between the pages of a tatty old notebook.

Portia picked up the diary and went over to the window. By the glow of a street light she flipped to the final page, from which the face of a wolf looked up at her with golden eyes. She traced the lines of the drawing with the tip of her finger.

Their adventure in the Otherworld had lasted twelve days. In the Human World only five days had passed, but that was enough for them to have been reported missing, and for their families and friends to have been thrown into turmoil. Luckily, Robin's oblivion powder had allowed the memories of the drama to fade and everyday life to return. At least for those who hadn't crossed over to Faerie.

Portia closed the notebook and smoothed out a wrinkle in the cover. Why was she so excited? She was only going to Wales, after all. The door to the Otherworld was now closed. But that shouldn't matter. It would be enough to sit in the conservatory at Afallon, drinking milky tea and making up stories for Ben to draw. The blank sketchbook she had bought for him was waiting in her suitcase.

Portia was just about to turn away from the window and put the notebook in her backpack when she noticed something moving in the park outside.

There! She leant her forehead against the glass. There was some rustling in a bush, and then a fox slid between the iron railings and onto the pavement. Portia clutched the diary tight to her chest. The fox trotted along by the railings with its head held low, until it reached a pool of light under the lamp post. Then it stopped and lifted its head. Portia held her breath. There were lots of foxes in London. Thousands of them. You saw them all the time once it got dark.

Portia couldn't be sure whether the shadow cast by the street light was that of a fox, or a man. *It can't be him*, she told herself. *You just wish it was.*

Down in the street below, the fox's ears twitched. Then he glanced up at Portia's window, and ran off into the night.

WELSH WORDS AND PHRASES

Yr Adar	The Birds
Ap	Son of
Caethiwa!	Lock them up!
Croeso	Welcome
Crwydriadgoch	Wretched red fleabag (approximately)
Damio	Damn
Ferch	Daughter of
Mwyalchod	Blackbird
Salamandrau	Salamanders
Swirne saff	Safe travels

William IV, Mrs, Jordan,
and the Family They Made

Daniel A. Willis

1

Dublin City Council
Comhairle Cathrach Bhaile Átha Cliath

Our ref: DB/P-1
Your ref: 3293709
Your Recal ref: RQ79288
Due: 1/9/2017

Dublin City Public Libraries, Information and Cultural Heritage Services
Leabharlanna Poiblí Chathair Bhaile Átha Cliath, Seirbhísí Eolais agus Oidhreachta Cultúrtha
E. email.publiclibraries@dublincity.ie

www.dublincitypubliclibraries.ie

with compliments
le dea-mhéin

TABLE OF CONTENTS

Preface

In recent decades, we have seen a great loosening of the restrictions against whom a member of the Royal Family may marry. All of the children of our current Queen have married, with permission, commoners, some more than once. This is a relatively recent change in attitude. It was only as recently as the children of the King George V, that marriage to a foreign Princess was not required for a son of the King. Imagine for a moment if this more relaxed attitude had been in effect in 1790, and William, Duke of Clarence, third son of King George III, were allowed to marry the woman with whom he chose to live in domestic bliss. Had this happened, the lady we currently call Queen Elizabeth II, would be merely Mrs. Philip Mountbatten, and the Sovereign would be the relatively unknown man now known as Patrick Elborough.

But who is Patrick Elborough you may ask? He is the heir-general, albeit through an illegitimate line, of King William IV and his 20-year paramour, Dorothea Bland (aka Mrs. Jordan, the actress). But Mr. Elborough is only one of roughly 900 people who descend from this union of Prince and Actress. This book will seek to introduce the reader to the rest of them.

Other prominent figures who will appear in these pages include the current Prime Minister, David Cameron; television presenter, Adam Hart-Davis; his literarily well-known father, Sir Rupert; a recent Grand Master of the Sovereign Order of Malta as well as the current Grand Prior of England; race-car driver Johnny (7th Marquess of) Bute; and a flurry of statesman, nobles, and maybe even a royal or two.

Every effort has been made to verify every fact mentioned in this book. There will be, without a doubt, errors. They are the nature of the beast when covering large numbers of people and more than 200 years of a family. For these, please accept my apologies at this time.

Daniel Willis
Denver, Colorado
March, 2011

Chapter 1: King William IV

On August 21, 1765, the world was on the brink of great change. The Holy Roman Emperor, husband of the remarkable Empress Maria Theresa, had died a few days previously. Mozart was changing the way the world viewed music. And the British parliament was about to pass the Stamp Act on the American Colonies, which proved to be the catalyst for the movement that culminated in the War of American Independence.

It was into this world that Britain's Queen Charlotte, with little fanfare, was delivered of a third healthy son, to be named William Henry. By this point, George III already had his "heir and a spare" in his older boys, George (later King George IV) and Frederick (later Duke of York), so while a third son was no less welcome, he was also not nearly as

7

prized as the elder two. In time, the King and Queen would become the parents of fifteen children, all but two of whom would survive to adulthood.

Prince William's early childhood was spent in almost constant companionship with his elder brothers at Kew House, some eleven miles up the Thames from Westminster. In 1772, the elder boys were given establishments of their own so William's education took place with his next younger brother, Edward (later Duke of Kent and father of Queen Victoria). Dr. Majendie, a Hugenot descendant from Exeter, had originally been given the job of governor for all of the young princes, but when they were separated, he remained with William and Edward. Majendie was assisted by General Bude, a Dutchman whose rank derived from military experience in the offices of high command rather than on the battlefield proper.

King George lived a rather austere life, especially when compared to the opulent courts of Versailles, Madrid, or Vienna. He expected the same frugality of his children. Meals were often simple but nourishing and outdoor exercise was plentiful. Discipline was the order of the day. The children were usually not permitted to sit in their parents' presence, and outfits were to be meticulously cared for, as

8

was their own personal appearance. In a day when children of the upper crust were generally kept out of sight of their parents, King George and Queen Charlotte actually gave a lot of attention to their children, and seem to have genuinely enjoyed their company, at least while they were young.

As Prince William grew, a problem developed: what to do with him. The eldest son's path in life was destined from birth, the second son typically was given over to the military, but a surviving third son was something of an anomaly in the Royal Family. King George himself had two younger brothers, but was very disappointed in both and felt theirs were wasted lives. Now he was faced with finding things to occupy six sons as Edward was followed by Ernest, Augustus and Adolphus. William was his first foray into this uncharted water of healthy younger sons. As it had already been determined that Frederick would pursue a career in the Army, William was given over to the Navy. This turned out to be a splendid match as William's temperament was well suited for a life at sea.

Midshipman William Guelph, as he preferred to be called, took his name from the ancient House to which his family belonged before their acquisition of Brunswick, and later Hanover, centuries earlier. It was a rather amazing piece of history that allowed the Hanovers to arrive at the British Throne at all. During the reign of the Tudors in the 16th century, many a battle was fought over the question of religion. It was, of course, Henry VIII, who had established the Church of England, and his children who battled royally over whether it should be a Catholic Church or a Protestant one. The Anglican form of Protestantism won out in the end and was pretty firmly established by the time James II ascended the Throne in 1685. However, James was married to the very Catholic Maria of Modena, and his heirs were being brought up as Catholics.

The parliament of the day was determined the Realm would remain Protestant, and so invited the King's son-in-law, the Prince of Orange, to overthrow James in the name of his wife Mary, who was James' eldest daughter by his first, and more importantly, Protestant, wife, Anne Hyde. The Prince staged what is remembered to history as the Glorious Revolution of 1688, placing himself and his wife jointly on the Throne as King William III and Queen Mary II. It was during William's reign that parliament passed the Act of Settlement, which established that the Kingdom would be ruled by a non-Catholic Sovereign forevermore. Under the new law, the Crown passed from William (whose wife Mary had predeceased him) to Anne, Mary's younger sister. Upon Queen Anne's death in 1714, dozens of Catholics were passed over to find a religiously appropriate heir.

Ultimately the Crown went to the descendants of James I's youngest daughter, Queen Elizabeth of Bohemia, whose youngest surviving daughter, Sophia, was married to the Elector of Hanover. The Electress Sophia missed becoming Queen herself by dying a mere two weeks before Queen Anne. Therefore, it was Sophia's eldest son who ascended the British Throne, as King George I, and was the great-grandfather of George III.

By the time Prince William joined the Navy in 1779, a mere lad of not quite fourteen, the Hanovers had successfully ruled the Kingdom for 65 years and crushed the last dregs of support for the Catholic descendants of King James II (called Jacobites). The pressing military matter of the day was the War of American Independence, still being waged across the Atlantic. The Prince's first taste of Navy life was aboard the *HMS Prince George*, a 98-gun warship, which joined the battle in America.

Much of William's naval career was spent carrying out the more mundane day-to-day tasks necessary to maintaining a ship at sea. He took to these chores with delight and insisted on being treated as any other midshipman and not as a Prince. However, being the son of the King, this could be accomplished only to a degree. Being as young as he was, William continued to have a tutor, even on shipboard. He was accompanied at sea by Rev. Henry Majendie, the son of his childhood governor at Kew House.

Once arriving at America, William's ship was briefly docked at New York, then still in the hands of loyalists. There were reports that Gen. George Washington was plotting to kidnap the Prince, and offer to make him King of a newly independent country. Looking at the situation with the 20/20 vision that hindsight offers, it seems more likely this plan was suggested to Washington by some of his officers, but that it was rejected. Just as well, as it would have been out of character for William to even entertain such a conspiratorial notion.

After a year and a half of two-to-three month cruises, broken up by brief visits to Kew, Prince William found himself at Windsor in time for the Christmas holidays of 1780. It had been during his time at sea that one of the greatest trials that a man faces hit full force: puberty. Now being on land, and no doubt prompted by his womanizing elder brothers, William had the opportunity to discover the opposite sex. For the next several years, the Prince would fall in and out of love with women of varying degrees of propriety, but none of which came close to the standards to be an appropriate wife. Therefore, William lived two love lives, one of properly conducted courtly pursuit, without capture, of nice girls and another of downright debauchery, reserved for the prostitutes of various ports-of-call. It became all too apparent to the King that William was following in the steps of his elder brothers in his love of sex, so it was decided to keep William at sea as much as possible.

For all of this time at sea, and not having seen much action during the war with the United States, William was not advancing in rank very fast. The King, in his efforts to control the amount of time William was on land, purposely held him back. This finally came to a head in 1790, when William demanded, unsuccessfully, his own command and ultimately resigned from the Navy, ironically being promoted to Rear-Admiral upon his retirement.

Having been created the Duke of Clarence the year previously, William now began living a life of courts and balls, along with many other members of his family. This included incursions into Parliament, usually defending the payment of the Prince of Wales's ever increasing debts.

13

William's financial issues were never as severe as his eldest brother's, but he lived in debt much of his single life. He was a very generous man and insisted on his guests always being as comfortable as possible. This comfort usually came at a price higher than his stipend from Parliament allowed.

This fateful winter of 1789-90 was momentous for another reason. It was the season William met the celebrated actress, Mrs. Jordan, which was the stage name of Dorothea Bland. Within the year a full fledged affair had begun, and their first child, George, was born in 1794. Over the course of the next sixteen years, Dora, as she was known to her intimates, would produce another nine children for the Duke, who were all duly recognized and surnamed FitzClarence.

William very happily settled into a comfortable domestic life with Dora and the children. This unorthodox family, which included Dora's children from previous relationships, melded into a blissful tribe, centered at Bushy Park, on the grounds of Hampton Palace. Bushy Park would be William's residence for the next twenty years. The subsequent chapters of this book will be devoted to Dora, the FitzClarence clan, and their descendants.

William's post-Dora life had further adventures. A short time after the birth of their last child, William faced, in addition to his approaching 50th birthday, what we now would call a "mid-life crisis," complete with the wandering eye, and less resistance of the body to follow. There was also pressure from his family to find a royal wife. By this point, there was only one eligible British grandchild of King George III to succeed to the Throne: Princess Charlotte of Wales. The remainder of the grandchildren were either illegitimate or members of foreign royal houses. William and Dora had an amicable break-up. Legal papers were drawn up to ensure proper care of the children, and it was all finalized by early 1812. Dora only lived on until 1815, dying impoverished, mostly due to her own generosity, in the south of France.

In 1817, a tragedy occurred which caused all of the royal brothers to step up the pace towards the altar. Princess Charlotte of Wales, only child of the Prince Regent (after 1820, King George IV) died, along with her baby, in childbirth. This event placed William directly in the crosshairs to become King, as his second eldest brother, the Duke of York, was childless and married to a Duchess who had passed child-bearing age.

The quest for a Princess to wed was slow and tedious. William, now 52, and already with a family of ten illegitimate children, was not a prize catch for young Princesses who were still chaste and pure. Arrangements were finally made, with significant help from all of his family, for him to marry the 25-year-old Princess Adelaide of Saxe-Meiningen. And just for good measure, the 1818 wedding would be a double ceremony with his next younger brother, the Duke of Kent, who had picked as his bride the widowed Princess of Leiningen, born Princess Victoria of Saxe-Coburg. To round out the marriages of the sons of George III, the Duke of Cumberland married, in 1815, their first cousin, Duchess Frederica of Mecklenburg. The youngest surviving son, the Duke of Cambridge, married Princess Augusta of Hesse-Cassel only a few days before William's marriage. The next to youngest son, the Duke of Sussex, proved to be the marital black sheep of the family. He entered into two alliances which did not conform to the Royal Marriages Act, therefore being declared illegal. Both would-be brides were from the British nobility and were perfectly nice ladies, but King George (and later William himself) would not grant permission for a marriage to a non-royal.

The new Duchess of Cambridge was immediately accepting of the large brood of FitzClarences which now lived with their father, their mother already being dead. It is probably good that William had so many children on which Adelaide could lavish her love and care, since her own children both died as newborns. In later years, all of William's children would remark on the extraordinary efforts made by their step-mother to make them feel loved, and to be sure they were properly introduced into society. The Queen, as Adelaide became in 1837, also helped her step-children find and make appropriate matches.

Old George III finally died in 1820, having long since been locked up as a lunatic, followed by his eldest son and heir, George IV, only ten years later. By the time of George IV's death in 1830, the Duke of York was already dead, so the Throne fell to William. After 64 years of having his life controlled by his father and brother, William accepted the crown with maybe a tad more glee than was respectful of his dead brother. Nonetheless, the seven-year reign of William IV had begun.

King William IV had done so much living during his time as Prince, that his reign as King was somewhat anti-climatic, although there was one major piece of legislation passed due to the King's direct influence. The Reform Bill of 1832 addressed what had become inequities in the country's electoral system, a system that had been unchanged since Tudor days. But getting the Reform Bill passed was more of a challenge than anyone had anticipated. William was faced with several difficult choices regarding Parliament during this period which led him to dissolve it at one point for fresh elections, and at another point, to personally admonish the House of Lords on their failure to pass the Reform Bill. Other laws passed during his reign, though without his personal input, were the abolition of slavery in the Colonies, and greater restrictions on child labor.

The year 1834 brought another round of disagreement between King and Parliament, and eventually the King dissolved parliament, again triggering new elections which did not go as the King had hoped. Parliament sent their choice of Prime Minister to the King, but he refused Lord Melbourne a second stint, instead selecting a Tory, Sir Robert Peel. Peel's administration never had a chance, as Melbourne's party was in control of the House of Commons. Ultimately Melbourne was restored as Prime Minister and continued as such for the remainder of William's reign.

King William and Queen Adelaide spent much of their reign trying to develop a friendship with, and to mentor, his niece and heir, Princess Victoria of Kent. These efforts were thwarted by Victoria's mother, the Duchess of Kent. The Duchess, for her part, had always gone to great lengths to shield her daughter from her paternal uncles as she viewed them all as lecherous old men. Though this assessment may have been accurate, the result lead to young Victoria ascending a Throne she was not groomed for. Fortunately, her ministers were well prepared for this situation, and she did just fine, having a Great Age of history named for her.

William IV died of a heart-attack, without much fuss or muss, just as he would have wanted, on the 20th of June, 1837, ending the Hanoverian era that had lasted since 1714. He was buried in the Royal Crypt at Windsor Castle where much of his family rests. Queen Adelaide lived on until the end of 1849. She was always remembered for the kindness she showed others, particularly her numerous step-children, and ever-growing army of step-grandchildren. Queen Victoria was always very fond of this aunt and remembered her when naming her own first daughter, Victoria Adelaide Mary Louise (later the German Empress). Her subjects also remembered the Dowager Queen fondly and named Adelaide, Australia, that country's only large interior city, after her.

Chapter 2: Dorothy Bland, aka Mrs. Jordan

If William IV was born into the pampered world of royalty, the mother of his surviving children was reared in the exact opposite. Dorothea "Dora" Bland was born in 1761 to parents whose own marriage was "everything but legal." Her father, Francis Bland, had parents devoted to religious service and not willing to accept aspiring actress, Grace Phillips, into their family, so a marriage was never performed. Francis and Grace simply lived away from his family "as if married" for appearances sake.

Dora was the third child of the Bland household, having an elder brother, George, and sister, Hester. The total number of children born to Grace has not been accuturately recorded, but is believed to be in the ballpark of nine, the last of whom was born in early 1774. Most of this time was spent in Dublin, where Grace was able to find work acting on a more or less regular basis.

One of the great disadvantages of not having a marriage certificate is that one cannot legally force a spouse to remain with the family or remit compensation if he doesn't. Thus, in 1774 Francis Bland left his "wife" and children, married an heiress and began a new family with the legal wife. Francis Bland did little to support his first family after this point, so it made little difference that he only lived four more years.

It was about this time that Dora began her own remarkable odyssey on the stage. She started in Dublin, following her mother's path. Just to be working, she initially tried out for all sorts of productions, both tragedy and comedy, but early on showed a genuine talent for the comedic roles. She quickly found herself in lead roles and working in Dublin's better theatres.

In 1780, Dora had the misfortune to begin performing in a theatre owned by Richard Daly. A year or so later, during their second season, he seduced her. It is generally accepted that this seduction was anything but romantic, with accounts ranging from what today would be called sexual harassment to outright rape. Whatever the true circumstances were, Dora removed herself from Daly's presence as soon as she could manage it, but not before finding herself pregnant with his child. In due course, Dora's first child, Frances, known as Fanny, was born.

Dora was an especially affectionate mother, but once Fanny reached adulthood, their relationship was stormy on the best of days. It is easy to imagine Dora resenting a child who was begotten in such an odious manner, but her biographers have generally agreed she made every effort to not punish Fanny for the crimes of her father.

Dora's life after Richard Daly improved considerably. Moving back to England with her mother and siblings in tow, she found work in Yorkshire with a chain of theatres owned by Tate Wilkinson. It was he who named her "Mrs. Jordan." The name was a biblical reference, just as she had crossed the water from Ireland to be free of Daly, it was as if she had crossed the River Jordan into a Promised Land. It was by this pseudonym that she would be known the rest of her life.

As her reputation as a great actress continued to blossom, she made, in 1785, the inevitable migration to London's Drury Lane, then the center of the theatrical world. It was here that she met and fell in love with Richard Ford a year later. The next three years were to bring relative personal happiness, a successful and profitable professional life, and three more children: Dorothea "Dodee" in 1787, a baby boy who sadly only lived a few hours in 1788, and Lucy in 1789. However, 1789 also saw the beginning of a lot of change for Mrs. Jordan.

In July of that year, Dora's devoted mother, Grace, passed away, leaving several of Dora's siblings in her care in addition to the three children of her own to raise. She had tried for three long years to nail Richard down on the prospect of marriage but he always managed to escape the noose. And this was the year that she caught the eye of a royal admirer: Prince William, the Duke of Clarence.

The Duke soon began efforts to woo Dora, but kept a respectable distance in public, as she was generally thought of as married to Richard Ford. In the meanwhile, Dora stepped up her efforts to get the ever-elusive legal marriage from Richard. He continued to hesitate and finally Dora delivered an ultimatum in early 1791: the Duke wanted her and would have her if Ford wouldn't marry her. Ford let her go.

From the get go, there was an understanding that William would never be able to marry Dora. He could and would be devoted and faithful to her, but the Royal Marriages Act made a marriage out of the question. Dora seems to have been very accepting of these conditions and soon moved in with the Duke. Prior to this arrangement, Dora had purchased a home in the Petersham district of London called Somerset House. It was here that the first two of her ten children with William would be born. The remainder were all born at Bushy House.

Bushy House was a royal residence that was provided for William in his titular role as Park Warden for Bushy Park, which is near Hampton Court. It was somewhat run down as it had been uninhabited for several years, but William and Dora set about putting it to rights and even adding a bit to the original buildings. Here, Dora again found herself in an "all but legal" marital relationship, now with the Duke.

Finances were always a major issue in Dora's life, as well as William's. When they got together, William was horribly in debt. This was mostly due to being a Prince. He was expected to entertain and live in a certain manner, one that was well outside the annual allowance Parliament was willing to provide. He often turned to his father for debt-relief, with mixed results. Dora, for her part, had been the primary money maker for much of her family, which included three children and three unwed sisters when she took up with the Duke. She also had cared for her mother until the latter's death. Yet she demonstrated a good head for money and actually helped her royal lover get his own debt under control.

The Clarence household was generally buoyed by Dora's continuing income as an actress. She continued to work through nearly the entirety of her relationship with William. If the Duke was not happy with this arrangement, he did not fuss about it. He was no doubt all too happy to have the income. As the family grew, this became even more important.

The Duke of Clarence and Mrs. Jordan would go on to have ten children together between 1794 and 1807, all surnamed FitzClarence. As the family continued to grow, and domestic bliss reigned supreme at Bushy House, even the most ardent opponents to this unorthodox royal arrangement were quelled. Dora began finding herself welcome in the highest social circles and often accompanied her lover to major social events. Even old King George III and Queen Charlotte came to appreciate the calming influence Dora had on their sometimes wayward son. They accepted these illegitimate grandchildren in their own way in private, but maintained a public distance in Court life.

Dora Jordan was well known to all as a devoted and loving mother. Nearly every farthing she earned went to their care, ultimately to her ruin. Between her and their royal father, the FitzClarence children received top-notch educations and, when their age dictated, were introduced into the best social circles. Some followed the Hanoverian tradition of being quarrelsome with their parents, but never to the point of a complete rupture within the family.

Eventually, Dora's remaining sisters married and went off to live their own lives. Her brother George remained an active part of her life. Of her children born prior to meeting the Duke, Fanny Daly married Thomas Alsop, a general waste of the flesh and blood it took to make him; Dodee Ford married Fred Marsh, the conniving illegitimate son of Lord Henry FitzGerald, himself a son of the Duke of Leinster; and Lucy Ford married a Colonel Hawker, moving with him to his various posts throughout the Empire.

By 1811, four years after their final child was born, Prince William had become restless in this not-quite-legal domestic situation. It was increasingly apparent that there might be a real chance for him to ascend the Throne, despite being the third son. His elder brothers were in their fifties and not likely to father any more children with their wives, and only one child survived: Princess Charlotte, daughter of the eldest brother, George (later King George IV). Furthermore, pressure from his family to marry a foreign Princess and make more heirs was mounting. Finally he decided to split with Dora.

In December 1811, a formal arrangement of separation was drawn up, with an allowance going to Dora for herself and each of her younger children until they reached age 13, at which point they would go to live with William. One provision that seemed out of character for the Duke, and was likely insisted upon by the Regent's advisors, required Dora to forfeit her allowance if she returned to the stage as a working actress. She had by this time been in a state of semi-retirement.

Dora left Bushy House in February 1812, having bought herself a house in Cadogan Place. Within the year, she found herself financially required to return to the stage giving up her allowance from William. She continued working until 1814, when she left the stage, never to return. Her last performance turned into an impromptu retirement party with the theatre packed to the rafters with well-wishers and not a dry eye in the house.

Unfortunately, even with her income from the stage, she could not keep up with her debts, many of which were created by her generosity to her children. Even though the older children were now married and theoretically on their own, she found she was usually still the one keeping them out of the poor house.

In 1815, she discovered her ne'er-do-well son-in-law, Fred Marsh had been spending her money and raising debt in her name. She soon found herself hounded by debt collectors for amounts she had no hope of paying off. She retained legal counsel to help with the debt situation and was advised to move to the Continent so the debt collectors could not reach her, and to allow her lawyers some time to gather proof that Fred had fraudulently been raising her debt.

She moved to Boulogne, France, her house and belongings having now been seized and auctioned off at well below their value. Little is recorded of her last months in France. She wrote to her children regularly, but the letters have not survived. Her health apparently deteriorated rapidly, and Dora Bland, known to the world as Mrs. Jordan, died in a very cheap rental on July 5th, 1816, aged 55, completely destitute and alone. What little she had left was sold off and her debts were paid at the rate of five shillings to the pound.

Her grave in St. Cloud went unmarked until her children found out and erected a simple tombstone for her. She is buried in a corner of a small churchyard, nearly as lonely as she died. There is irony worthy of Shakespeare in that the greatest comedic actress of her day ended life in such tragic circumstances.

Chapter 3: The FitzClarences

In the thirteen year interval between 1794 and 1807, Mrs. Jordan bore 10 healthy children to the Duke of Clarence. All of these children would grow to adulthood. It was tradition in the day for illegitimate children to take as a surname Fitz plus their father's name. So a child of Gerald would be named FitzGerald. The children of William and Dora though were named FitzClarence in reference to their father's title rather than his name.

The children were generally raised at Bushy Park, near Hampton Court. This more rural setting provided not only a physically healthy environment to grow in, but also afforded a certain amount of privacy for a family that was not quite proper. The press had been particularly cruel in their depictions of William and Dora's arrangement in the beginning. Once it became apparent that this was going to be a lasting relationship, they quieted down a bit.

The first born child was named George, after the Prince of Wales, to whom William was always devoted. William had been somewhat on the outs with his parents for quite some time at this point, so perhaps this was his way of sticking his tongue out at them. George, as well as his next younger brother, Henry, were the only children of William and Dora not to be born at Bushy Park. They were both born at Dora's home in Petersham.

George was educated at Harrow, as were all of his brothers, and was an average student. He would later show interest in Asian military history, travelling extensively throughout the Far East as a young man. He collected and amassed a large catalogue of information from libraries all over the European and Asian continents whichhe published, 1817, as *A History of the Art of War among Eastern Nations* to very favorable reviews from the halls of academia. He followed this up by publishing a book about his travels, *Journal of a Route Across India*, a year later.

With an income from his books, he was able to start a family and did so by marrying Mary Wyndham, an illegitimate daughter of the 3rd Earl of Egremont. One would think George and Mary would have been well suited to each other as they both came from non-traditional families and understood the various societal inconveniences that situation handed them. The marriage produced seven children, although one lived only a month. However happy the marriage started, it did not continue that way, George often finding other sleeping accommodations.

Like so many men in the Hanover family, George felt it was his duty, as eldest son, to be the most quarrelsome with his father. Early on, these quarrels were often over money. Both William and Dora provided their children an adequate upbringing. It was not as opulent as William himself had experienced, but it was not exactly frugal either. When William and Dora separated in 1811, George embarked on a resentment of his father that was never alleviated.

However, this did not stop William, who was now King, from using his newfound royal powers in 1830 to do all he could to help his firstborn[1]. He gave him some royal

---

[1] William reportedly had fathered one other son prior to his relationship with Dora, by an unknown lady. This child supposedly

functions to carry out and, three months prior to his coronation, created George the 1ˢᵗ Earl of Munster, a secondary title that William himself had carried prior to his ascension. Even this led to a bitter row between father and son as George, being the King's eldest son, believed he should have a role in the coronation ceremony. Decorum of the day, as well as the Archbishop of Canterbury who oversaw the ceremony, simply would not permit it.

In an effort to appease his son, William made him a member of the Privy Council. This was not for George, who found himself estranged from Court for much of his father's reign. Queen Victoria, always rather fond of the FitzClarence clan, made him her aide-de-camp until 1841 when he seems to have again fallen out of favor. His bitter resentment of his life in general, his unhappy marriage, and his bleak financial situation finally got the better of him on 20 March 1842 when he shot himself, using a pistol presented to him by his uncle and namesake, King George IV, when the latter was Prince of Wales. George's estranged wife followed him to the grave that December. They were

---

was also named William, however evidence of his existence is fleeting. According to Tomalin, this child died in the Navy at sea in late 1806 or early 1807.

survived by their six remaining children, two girls and four boys, ranging in age from 6 to 22.

The eldest child, a daughter named Adelaide in honor of William's Queen, lived a quiet life away from Court and never married. She died at the age of 63. Her only surviving sister, Augusta, fell in love with a handsome Swedish diplomat, Baron Bonde, while studying in Paris. She eloped to Sweden where they lived at the Bonde estate in Grimmersta. Sadly Augusta's happiness was short lived. She died in 1846, less than a week after delivering a healthy daughter named in her memory.

The younger Baroness Augusta Bonde grew up in Grimmersta with her father, who remarried to Helena Robinson, another English girl, perhaps to replace the mother little Augusta had lost. Augusta made a brilliant matrimonial coup by marrying Gustave Fouché, the heir of the Duke of Otrante, Sweden's wealthiest noble at the time. But, like her mother, Augusta's married life was cut short by her death in 1872. Also like her mother, she left a young daughter, this one named Augustine, later Mrs. Frederik Peyron. The Peyron descendants immigrated to the United States in the middle of the 20th century and are now settled there in New England.

The eldest son of the Earl of Munster was named William in 1824, despite his father's ongoing disagreements with the child's namesake and grandfather. William succeeded his father as Earl in 1842. Having also been educated at Harrow, William sought a military career, serving in the Life Guards until he retired as a Captain upon his succession to the peerage. In 1855, he married his first cousin, Wilhelmina Kennedy-Erskine, daughter of his father's sister, Augusta. They also had a large family of seven boys and two girls.

The first two sons of the 2nd Earl both died young, as did the fourth son, leaving the third son, Geoffrey to inherit the title. Like his father, he was also a career military man, serving in the 1879-1880 Afghan War and the Boer War a year afterwards. He later fought in the South African War of 1899-1902, where he earned the Distinguished Service Order (DSO). Having survived many military campaigns, he was killed in a mining accident, unmarried, while still in South Africa in 1902.

The fifth son, Aubrey, also a bachelor, succeeded Geoffrey as the 4th Earl. He carried the title with little distinction and, having remained unmarried, passed it on, upon his death in 1928, to the son of his youngest brother,

Harold. Being sixth and seventh sons, there was no reason to believe either William or Harold FitzClarence would ever inherit the title. But, had William not succumbed to "jungle fever" in Africa in 1899, he would have done just that. Although he did marry, William produced only daughters, so the titles were not able to go to his descendants.

William FitzClarence's elder daughter, Dorothy, named in honor of her famous ancestress, married Cadogan Elborough, in 1909, and had five children over the next eleven years. Today, the Elboroughs are quite numerous, living in pockets around England. One of the younger generation has immigrated to Hawaii, where he is now building his own family. This family is headed up by Patrick, born in 1937. He caught the attention of the media in 1981, when an industrious reporter figured out he would be the King had William IV and Mrs. Jordan married.

William FitzClarence's younger daughter, Wilhelmina, married in 1918 to Cecil Maunsell, a Justice of the Peace and Lord of Rothwell Manor in Kettering, Northamptonshire. Their only child was Cecilia, first wife of George Kennard, who would later become the last Baronet of that name. George married another royal descendant as his fourth wife, Georgina Werhner, a granddaughter of Grand Duke Michael of Russia. George and Cecilia's daughter, Zandra, now approaching 70, has been married since 1962 to John Powell and is a noted artist living near Kettering. She has two grown children and three school-aged grandchildren.

The 2nd Earl's seventh son, Harold, followed the "family business" by joining the military, ultimately achieving the rank of Major. He married Frances Keppel, a scion of the Earl of Albemarle's family, in 1902. They had two children: Joan and Geoffrey. Lady Joan, having been raised to the rank of an Earl's daughter in 1928, married Oliver Birkbeck, of an old landed family from Norfolk. In her widowhood, Joan remarried to Henry Cator, a man 18 years her junior.

Lady Joan's younger brother, Geoffrey, succeeded his uncle as Earl in 1928. Geoffrey Munster, as he was commonly called, followed a career in politics. After taking a seat in the conservative benches in the House of Lords, he was appointed a Lord-in-Waiting, as well as the government whip in the Lords, during the Macdonald, Baldwin and Chamberlin governments. When World War II broke out, he moved to the State Department, where he started as Paymaster General but soon moved up to Undersecretary of State for War. After the war, he continued to hold several high-ranking positions within government, mostly dealing with the Colonies. He ultimately died in 1975, leaving a widow, the former Hilary Wilson, but - like many of his predecessors, - no children. His title would go to a second cousin.

The two daughters of the 2nd Earl of Munster, Ladies Lillian and Dorothea, each married in the 1890s and each had two children. Lillian married William Boyd and Dorothea married Chandos Lee-Warner. But these two lines quickly became extinct, as none of their children had any children of their own. Lillian's daughter, Phyllis, was the only one of them to marry. Her husband was a French nobleman, Vicomte Henri de Janzé, brother of the Comte de Janzé. The Comte figures into the tail of another William IV descendant, as he was the ex-husband of a mistress of the 22nd Earl of Erroll.

The second son of the 1st Earl, the Hon. Frederick FitzClarence, was born in 1826 and, after marrying his first cousin, the Hon. Adelaide Sidney, added Hunloke to his surname. The Sidney family had become the heirs of the Hunloke family, which was now extinct in the male line. However, Fredrick and Adelaide had no children to whom to pass this name. It would devolve to a nephew of Adelaide's,

Sir Philip Hunloke. Between Frederick and his next younger brother, George, was a baby girl who survived only a few days.

While many of the FitzClarences pursued Army careers, George joined the Royal Navy and was raised to the rank of Captain. He married Lady Maria Scott, daughter of the 3rd Earl of Clonmell, and heiress of the estate, "Bishopscourt," in co. Kildare. The four sons of George and Maria, - Charles, Edward, William, and Lionel, - all joined the army, the elder two eventually being killed in action. The two daughters lived in relative obscurity, the younger, Mary, being the only one to marry. She and her husband, Frederick Wing, had only one child, Gertrude, who died an elderly, but unmarried, lady in 1983.

The eldest son, Charles, became the war hero of the family. Serving in Africa with a few different regiments late in the 19th century, he was decorated with the Victoria Cross for his bravery at Mafeking. Ultimately he was killed in action during World War I, in Ypres, France. His brother, Edward, was killed fighting with the Egyptian army in what is now the Sudan, while the youngest son, Lionel, died in the early days of World War II in the Crimea.

Only Charles and Lionel left descendants, the former's becoming the last Earls of Munster and the latter's being an only daughter, Mary, who lived a quiet life in Sussex with her Polish husband, Adam Gluskiewicz. Their only child, Anna, now a "lady of a certain age," has never married.

Charles' eldest son, Edward, eventually inherited the Earldom of Munster from his second cousin, Geoffrey, when he was already a 75-year-old man, but carried the title for eight years until his death in 1983. During his years as plain Mr. FitzClarence, he served in the Army during World War II in Egypt, mostly in a staff position, and married twice. His first marriage, to Monica Grayson, the daughter of a Baronet, played out in the years between the wars and produced his only children. A second marriage, to Vivian Scholfield, turned out to be much longer, lasting until his death.

The son of the 6th Earl was Anthony, 7th and last Earl of Munster. By the time of his death in 2000, all other branches of the FitzClarence family had become extinct in the male line. After being educated at St. Edward's School in Oxford, and in Switzerland, Tony FitzClarence joined the Royal Navy, at age 16 in 1942, and served until 1947, being wounded in action along the way.

41

Being from a junior line of the family in his early adulthood, Tony had no real hereditary income of his own. After training at the Central School of Crafts and Arts in London, he began a career as a graphic designer, working for the Daily Mirror and then the Sun, finally working his way into being a sustainable freelancer. Later in life he developed an expertise in stained glass. After becoming Lord FitzClarence and heir to the Earldom, he took first a staff position at the Burrell Collection in Glasgow, and later with Chapel Studio.

His marital career was as varied as his professional one, having had four wives: Diane Delvigne, Pamela Hyde, Alexa Maxwell, and Halina Winska. The first and last wives survive today, as well as his four daughters, two from each of his first two wives. The last Countess of Munster also has a daughter from a previous relationship, who assumed the FitzClarence name.

Tony's eldest daughter, Lady Tara, is married to Ross Heffler and has two college-aged children. The second daughter, Lady Finola, divorced her husband of 25 years, Jonathan Poynton, in 2007. The couple had two children of their own, who are also in their twenties. The third daughter, born with the name Oonaugh, was born two years prior to the marriage of her parents and was shortly thereafter adopted by John Lawrence Mills. Now known as Charlotte Lawrence Mills, she is married to Raymond Burt and has three children. The youngest daughter, Lady Georgina, married briefly to Paul Phillips before remarrying to John Adam and having one son by the latter.

Tony's only sibling was his sister, Lady Mary-Jill, who died rather young at age 42, but not before she married twice. Perhaps it was a blessing she had no children to leave motherless.

Like his son, the 6th Earl also only had one sibling, a younger sister named Joan. Unlike her niece, though, Joan has descendants. She had married, in 1933, to Francis Barchard, who was later killed in World War II, leaving Joan with two young daughters, Jane and Elizabeth. Both have married and have had only daughters themselves. Now there are grandchildren ranging in age from teens on down.

Edward, the youngest son of the 1st Earl, like so many of his relatives, began a military career. However, his career and his life were cut tragically short as he was killed in action in the Crimean War in 1855, only two weeks after his eighteenth birthday.

The eldest daughter of Mrs. Jordan and the Duke of Clarence was Sophia, the apple of her father's eye nearly from birth. Her life and descendants will be discussed in the next chapter.

For all of the disagreement that Prince William had with his eldest son, he was a doting father to his second, named Henry Edward. Of all of their children, young Henry seems to have had the hardest time coping with the separation of his parents. It appears to be what motivated him to sign on to a campaign going to India. It was here that he learned of his mother's death in 1815, and also here that he met with a fatal illness himself two years later. Young Henry FitzClarence died without having been married, one of three of the FitzClarence children of King William IV not to produce additional descendants.

Lady Mary FitzClarence, the second daughter of the Duke of Clarence and Mrs. Jordan, was another of these three siblings. She married in 1824 to another notable bastard, Charles Richard Fox. Fox was the illegitimate son of the 3rd Baron Holland and his mistress, Lady Webster, whom he would later marry. Young Fox made his way through the ranks of the army, eventually becoming a general. After his military career, he entered politics, being a Whig MP for various constituencies in the 1830s and 40s. He was also a renowned collector of ancient Greek coins. After his death, his collection was sold to the royal museum in Berlin.

William and Dora's third son, Frederick, made the military his life's work. Most notably, he was the military governor of Portsmouth in the mid-19th century. He was a well respected administrator, with several plaques and monuments devoted to his memory. He married Augusta Boyle, a daughter of the 4th Earl of Glasgow, and by her had two daughters, one who died in infancy and another, who lived to adulthood, but did not marry.

The third daughter of William and Dora, Elizabeth, was to be the most prolific in terms of descendants. No fewer than four subsequent chapters will be devoted to the descendants of Lady Elizabeth FitzClarence and her husband, the 18th Earl of Erroll.

A hereditary insanity ran through several of the Hanoverian men. It has been most famously documented in King George III. However, the behavior of Lord Adolphus FitzClarence, William and Dora's fourth son, left little doubt he was of the same gene pool as "Mad King George." Lolly, as he was called by his mother, carried out a very respectable, even notable, naval career. But, the older he got, the more peculiar he became, often to the entertainment of his numerous nieces and nephews. His odder behavior was never a threat, and was generally tolerated by his family as all in good fun. Lolly FitzClarence never married, so if there was a hereditary taint, at least he didn't pass it along.

The next FitzClarence child, Augusta, was the progenitress of the Kennedy-Erskine line of descendants, more of whom we will meet in the last chapter.

The youngest son, Augustus, turned his energies toward the church. He ultimately became the Vicar of Mapledurham in Oxfordshire. He married Sarah Gordon, a granddaughter of the 9th Marquess of Huntly. They had six children, of whom, only Dorothea and Henry married.

Dorothea FitzClarence married Thomas Goff in 1863. Their only surviving descendants are through their granddaughter, also named Dorothea, who married Harold Swann. The Swann family is now also gone, as their only grandchildren were all daughters and have now married into other families. Henry FitzClarence's family has not proven as resilient. His son, Augustus, was killed in World War I, leaving no children. Henry's daughter, Cynthia, had two daughters of her own, by husband Roland Orred, but they too died childless.

For a family that started with ten children two hundred years ago, the FitzClarence name is all but gone at this point, being held only by the daughters of the last couple of Earls. However, many descendants in the female line remain. We will be exploring those lines in the next several chapters.

Chapter 4: The Sidneys

Having such a large number of children who were not royal, William and Dora gave the British nobility a rare opportunity to marry children of a King. Royal princes and princesses were generally expected to marry foreign royalty in the early 19th century as the noble classes of the home land were not considered good enough. However, since Mrs. Jordan's children were not royal in name, they were eligible, and very desirable, as spouses for British peers. And, not since the reign of Charles II, had a king provided such a bounty of children for them to choose from. In order to equate their rank to the nobles they hoped to marry, upon his ascension to the Throne, William elevated them all to the rank of a Marquess's child, save the eldest son who was given his own peerage title as the Earl of Munster.

William and Dora's eldest daughter, Sophia, was the apple of her father's eye. While he loved all his children, she presented the first opportunity for William to have a "daddy's little girl." This may have contributed to his allowance for her to marry for love to the heir of a mere Baronet, albeit a wealthy one, Philip Sidney.

Baronets can be best described as a hereditary knighthoods. Their numbers are not considered peers, they do not sit in the House of Lords, and they are styled the same as a knight: Sir before their given name. However Baronets are not knights in the sense of belonging to any order of chivalry and rank in precedence above such knights except those of the Orders of the Garter and the Thistle.

So it was into this "neither Lord nor Knight" realm that Lady Sophia FitzClarence married in 1825. Philip's father, Sir John, had inherited the historic Penhurst Place, a 14th century manor house in Kent from his maternal ancestors, the Earls of Leicester. Penhurst has remained the seat of the Sidney family ever since. Now open to the public, some of its visage has been made famous by being used as a set for movies such as *The Princess Bride* and *The Other Boleyn*

Girl and is presently being used to represent Camelot in the BBC (SyFy Channel in the US) series *Merlin*.

After ten years of marriage, William, now King, saw fit to raise his son-in-law to the Peerage as Baron de L'Isle and Dudley. While there is little doubt this was done as a service to his daughter, publicly it was a reward for Sir Philip's service to the people as an MP from Eye followed by service to the Crown as the King's Equerry. After the creation he was also appointed a Lord of the Bedchamber, a particularly high post within the King's household.

The choice of titles was an acknowledgement of Sir Philip's ancestry. His ancestors, the Earls of Leicester, also held the title Viscount de L'Isle, and were themselves descended from Mary Dudley, sister of Elizabeth I's great love, Robert Dudley.

Within a year of her marriage, Sophia found herself giving birth to her first child, a daughter named Adelaide in honor of her step-mother, the future Queen Adelaide. The following decade would bring three more children: only son, Philip, in 1828; and daughters Ernestine and namesake Sophia in 1834 and 1837, respectively.

Like her husband, Sophia was appointed to a royal household position, Housekeeper of Kensington Palace. This does not mean she was cleaning the woodwork or polishing the silver. Housekeeper in this context refers to the person who manages the household staff and essentially keeps the palace running. In this position, Sophia was also able to keep her father apprised of the goings on there, as it was the home of William's heir, Princess Victoria of Kent. Young Victoria was generally kept away from her Hanoverian uncles by her widowed mother, deeming them all as unsavory influences. So, having a much loved and trusted daughter in the house was probably William's best source of information about his niece's upbringing.

Baroness de L'Isle died rather suddenly at the young age of 40 at Kensington Palace in April 1837. The loss of his favorite daughter likely prevented the King from rallying from his final heart attack. He followed her to the grave only two months later. Philip, her widowed husband, would live on to 1851, dying at Penhurst.

Philip Jr. led a reasonably quite life. Prior to succeeding his father, he was an officer in the Royal House Guards. When he became the 2nd Baron de L'Isle and Dudley in 1851, he took his seat in the conservative benches of the House of Lords. He married twice. His first wife, Mary Foulis, was the heiress of Ingleby Manor in Yorkshire. She was also the mother of all five of Philip's children before her sudden death in 1891. Two years, later he married Frances Ramsay, only to make her a widow five years after that.

Of Philip Jr.'s four sons, three would become Baron de L'Isle in their own turn. The only daughter, Mary, died unmarried at age 42, in 1903. She lived only seven years after the death of her unmarried brother, Henry.

The 3rd Baron, another Philip, did marry, to Elizabeth Vereker, daughter of the Viscount Gort, but they remained childless during their 20 years of marriage. This Philip was succeeded by his next younger brother Algernon who, remaining a bachelor, was succeeded in turn by the youngest brother, William, although the latter was only Baron for two months before his own death in June 1945.

When William Sidney, 5th Baron de L'Isle and Dudley died, he left two children by his wife, the former Winifred Yorke Bevan. These children were, by 1945, both married and had families of their own, but it was only that spring that an heir to the title was born.

William's daughter, Mary, who had married Walter Garnett in 1939, died prematurely a few days after her 53rd birthday, leaving a teenaged son.

Mary's brother, also named William, succeeded his father, in 1945, as the 6th Baron. By this time, he had already served with distinction in World War II, being wounded while fighting in France and Italy, earning him the Victoria Cross, Britain's highest military honor, for "showing valor in the face of the enemy." In later years when recounting his war record, if asked where he was shot, he would reply "in Italy" to avoid the embarrassment of talking about being shot in the buttocks.

After returning from the war, William quickly entered politics, being elected in 1944 to serve Chelsea in Parliament. The term only lasted a few months, as he succeeded to the Barony the following June. Steering his public service to a more diplomatic heading, the new Baron was appointed by Winston Churchill, to Secretary of State for Air, a position that oversaw the Royal Air Force before its incorporation into the Ministry of Defense. His efforts as veteran and Secretary were rewarded with an elevation in title to Viscount de L'Isle in 1956.

During his days in Churchill's cabinet he made a trip to Australia to research weapons production there and met often with that country's Prime Minister, Robert Menzies. When the position of Governor-General came open in 1961,

William was appointed to it, serving until retiring from public life in 1965.

On the home front, William had married, in 1940, the grand-niece of his Uncle Philip's wife, Jacqueline Vereker. They have five children, the middle one being his only son and heir, Philip, now the 2nd Viscount de L'Isle. The four daughters have, so far, racked up nine marriages among them, and mostly live in the London or Kent areas with their ever-growing numbers of grandchildren.

The current Viscount followed a military career until taking early retirement in 1979. Having succeeded his father in 1991, he was also appointed Vice-Lieutenant of Kent in 2002 and has since focused on the promotion of commerce for his ancestral home. He and his father were largely lauded for refurbishing Penhurst Place and its splendid gardens, now both open for the public to enjoy.

Viscount de L'Isle has been married since 1980 to the former Isobel Compton. The couple has two children named after their forebears, Sophia and Philip, and who are entering an age when it will soon be their turn to marry and continue the family lines.

Of the daughters of Lady Sophia FitzClarence and the 1st Baron de L'Isle, only Ernestine had children. However, the eldest daughter, Adelaide received an inheritance to pass on to them. Adelaide was determined to be the heiress to the last Hunloke Baronet who died in 1856. This inheritance included the 12th century manor house, Wingerworth, in Derbyshire. Adelaide and her husband, and cousin, Frederick FitzClarence, made Wingerworth their home until Frederick's death in 1878. Adelaide then moved back to London, putting the house up for rent.

Meanwhile, Adelaide's sister Ernestine had married Philip Perceval and began a family. Twins, Philip and Kathleen, were born in 1868 and wer followed by a sistes and a brother, of which, only the twins lived past the age of twenty. Kathleen died, unmarried, in 1931.

Philip Perceval thus became the heir to his childless aunt, Adelaide FitzClarence-Hunloke, who, with her husband, added the Hunloke name after their inheritance of that family's estate. As heir, Philip would change his name to Hunloke in 1904 upon Adelaide's death. In 1918, Philip returned to Wingerworth, but quickly found the expense of running such an estate to be beyond his means. He placed the manor up for sale, but without any takers, the house was eventually demolished in 1923.

Philip Perceval, as he was still named then, grew up at Villa Rothesay in London, near the water. He developed a love of sailing boats early on, starting a successful career in competitive sailing through the 1890s and on. In 1908, now named Hunloke, he represented Great Britain at the Olympic Games, bringing home a bronze medal in yachting. In 1914, he was appointed to royal service as a Groom-in-Waiting to King George V, moving on to becoming His Majesty's Sailing Master in 1920. Even in later life, he remained close to the sea, being a Commodore of the Royal Yacht Squadron from 1941 until his death in 1947.

Philip married, in 1892, to Silvia Heseltine, but his true wife remained the sea. In his authorized biography, which also doubled as a history of yachting, author Douglas Dixon did not even see fit to mention that Philip had a wife or children. But he did, - three children , in fact, - two daughters and a son to carry on the Hunloke name.

The elder daughter, Joan Hunloke, married the fabulously wealthy Philip Fleming of the Fleming banking family. He was also a cousin of Ian Fleming, creator of the famed spy, James Bond, as well as the beloved children's story, *Chitty Chitty Bang Bang*. Although the family has sold its share in the banking firm, they remain one of Britain's wealthiest families.

In recent years, the family has been in the news for another reason. Joan and Philip's grandson, Rory, entered into a high-profile society marriage with Denmark's Baroness Caroline Iuel-Brockdorff, herself a successful model. After seven years and two children, the couple began divorce proceedings. The protracted financial negotiations caused the divorce to drag on for quite some time, ultimately costing Rory Fleming a reported £400,000,000. For her part, Caroline has moved on to soccer star Niklas Bendtner, with whom she had a child at the end of 2010.

The Hunloke name was carried on by Philip and Silvia's son, Henry, and, after his death in 1978, his sons Timothy and Nicholas, the younger of whom is married with children and grandchildren. The Hunlokes have continued to marry well through the 20th century and to a smattering of British nobles. Henry's first wife, and mother of his sons, was Lady Anne Cavendish, daughter of the 9th Duke of Devonshire. Their only daughter, Philippa, married the 3rd Viscount Astor.

Nicholas, the current head of the family, is married to Lady Katherine Montagu, daughter of the 10th Earl of Sandwich, and their elder daughter, Henrietta, is married to a grandson of the 6th Marquess of Bath. Not bad for the descendants of a Drury Lane actress who started off on the wrong side of the blanket.

Chapter 5: The Hays

Lady Elizabeth FitzClarence, 3rd daughter of King William, is probably the only daughter to have been generally thought ill of. In 1824, and only at the age of 23, she was summed up by one her of contemporaries as "a domestic, lazy, fat, woman."[2] That was a pretty harsh appraisal of a daughter of the heir-presumptive to the Throne and wife of one of Scotland's premiere Peers.

In 1820, Elizabeth had married William Hay, the 18th Earl of Erroll. The Hay family is ancient enough to have their beginnings told in myth. The story goes that they descended from a farm worker who sent his sons to block the way of a retreating 11th century Scottish army forcing them to

---

[2] Gibbs, Vicary. *The Complete Peerage.* vol. VI, p.102

return to battle with the invading Danes ultimately winning the day. An interesting story, but more likely a later invention. There were, however, several true stories of the family's brave and gallant service to the Kings of Scotland in the 14th and 15th centuries. The Earls of Hay also serve as the hereditary High Constables of Scotland, a position which places them second only to the Royal Family in Scottish precedence.

By the time we get to the early 19th century, the Earls of Erroll of settled into just another noble Scots family of no particular distinction. They made their seat at Slains Castle near Cruden Bay in Aberdeenshire. Built in 1597 by the 9th Earl, the building was in bad need of repair by the 1830's and William made a complete overhaul. The Castle remained with the Hays until 1916, by which time financial misfortune forced them to sell the castle. The buyers also had to abandon the property and removed the roof to avoid paying taxes, reducing this once noble monument to a lonely ruin, overlooking the North Sea. Fortunately, the Aberdeenshire Council has taken a renewed interest in the historic landmark. In October 2007, public access to the castle was discontinued so that restoration construction could begin to convert the old castle into holiday apartments.

With the Duke of Clarence now being very likely to ascend the Throne, the Earl of Erroll found it quite convenient to be married to his daughter. He was able to use this position to be appointed a Lord of the Bedchamber to King George IV and later Master of the Horse to Queen Adelaide. Upon William IV's ascension, the Earl was also given a knighthood in the Royal Guelphic Order, more commonly called the Royal Hanoverian Order, followed a few years later by the Order of the Thistle, the highest chivalric order in Scotland.

In 1834, the Earl was given the additional title of Baron Kilmarnock. This title referred to a second Earldom the Hays family enjoyed prior to joining in the Jacobite rebellion against King George II in 1746, resulting in a forfeiture of the titles. The current creation is in the peerage of the United Kingdom, whereas the other titles held by the Earl of Erroll are created in the peerage of Scotland. The result being these two sets of titles having different succession rules. Titles created in the United Kingdom generally follow the rule of Salic law, meaning they can only be inherited by the male line descendants of the person for whom the title was created. However, Scottish titles typically allowed for female succession if a peer died without sons but had surviving daughters. This leads to the possibility of the titles separating and being inherited by different people, an event that would take place in 1941.

William and Elizabeth had four children: Ida, William, Agnes, and Alice. Ida would marry the Earl of Gainsborough and become the ancestress to the bulk of William IV's living descendants today. Agnes married the Earl Fife and her descendants will bring this line of illegitimate royal descendants to marry members of the legitimate royal family. Conversely, Alice remained childless but made an interesting marriage, nonetheless.

Lady Alice Hay married in 1874 to Charles Allen, a charlatan who, with much of his family, claimed to be a male line descendant of the Stuart Kings of England and Scotland. The story, as they told it, was that that Charles's father and uncle, named Charles and John respectively were the grandsons of Prince Charles Stuart, generally known to history as the "Young Pretender," himself being a grandson of King James II.

The brothers, John and Charles, concocted the whole tale after the death of their father, one Thomas Allen, a naval officer from Wales. They contended that Thomas was a child of Prince Charles and his wife, Luise of Stolberg, and that he

had been hidden fearing reprisals from the last Jacobite
Rebellion. The story is completely without foundation, but
that does not prevent this dubious duo of brothers from
styling themselves Count of Albany. Actually they used the
more romantic French spelling, Count d'Albanie, based on
the alias that Prince Charles used throughout his later life in
exile. Luckily the Charles "Stuart" who married Lady Agnes
Hay was the last of this suspicious line so their pretentions
died with him when he left the earth childless in 1880.

The 18th Earl of Erroll was succeeded by his only son,
also named William, in 1846. He spent much of his life
tending to Slains Castle and the Cruden Bay area. He
sometimes worked with an architect also named William
Hays, a distant cousin. Around the time he inherited the
castle and the title, he organized a small fishing village into a
functional port which was named for him, Port Erroll.
Shortly after he joined the Rifle Guards, seeing action in the
Crimean War and being wounded at the Battle of Alma.

In the early days of his military career, he was stationed
in Canada where he met his wife, Eliza Gore, a
granddaughter of the 2nd Earl of Arran. William and Eliza
mostly retired to their Castle on the North Sea after his
military career, entertaining the celebrities of the day during

the later part of summer when it was desirable to not be in muggy London. Although he was not a guest at the Castle, it did capture the attention of a struggling novelist named Bram Stoker during a visit to the area. He documented that Slains inspired his descriptions of Castle Dracula is his most famous novel.

Although William and Eliza would have seven children, two would tragically die in their infancy, one being the heir-apparent, if only for two days. Of the five surviving children, the two daughters, Cecilia and Florence would each marry, but neither had children. The two younger sons, Arthur and Francis, would not even marry. Arthur lived a military life, serving as a Gentleman Usher to three monarchs, Victoria, Edward VII and George V. Francis travelled the world, but committed suicide in Australia at the age of 34.

This leaves Charles, who succeeded as the 20th Earl of Erroll in 1891. He spent much of his early life in the military, retiring from active duty in 1900 and being granted a knighthood in the Order of the Thistle the following year. Now home from the service, he concentrated on his duties as a member of the House of Lords, serving as Lord-in-Waiting (the title given the government Whip) during the administration of Arthur Balfour. He returned to active duty as a Brigadier General during the First World War.

Charles had married in 1875 to Mary L'Estrange, a descendant of the Earls of Scarborough. They had three sons, Victor, Serald, and Ivan, the younger two also seeing action during World War I. Serald would not leave children, and Ivan's descendants are via two of his three daughters, the Gurneys and Dares of London.

Victor's life was fully lived prior to becoming an Earl as he only outlived his father by seven months. He had entered the Diplomatic Services in 1900, serving the next 20 years as various under-secretaries. During the Great War, he was stationed in Denmark as a first Secretary, which was followed up by becoming the British Chargés d'Affaires in Berlin when diplomatic ties were restored following the War until a new Ambassador could arrive. He remained in Berlin as a Councilor until 1921, moving on to the commission which oversaw the occupation of the Rhineland.

Lord Kilmarnock, as he was known most of his life, also was an aspiring writer. His only novel to get published, *Ferelith*, came out in 1903. He later wrote two plays in the 1920's.

Upon entering the Diplomatic Service, Victor married Lucy Mackenzie, daughter of a Scottish Baronet, and promptly had three children, two sons and a daughter. The daughter, Rosemary, met and married an army officer during the time her father served on the Rhineland Commission, Lt. Col. Rupert Ryan. Born in Australia but educated in Britain, Ryan would replace his father-in-law on the Commission after the latter's death in 1928 and serve until the end of the occupation.

Retiring from the military, he became a salesman for an arms manufacturing firm assigned to territory throughout southeast Asia. After leaving this position and divorcing Rosemary, all within a year, he returned to his native Australia to oversee a large ranch he had inherited from his parents, taking his and Rosemary's only child, Patrick, with him. Rupert would go on to serve in World War II, then in the Australian House of Representatives. Today Rupert and Rosemary's descendants continue to live in Australia. Their son, Patrick passed away in 1989 leaving a son and daughter.

Victor and Lucy's elder son would become the subject of books and movies. Well, at least his death would. Josslyn Hay lived want many might call a squandered life. Born into the one of the most ancient noble families of Scotland, in

1901, young Hay had no trouble getting into Eton. But he did have trouble staying there, being dismissed after two years of letting a lascivious lifestyle get in the way of his studies. In an effort to keep some control of his wayward son, his father took him with him to Berlin and put him to work as an honorary attaché. However, when Lord Kilmarnock was appointed High Commissioner in the Rhineland, young Josslyn remained in Berlin to serve under the new Ambassador, Viscount D'Abernon.

In 1922, Josslyn returned to London, ostensibly to take the necessary test to enter full diplomatic service. However, he quickly took up with Lady Edina Gordon, a married woman with one divorce already under her belt. Being the daughter of the 8th Earl de la Warr, Edina was born into the same society as Josslyn, but also shared his taste for sexual adventures. She quickly dumped poor Mr. Gordon and married Josslyn, eight years her junior, in September 1923, her third of what would eventually become five marriages.

British society had come quite a ways in the past twenty years, but not far enough to accept Josslyn and Edina's unconventional marriage and even more unconventional lifestyle. So they escaped the notoriety by moving to Kenya, financed with Edina's money. In Kenya, they settled among several other expatriates in an area outside Nairobi known as Happy Valley. These young, wealthy settlers were notorious for their hedonistic lifestyles. Alcohol and drugs flowed freely, sexual inhibitions thrown to the wind. However, to play in these games, one had to have money and Josslyn did not have his own. The Hay family fortunes were no longer what they had been in their heyday and by now the family estate, Slains Castle had even been sold. Josslyn's debts were rising and he started stealing from his wife to cover them.

Edina discovered she was being swindled and returned to London to obtain a divorce in early 1930. As soon as he received word he divorce was final, Josslyn remarried Molly Ramsay-Hill, another former wife of two other men. Molly quickly fell in with the debauchery of the Happy Valley set, but it consumed her. She died of a drug overdose in 1939.

The widowed Josslyn Hay, now 21st Earl of Erroll, remained in Kenya carrying on affairs with one married lady after another, and sometimes not after. This wanton behavior caught up to him in 1941 when his body was discovered in his car on the side of the road with a bullet in his head.

The murder investigation captured the imagination of a world gripped by war. As more and more details about the Earl's lifestyle became known, the list of suspects became longer and longer. The murder became the subject of a bestselling book, *White Mischief*, and a movie by the same name. It is now known that the culprit was the man who was tried and acquitted of the murder, Sir "Jock" Broughton, a Baronet whose much younger wife was one of Erroll's many lovers. Lack of evidence at the time prompted the acquittal but guilt still persecuted the killer, leading to his suicide a year later.

When the 40-year-old Earl was murdered, his titles were divided. His only child, Diana, who was raised by her mother, Edina, in England, inherited his Scottish titles becoming the Countess of Erroll and Lady Hay. The Barony of Kilmarnock did not allow female succession so it passed to Josslyn's younger brother, Gilbert.

The Countess of Erroll was among the dozen peeresses to take their seats in the House of Lords in 1963 when the law was changed to allow women admittance. Prior to this peeresses *suo jure*, the term for peeresses in their own right, were typically considered place holders until the title passed to on to their son or other male relative. In older days, husbands of such ladies shared the title and were usually treated at the peer instead of their wife. Today, succession to a title by a lady is rather uncommon, but at least when they get there, they are treated with a little more equality than their ancestresses.

In 1946, Diana married Iain Moncreiffe, who would eventually succeed as the Chief of his Clan and the baronetcy that accompanied it. Iain had served in World War II in the Scots Guards, afterwards being made an attaché in Moscow. His true love was genealogy and he authored or co-authored several works relating to Georgian and Byzantine nobility as well as Scottish heraldry. After his brief diplomatic career, he served several positions under the Lyon King of Arms, the senior heraldic official of Scotland. He eventually became a barrister specializing in heraldic and inheritance issues. Iain and Diana had three sons before divorcing in 1964. Although he remarried, Iain had no further children.

After the divorce, Diana also remarried, to Raymond Carnegie, a grandson of the 7th Earl of Southesk and cousin to the 11th Earl who married Princess Maud of Fife, also a William IV descendant. Diana and Raymond had one more child, Jocelyn, who lives today with his wife and children in France.

Of the three sons of the Countess's first marriage, the eldest, Merlin, followed his mother as Earl after her death in 1978, keeping the Hay family name. His siblings would carry their father's name, Moncreiffe. Today the 24th Earl is an acknowledged expert in information technology and maintains his seat as his wife's ancestral home, Woodbury Hall in Bedfordshire. He is the father of four twenty-something children.

Diana's younger son, Peregrine Moncreiffe succeeded his father as the Chief of the Clan in 1985, confirmed by the Lord Lyon King of Arms in 2001. As the Earldom of Erroll is historically closely tied to the Hay family it was determined the Moncreiffes would be represented by the line of the 2nd son. Peregrine and his family make their home at the Moncreiffe family seat in Perthshire.

Diana's only daughter, Alexandra, had a relationship with Michael Wigan, later the 6th Baronet, in the later 1970's producing a son Ivar. She later married Jocelyn Connell and has two more daughters. Although Ivar is Sir Michael's only son, he is ineligible to inherit the baronetcy since his parents never married.

When Josslyn, Earl of Erroll was murdered in 1941, his title, Baron Kilmarnock, went to his younger brother, Gilbert. He adopted the name Boyd, the ancestral name associated with his paternal ancestry, the Earls of Kilmarnock, a title that was forfeited in 1745 when the 4th Earl joined in

73

rebellion against King George II. The family name had been changed to Hay in 1758 with the inheritance of the Earldom of Erroll.

Gilbert, now the 6th Baron Kilmarnock, had married Rosemary, a daughter of Viscount Wimborne in 1926, with whom he had six children, although a set of twin girls were both dead within 48 hours of their birth. Gilbert and Rosemary divorced in 1955 and Gilbert remarried the same year to Denise Coker. She would give him two more children. Gilbert died in 1975 and was succeeded by his eldest son, Alastair.

Alastair Boyd was born in 1927 and had a standard upbringing of the titled class with only an upper-middle class income. He went to King's College in Cambridge and served a stint in the Irish Guards in the late 1940's. After his parents' divorce in 1955, he moved to the Andalusia region, in southern Spain, to the town of Ronda which he had discovered on a trip two years earlier. We would remain in Spain for the next 20 years with the wife he married shortly before the move, Diana Gibson. Ultimately the marriage ended, childless, with Diana returning to England.

While in Spain, Alastair founded a language school and began his own career as a writer. He wrote several books about his adopted country, a few are travel guides which continue to be updated. Alastair found love again with the mother of one of his language school students, Mrs. Hilary Bailey, known as Hilly.

Hilly Bailey's first husband had been novelist Kingsley Amis, who was the father of her children. In his last years of life, becoming something of a cantankerous old man, Amis lived with Alastair and Hilly. When Hilly became pregnant with Alastair's only child, James, known by his Spanish name, Jaime, she was still legally married to Shackleton Bailey. He dragged his feet through the divorce proceedings causing Jaime to be born prior to his parents' marriage and making him ineligible to inherit the Barony of Kilmarnock.

After becoming Baron in 1975, Alastair returned to England, serving actively in the House of Lords until so-called reform measures removed most hereditary Peers from that body. He embraced the Social Democrats Party and nurtured the careers of up and coming politicians through the party.

When being a hereditary peer no longer had meaning in the House of Lords following passage of the House of Lords Act of 1999, Kilmarnock and his wife returned to their beloved Andalusia where died in 2009, followed by Hilly a year later. Since Jaime was ineligible to succeed due to being born prior to his parents' marriage, the Barony passed to Alastair's next younger brother, Robin, who is known as "Tiger." The future succession seems secure as Tiger Kilmarnock has two sons, the eldest of whom, Simon, is also father to a son, Lucien, born in 2007.

The remainder, and majority, of the large number of descendants of Lady Elizabeth FitzClarence and the 18th Earl of Erroll come through their daughters, Ida, Countess of Gainsborough and Agnes, Countess of Fife, and will be examined over the next three chapters.

Chapter 6: The Noels

Lady Ida Hay was the eldest daughter of the 18th Earl of Erroll and, through her mother, granddaughter of King William IV and his long-time paramour, the actress Mrs. Jordan. She married, in 1841, Charles Noel, later the 2nd Earl of Gainsborough.

The Gainsborough title and Noel name both have a bit of a convoluted history. These Earls were of a second creation of the title, the first having been created for one Edward Noel in 1682. In due course of time, the first creation became extinct with the death of the 6th Earl in 1798. The sister of this last Earl, Lady Jane Noel, married Gerard Edwardes, himself an illegitimate grandson of the 4th Duke of Hamilton.

Jane and Gerard's son, also named Gerard, adopted his mother's maiden name of Noel in 1798 and married Diana, Baroness Barham in her own right. Through a special remainder created for his father-in-law, Gerard Noel also inherited a baronetcy, which was, in turn, passed to his and Diana's son, Charles, who was created Earl of Gainsborough, and became the father of Lady Ida Hay's husband.

In an interesting genealogical twist, had the parents of Gerard Edwardes been married, as has been proposed by some historians but lacking in proof, the present day Earls of Gainsborough would also be the Dukes of Hamilton. The senior line of the Hamiltons became extinct in 1895 at which time the descendants of the peculiarly named Lord Anne Hamilton, Gerard Edwardes' father, inherited the Dukedom. If Lord Anne and Mary Edwardes had indeed married, Gerard would be the eldest legitimate son and his descendant, the 3rd Earl of Gainsborough would have succeeded as Duke in 1895.

However, no proof has been found of a marriage between Lord Anne and Mary Edwardes so their son continues to be determined as illegitimate. Therefore the Dukedom passed to the descendants of a later, proven marriage for Lord Anne instead.

The Earl of Gainsborough and his wife converted to Catholicism in 1851, an act that generally kept the family at arm's length from the then Queen Victoria - at least at further length than her other cousins descended from her "Uncle King." Previously, Lady Ida had been quite close to the Queen and was even one of her bridesmaids at her wedding to Prince Albert.

Charles and Ida had five children: Blanche, Constance, Charles, Edith and Edward. Blanche married an organist and lived quietly, dying without children in 1881. Edith entered the Church as a nun. The remaining three children have plenty of descendants to make up for the two who do not.

Lady Constance Noel married Sir Henry Bellingham, 4th Baronet, in 1874. The title Baronet was created for Henry's great-grandfather, Sir William, a naval commissioner. Sir William's claim in history is his close involvement with outfitting the exploration team of George Vancouver. for whom the Canadian city is named. Appropriately enough, a bay near Vancouver is now named for Bellingham, as is a town in the U.S.A.'s state of Washington - All of this despite the fact that Bellingham never even saw the Pacific Ocean.

The Bellinghams were an Irish family from county Louth. Sir Henry pursued a career in public service. He served Louth in the British Parliament in the 1880s followed up by serving as High Sheriff and later Lord Lieutenant back in his home county. In addition to serving his homeland, he served his Pope as Private Chamberlain, - actually three Popes: Pius IX, Leo XII, and Pius X.

Of Henry and Constance's four children, the elder daughter became a nun as Sister (later Mother) Mary Emanuel, and the younger daughter, the Marchioness of Bute. The Crichton-Stuarts of Bute will be discussed in the next chapter.

The elder son, Edward, succeeded his father as Baronet, in 1921, as well as Lord Lieutenant of county Louth, a title he would hold only a year until Irish independence. He lived most of his life as a soldier serving in the Boer Wars, and both World Wars. He briefly served in the Seanad Éireann, the first upper house in Ireland's parliament, between the wars. Late in life he also served as Vice-Consul in the British embassy in Guatemala.

In 1904, Edward married a widow, Mrs. Charlotte Gough and with her had an only daughter, Charlotte. Charlotte married Ronald Hawker, a descendant of Dorothy Jordan's daughter Lucy Ford. Charlotte's only son is now elderly and unmarried.

Sir Edward was the last of the Baronets to live in Castle Bellingham in county Louth. He sold the 17th century castle to the Irish State which, in turn, sold it to one Dermot Meehan who developed it into a hotel, which is how it remains today.

Since Edward only had a daughter, his baronetcy passed to the son of his younger brother, Roger, who is also named Roger. Sir Roger made his home in Cheshire, in western England. There he raised his two sons who would each become Baronet. The elder, Sir Noel, died childless in 1999. The younger, Sir Anthony, is the present Baronet and currently lives in Thailand. His only child is his heir, William. In his late teens, William now makes his home in California near his mother, where he has fallen in with the children of some of Hollywood's biggest names.

In 1881, the Earldom of Gainsborough passed to Charles Noel, elder son of the 2nd Earl and Lady Ida Hay. Charles was born and died at Campden House in Chipping Campden, Gloucestershire. Campden House is a rebuilt mansion, the original manor house being burnt during the Civil War, and served as home to the Earls of Gainsborough in the 19th Century. More recently they have tended toward their principal estate at Exton Park, Rutland.

Charles, while still heir to his father and thus styled
Viscount Campden, married firstly to Augusta Berkeley, a
maternal granddaughter of the Irish Earl of Kenmare. She
died in 1877, four years before she could become Countess of
Gainsborough. Her only child, Agnes, died unmarried
in1915. It is Charles' second wife who became Countess and
ancestress of the subsequent Earls. She was Mary-Elizabeth
Dease, a descendant of King Charles II through her mother,
Charlotte Jerningham. Charles and Mary-Elizabeth would
have five more children, three sons and two daughters.

The eldest son, Arthur, succeeded to the Earldom in
1926. His 1915 marriage to Alice Eyre produced three
children: Maureen, later Baroness Dormer, Anthony, the 5th
Earl, and Gerard. Prior to becoming Earl, Arthur, as well as
both of his brothers, saw action in the First World War, the
youngest brother, Robert, dying in Africa from disease
contracted while on active duty. Arthur would be the Earl of
Gainsborough for only eight months as he died in 1927.

Arthur was succeeded by his elder son, Anthony.
Described in his obituary as the largest landowner in
England's smallest county, Rutland, the 5th Earl of
Gainsborough was an adamant defender of rural self-
government. Serving on several boards and commissions,

not to mention in the House of Lords, he opposed dictates from London about how resources of the rural area should be managed. He fought against the absorption of Rutland by Leicestershire, which happened in 1974, professing it would never work. He lived long enough to be proven right and saw the 1997 re-establishment of the Rutland County Council, a body on which he once served.

Married in 1947 to Mary Stourton, granddaughter of the 25th Baron Stourton, Anthony sired a large brood of a family with eight children, evenly divided between sons and daughters Sadly, one daughter died in infancy. His descendants include not only the current Earl and his son and heir, but also Viscount Flojambe, heir to the Earl of Liverpool.

Anthony's brother, the Hon. Gerard Noel, also has a connection to the Royal Family among his family, albeit somewhat roundabout. His daughter, Elizabeth is married to the step-son of Andrew Parker-Bowles, first husband to Her Royal Highness the Duchess of Cornwall.

The 4th Earl of Gainsborough's sister, Lady Norah, married into another prominent titled family of Britain, the Bentincks. This family is actually a foreign import as they came to Britain with the Glorious Revolution that brought

William and Mary to the Throne in 1689. Count Hans Willem Bentinck was a chief advisor to Willem, Prince of Orange, and came with him to Britain when Willem became King William III to sit alongside his wife Queen Mary II. There are long standing rumors that Bentinck may have been not only an advisor, but also a lover to the new King. His descendant, the current Earl of Portland, has a novel way of refuting this; he claims Count Bentinck was just too dull to be gay.

Whatever Count Bentinck's orientation, he was married and produced heirs. Bentinck himself was created Earl of Portland and his eldest son was later elevated to Duke. The Dukes of Portland continued over the centuries but became extinct in 1990. Since the Earldom had been created for a previous generation of the family, it was able to pass to the younger sons of Count Bentinck, which brings us to one Robert Bentinck, who married Lady Norah Noel. In addition to any British titles they may inherit, this family also has the right, by special permission of Queen Victoria, to continue to use their countly title from the Holy Roman Empire. So Robert was styled Count Robert Bentinck.

Count and Countess Bentinck had two children, Brydgytte and Henry. Brydgytte returned to the land of her ancestors when she married Dutch nobleman Adriaan van der Wyck. Adriaan carried the title Jonkheer, a title which does not have an accurate translation into English. Perhaps saying the Noble Adriaan van der Wyck would be the best way to capture the sense of the meaning. Adriaan and Brydgytte's five children and their descendants have remained in the Netherlands.

Count Henry ultimately inherited the Earldom of Portland upon the extinction of the ducal line in 1990. Henry, who discontinued using the title Count, was the first to break from the traditions of European aristocracy and entered the regular workforce. He is best known as a producer of television commercials and for the BBC, but he also did a stint as a farm hand in Tasmania. It should therefore not be surprising that neither of his marriages were with members of the titled elite. Henry had the title Earl for only seven years before his own death in 1997.

Being raised by a television producer, it is no wonder that his only son and heir, Timothy, entered a similar field: acting. Tim Bentinck, as he is known professionally, was born during his father's time in Tasmania. After a somewhat aimless start, he has found a successful career in both voice-over and stage performances. A thoroughly down-to-earth fellow, he prefers Tim to "your Lordship." Married since 1979, he is the father of two twenty-something boys, William and Jasper, who he describes on his website as being a major intellect (William) and a future rock deity (Jasper).

Tim Bentinck's two elder sisters are also occupied with their own families, the elder, Sorrel, being formerly married to the Lister-Kaye Baronet and the younger, Anna to a couple of fellows before starting a family without a husband. The Bentinck siblings have done many things during their lives and been many people. They have also known tragedy, as Anna lost a set of twins within minutes of their birth.

Several of the families that have married into the descendants of King William and Mrs. Jordan have belonged to the Peerage, that is, the titled nobility of the British Isles, but others have belonged to what is known as the Landed Gentry, a series of families that, though not noble, have long family histories typically associated with a particular place or estate. A classic example of such a family is the Steuart Fothringhams, Lairds of Murthly, in Perthshire.

Laird is an ancient Scottish designation that is derived from "Lord of the Manor," and has come to be used to differentiate between these types of lords and the noble title "Lord" which has been ranked at the same level as an English

Baron. Thus it is as the owners and caretakers of the Estate of Murthly that the Steuart Fothringhams can be termed as Lairds.

Carola Noel, granddaughter of the 3rd Earl of Gainsborough, brought this landed family into the fold of William IV descendants by marrying Thomas Steuart Fothringham in 1936. The Murthly estate is famous for its beautifully maintained international woods, comprised mostly of conifers such as Douglas firs brought to Scotland from the United States in the early 1800s, Serbian spruce, Chilean pine, and varieties of hemlock. There continue to be additions made and a more diverse choice of trees planted.

The Steuart Fothringhams, like the trees they care for, are on the brink of becoming a very large family. Carola and Thomas had only three children, but they multiplied into nine grandchildren who are now the parents of a growing army of great-grandchildren.

Chapter 7: The Crichton-Stuarts

The 1905 marriage of Augusta Bellingham to John Crichton-Stuart, 4th Marquess of Bute, marked the joining of a descendant of the newer Germanic Hanover/Saxe-Coburg dynasty of British Kings with a descendant of the old regime of the Stuart Kings of Scotland.

The Crichton-Stuarts, named only Stuart until 1805, are direct male line descendants of King Robert II of Scotland (died 1390), the first of the Stuart Kings, through his illegitimate son, John, the Black Stewart, so named because of his dark complexion.

Over the centuries, the Stuarts picked up several titles, beginning with a baronetcy in 1627. This was followed by the Earldom of Bute, with its subsidiary viscountcy and three lordships, in 1703. The first title in the Peerage of Great Britain, the previous ones all being in that of Scotland, was given to the 3rd Earl's wife as Baroness Mount Stuart, a title that merged with the others when their son succeeded both of his parents. In addition to his own inheritance, he married the heiress of vast Welsh lands and in recognition of this was created in Baron Cardiff in 1776. This Lord Bute was further titled Earl of Windsor and Viscount Mountjoy, revivals of titles held by his wife's family, and Marquess of Bute in 1796. His grandson, the 2nd Marquess, also succeeded his maternal grandfather as the 7th Earl of Dumfries, Viscount Ayr and 15th Lord Crichton. The current Marquess carries this lengthy list of titles to this day.

Of the more notable ancestors, none are more so than the 3rd Earl of Bute, Prime Minster of Great Britain 1762-1763, the first Scot to hold the position after the Act of Union of 1707, which created Great Britain. Though a brief term, it was at a momentous one, seeing the end of the Seven Years' War, alternately known outside Britain as the French and Indian War, the 3rd Silesian War, or the Pomeranian War.

The title Marquess itself is an interesting story. The titles of the British Peerage system typically have their roots in foreign languages. For example, Duke comes from the

Latin dux. Earl is the only one that is uniquely British, being derived from an ancient Celtic term. The term Marquess came to Britain with the conquering Normans in 1066 and is an attempt to anglicize the French title Marquis. This title has recognizable variations in other languages such as Marqués or Marchese. Many try to tie the word also to the German Markgraf, but this term seems to have a different origination. In present-day Britain, with worldwide media available 24 hours a day, the term Marquess has become nearly interchangeable with Marquis in day-to-day usage.

It is with all of this history and all of these titles that the 4th Marquess, or Marquis, traditionally named John Crichton-Stuart, married Augusta Bellingham, direct matrilineal descendant of Mrs. Jordan and her royal lover, the Duke of Clarence, later King William IV. By this point, not only had the Marquess acquired many titles, but also had amassed extremely large tracts of property, becoming the largest land owner in the British Isles.

John also held an interest in Morocco and bought several acres there as well, founded a hotel in Tangier, and became proprietor of an English-language newspaper, *The Tangier Gazette*. In the 1930s he oversaw the sale of much of his Welsh land holdings, the unparalleled sale causing quite the media sensation just as much the world was working its way out of a Depression and into a World War.

John and Augusta, who was herself honored as a Dame of the British Empire in 1918, had seven children, five of them boys. Through their eldest daughter, Lady Mary, the Crichton-Stuarts are now connected to European nobility. Mary's elder daughter, Ione, married Baron Christian von Oppenheim and made their home in Spain. The younger daughter, Lady Jean, married a son of the 7th Earl of Abington, the Hon . James Bertie. James and Jean had two sons, the elder of whom became the Grand Master of the Sovereign Military Order of Malta, the first Brit to do so since 1258.

The eldest Crichton-Stuart brother, of course named John, succeeded his father as 5th Marquess of Bute in 1947. After serving in the Royal Navy during World War II, he made his mark in the world of ornithology. He purchased the islands of St. Kilda as a means of preserving the delicate eco-systems there. He then gifted the islands to the National Trust for Scotland so they could be properly maintained for future generations. He also gifted his remaining Welsh property, Cardiff Castle, to the City of Cardiff. Today the

Castle houses museums and, sitting in luscious Bute Park, is used as a concert venue.

The 5th Marquess married Lady Eileen Forbes, daughter of the 8th Earl of Granard, in 1932. They had four children, three sons and a daughter. The daughter, Lady Fiona, and her husband, Michael Lowsley-Williams, moved to Spain, making their living there in real estate with their four sons. The three sons remained in Britain and their descendants make up the core of the Crichton-Stuart family today.

The eldest son, - yes, he too is named John, - succeeded to the Marquessate in 1956. Dedicated to historic preservation, the 6th Marquess sat on several boards, most notably the National Trust for Scotland, serving as its chair. He began an ambitious restoration of his home estate, Mount Stuart, in the late 1980s, work that has continued under his son, the current Marquess.

Johnny Dumfries, as the 7th and current Marquess was known during his father's lifetime, was a professional race car driver, winning several formula races, crowning his achievements with a win at Le Mans in 1988. Since the death of his father, in 1993, he still prefers to be called Johnny, but now it is Johnny Bute.

A very modern individual, Johnny Bute places less emphasis on his title and more on what he can do for Scotland and the rather large corner of it that he owns. Continuing the restorative work begun by his father, Johnny has proven his dedication to the land he owns and preserving its heritage for future generations.

Over the course of two marriages, Johnny is now the father of four children: three girls and a boy, now styled Earl of Dumfries. In a nod to the conventional from an unconventional Marquess, the boy is also named John.

Of the several living Crichton-Stuart cousins descended from the 4th Marquess and Augusta Bellingham, one of the more notable is their grandson, Frederik Crichton-Stuart. He is the son of Lord Rhidian, Augusta's youngest son, and Selina Gerthe van Wijk, herself the daughter of a Dutch diplomat.

Freddy, as he is universally known, followed a similar path as his cousin, Andrew Bertie, becoming heavily involved with the Sovereign Military Order of Malta, known colloquially as the Order of St. John. In 2008, when Bertie died, he was succeeded as the Grand Master by Matthew Festing, until then Grand Prior of England. In the position of

Grand Prior, Festing has been succeeded by Freddy Crichton-Stuart.

His installation as Grand Prior completes a circle begun when his ancestors staunchly supported Mary, Queen of Scots, until her execution was ordered by her cousin, Queen Elizabeth I of England. One of Elizabeth's acts to end the religious war in England in favor of a protestant Church of England was to dismember the Priory. It lay in abeyance for the next fours and a half centuries until Elizabeth's namesake, Elizabeth II, restored the Grand Priory in 1993. And now another Stuart is its Grand Prior.

Chapter 8: The Duffs

Lady Agnes Hay (I1829-1869) married, in 1846 in Paris, James Duff, who after 1857, was the 5th Earl of Fife. Life with the Earl was nearly the opposite of life with her parents. The Errolls had been a very social family and always a presence at Court. The Earl was a notorious recluse, who wandered from his home, "Duff House," near Banff, only when he could otherwise not get out of doing so. This staying at home business did have one happy side affect: children, of whom they had five.

The eldest Duff daughter was Anne, born in 1847. She married the future 5th Marquess of Townshend. Like many Lords-in-waiting, John Townshend served first in the House of Commons, having been elected from Tamworth in

Staffordshire. His term was from 1856 to 1863, when he succeed his father as Marquess. John and Anne Townshend had two children, John and Agnes.

John, the 6th Marquess of Townshend after 1899, married in 1905 Gwladys Sutherst, who became one of the earliest ladies to be what we now would call a screenwriter. She was also a playwright and novelist and was associated with the Claredon Film Company early in its existence.

Gwladys Townshend also became known for a more "spirited" matter. She is one of the many occupants of Raynham Hall, seat of the Marquesses of Townshend, to have encountered, and discussed at length, its celebrated ghost, the Brown Lady. The spirit is so named because she reportedly appears as a brown haze, lacking real definition, but seeming like a lady in dresses and a veil. She is believed to be the ghost of Audrey, Viscountess Townshend, mother of the 1st Marquess. The story goes that after being discovered of infidelity, she was kept prisoner in Raynham Hall and never allowed to see her children again. Whatever the story, a photograph of the Brown Lady taken in 1936 is considered one of the best "ghost pictures" ever taken.

Like his own parents, John & Gwladys also had only two children, one son and one daughter. The son, the 7th

Marquess of Townshend, has the distinction of being the longest serving member of the British Peerage. On March 2nd, 2009 he broke the record, and at the time of his death thirteen months later, at age 93, he had been a Peer for 88 years, 5 months and 10 days. Like his mother, he was in the theater arts, serving as Chairman of Anglia Television for three decades until his retirement in 1986. This Marquess was married three times, first to Elizabeth Luby (later Lady Galt, wife of Sir James), then to Ann Darlow, who died in 1988, and finally to Philippa Montgomerie, who was the widow of Humphrey Swire. By his first two wives, he became the father of five children: Carolyn, Joanna and Charles by Elizabeth, and John and Katherine by Ann.

Lady Carolyn Townshend, the name she continues to be known by after two failed marriages, is a London event and party planning socialite who married two wealthy business men. First, she married Goodyear executive Antonio Capellini, and then briefly to Seagram's CEO, Edgar Bronfman Sr. She has one grown son by Capellini who is now married with a family of his own.

Lady Joanna, who also has retained her maiden name, is now on her third marriage, this one to Christian Boegner.

She also has one grown son, Francis, by her first husband, Jeremy Bradford.

Charles, now the 8th Marquess, was the elder son and heir to his father. He is very involved with the local community surrounding Raynham Hall. One notable example is his devotion to renovations was adding new bells to the Church of East Raynham, whose renovation caught the interest of even the Queen, prompting a 2002 royal visit during the construction. While still Lord Raynham, his first wife, Hermione Ponsonby, sadly was killed in a car crash in 1985. Charles remarried five years later to Mrs. Alison Marshall. Lord Townshend has two grown children by his first wife, including heir, Thomas.

The 7th Marquess's younger children, John and Katherine have each married twice and each have young children still at home. Katherine's first husband, Piers Dent has made a name for himself as an aerial photographer. Lord Townshend's lone sister, Lady Elizabeth, married a Baronet named Richard White and had one child, the current holder of that Baronetcy, Sir Christopher.

The only sibling of the 6th Marquess, Lady Agnes, married James Cunnighame-Durham, son of a diplomat by the same name. Their son, Nicholas was killed in World War

II, and their daughter, Victoria, died unmarried, aged 94, in 2002.

The Countess of Fife's second daughter, Ida, was born in 1848 at Duff House. Ida married twice, to Adrian Hope and William Wilson, and was divorced both times. With Adrian, she had three daughters: Agnes, Mildred, and Ethel. The eldest daughter, Agnes, married Edwin Phillips de Lisle, whose father, Ambrose, was a prominent layman of the Catholic Church. They had a large family of eight children, which today have turned into dozens of descendants. The second daughter, Mildred, remained unmarried.

The youngest daughter, Ethel, married John Lockhart-Mummery, a doctor of a Landed Gentry family. John became well-respected in the medical community and published works connecting heredity to likeliness to develop cancer. Ethel died childless, but John has descendants still living through his second marriage.

Lady Fife's only son, Alexander was born in 1849 in Edinburgh. It was through his father's friendship with the Prince of Wales (later Edward VII,) that he married Princess Louise, the Prince's eldest daughter. This marriage not only brought him into the British Royal Family, but also made him a brother-in-law to the future Queen of Norway, Louise's youngest sister, Maud. In preparation for marrying a royal princess, it was determined that being an Earl wasn't good enough so he was elevated to become the first Duke of Fife.

The Duke and the Princess had two surviving daughters, their only son being stillborn in 1890. When it became obvious there would be no more children, and Louise's father had finally succeeded his long-living mother, Queen Victoria, the creation of the Dukdom of Fife was reconstituted to allow the succession of the daughters and any male heirs they may have. The two girls, now teenagers, were also raised to the rank of Princess of Fife by their doting grandfather in 1905.

The elder daughter, Princess Alexandra, Duchess of Fife after 1912, married her first cousin, Prince Arthur, who was the only son and heir to the Duke of Connaught. As it happened, the old Duke outlived Arthur and that title passed to Arthur and Alexandra's only child, Alastair, who himself died unmarried in 1943 before he could also succeed as Duke of Fife.

The younger daughter, Princess Maud, married the Earl of Southesk and had one child, a son James, who today is the 3rd Duke of Fife, and has been since Princess Alexandra's death in 1959. James' mother had died in 1945, but his father lived on until 1992, dying at the age of 98. The current Duke, who now is also the Earl of Southesk, married Caroline, daughter of the 3rd Baron Forteviot in 1954, but divorced twelve years later. They have two grown children, David, styled Earl of Southesk by courtesy, and Lady Alexandra. Both are married with children, - Charles' three are in their teens, and Clare's only daughter is still in early primary school.

Lady Fife's third daughter, Agnes, was born in 1849. Agnes' marital adventures could be a book unto themselves. The short version is, at age 19, she eloped with Viscount Dupplin, the heir to the Earl of Kinnoull, and two years later had her first daughter, also named Agnes, but quickly grew tired of the boring Viscount. She eloped again in 1876, - losing her child to Dupplin in the process, - with Herbert Flower, whose brother, Cyril, was created Lord Battersea. This match suited her much better and they were truly happy together, according to family and friends, for the four years until Herbert died. Penniless and a social outcast, Agnes went to work in a hospital doing menial labor hoping to learn enough to become a nurse. While there, she met and was swept off her feet by a surgeon, Dr. Alfred Cooper, who became her third husband in 1882.

Alfred had a knack for being in the right place at the right time. It is how he met Agnes, and it is how he happened to be visiting friends in St. Petersburg, Russia at the same time as the then Duke of Edinburgh (2nd son of Queen Victoria) was marrying the Tsar's daughter. The Prince of Wales was also in attendance of the wedding and fell ill. Cooper was the first British doctor they could locate, so he cared for the ailing Prince, getting him back on his feet, and becoming friends at the same time. Edward did not forget this kindness shown him and awarded Alfred with a knighthood when he became King. One more tidbit about Alfred Cooper (later Sir Alfred): his medical specialty was venereal disease, and his clients were mostly the upper crust of society. Even though he must have had some truly sordid gossip to share, he never did.

Agnes, the daughter by Viscount Dupplin, married German diplomat Herbert von Hindenburg, a relative of the Imperial Field Marshal and later President of the German Republic. Their life was lived in relative obscurity, with one sadness being their only child, a daughter, who died at birth.

The eldest Cooper child was Stephanie, born in 1883. Her first marriage to stockbroker Arthur Levita brought financial security, which served her well after his death, in

1910, and also gave her the ability to take in her family members as needed during the lean years of the First World War. In the midst of the war, in 1916, Stephanie married Maurice Wingfield, known to his friends as Tolly. Stephanie had lovely daughters by Levita, Violet and Enid. Violet's line ended with the death of her only child, Nicholas Hirsch, in 1983. Enid married Euen Cameron and by him had an only son, Ian. Ian Cameron married Mary Mount, the daughter of a Baronet and by her has four children including the current Prime Minister, David Cameron.

The second Cooper daughter, Hermione (known as Mione to her family), married in 1904, at age 19, to Neil Arnott. The marriage was not a happy one but did produce one child, a son Ian. Ian died prematurely in 1950 and left a sole daughter, Portia. Portia ended her days in 2009 on the island of Cyprus, having been married to James Lord and leaving a son and a daughter as well as five grandchildren.

Agnes's fourth daughter, the third by Cooper, Sybil, came in 1886 and only lived to the age of 41. During that time she married Richard Hart-Davis of a landed family in Surrey. Sybil had two children, but it was believed by them that Richard was not their father. Sybil herself was always unsure of the paternity of her children, but Richard accepted them and raised them as his own. It is perhaps a blessing that Sybil's life was short, as it was tormented by mental illness which led her to living a religious-based life at the end in hopes of finding relief. But ultimately, she lost that battle, committing suicide.

The son, Rupert, born in 1907, went on to become a very well-known publisher, editor, author, and even briefly an actor. It is uncommon to come across his name without the term "Man of Letters" attached. In addition to his meticulous editing of hundreds of the letters of Oscar Wilde, he is also the author of a superb biography of Hugh Walpole, and published his own weekly correspondence with his old Eton professor, George Myttleton. Furthermore, he was an active member of the London Library and the Literary Society. In 1967, he was awarded a knighthood for his literary contributions.

Even though Rupert Hart-Davis spent a hectic schedule of dining with this group or attending that gala, he did not consider himself a social person. In one of his published letters he wrote:

> The fact that I am tolerably good at coping with
> people is misleading. I much prefer near-solitude,
> at any rate for long periods. Maybe too much of
> it would drive me back to the world of men, but

I've never had enough leisure to test the theory.[3]

This, "preference for solitude" did not include solitude from marriage. He did it four times; firstly and briefly to the actress Peggy Ashcroft; secondly to the mother of his three children, Comfort Borden-Turner; thirdly to Ruth Simon, whom he had loved for 17 years before marrying her and who died suddenly in his arms in a taxi; and fourthly to his former secretary, June Williams, who provided him companionship in his last years before dying at the age of 92.

Rupert's three children have made marks in the world in their own ways. The eldest, Bridget, married Baron Silsoe, and has lived the life of a political wife and mother of two. Duff, the elder of two sons, is himself a noted biographer and journalist, and the youngest, Adam, has also published several works, mostly on scientific or technical concerns, and like his father, has had a career so varied as to include television production and being an expert on toilets. Each of Rupert's children has married and each has two children of their own, with a new generation just starting to appear.

---

[3] Hart-Davis, Rupert. *The Lyttleton Hart-Davis Letters, Vol. III* (1981)

Sir Rupert's only sibling, Deirdre, also visited the altar four times. Her first husband, Ronald Balfour, the father of first two children, was killed in a car crash in 1941. The only thing worth remarking on her three subsequent marriages is that she had a third daughter by her third husband, Tony Bland.

The youngest of the Cooper kids, Duff, was the one to lead the most public life. After attending Eton he joined the foreign service, which spared him active duty in World War I until 1917 when he joined the Grenadier Guards. He received a DSO for his service. The most remarkable event of war life is that he survived it. He was the only one a tight knit group of friends from Eton to do so. This shared loss brought him closer to the only lady in the group, Lady Diana Manners, the "Lady Di" of her day. They married after the war, in 1919, and after much debate with the Diana's parents, the Duke and Duchess of Rutland. The Rutlands initially did not want the match, after all Duff was not a Peer or even the son of one, but in the end Diana and Duff won out.

After the war, Duff returned to the foreign service, mostly in Egypt and Turkey. In 1924, he won a seat in Parliament from Oldham. He was a supporter of Baldwin, support which led to him losing his seat, along with many other Conservatives in 1929. He turned to literature while out of office and wrote a well-received biography of Talleyrand. With the threat of War once again looming on the Continent, he returned to government in the 1930s working his way up to First Lord of the Admiralty in 1937, only to resign a year later in protest of Neville Chamberlain's appeasement policies towards Hitler's Germany. He later served again, this time under Churchill, in minor roles during the war, eventually being the British liaison to the Free French and then Ambassador to Paris in 1944. He retired from public service in 1947, receiving a knighthood, and later a peerage as Viscount Norwich, and devoted the remaining seven years of his life to literature.

The Cooper-Manners marriage lasted 35 years but was wrought with infidelities. One such affair on Duff's side in 1947 lead to the birth on an illegitimate son, William Patten, who only learned this truth after he was 50. William is a Unitarian pastor in Massachusetts. His mother was the quintessential political hostess, Susan Alsop. The story of this "long-lost" child became public only after the death of both biological parents involved. William recently wrote a memoir of his life, his relationship with his mother and the three men he called "father" at various times.

By Lady Diana, Cooper also fathered a son, the current Viscount Norwich. John Julius Norwich, as he is listed in television credits, has had a successful career as an author and in television. His areas of specialty are history and travel documentary, with a long list of productions he wrote and/or produced. Lord Norwich has been married twice and is the father of Artemis Cooper, who has followed in her father's footsteps as a historian, and of Jason Cooper, the heir to his title. Lord Norwich also has a daughter named Allegra by the late Enrica Huston, who, at the time, was the estranged wife of filmmaker, John Huston.

Lady Fife's youngest child, Alexina, born in 1851, is the one almost forgotten to history. She married a grandson of the Earl of Coventry, but died in 1882 at the young age of 31, leaving no children.

Chapter 9: The Kennedy-Erskines

Lady Augusta FitzClarence was only eight when her parents separated. Under the separation agreement between her father and mother, Augusta remained with her mother until she turned 13 and, at which time she went to live with her father. By the time she reached the height of her teen-aged years, Dora Jordan was dead and William had married Princess Adelheid of Saxe-Meiningen. Augusta, and the younger half of her siblings, found very close relationships with their step-mother. It was this soon-to-be Queen who facilitated most of the meetings of William's children with their spouses.

This was the case with Augusta when she met her future husband, John Kennedy, the younger son of the Earl of

Cassilis, who would later be elevated to the Marquessate of Ailsa. John's mother was Margaret Erskine, eventual heiress to the Lairdship Erskine of Dun, which was passed to her children. Since John's elder brother, Archibald, was heir to their father, the maternal Erskine inheritance fell to John. To reflect this inheritance, he changed his name to Kennedy-Erskine prior to his marriage to Augusta.

John and Augusta's marriage would only last not quite four years, as John died in 1831. However, the marriage did produce three children, William, Wilhelmina, and Millicent. Wilhelmina, the elder daughter would one day marry her cousin the 2nd Earl of Munster, but it is her childhood that she chose to write heavily about in a memoir published later in her life. It is through this memoir that we today can understand the lives of the children and grandchildren of King William during his later life.

While married to John, the family lived on the outskirts of London along the River Thames at an estate called Railshead next door to the estate of his parents. After his death, Augusta remained there until she remarried, an act ardently disapproved of by her in-laws. She was obliged to find a new home, so she turned to her father for help. Now

King, William was able to offer her and her family apartments in Kensington Palace.

Augusta's second marriage was to Lord John Gordon, a younger son of the 9th Marquess of Huntly. The Gordon family is one of the oldest and most distinguished families of Scotland. The Marquessate of Huntly is also the oldest Marquessate in Scotland, having been created in 1599. The 4th Marquess was further created Duke of Gordon and the two titles remained combined until the death of the 5th Duke and 8th Marquess in 1836. While the Dukedom then became extinct, the Marquessate passed to a more distant relative, Lord John's father. John and Augusta would not have any children.

Through Augusta's only son, William, named in honor of his royal grandfather, the Kennedy-Erskine name continued a couple more generations, but came extinct in 1980 with the death of Mrs. Millicent Lovett, the last child of William's only son, Augustus. Augustus's other children were twin boys, - one who died young and the other died childless, in 1963 - and a daughter, Violet.

Violet Kennedy-Erskine died most unusually, aged only 37. She was discovered dead in her room at the Empress Club in London on Christmas Day, 1934. The Coroner ruled she had committed suicide based on the fact that the room had been locked from the inside. However, she was discovered with her bed jacket wrapped around her throat and a dressing gown shoved into her mouth. It was an odd means for committing suicide. At the Coroner's Inquest, it was mentioned that the club's engineer entered through a window when it was discovered the door was locked and she was not responding to calls from the hall. Could someone have entered, or at least exited, that same way? Perhaps the Coroner was too quick to rule out foul play.

Violet had been named for her father's elder sister, Violet Erskine-Kennedy, who, by marriage, became Violet Jacob, the well known Scottish poet and author. This elder Violet married Arthur Jacob, and with him, had an only child, also named Arthur. The younger Arthur was still unmarried when he was killed in action in World War I, in Belgium.

The youngest child of Lady Augusta, Millicent Kennedy-Erskine, is the only one to have living descendants today. When Millicent married in 1855, she got to keep part of her name. Her husband was also a distant cousin, James Erskine-Wemyss. Just as her grandmother had been the heiress of the Erskines of Dun, James' mother was the heiress of the Erskines of Torriehouse. James' father was an heir in his own right to the Lairdship of Wemyss of Wemyss Castle. The names were joined by his parents' marriage to be Erskine-Wemyss.

Millicent and James had five children: Dora, Mary, Randolph, Hugo, and Rosslyn. Hugo died unmarried in 1933. Mary married Cecil Paget, a grandson of the 1st Marquess of Anglesey, and had three children, but they all died childless.

Dora married quite well in 1887 when she married the Lord Henry Grosvenor, son of the 1st Duke of Westminster, owner of extensive, and exclusive, properties throughout London. The title would eventually pass to their son, - but as he never married, - it would move onto a collateral branch of the family, where it remains today.

The youngest son was Rosslyn, who became a naval officer and eventually Admiral of the Fleet. His distinguished service in the Royal Navy through the First World War earned him a knighthood and, upon his retirement, a peerage as Baron Wester Wemyss. With his wife, Victoria Morier, daughter of noted diplomat, Sir Robert Morier, Rosslyn fathered only one child, a daughter, Alice. Therefore his Barony would expire upon his death in 1933.

The remaining Erskine-Wemyss, eldest son Randolph, would succeed his father in due course to the Lairdship of Wemyss of Castle Wemyss, was followed by his son, Michael, who ultimately succeeded to the headship of the entire clan of Wemyss. With this inheritance comes Wemyss Castle, a historically important building dating from 1421. Among its other historical events, it is the location where Mary, Queen of Scots, met her husband, Lord Darnley.

The Wemyss family today is headed by Michael's grandson and namesake, Michael Wemyss of that Ilk, whose maternal ancestry may be even more impressive, as his mother was from the Bruce family, this branch being the earls of Elgin and Kincardine. As Michael has only two grown daughters, the elder, as heiress, will presumably pass the name Wemyss on to any children she may have. The male line of the family will be continued by Michael's brother, Charles who has a son in his early twenties.

The Detailed Genealogy of the Descendants of King William IV

This genealogy attempts to list every descendant of King William IV, both legitimate and illegitimate. In any work of this nature there are bound to be errors and omissions. Corrections and additions are always welcome and shule be sent by email to daniel@dan-willis.com or by post to Daniel Willis, 354 Lincoln St, Denver CO 80203 USA.

Symbols & Abbreviations:

* Born
= Married
+ Died
cr. created
DBE Dame of the Order of the British Empire
DCB Dame Commander of the Order of the Bath
DCMG Dame Commander of the Order of St. Michael and St. George
DCVO Dame Commander of the Royal Victorian Order
dv. divorced
GBE Knight Grand Cross of the Order of the British Empire
GCB Knight Grand Cross of the Order of the Bath
GCH Knight Grand Cross of the Order of Hanover
GCMG Knight Grand Cross of the Order of St. Michael and St. George
GCVO Knight Grand Cross of the Royal Victorian Order
HGDH His/Her Grand Ducal Highness
HH His/Her Highness
HIH His/Her Imperial Highness
HI&RH His/Her Imperial and Royal Highness
HM His/Her Majesty
HRH His/Her Royal Highness
HSH His/Her Serene Highness
KCB Knight Commander of the Order of the Bath
KCH Knight Commander of the Order of Hanover
KCMG Knight Commander of the Order of St. Michael and St. George
KCVO Knight Commander of the Royal Victorian Order
KG Knight of the Order of the Garter
KBE Knight of the Order of the Britsh Empire
KH Knight of teh Order of Hanover
KP Knight of the Order of St. Patrick
KT Knight of the Order of the Thistle
Kt. Knight Bachelor
ph. posthumous
suc. succeeded

HM William IV Henry, **King of the United Kingdom of Great Britain and Ireland, Elector of Hanover, Duke of Brunswick-Luneburg** (21 Aug 1765 London – 20 Jun 1837 Windsor) son of George III, King of the United Kingdom, etc.& Duchess Charlotte of Mecklenburg; cr. Duke of Clarence and St. Andrews, Earl of Munster 20 May 1789; suc. brother, George IV, as King, Elector, and Duke 26 Jun 1830

= 11 Jul 1818 London; **HSH Princess** Adelheid (**Adelaide**) Luise Therese Karoline Amelie **of Saxe-Meiningen, Duchess of Saxony** (13 Aug 1792 Meiningen – 2 Dec 1849 Middlesex) daughter of Georg I, Duke of Saxe-Meiningen Princess Luise Eleonore of Hohenlohe-Langenburg

issue by **Dorothy Bland** (known professionally as **Mrs. Jordan**) (22 Nov 1761 London – 5 Jul 1816 St. Cloud, France) daughter of Francis Bland & Catherine Mahoney:

Granted the style of children of a Marquess 24.5.1831:

I. **George** Augustus Frederick **FitzClarence, 1ˢᵗ Earl of Munster,** Viscount FitzClarence, Baron Tewkesbury (29 Jan 1794 London – 20 Mar 1842 London) cr. Earl 4 Jun 1831

= 18 Oct 1819 London; **Mary Wyndham** (… - 3 Dec 1842 Middlesex) natural daughter of George Wyndham, 3ʳᵈ Earl of Egremont & Elizabeth Ilive

A. **Lady Adelaide** Georgiana **FitzClarence** (28 Aug 1820 Bushy Park, Middlesex – 11 Oct 1883 Hove, Sussex)

B. **Lady Augusta** Margaret **FitzClarence** (29 Jul 1822 Bushy Park – 5 Sep 1846 Gimmersta, Sweden)

= 10 Apr 1844 Paris; **Baron Knut** Filip **Bonde** (9 Mar 1815 Eriksberg, Sweden – 17 Oct 1871 Stockholm) son of Baron Carl Bonde & Agneta Hildebrand; =2ⁿᵈ Helena Robinson

1. **Baroness** Adelaide **Augusta Bonde** (30 Aug 1846 Gimmersta – 4 Mar 1872 Stockholm)

= 2 May 1865 Stockholm; **Count Gustave Fouché, Duke d'Otrante** (17 Jun 1840 Paris – 5 Aug 1910 Stjarnholm) son of Count Athanase Fouché, Duke d'Otrante & Baroness Adelheid von Stedingk; suc.father as Duke 10 Feb 1886; =2ⁿᵈ Baroness Therese von Stedingke

a. **Augustine Fouché d'Otrante** (2 May 1866 Paris – 12 Nov 1943 Stockholm)

= 14 Oct 1893 Stockholm; **Frederik** Mauritz **Peyron** (2 Jul 1861 Karlskrona – 8 Jan 1915 Stockholm) son of Edvard Peyron & Katinka Due

119

I) **Maud** Therese Anna **Peyron** (15 Mar 1895 Stockholm - 1977)

II) **Victor** Oscar Knut Gustaf **Peyron** (16 Sep 1897 Stockholm - Sep 1971 Stockholm)
= 12 Jul 1922 Stegeborg; **Dagmar Westerberg** (29 Dec 1902 Goteborg – 10 Oct 1990 Stockholm)

A) **Frederik Peyron** (*8 Sep 1923 Stockholm)
= 13 Nov 1951 Memphis, Tennessee; **Gertrud Carlsson** (*27 Dec 1922 Paskallavik) daughter of John Carlsson & Tekla Nygren

1) **Elisabeth Peyron** (*7 Jul 1953 Worcester, Massachusetts)

2) Fredrik **Edward Peyron** (*10 Jun 1955 Worcester)
= 22 June 1982; **Susan Ludwig** (*29 Feb 1956)

a) **Sarah** Elisabeth **Peyron** (*7 Nov 1983 Mancherster, New Hampshire)
= 30 May 2009; **Hugh** Goodwin **Murphy** (...)

B) **Christina Peyron** (*24 Dec 1924 Stockholm)

C) **Carl-Gustaf Peyron** (6 Apr 1928 Stockholm – 4 Sep 1947 Stockholm)

III) **Adine Peyron** (6 Feb 1900 Stockholm – Aug 1989 Stockholm)
= 2 Aug 1931 Stockholm; **Ragnar** Adolf **Wollert** (25 Jul 1886 – Sep 1967 Stockholm) son of Rudolf Wollert & Fanny ...

A) **Rolf** Ragnar **Wollert** (*26 Nov 1932 Stockholm)
= 23 Jun 1957 Copenhagen; **Inger Lise Steen** (28 Jul 1932 Copenhagen – 25 Aug 2008 Mellbystrand, Sweden)

1) **Madeleine** Louise **Wollert** (*3 Mar 1967 Göteborg)
= 2001; **Imad Abou Daher** (*11 May 1966 Beirut, Lebanon) no issue

C. **William** George **FitzClarence, 2ⁿᵈ Earl of Munster** etc.(19 May 1824 Bushy Park – 30 Apr 1901 Brighton) suc.father as Earl 20 Mar 1842
= 17 Apr 1855 Knightsbridge; (his first cousin) **Wilhelmina Kennedy-Erskine** (27 Jun 1930 – 9 Oct 1906 Brighton) daughter of Hon. John Kennedy-Erskine & Lady Augusta FitzClarence *see below*

1. **Edward, Viscount FitzClarence** (29 Mar 1856 London – 20 Nov 1870 Hove, Sussex)

2. **Hon. Lionel** Frederick Archibald **FitzClarence** (24 Jul 1857 London – 24 Mar 1863 London)

3. **Geoffrey** George Gordon **FitzClarence, 3ʳᵈ Earl of Munster** etc.

(8 Jul 1859 London – 2 Feb 1902 in South Africa) suc.father as Earl
30 Apr 1901
4. **Hon. Arthur** Falkland Manners **FitzClarence** (18 Oct 1860
Edinburgh – 20 Apr 1861 Edinburgh)
5. **Aubrey FitzClarence, 4ᵗʰ Earl of Munster** etc.(7 Jun 1862
London – 1 Jan 1928) suc.brother as Earl 2 Feb 1902
6. **Hon. William** George **FitzClarence** (17 Sep 1864 Hove – 4 Oct
1899)
= 1887; **Charlotte** Elizabeth Alice **Williams** (1859 – 5 Sep 1902)
daughter of Richard Williams
  a. **Dorothy** Margaret Aline **FitzClarence** (23 Sep 1888 East
  Preston - 1952)
    = 11 Sep 1909 Shoreham; Cecil **Cadogan Elborough** (1885
    London - 1953) son of Alfred Elborough & Fanny Hadlands
    I) **Wilhelmina** Susan **Elborough** (7 Aug 1910 Lancing,
    Sussex - 1970)
    II) William **George** Edward **Elborough** (1912 Lewisham,
    Kent - Dec 1993)
      = 1937 Rochfort, Essex; **Joan O'Grady** (*1918 Essex)
      daughter of Hugh O'Grady & Nora Jarvis
      A) George **Patrick** A **Elborough** (*1937)
        = 1961 Brighton; **Rosemary McQuaker** (*12 Oct 1940)
        1) **Nicholas J Elborough** (*10 Jan 1964)
          =1 Nov 1986 (dv.); **Sally Alexander** (...)
          =2 Apr 1997; **Katherine Duchesne** (...)
          issue of 1ˢᵗ:
          a) **Charlotte** Blue **Elborough** (*17 Jun 1986)
          b) **Tobias** George **Elborough** (*Sep 1989)
          c) **Charlie** James **Elborough** (*Aug 1994)
          issue of 2ⁿᵈ:
          d) **Zachary** Roderick **Elborough** (*31 Jul 1997
            Winchester, Hampshire)
          e) **Madeleine** Rose **Elborough** (*2000 Winchester)
          f) **Bella Elborough** (*...)
        2) **Philip** Alan **Elborough** (*27 Feb 1966)
          = Oct 1999; **Michelle Treacher** (...)
          a) **Joshua** Alan **Elborough** (*6 May 1988)
        3) **Michael** Patrick **Elborough** (*19 Sep 1968)
          = ...; **Judy Larsson** (...)
          a) **Jasper Elborough** (...)
          b) **Tonto Elborough** (...)

   c) **Brianna Elborough** (...)
B) **Roger** J E **Elborough** (*1940 Essex)
  =1 1961; **Gillian Breaker** (1940 - Jan 1985)
  =2 1986; **Lynda ...** (...)
  issue of 1st:
  1) **Julie Elborough** (*1965)
   = Jul 1993; **Sunil Coutinho** (...)
  2) **Alan Elborough** (*27 Jan 1967)
C) **Anthony** M J **Elborough** (*1941 Sussex)
  = 1968; **Gillian Allen** (..)
  1) **Travis** Darren **Elborough** (*1971)
  2) **Justin** Dale **Elborough** (*13 Sep 1973)
   = Aug 2002; **Helen Norton** (...)
  3) **Saffron** Fay **Elborough** (*1976)
D) **David** William Cadogan **Elborough** (*4 Oct 1942)
  = 1965; **Brenda Sharman** (...)
  1) **Amanda J Elborough** (*2 Jun 1965)
   = May 1998 (dv.); **Martin Cannard** (...)
   a) **Jacob** William George **Cannard** (*15 Jan 1999)
E) **Michael** G **Elborough** (*1945)
  =1 1967; **Theresa Woodford** (*1949 London) daughter
  of Roy Woodford & Helena Light
  =2 1993; **Kay Reynolds** (...)
  issue of 1st:
  1) **Heide** Helena **Elborough** (*1968)
   = Aug 1987; **Craig Barnes** (...)
   a) **Luke** Craig **Barnes** (*Oct 1988)
   b) **Thomas** Michael **Barnes** (*Nov 1989)
   c) **George** Francis **Barnes** (*Mar 2003)
  2) **Jonathan** Michael **Elborough** (*1971)
F) **Jayne Elborough** (*1951 Sussex)
  =1 1970; **Malcolm Wright** (...)
  =2 Dec 1985; **Lloyd Southern** (*1954) son of William
  Southern & Hazel North
  issue ?
III) **Dorothy** Katherine Elizabeth **Elborough** (1914 Hove -
2005)
=1 1936 Sussex; **Alan M Adamson** (1913 - ...)
=2 ...; **John O'Grady** (... – 8 Apr 2009 Southwark)
issue of 1st:
A) **Alan** H **Adamson** (*1938)

B) **Janet** A **Adamson** (*1943)
issue of 2nd:
A) **Linda O'Grady** (...) [married with children]
IV) **Edward** Frederick Fitzclarence **Elborough** (1919 West Derby - Aug 1995)
=1 1945; **Mabel** F **Instrall** (1919 -) daughter of Albert Instrall & Elizabeth Veale
=2 1968; **Ivy** Kathleen **Carter** (1927 - 1973)
issue of 1st (none by 2nd):
A) **Michael** J **Elborough** (*1948 Sussex)
B) **John** A **Elborough** (*1953)
= 1977; **Julie Bridger** (*1957) dau of Frank Bridger & Gladys Nicolaides
1) **Daniel** Lee **Elborough** (*Mar 1974)
2) **Mark** Duncan J **Elborough** (*Mar 1978)
C) **Peter** K **Elborough** (*1956)
= 1979; **Maureen Budgen** (*1958)
1) **Natalie Elborough** (*Jun 1983) (twin)
2) **Sarah Elborough** (*Jun 1983) (twin)
V) **Patrick** Cecil **Elborough** (1920 Hove – 25 Sep 1934 East Grinstead, East Sussex)
b. **Wilhelmina** Violet Eileen **FitzClarence** (17 Jul 1894 – 12 Feb 1962 Thorpe Malsor Hall, Kettering, Northamptonshire)
= 19 Jan 1918 London; **Cecil** John Cokayne **Maunsell** (2 Feb 1881 – 11 Feb 1948 Thorpe Malsor Hall) son of Thomas Maunsell & Catherine Cavendish
I) **Cecilia** Violet Cokayne **Maunsell** (24 Feb 1919 – 11 Jan 2001 Thorpe Malsor Hall)
= 12 Oct 1940 Rothwell, Leeds (dv.1958); **George** Arnold Ford **Kennard** (later 3rd Baronet) (27 Apr 1915 – 13 Dec 1999 London) son of Sir Coleridge Kennard, 1st Baronet & Dorothy Barclay; suc.brother as Baronet 3 May 1967; =2nd Mollie Wyllie; =3rd Nicola Carew; =4th Georgina Wernher; upon his death the Baronetage became extinct
A) **Zandra Kennard** (*17 Jun 1941 Thorpe Malsor Hall)
= 18 Aug 1962 Rothwell; **John** Middleton Neilson **Powell** (*10 Nov 1936 London) son of John Powell & Fortune Middleton
1) **Edward** Coleridge Cokayne **Powell** (*2 Feb 1964)
2) **Louise** Cecilia Middleton **Powell** (*20 Nov 1966 Northampton)

123

= 30 Jul 1994 Rothwell; **Crispin** David Jermyn **Holborow** (*7 Mar 1963 Truro) son of Geoffrey Holborow & Lady Mary Stopford

    a) **George** Maunsell Jermyn **Holborow** (*21 Jun 1997)

    b) **William Holborow** (*18 Apr 1999)

    c) **Benjamin Holborow** (*22 Apr 2003)

7. **Hon. Harold** Edward **FitzClarence** (15 Nov 1870 Hove – 28 Aug 1926)

= 14 May 1902; **Frances** Isabel Eleanor **Keppel** (20 Jul 1874 Mitford, Norfolk – 1 Feb 1951) daughter of William Keppel & Hon. Charlotte Fraser

Issue was raised to the rank of children of an Earl 1928:

a. **Lady** Wilhelmina **Joan** Mary **FitzClarence** (17 Nov 1904 - 1992 Little Massingham, Norfolk)

=1 21 Apr 1928; **Oliver Birkbeck** (6 May 1893 Henstead, Norfolk – 27 May 1952) son of Edward Birkbeck & Emily Seymour

=2 28 Apr 1961; **Henry** John **Cator** (23 Jan 1923 – 27 Mar 1965) son of John Cator & Maud Adeane

issue of 1st (none by 2nd):

  I) **Edward** Harold **Birkbeck** (2 May 1929 Little Massingham– 9 Feb 2005 Dumfries)

  = 11 Jun 1958; **Sarah** Anne **Brook** (*9 Aug 1934) daughter of Edward Brook & Hon. Catherine Gretton

    A) **Elizabeth** Mary **Birkbeck** (*17 Oct 1960 Bowley Court, Herfordshire)

    B) **Nicola** Susan **Birkbeck** (*2 Dec 1962 Skeffington Hall, Leicestershire)

    C) **George** Charles Edward **Birkbeck** (*8 Dec 1964 Skeffington Hall)

    = 4 Sep 1998 London; **Fiona Gamble** (…)

      1) a son (*19.5.2004)

  II) **Mary** Joan **Birkbeck** (*13 Sep 1931 Litle Massingham)

  III) **John** Oliver Charles **Birkbeck** (*22 Jun 1936 Little Massingham)

  = 2 May 1964; **Hermoine** Anne **Dawes** (*5 Dec 1941 Ainderby, Yorkshire) daughter of D'Arcy Dawes & Naomi Thompson

    A) **Lucy** Claire **Birkbeck** (*7 Oct 1966 Kench Hill, Kent)

    = 8 Jul 1995 Litcham, Norfolk; **Robert Leitao** (*1963)

      1) **Felix** Edward **Leitao** (*Jul 1998 London)

      2) **Tobias** Alexander **Leitao** (*Sep 1999 London)

3) **Hermione** Sophie **Leitao** (*Jul 2003 London)
  B) **Oliver** Benjamin **Birkbeck** (*3 Apr 1973 Norwich)
  C) **Rosanna** Mary **Birckbeck** (*11 Sep 1974 Norwich)
    = 5 Jul 2003 Litcham; **Michael** W **Tremayne** (*1974 London)
    son of John Tremayne & Vivienne Cullimore
    1) **Emily** Rose **Tremayne** (*15 Jul 2004 London)
    2) **Benjamin** William **Tremayne** (*31 Mar 2006 London)
  b. **Sir Geoffrey** William Richard Hugh **FitzClarence KBE, 5th**
  Earl of Munster etc.(17 Feb 1906 – 27 Aug 1975) suc.uncle
  as Earl 1 Jan 1928; KBE 1957
  = 9 Jul 1928; **Hillary Wilson** (19 Mar 1903 – 29 Oct 1979
  Bletchingley, Surrey) daughter of Edward Wilson & Adela
  Hacket
  no issue
8. **Lady Lilian** Adelaide Katherine Mary **FitzClarence** (10 Dec
  1873 Hove – 15 Jul 1948)
  = 17 Jan 1893 Brighton; **William** Arthur Edward **Boyd** (6 Apr
  1845 – 6 Dec 1931) son of Curwen Boyd & Margaret Campbell
  a. **Phyllis** Meata **Boyd** (1894 – 19 Mar 1943)
    = 17 Jan 1922 (dv.); **Viscount Henri** Louis Leon **de Janzé**
    (…) son of Viscount François Leon de Janzé & …
    no issue
  b. **Benjamin** Harold Alan **Boyd** (16 Dec 1912 – 22 Nov 1930)
9. **Lady Dorothea** Augusta **FitzClarence** (5 May 1876 Hove – 28
  Jan 1942 Hereford)
  = 20 Nov 1899 London; **Chandos** Brydges **Lee-Warner** (11 Jun
  1863 – 1 Oct 1944 Hereford)
  a. Dorothy **Jean** Mary Essex **Lee-Warner** (21 Nov 1900
    Steyning - …)
  b. Olive **Irene** Wilhelmina **Lee-Warner** (31 May 1902 Steyning–
    11 Mar 1975 Herford)
D. **Hon. Frederick** Charles George **FitzClarence-Hunloke** (1 Feb
  1826 – 17 Dec 1878) assumed additional name Hunloke 1865
  = 2 Dec 1856 Penhurst, Kent; (his first cousin) **Hon. Adelaide**
  Augusta Wilhelmina **Sidney** (1 Jun 1826 Dingerworth, Derbyshire –
  20 Sep 1904) daughter of Philip Sidney, 1st Baron De L'Isle & Lady
  Sophia FitzClarence *see below*
  no issue
E. **Lady Mary** Gertrude **FitzClarence** (31 Oct - … Nov 1834 London)
F. **Hon. George FitzClarence** (15 Apr 1836 London – 24 Mar 1894
  Uxbridge, Middlesex)

= 5 Jul 1864 London; **Lady Maria** Henrietta **Scott** (1841 – 27 Jul 1912) daughter of John Scott, 3rd Earl of Clonmell & Hon. Anne de Burgh

1. **Charles FitzClarence** (8 May 1864 Bishopscourt, co. Kildare – 12 Nov 1914 Ypres) killed in action (twin)
   = 20 Apr 1898; **Violet Churchill** (11 Jun 1864 London – 22 Dec 1941 Buckingham) daughter of Lord Alfred Churchill & Hon. Harriet Hester
   a. **Edward** Charles **FitzClarence, 6th Earl of Munster** etc.(3 Oct 1899 London – 15 Nov 1983) suc. 2nd cousin as Earl 27 Aug 1975
      =1 30 Jul 1925 (dv.1930); **Monica** Sheila Harrington **Grayson** (1907 - 5 Oct 1958) daughter of Sir Henry Grayson, 1st Baronet & Dora Harrington; =2nd Robert Symonds
      =2 28 Sep 1939; **Vivian Scholfield** (14 Jul 1908 – 7 May 2008) daughter of Benjamin Scholfield & …
      issue of 1st:
      I) **Anthony** Charles **FitzClarence, 7th Earl of Munster** etc.(21 Mar 1926 Dorking, Surrey – 30 Dec 2001 London) suc. father as Earl 15 Nov 1983; upon his death his titles became extinct
         =1 28 Jul 1949 London (dv.1966); Louise Marguerite **Diane Delvigne** (*10 May 1923 Liège, Belgium) daughter of Louis Delvigne & Margaret Waite
         =2 18 Jun 1966 (dv.1979); **Pamela** Margaret **Spooner** (1921 - 2000) daughter of Arthur Spooner & Evelyn Hinckley; =1st … Hyde
         =3 1979; Dorothy **Alexa Maxwell** (22 Dec 1924 – 13 Jun 1995) daughter of Edward Maxwell & Sybil Lubbock
         =4 3 May 1997 Cowhurst, Surrey; **Halina Winska**[4] (…) daughter of Mieczlaw Winski-Lubicz
         issue of 1st:
         A) **Lady Tara** Francesa **FitzClarence** (*6 Aug 1952 Paris)
            = 22 Apr 1979 London; **Ross** Jean **Heffler** (10 Nov 1952 London) son of Leon Heffler & Elizabeth Defries
            1) **Alexandra** Louise **Heffler** (*1 Nov 1982 London)
            2) **Leo** Edward Michael **Heffler** (*17 Dec 1985 London)
         B) **Lady Finola** Dominique **FitzClarence** (*6 Dec 1953)
            = 1981 (dv.2007); **Jonathan** Terence **Poynton** (*1957) son of Desmond Poynton & Nancy Eva

---

[4] Halina, Countess of Munster had a daughter by a previous relationship who took the FitzClarence name but was not a child, and not adopted, by the 7th Earl.

1) **Chloe** Nona **Poynton** (*29 May 1982)
2) **Oliver** Maximilian Christo **Poynton** (*20 Jun 1984)
issue of 2nd:
C) **Charlotte** Catherine **Lawrence Mills** (*1964) née Oonaugh
Sarah FitzClarence; adopted 1965 by John Lawrence Mills
= … 1987; **Raymond Burt** (…)
  1) **Christopher** James **Burt** (*1987)
  2) **Jennifer** Emily **Burt** (*1989)
  3) **Stephanie** Louise **Burt** (*1991)
D) **Lady Georgina FitzClarence** (*19 Dec 1966)
=1 1993 (dv.1995); **Paul** Robert **Phillips** (…) son of Peter
Phillips
=2 1997; **John Adam** (…)
issue of 2nd (none by 1st):
  1) **Thomas** Charles **Adam** (*31 Mar 1999)
II) **Lady Mary-Jill FitzClarence** (6 Feb 1928 – 17 Jan 1971)
=1 4 Jun 1953 (ann.1960); **Melvin Flyer** (…)
=2 28 Mar 1968; **John Walter** (31 Oct 1908 - 1980) son of
John Walter & Charlotte Foster; =1st Florence Cole
no issue
b. **Joan** Harriet **FitzClarence** (23 Dec 1901 – 6 Jan 1971)
= 30 Mar 1933 London; **Francis Barchard** (1903 Sussex - 25
Nov 1941) killed in action; son of Francis Barchard & Emma
Lawrence
I) **Jane** Ann Violet **Barchard** (*5 Nov 1935)
=1 10 Mar 1962; **Geoffrey** Ewart **Martin** (… - 8 Apr 1978)
son of Melton Martin
=2 9 May 1981; **Alastair** Jackson Wallace **Reid** (...)
A) **Lucinda** Katharine **Martin** (*20 Oct 1966)
  = 17 Feb 1990; **Peter Williams** (…)
  1) **Sophie** Elizabeth Rose **Williams** (*30 May 1992)
  2) **Eleanor** Jane **Williams** (*3 Mar 2000)
II) **Elizabeth** Maud **Barchard** (*18 Apr 1939)
  = 13 Jul 1967; **David** Leslie **Scott** (…) son of Thomas Scott
A) **Juliet** Catherine **Scott** (*23 Nov 1968)
B) **Sara** Frances **Scott** (*16 Dec 1970)
2. **Edward FitzClarence** (8 May 1864 Bishopscourt, co. Kildare –
7 Aug 1897 Abu-Hamed, Sudan) (twin) killed in action
3. **William** Henry **FitzClarence** (17 Dec 1868 – 24 Nov 1921)
= 11 Aug 1908 London; **Hilda** Charlotte **Sankey** (1876 Thanet,
Kent - 3 Jan 1959) daughter of Richard Sankey

127

no issue
- 4. **Lionel** Ashley Arthur **FitzClarence** (30 Nov 1870 London – 19 Dec 1936 the Crimea)
  = 16 Jul 1913; **Theodora** Frances Maclean **Jack** (1880 London – 12 Apr 1948) daughter of Evan Jack
  - a. **Mary** Theodora Annette **FitzClarence** (10 May 1914 – 14 Aug 2002 Chichester, Sussex)
    = 1948; **Adam Gluskiewicz** (…)
    - I) **Anna** Judith **Gluszkiewicz** (*28 Oct 1949)
- 5. **Annette** Mary **FitzClarence** (15 Jun 1873 London – 7 Jul 1970)
- 6. **Mary FitzClarence** (17 Aug 1877 London – 19 Feb 1939 Lyndhurst, Hampshire)
  = 5 Oct 1905 London; **Frederick** Drummund Vincent **Wing** (29 Nov 1860 Christchurch, Hampshire – 2 Oct 1915 in France) killed in action; son of Vincent Wing & Gertrude Vane
  - a. **Gertrude** Iris **Wing** (1 Aug 1906 London - 28 Jul 1983 Milford-on-Sea, Hampshire)
- G. **Hon. Edward FitzClarence** (8 Jul 1837 London – 23 Jul 1855 Redan, Crimea) died of wounds received in battle

II. **Lady Sophia FitzClarence** (4 Mar 1795 London – 10 Apr 1837 Kensington Palace, London)
= 13 Aug 1825 London; **Sir Philip** Charles **Sidney, 2nd Baronet, 1st Baron De L'Isle and Dudley, GCH** (11 Mar 1800 Penhurst, Kent – 4 Mar 1851 Penhurst) son of Sir John Shelley-Sidney, 1st Baronet & Henrietta Hunloke; cr. Baron 13 Jan 1835, suc.father as Baronet 14 Mar 1849; GCH 1831

A. **Hon. Adelaide** Augusta Wilhelmina **Sidney** (1 Jun 1826 Dingerworth, Derbyshire – 20 Sep 1904)
  = 2 Feb 1856 Penhurst Place; (her first cousin) **Hon. Frederick** Charles George **FitzClarence-Hunloke** (1 Feb 1826 – 17 Dec 1878) son of George FitzClarence, 1st Earl of Munster & Mary Wyndham *see above*
  no issue

B. **Sir Philip Sidney, 2nd Baron De L'Isle and Dudley, 3rd Baronet** (29 Jan 1828 London – 17 Feb 1898 London) suc.father as Baron and Baronet 4 Mar 1851
  =1 23 Apr 1850 London; **Mary Foulis** (19 May 1826 Ingleby, Yorkshire – 14.6.1891 London) daughter of Sir William Foulis, 8th Baronet & Mary Ross
  =2 25 Jan 1893 London; Emily **Frances Ramsay** (1864 Brackely, Northamptonshire – 3 Nov 1926) daughter of William Ramsay &

Emily Tredcroft; =2nd Sir Walter Stirling, 3rd Baronet
issue of 1st (none by 2nd):
1. **Hon. Mary** Sophia **Sidney** (5 May 1851 London – 25 Nov 1903
   London)
2. **Sir Philip Sidney, 3rd Baron De L'Isle and Dudley, 4th Baronet**
   (14 May 1853 London – 24 Dec 1922) suc. father as Baron etc. 17
   Feb 1898
   = 12 Jun 1902 London; **Hon. Elizabeth** Maria **Vereker** (26 Nov
   1860 London – 19 Jul 1958) daughter of Standish Vereker, 4th
   Viscount Gort & Hon. Caroline Gage; =1st William Astell
   no issue
3. **Sir Algernon Sidney, 4th Baron De L'Isle and Dudley, 5th
   Baronet** (11 Jun 1854 Penhurst – 18 Apr 1945) suc.brother as
   Baron etc. 24 Dec 1922
4. **Hon. Henry Sidney** (17 Jan 1858 London – 13 Apr 1896
   Durham)
5. **Sir William Sidney, 5th Baron De L'Isle and Dudley, 6th
   Baronet** (19 Aug 1859 London – 18 Jun 1945) suc.brother as
   Baron etc.18 Apr 1945
   = 5 Dec 1905 London; **Winifred** Augusta **Yorke Bevan** (1874 –
   11 Feb 1959) daughter of Roland Yorke Bevan & Hon. Agneta
   Kinnaird
   a. **Hon. Mary** Olivia **Sidney** (20 Nov 1906 London – 24 Nov
      1959)
      = 3 Jun 1939; **Walter** Hugh Stewart **Garnett** (1875 -)
      son of Frank Garnett & Jeanne Buddicom; =1st Enid Evans
      I) **Andrew** William **Garnett** (*31 Aug 1943)
         = 24 Aug 1968 London; **Maria Constantinidou** (*1946)
         daughter of Noikis Constantinides
         A) **Tara** Olivia **Garnett** (*1969 London)
            = May 2002 London; **Benjamin J Glasstone** (*1970)
            1) **Ezra** Daniel **Glasstone** (*May 1998 London)
            2) **Rachel** Deborah **Glasstone** (*Nov 2001 London)
         B) **Michael** Nicholas **Garnett** (*1981 London)
   b. **Sir William** Philip **Sidney KG, GCMG, GCVO, 1st Viscount
      De L'Isle, 6th Baron De L'Isle and Dudley, 7th and 9th
      Baronet** (23 May 1909 London – 5 Apr 1991 London) suc.
      father as Baron etc.18 Jun 1945; cr. Viscount 12 Jan 1956 suc.
      distant cousin, Sir Sidney Shelley as 9th Baronet 25 Jul 1965;
      Governor-General of Astralia 1961-1965
      =1 8 Jun 1940 London; **Hon. Jacqueline** Corinne Yvonne

Vereker[5] (20 Oct 1914 London – 15 Nov 1962 London) daughter of John Vereker, 6th Viscount Gort & Corinne Vereker[6] =2 24 Mar 1966 Paris; **Margaret** Eldrydd **Shoubridge** (1913 Chester – 22 Jan 2002 Crickhowell, Wales) daughter of Thomas Shoubridge & … Dugdale; =1st Wilfred Bailey, 3rd Baron Glanusk issue of 1st:

I) **Hon. Elizabeth** Sophia **Sidney** (*12 Mar 1941)
  =1 10 Oct 1959 (dv.1966); George Silver **Oliver** Annesley **Colthurst** (1 Mar 1931 - 16 Aug 2008 Beaulieu, France) son of Sir Richard Colhurst, 8th Baronet & Denys West; =2nd Caroline Combe
  =2 1 Jul 1966 (dv.1971); **Sir** Edward **Humphrey** Tyrell **Wakefield, 2nd Baronet** (*11 Jul 1936) son of Sir Edward Wakefield, 1st Baronet & Lalage Thompson; =1st Priscilla Bagot and =3rd Hon. Katharine Baring
  =3 26 Jan 1972 Gibralter (dv.1989); **James** Sylvester **Rattray of Rattray** (3 Aug 1919 – 1999) son of Paul Burman-Clerk-Rattray
  =4 Nov 1989 London; Robert **Samuel** Clive **Abel Smith** (*17 Apr 1936)
  issue of 1st:
  A) **Shaunagh** Anne Henrietta **Colthurst** (*30 Apr 1961)
    =1 1980 Shropshire (dv.1990); **Thomas** Peter William **Heneage** (*1950) son of Peter Heneage & Jean Douglas; =2nd Carol Vogel
    =2 2 Aug 1995; **Crispin** James Alan Nevill **Money-Coutts, 9th Baron Latymer** (*8 Mar 1955) son of Hugo Money-Coutts, 8th Baron Latymer & Hon. Penelope Emmet; =1st Hon. Lucy Deedes; suc.father as Baron 10 Nov 2003
    issue of 1st (none by 2nd):
    1) **Elizabeth** Anne Sophia **Heneage** (*1981)
      = 2006; **Hon. Quintin** John Neil Martin **Hogg** (*1973) son of Rt.Hon. Douglas Hogg, 3rd Viscount Hailsham & Sarah Boyd-Carpenter, (life) Baroness Hogg; heir apparent to father
      a) **Eleanor Hogg** (*Nov 2010)
    2) **Henry** Robert **Heneage** (*1983)
  issue of 2nd:
  B) **Maximilian** Edward Vereker **Wakefield** (*22 Feb 1967

---

[5] Jacqueline was the grand-niece of Elizabeth, Baroness De L'Isle.
[6] The 6th Viscount Gort and his wife were first cousins to one another.

Lough Coltra Castle, Gort) heir-apparent to Baronetcy
= 5 Nov 1994 Winchester; **Lucinda** Catherine **Pipe**
(*1969) daughter of David Pipe & Patricia Coombes
  1) **William Wakefield** (*9 May 1998)
  2) **Edward** Gort **Wakefield** (*22 Jun 2000)
issue of 3rd (none by 4th):
C) **Robert** Surtees Predergast **Rattray** (*11 Oct 1972)
D) a daughter (*25 Mar 1983)
II) **Hon. Catherine** Mary **Sidney** (*20 Oct 1942)
=1 1 Dec 19641 Canberra, Australia (dv.1983); Martin **John
Wilbraham** (*3 Jun 1931 London) son of Edward
Wilbraham & Evelyn Martin
=2 9 May 1983; **Nicholas** Hyde **Villiers** (10 Apr 1939 – 31
Aug 1998 at sea) son of Sir Charles Villiers & Pamela
Flower
=3 Nov 2002 London; **Nigel** Samuel **Wass** (*1942) son of
Lawrence Wass & Margaret Wilson; =1st Sean Oyler
issue of 1st (none by others):
A) **Alexander** John **Wilbraham** (*22 Oct 1965 Cheshire)
  = 3 Sep 1996; **Fernanda Amaral Valentini** (…)
  daughter of Arnoldo Valentini & Valeria Amaral
  1) **Marina Wilbraham** (*31 Jan 1997) (twin)
  2) **Camilla Wilbraham** (*31 Jan 1997) (twin)
B) **Rupert** Edward Robert **Wilbraham** (*26 Feb 1967
  Cheshire)
  = 14 Jun 2007 Moscow; **Anna Yevdokimova** (*4 Jun
  1973) daughter of Oleg Yevdokimov & Ludilla …
  no issue
C) **Jocelyn** Thomas Ralph **Wilbraham** (*30 Apr 1970
  Cheshire)
  = 24 Jun 2005 London; **Fiona Butler-Adams** (*9 Jul
  1973) daughter of David Butler-Adams & Rosalie
  Bradshaw
  1) **Oscar** David John **Wilbraham** (*25 Jul 2006)
III) **Sir Philip** John Algernon **Sidney, 2nd Viscount De L'Isle,
7th Baron De L'Isle and Dudley, 8th & 10th Baronet** (*21
Apr 1945 Dailly, Scotland) suc.father as Viscount etc.5 Apr
1991
= 15 Nov 1980 Penhurst; **Isobel** Tresyllian **Compton** (*18 Mar
1950 London) daughter of Sir Edmund Compton & Betty
Williams

A) **Hon. Sophia** Jacqueline Mary **Sidney** (*25 Mar 1983 London)
B) **Hon. Philip** William Edmund **Sidney** (*2 Apr 1985 London) heir apparent to father
IV) **Hon. Anne** Marjorie **Sidney** (*15 Aug 1947 Penhurst, Kent)
= 3 Jun 1967 Penhurst; **David** Alexander **Harries** (*14 Apr 1938 Sydney, Australia) son of David Harries & Margaret Street
A) **Alexandra** Victoria Corinna **Harries** (*12 Jul 1968 Long Beach, California[7])
= 19 Jun 2004 Benenden; **Piers** Adrian Carlyle **Hillier** (*24 Sep 1968 Nassau, Bahamas) son of Philip Hillier & Geraldine Matthews
1) **Hugh** Alexander Philip **Hillier** (*29 Jun 2005 London)
2) **Penelope** Elizabeth Anne **Hillier** (*23 Jan 2008 London)
3) **Audrey** Camilla Hester **Hillier** (*24 Sep 2009 London)
B) David **Henry Harries** (*4 May 1970 Sydney, Australia)
= 14 Dec 2001 London; **Sophy** Emma **Maclean** (*15 Feb 1972) daughter of Roddy Maclean & Hon. Sarah Corbett
1) **Lara** Constance **Harries** (*25 Mar 2004 London)
2) **Miranda** Violet **Harries** (*17 May 2006 London)
3) **David** Edward **Harries** (*7 Apr 2010 London)
C) **James** Hugh **Harries** (*28 Jun 1972 London[8])
= 19 Sep 2003 London; **Harriet** Florence **Pugh** (*6 Mar 1973) daughter of Richard Pugh & Diana Coley
1) **Robert** Alexander **Harries** (*18 Jun 2008 London) (twin)
2) **Charles** Richard **Harries** (*18 Jun 2008 London) (twin)
V) **Hon. Lucy** Corinna Agneta **Sidney** (*21 Feb 1953 Tonbridge)
= 26 Feb 1974 Tonbridge; **Hon. Michael** Charles James **Willoughby** (*14 Jul 1948 London) son of Michael Willoughby, 12th Baron Middleton & Janet Cornwall; heir-

---

[7] Most sources say Alexandra was born in San Diego, but her father clarified it was Long Beach.
[8] Again, James' father corrected published sources which state James was born in Ashford, Kent.

apparent to Barony

A) **James** William Michael **Willoughby** (*8 Mar 1976 York)
= 10 Sep 2005 Petworth, Sussex; **Lady Cara** Mary Cecilia
Boyle (*16 Jun 1976 Winchester, Hampshire) daughter of John
Boyle, 15th Earl of Cork and Orrery & Hon. Rebecca Noble
  1) **Thomas** Michael Jonathan **Willoughby** (*23 Aug 2007)
  2) **Flora** Rebecca Lucy **Willoughby** (*7 Jan 2009)
  3) due Feb. 2011
B) **Charlotte** Jacqueline Louise **Willoughby** (*20 Sep 1978
Malton)
= 8 Jul 2006 London; **Martin Taylor** (*21 Jul 1971 East
Kilbride, Lanarkshire) son of James Taylor
  1) **Matilda** Jacqueline Azvina **Taylor** (*30 Jan 2009)
C) **Emma** Caralie Sarah **Willoughby** (*7 Sep 1981 Malton)
D) **Rose** Arabella Julia **Willoughby** (*25 Sep 1984 Malton)
E) **Charles** Edward Henry **Willoughby** (*27 Jul 1986
Scarborough)

C. **Hon. Ernestine** Wellington **Sidney** (9 Jan 1834 London – 20 Sep
1910 London)
= 9 Jan 1868 London; **Philip Perceval** (19 Mar 1814 London – 28
Mar 1897) son of Alexander Perceval & Jane L'Estrange
1. **Sir Philip Hunloke, GCVO** (26 Nov 1868 London – 1 Apr 1947
London) (twin) ne Perceval, assumed name Hunloke 1904
= 12 Feb 1892 London; **Silvia Heseltine** (1872 London - 1951
London) daughter of John Heseltine & Sarah Edmundson
a. **Joan** Cecil **Hunloke** (14 Apr 1901 London - Jan 1991) née
Perceval
= 28 Apr 1924 London; **Philip Fleming** (15 Aug 1889 – 13
Oct 1971) son of Robert Fleming
I) **Anne** Kathleen **Fleming** (4 Jan 1926 - Jul 1996)
= 9 Feb 1952; **Jesse Hughes** (…)
II) **Silvia** Catriona **Fleming** (14 Feb 1930 - Jun 1987)
= 25 Nov 1951; George **Christopher Rittson-Thomas** (1927
Cardiff - ...) son of Geoffrey Rittson-Thomas & Grace Cotter
A) **Michael** P **Rittson-Thomas** (*1953 London)
B) **Hugo Rittson-Thomas** (*1957 London)
= 2009/2010; **Silke Taprogge** (...) daughter of Ludwig
Taprogge
C) **Rupert Rittson-Thomas** (*1963 Oxford)
= ...; **Kate ...** (...)
  1) **Walter** Robert **Rittson-Thomas** (...)

2) **Theodore** George **Rittson-Thomas** (*29 Jun 2009)
III) **Robert Fleming** (*18 Sep 1932)
  = 28 Apr 1962; **Victoria** Margaret **Ackroyd** (*1 Apr 1939)
  A) **Joanna** Kate **Fleming** (*1963)
    = 1997; **James King** (…)
    1) **Elva** Silvie **King** (*1998)
    2) **Valentine** Jack Naisbett **King** (*2000)
  B) **Philip Fleming** (*1965)
    = 1997; **Jane Carter** (…)
    1) **Robert Fleming** (*1998)
    2) **Lorna** Hebe Louise **Fleming** (*2000)
  C) **Rory** David **Fleming** (*1968)
    = 31 Oct 2001 Valdemars Slot, Denmark (dv.2010);
    Baroness Caroline Iuel-Brockdorff (*9 Sep 1975)
    daughter of Baron Niels Iuel-Brockdorff & Margarethe
    Lundgren
    1) **Alexander** William **Fleming** (*7 Apr 2004 London)
    2) **Josephine** Margarethe Victoria **Fleming** (*20 Dec 2006)
b. **Alberta** Diana **Hunloke** (1898 - 10 Feb 1972) nee Perceval
= 5 Feb 1921 London; **Sir George** Camborne Beauclerk
Paynter, KCVO (2 Aug 1880 London – 15 Aug 1950 near
Grantham) son of George Paynter & Frances Beauclerk;
KCVO 1950
I) **Janetta** Alba **Paynter** (*26 Jan 1922)
  =1 2 Aug 1946 (dv.1948); **Richard** Boycott **Magor** (1918 - Oct
  2003) son of Richard Magor & Frances Boycott
  =2 5 May 1954; **John** Anthony **Warre** (4 Dec 1912 London -
  Sep 1999) son of John Warre & Marie Scott; =1st Arabella
  Mackintosh
  issue of 1st (none by 2nd):
  A) **Carolyn Magor** (*ca.1947)
    =1 6 Jan 1977 London (dv.); **Broderick** Giles Edward **Munro-
    Wilson** (…) son of Donald Munro-Wilson; =2nd Samantha
    Bleby
    =2 Jul 1996; **Michael Peacock** (…)
    issue of 1st:
    1) **Charlotte** Alba Louise **Munro-Wilson** (*26 Nov 1977)
      = 2006; **Ross** Lindsay **Henderson** (…) son of Lindsay
      Henderson
      a) **Edward** Ross Beauclerk **Henderson** (*9 June 2008)
II) **Yvery** Silvia **Paynter** (*16 Dec 1924)

= 18 Dec 1952 London; **Hamish** Edward Lachlan **Wallace** (*19 Sep 1924) son of Harold Wallace & Elizabeth MacPherson

A) **James** George Chisholm **Wallace** (*1954)

B) Elizabeth **Anna** Francesca **Wallace** (*1955)

=1 2 Dec 1980 (dv.1986); **Hon. John Fermor-Hesketh** (*15 Mar 1953) son of Frederick Fermor-Hesketh, 2nd Baron Hesketh & Christian McEwen; =2nd Helena Hunt

=2 1991; **Thomas Oates** (…)

issue of 2nd (none by 1st):

1) **Ophelia** Rose **Oates** (*1992 London)

III) **George Paynter** (2 Aug 1933 – 14 Apr 1954 Fayid, Egypt)

c. **Henry** Philip **Hunloke** (27 Dec 1906 London – 13 Jan 1978 London)

=1 28 Nov 1929 (dv.1945); **Lady Anne Cavendish** (20 Aug 1909 – 1981) daughter of Victor Cavendish, 9th Duke of Devonshire & Lady Evelyn Fitzmaurice; =2nd Christopher Holland-Martin; =3rd Alexander Victor Montagu, 10th Earl of Sandwich[9]

=2 19 May 1945 (dv.1972); **Virginia** Archer **Clive** (14 Mar 1913 Ludlow – 14 Feb 1995) dau of Percy Clive & Alice Dallas

=3 1972; **Ruth** Mary **Holdsworth** (1917 - Jun 1998 Marlborough) daughter of Frederick Holdsworth & Mary Arundell; =1st Clarence Percival

issue of 1st:

I) **Philippa** Victoria **Hunloke** (10 Dec 1930 London - 20 Jul 2005)

= 26 Apr 1955 London (dv.1960); **William** Waldorf **Astor, 3rd Viscount Astor** (13 Aug 1907 Cliveden, Buckinghamshire – 8 Mar 1966 Nassau, Bahamas) son of Waldorf Astor, 2nd Viscount Astor & Nancy Langhorne; suc. father as Viscount 30 Sep 1952; he =1st Hon. Sarah Norton, =3rd Bronwen Pugh

A) **Hon. Emily** Mary **Astor** (*9 Jun 1956)

=1 1984 (dv.); **Alan Gregory** (…) son of David Gregory

=2 1988 (dv.1996); **James** Ian **Anderson** (*1 Nov 1952) son of John Anderson & Lady Gillian Drummond

issue of 2nd (none by 1st):

1) **Thomas** Alexander **Anderson** (*1990)

2) **Rory** John **Anderson** (*2 Nov 1991)

---

[9] By her 3rd marriage, Lady Anne became the step-mother of her daughter-in-law, Lady Katherine (Montagu) Hunloke.

3) **Liza** Kate **Anderson** (*1993) (twin)
4) **Isobel** Nancy **Anderson** (*1993) (twin)
II) **Timothy** Henry **Hunloke** (*30 Dec 1932 London)
III) **Nicholas** Victor **Hunloke** (*22 Apr 1939 London)
= 15 Jul 1965 London; **Lady Katherine** Victoria **Montagu**
(*22 Feb 1945 London) daughter of Victor Montagu, 10th Earl of
Sandwich & Rosemary Peto
  A) **Henrietta** Yvery **Hunloke** (*14 May 1968)
    = 17 Oct 1998; **Lucien** Henry Valentine **Thynne** (*2 June
    1965) son of Lord Valentine Thynne & Veronica Jacks
    1) **Atalanta** Xenia **Thynne** (*27 Dec 2000 London)
    2) **Cassia** Victoria **Thynne** (*15 Jul 2002 London)
  B) **Edward** Perceval **Hunloke** (*1 Nov 1969)
    = 16 Jul 2005 London; **Philippa Collett** (*17 Feb 1965
    Swindon) daughter of David Collett & Glenda Pratt
    1) **Molly** Evelyn **Hunloke** (*6 Feb 1999 London)
    2) **Delilah** Rose **Hunloke** (*4 Dec 2003 London)
  C) **Matilda Hunloke** (*25 Jul 1972 London)
    = 19 Jul 2003; **Edward** William P. **Cartlidge** (*11 Sep 1970
    London) son of William Cartlidge & Denise Rayner
    1) **Wilfred** Victor P. **Cartlidge** (*30 Sep 2004 London)
    2) **Samson** Edward P. **Cartlidge** (*25 Apr 2006 Salisbury)
    3) **Cecily** May **Cartlidge** (*10 Feb 2010 London)
issue of 2nd (none by 3rd):
IV) **Clare Hunloke** (10 Jan 1947 – 23 Nov 1964)
V) **Sarah Hunloke** (*17 Apr 1949)
= …; **Antônio Correa de Sá** (*1950) son of José Correa de Sá
& Lilias van Waterschoot Pinto da Rocha
  A) **Marta Correa de Sá** (…)
  B) **Inèz Correa de Sá** (…)
  C) **Sofia Correa de Sá** (…)
2. **Kathleen** Sophy **Perceval** (26 Nov 1868 London – 10 Aug 1931
Yvery, Cowes, Isle of Wight) (twin)
3. **Ernestine Perceval** (6 May 1870 London - 1887 Isle of Wight)
4. **Ernest Perceval** (19 Nov 1871 Hamble, Southampton - ca.1890 in
Australia)
D. **Hon. Sophia** Philippa **Sidney** (11 Mar 1837 – 12 May 1907)
= 20 Apr 1871 London; **Count Alexander** Friedrich Carl **von
Kielmansegg** (13 Aug 1833 Hanover - Aug 1914) son of Count
Eduard von Kielmansegg & Juliane von Zesterfleth
no issue

136

III. **Henry** Edward **FitzClarence** (27 Mar 1796 Bushy Park - Sep 1817 in India)

IV. **Lady Mary FitzClarence** (19 Dec 1798 Bushy Park – 13 Jul 1864 London)

= 19 Jun 1824 London; **Hon. Charles** Richard **Fox** (6 Nov 1796[10] London – 13 Apr 1873 London) son of Henry Fox, 3rd Baron Holland & Elizabeth Vassall

no issue

V. **Lord Sir Frederick FitzClarence, GCH** (9 Dec 1799 Bushy Park – 30 Oct 1854 Glendale, Northumberland)

= 9 May 1821; **Lady Augusta Boyle** (14 Aug 1801 London – 28 Jul 1876 Etal, Northamptonshire) son of George Boyle, 4th Earl of Glasgow & Lady Augusta Hay

A. **Augusta** Georgiana Frederica **FitzClarence** (Dec 1823/4 Belfast – 18 Oct 1865)

B. **William** Henry Adolphus **FitzClarence** (16 – 27 Jul 1827 Belfast)

VI. **Lady Elizabeth FitzClarence** (17 Jan 1801 Bushy Park – 16 Jan 1856 Edinburgh)

= 4 Dec 1820 London; **William** George **Hay KT, GCH, 18th Earl of Erroll,** Lord Hay, Lord Stains, **1st Baron Kilmarnock** (21 Feb 1801 Slains Castle, Aberdeenshire – 19 Apr 1846 London) son of William Hay, 17th Earl of Eroll & Alcia Eliot; suc.father as Earl 26 Jan 1819; cr. Baron Kilmarnock 17 Jun 1831; GCH 1830, KT 1834

A. **Lady** Adelaide **Ida** Harriet Augusta **Hay** (18 Oct 1821 – 22 Oct 1867 Exton, Rutland)

= 1 Nov 1841 London; **Charles** George **Noel, 2nd Earl of Gainsborough,** Viscount Campden, Baron Noel (5 Sep 1818 – 13 Aug 1881 London) son of Charles Noel, 1st Earl of Gainsborough & Elizabeth Grey; suc. father as Earl 10 Jun 1866

1. **Lady Blanche** Elizabeth Mary Annunciata **Noel** (22 Mar 1845 - 21 Mar 1881 North Conway, New Hampshire)

= 6 Mar 1870 London; **Thomas Murphy** (1846 – 11 Oct 1890)

no issue

2. **Lady Constance** Julia Eleanor Georgiana **Noel** (19 Oct 1847 London – 8 Apr 1891)

= 13 Jan 1874 Canterbury; **Sir** Alan **Henry Bellingham, 4th Baronet** (23 Aug 1846 Bellingham Castle, Louth, Ireland – 9 Jun 1921) son of Sir Alan Bellingham, 3rd Baronet & Elizabeth

---

[10] Charles Fox was born illegitimate but his parents subsequent marriage allowed him ot be styled as a son of a Baron.

Clarke; suc. father as Baronet 19 Apr 1889; =2nd Hon. Leigar de Clifton
a. **Mother** Ida **Mary (Emanuel)** Elizabeth Agnes **Bellingham** (26 Jan 1876 London – 28 Nov 1945 St. Leonards)
b. **Sir Edward** Henry Charles Patrick **Bellingham, 5th Baronet** (26 Jan 1879 Oakham – 19 May 1956 Dublin) suc.father as Baronet 9 Jun 1921
= 11 Jun 1904; **Charlotte** Elizabeth **Payne** (1880 – 25 May 1964 Coptford, Essex) daughter of Alfred Payne & ...; =1st Frederick Gough
   I) **Gertrude** Mary **Bellingham** (23 Jul 1906 in Guatemala – 16 May 1983 London)
   = 15 Feb 1927; **Ronald** Derwent **Hawker**[11] (28 Jul 1901 London – 26 Jan 1972) son of Rev. Bertram Hawker & Constance Buxton
   A) **Martin Hawker** (*10 Feb 1929)
c. **Dame Augusta** Mary Monica **Bellingham, DBE** (19 Aug 1880 Oakham – 16 May 1947) DBE 1918
= 6 Jul 1905 Mount Stuart, Isle of Bute; **Sir John Crichton-Stuart KT, 4th Marquess of Bute,** Earl of Windsor, Viscount Montjoy, Baron Cardiff, **9th Earl of Dumfries,** Viscount Ayr, **7th Earl of Bute,** Viscount Kingarth, Lord Mountstuart, Cumra and Inchmarnock, **5th Baron Mount Stuart of Wortley, 17th Lord Crichton** (20 Jun 1881 London – 25 Apr 1947) son of John, 3rd Marquess of Bute & Hon. Gwendolen Fitzalan-Howard; suc. father as Marquess etc. 9 Oct 1890; KT 1922
   I) **Lady Mary Crichton-Stuart** (8 May 1906 Edinburgh - 1980) after her marriage she was known as Lady Mary Stuart-Walker
   = 8 May 1933 London; **Edward** Alan **Walker** (6 Dec 1894 Cambridge - ...) son of Arthur Walker & Ellen Church
   A) **Ione** Mary Stuart **Walker** (*3 Aug 1934 Athens, Greece)
   = 23 Jul 1955 London; **Baron Christian** Johan Manuel Marie **von Oppenheim** (4 Feb 1926 Antibes, France – 8 Oct 1967 near Lagos, Nigeria) killed in a car crash; son of Baron Harold von Oppenheim & Manuela de Rivera
      1) **Baroness Corinna** Maria de Roccio Pimpinella Fernanda **von Oppenheim** (*30 May 1956 Madrid)
      = 29 Dec 1983 San Roque, Spain; **William Hettinger** (*30

---

[11] Ronald Hawker is also descended from Dora Bland (aka Mrs. Jordan) via her daughter Lucy (Ford) Hawker (not a child of William IV).

May 1956 Madrid) son of John Hettinger & Elisabeth ...
a) **Caroline Hettinger** (*5 Dec 1984 New York City)
b) **Charles Hettinger** (*1 Nov 1986 Pawling, New York)
2) **Baron Eduard** Harold Manuel Maria Rodrigo **von Oppenheim** (*13 Mar 1958 Madrid)
=1 Aug 1974 Sabeti Spiritu, Argentina (dv.); **Telma Carlini** (...)
=2 9 May 1980 Madrid; **Ana Maria Fernandez y Smith** (...) daughter of Manuel Fernandez & Shirley Smith
issue of 1st:
a) **Baroness Christia von Oppenheim** (*23 May 1975 Sancti Spiritu)
issue of 2nd:
b) **Baroness Maria Manuela von Oppenheim** (*31 Aug 1985 Madrid)
c) **Baroness Maria Almudena von Oppenheim** (*8 Oct 1988 Madrid)
3) **Baroness Flora** Claudia Maria del Mar Monica **von Oppenheim** (*4 May 1960 Madrid)
= 1991; **Jesus Medrano y Yllera** (...)
issue ?
4) **Baroness Maria Gabriela** Isabel **von Oppenheim** (*22 Feb 1963 Madrid)
= 3 Jun 1988 San Roque; **Fidel de Sandagorta y Gomez del Campillo** (...) son of Jesus de Sandagorta & Maria Soledad Gomez del Campillo
issue ?
B) **Hella** Immaculate Stuart **Walker** (*8 Dec 1935 Athens)
= 3 Jun 1957; **Frederick** Villeneuve **Nicolle** (...) son of Arthur Nicolle
1) **Miranda** Camilla **Nicolle** (*29 Oct 1958)
= Aug 1986 London; **Paul Berrow** (...)
a) **Grace Berrow** (*May 1987 London)
b) **Augustus** Peter **Berrow** (*Oct 1989 London)
c) **Daisy** Stuart **Berrow** (*Aug 1992 London)
d) **Joya Berrow** (*Mar 1994 London)
2) **Edwina** Mary **Nicolle** (*2 Feb 1961)
=1 May 1991; **Timothy** M C **Copping** (*1962) son of Austin Copping & Haidee Cockroft
=2 May 2000 London; **Hon. Alexander** David **Smith**

(*11 Mar 1959) son of William Smith, 4th Viscount
Hambleden & Donna Maria Carmela Attolico di
Adelfa
issue of 1st (none by 2nd):
  a) **Olivia** Rose A **Copping** (*Jan 1994 York)
  b) **Benedict** Oscar F **Copping** (*Jun 1995 York)
 3) **Hugo** Arthur Villeneuve **Nicolle** (*12 Jan 1963)
  = Jul 1996; **Rebecca** M **Crawley** (*1965 London)
  daughter of Eustace Crawley & Dorothy Bacon
  a) **Mamie** Elspeth **Nicolle** (*Oct 1997 London)
  b) **Dora** Rose **Nicolle** (*Aug 1999 London)
  c) **Arthur** Eustace Villaneuve **Nicolle** (*Jul 2003
  London)
II) **Sir John Crichton-Stuart KT, 5th Marquess of Bute** etc.
  (4 Aug 1907 – 14 Aug 1956) suc. father as Marquess 25 Apr
  1947
  = 26 Apr 1932; **Lady Eileen** Beatrice **Forbes** (1 Jul 1912 -
  1993) daughter of Bernard Forbes, 8th Earl of Granard &
  Beatrice Mills
  A) **Sir John Crichton-Stuart KBE, 6th Marquess of Bute**, etc.
    (27 Feb 1933 London – 22 Jul 1993 Mount Stuart) (twin) suc.
    father as Marquess 14 Aug 1956
    =1 19 Apr 1955 London (dv.1977); Beatrice **Nicole** Grace
    Wild-Forester (*19 Nov 1933) daughter of Wolstan Wild-
    Forester & Anne Home-Douglas-Moray
    =2 12 Nov 1978; **Jennifer Home-Rigg** (…) =1st Gerald Percy
    issue of 1st:
    1) **Lady Sophia** Anne **Crichton-Stuart** (*27 Feb 1956)
      =1 23 Jun 1979 London (dv.1988); **James** Stewart **Bain** (…)
      son of Alistair Bain
      =2 1990; **Alexius** John Benedict **Fenwick** (*1959 London)
      son of David Fenwick & Susan Heber-Percy; =1st Briony
      Gyngell
      issue of 1st:
      a) **Samantha** Ella **Bain** (*25 Jun 1981)
      issue of 2nd:
      b) **Georgia** Jessie **Fenwick** (*Aug 1990 London)
    2) **Lady** Eileen **Caroline Crichton-Stuart** (21 Feb
      1957 – 1984 Cranwell, Lincolnshire) killed in a car
      crash
    3) **John** Colum **Crichton-Stuart, 7th Marquess of Bute**

etc.(*26 Apr 1958) suc.father as Marquess 22 Jul 1993
=1 1984 (dv.1993); **Carolyn Waddell** (…) daughter of
Bryson Waddell
=2 13 Feb 1999; **Serena** Solitaire **Wendell** (*1960
London) daughter of Jack Wendell & Anthea Hyslop;
she =1ˢᵗ Robert De Lisser
issue of 1ˢᵗ:

  a) **Lady Caroline Crichton-Stuart** (*26 Sep 1984
  London)
  b) **Lady Cathleen Crichton-Stuart** (*14 Sep 1986)
  c) **John** Bryson, **Earl of Dumfries** (*21 Dec 1989)
  issue of 2ⁿᵈ:
  d) **Lady Lola** Affrica **Crichton-Stuart** (*23 Jun 1999
  London)
 4) **Lord Anthony Crichton-Stuart** (*14 May 1961)
  = 8 Sep 1990 Great Snoring, Norfolk; **Alison Bruce**
  (…) daughter of Keith Bruce
  a) **Flora** Grace **Crichton-Stuart** (*10 Nov 1994 New
  York)
  b) **Eliza** Rose **Crichton-Stuart** (*7 Mar 1996 New
  York)
  c) **Arthur** Alec **Crichton-Stuart** (*23 Jan 2001 New
  York City)
B) **Lord David** Ogden **Crichton-Stuart** (27 Feb 1933
London - 1977) (twin)
 = 24 Feb 1972; **Helen McColl** (…) daughter of William
McColl
 1) **Elizabeth** Rose **Crichton-Stuart** (*10 Mar 1973)
 2) **Kenneth** Edward David **Crichton-Stuart** (*27 Jun
 1975)
  = 27 Aug 2005 London; **Kaye Smith** (…) daughter of
  George Smith
  a) **Georgina** Elizabeth Helen **Crichton-Stuart** (*29
  Sep 2010)
C) **Lord James** Charles **Crichton-Stuart** (17 Sep 1935 – 5
Dec 1982 Upton Grey, Hampshire)
=1 25 Jun 1959 London (dv.1968); **Sarah** Frances
Croker-Poole (*28 Jan 1940 New Delhi, India) daughter
of Arthur Poole; =2ⁿᵈ Karim IV, Aga Khan
=2 1970 London; **Anna-Rose Bramwell** (…) daughter of
Henry Bramwell; =2ⁿᵈ Peter Knatchbull-Hugessen

issue of 2nd: (none by 1st):
1) **William** Henry **Crichton-Stuart** (*2 Jan 1971
London)
= 2009; **Susan Daniels** (...) daughter of Robert Daniels
& Claire ...
no issue
2) **Hugh** Bertram **Crichton-Stuart** (*20 Mar 1973
London)
= 11 Sep 1999 Paarl, South Africa; **Kerry-Anne Reid**
(...) daughter of Leo Reid
a) **Philippa** Jane **Crichton-Stuart** (*16 Oct 1999
Capetown, South Africa)
b) **Katharine** Morgan **Crichton-Stuart** (*28 May
2003 Capetown)
3) **Alexander** Blain **Crichton-Stuart** (*26 Apr 1982
London)
= 2007; **Susannah Collett** (*Jun 1984 London)
daughter of Alan Collett & ... Bennett
issue ?
D) **Lady** Caroline Moira **Fiona Crichton-Stuart** (*7 Jan
1941)
= 4 May 1959; **Michael Lowsley-Williams** (...) son of
Francis Lowsley-Williams & Monica Makins
1) **Patrick** David Edward **Lowsley-Williams** (*10 Feb
1960)
2) **Mark** Ogden Francis **Lowsley-Williams** (*26 Feb
1961 London)
3) **Paul** John Fermin **Lowsley-Williams** (*22 Mar 1964
London)
= 27 Jun 1992 Orleans, Massachusetts; **Elizabeth**
Compton **Allyn** (...) daughter of Rev. Compton Allyn
& Elizabeth ...
4) **Michael** Charles Javier **Lowsley-Williams** (*... 1967)
III) **Lady Jean Crichton-Stuart** (28 Oct 1908 Edinburgh – 23
Oct 1995 Rome)
= 12 Jun 1928; **Hon. James** Willoughby **Bertie** (22 Sep
1901 – 11 May 1966 Malta) son of Montagu Bertie, 7th Earl
of Abingdon & Gwendoline Dormer
A) **Fra Andrew** Willoughby Ninian **Bertie, 78th Grand
Master of the Sovereign Order of Malta** (15 May 1929
London – 7 Feb 2008 Rome) elected Grand Master 8 Apr 1988

142

B) Charles **Peregrine** Albemarle **Bertie** (*2 Jan 1932 London)
= 20 Apr 1960 London; **Susan** Giselda Anne Lyon **Wills** (*8 Apr 1940 London) daughter of John Wills & Hon. Jean Elphinstone
  1) **David** Montagu Albemarle **Bertie** (*12.2.1963 Windsor)
    = 12 Feb 1994 Burton-on-Kendal; **Catherine** Cecily **Mason-Hornby** (*7 May 1964) daughter of Antony Mason-Hornby & Cecily Carter
    a) **Charlotte** Iona Rose **Bertie** (*27 Mar 1995 Windor)
    b) **Lucy** Victoria Isabella **Bertie** (*5 Feb 1998 Windsor)
    c) **Hugo** Peregrine Anthony **Bertie** (*18 May 2001 Windsor)
    d) **Rory** Willoughby James **Bertie** (*9 Sep 2003 Windsor)
  2) **Caroline** Georgina Rose **Bertie** (*6 Mar 1965)
    = 3 Sep 1991 Tattendon, Berkshire; **Andrew Carrington** (*5 Dec 1959) son of Norman Carrington & Caroline Campbell
    a) **Georgia** Elizabeth Jean **Carrington** (*9 Jul 1994 Bath)
    b) **Charles** Alexander Francis **Carrington** (*27 Jul 1996 Bath)
IV) **Lord Robert Crichton-Stuart** (12 Dec 1909 - 1976)
= 18 Apr 1934 Windsor; **Lady Janet** Egidia **Montgomerie** (13 May 1911 – 30 Dec 1999) daughter of Archibald Montgomerie, 16th Earl of Eglinton and Winton & Lady Beatrice Dalrymple
A) **Ninian Crichton-Stuart** (31 Oct 1935 London - 1992)
B) **Henry** Colum **Crichton-Stuart** (*1 Apr 1938 London)
  = 20 Jul 1963 (dv.1985); **Patricia** Margaret **Norman** (*27 May 1940) daughter of Hugh Norman & Margaret Griffin; she =2nd Robert Kindersley
  1) **Camilla Crichton-Stuart** (*15 Apr 1964)
    = Dec 1994; Martin **Andreas Carleton-Smith** (*1967) son of Sir Michael Carleton-Smith & Helga Stoss
    a) **Joshua** Michael **Carleton-Smith** (*1998)
    b) **Katinka Carleton-Smith** (*2000)
  2) **Serena Crichton-Stuart** (*9 Jul 1965)
    = 1993; **Morgan** Jonathan **Watts** (…) daughter of Dennis Watts
    a) **Megan** Isabella **Watts** (*May 1994 London)
    b) **Lily** Eve **Watts** (*Jun 1997)

3) **Alexander** Colum **Crichton-Stuart** (*4 Feb 1967 London)
= 2001; **Isabella Martin** (…)
issue ?
4) **Teresa** Clare **Crichton-Stuart** (*1971 London)
= 1995; **Toby Mermagen** (…)
a) **Sam** Timothy **Mermagen** (*Sep 1999)
b) **Jake** Henry **Mermagen** (*Nov 2001)
c) **Ella** Jean **Mermagen** (*Jun 2004)

V) **Lord David Stuart** (8 Feb 1911 - 1970) discontinued use
of Crichton 1934
= 24 May 1940 Edinburgh; **Ursula** Sybil Clifton **Packe** (2
Feb 1913 - 1989) daughter of Sir Edward
Packe & Hon. Mary Colebrooke; =1st Peter Clifton
A) **Flora Stuart** (3 Aug 1941 Isle of Bute – 27 Feb 2005)
B) **Rose Stuart** (6 Apr 1946 – 5 Jan 1962) killed in a car crash

VI) **Lord Patrick Crichton-Stuart** (1 Feb 1913 - 5 Feb 1956)
=1 14 Oct 1937 London; **Jane von Bahr** (… - 18 Dec 1944
Stockholm)
=2 16 Apr 1947; **Linda** Irene **Evans** (16 Apr 1922 - 1974
London) daughter of William Evan
issue of 1st (none by 2nd):
A) **Charles** Patrick Colum Henrey **Crichton-Stuart** (10 Mar
1939 – 3 Jul 2001)
=1 7 Jul 1967 London (dv.); **Shirley Anne Field** (*27
Jun 1938 Bolton, Lancashire) née Broomfield; was raised
in an orphanage; took name Field as an actress
=2 1980; **Jennifer** A **Collie** (*1959)
issue of 1st:
1) **Nicola** Jane **Crichton-Stuart** (*1967 London)
= Apr 1994 London; **Stuart Gill** (…)
a) **Charlie Gill** (*Sep 1998 London)
b) **Max Gill** (*Mar 2001 London)
issue of 2nd:
2) **Sophie Crichton-Stuart** (*1980 London)
3) **Patrick** James **Crichton-Stuart** (*1982 Oxford)
B) **Angela** Mary Monica **Crichton-Stuart** (*25 Mar 1940)
= 19 Feb 1963 London (dv.); **Simon** Mark **Pilkington**
(1938 London - 25 Mar 2009) son of Mark Pilkington &
Susan Henderson; =2nd Caroline Ramsay
1) **Rupert** Charles **Pilkington** (*21 Feb 1964 London)
2) **Mark** Patrick **Pilkington** (*6 Oct 1965 London)

144

= 1999; **Gaynor Driscoll** (…)

a) **Iain Pilkington** (*2004)

3) **Jane** Susan **Pilkington** (*7 Nov 1966)

= 1996; **Brett Marshall** (…) son of Stanley Marshall

a) **India** Rose **Marshall** (*2001)

b) **Amber Marshall** (...)

4) **Kate** Susan **Pilkington** (*23 May 1970 Ayr)

= 24 Sep 2004; **Tom Shepherd** (...)

a) **Amelie** Janey McEwen **Shepherd** (*2005)

b) **Isla** Monique Curzon **Shepherd** (*2007)

VII) **Lord Rhidian Crichton-Stuart** (4 Jun 1917 Cardiff – 25 Jun 1969 London)

= 20 Jul 1939 London; **Selina Gerthe van Wijk** (24 Apr 1913 – 4 May 1985) daughter of Fredrik van Wijk & Charlotte de Casarotto

A) **Fredrik** John Patrick **Crichton-Stuart** (*6 Sep 1940)

= 3 Oct 1964 London; **Elizabeth** Jane Douglas **Whitson** (*3 Mar 1944) daughter of Ernest Whitson & Jean Miller

1) **Ione** Jane **Crichton-Stuart** (*22 Nov 1965)

= 2005; **Collin Tulloch** (...)

2) **Rhidian** Colum **Crichton-Stuart** (*3 Aug 1967)

= 16 Sep 1997; **Claire Stead** (…)

a) **Isabelle** Alexandra **Crichton-Stuart** (*2 Feb 1997 London)

3) **Amanda** Mary **Crichton-Stuart** (*31 Oct 1968)

4) **Alexandra** Victoria **Crichton-Stuart** (12 Jul 1973 – 5 Jun 1978)

5) **Edward** James Neil **Crichton-Stuart** (*27 Dec 1974)

B) Mary **Margot** Patricia **Crichton-Stuart** (*18 Mar 1942)

= 20 Jun 1962; **Edward** Henry **Lovell** (…)

1) **Nicola** Mary **Lovell** (*23 Aug 1963 London)

= 1983 (dv.); **Francis Maxwell of Kirkconnel** (…)

a) **Georgia Maxwell** (…)

b) **Bettina Maxwell** (…)

c) **Clementina Maxwell** (…)

d) **Merlin Maxwell** (…)

e) **Robert Maxwell** (…)

2) **Peter** Henry James **Lovell** (*21 Feb 1965)

= 1988; **Nicola Fazakerley** (…)

a) **James** Alexander **Lovell** (*1990)

b) **Alexander** Hugh **Lovell** (*1993)

3) **Henrietta** Margaret **Lovell** (*1971)

C) Jerome **Niall** Anthony **Crichton-Stuart** (*1 Jan 1948)
= 1971 London; **Susan Dwyer-Joyce** (...) daughter of
Patrick Dwyer-Joyce

   1) Rhidian **Charles** Patrick **Crichton-Stuart** (*1974)
= 2007; **Olivia** Rosemary **Blomfield-Smith** (*1976)
daughter of Clive Blomfield-Smith & Eirenice Gore-
Booth
no issue

   2) Niall **Rollo** Robert **Crichton-Stuart** (*1977)
= Sep 2005 London; Eun-Lee **Isobella** Gage **Heygate**
(*1977) daughter of Sir Richard Heygate, 6th Baronet &
Jong-Ja Hyun

     a) **Henry** Richard Niall **Crichton-Stuart** (*20 Jan 2010)

   3) **Archie** Michael John **Crichton-Stuart** (*Jan 1984 London)

d. **Roger** Charles Noel **Bellingham** (28 Apr 1884 Oakham,
Sussex – 4 Mar 1915 Flanders, Belgium) killed in action
= 18 Jan 1910 Brighton, Sussex; **Alice** Maud **Naish** (1878 -
10 Jan 1949)

I) **Sir Roger** Carroll Patrick Stephen **Bellingham, 6th Baronet**
(23 Aug 1911 – 6 Feb 1973 Stockport, Cheshire) suc. uncle
as Baronet 19 May 1956
= 27 Dec 1941; **Mary Norman** (...) daughter of William
Norman

A) **Sir Noel** Peter Roger **Bellingham, 7th Baronet** (4 Sep 1943 –
12 Jul 1999) suc. father as Baronet 6 Feb 1973
= 1977; **Jane Taylor** (...) daughter of Edwin Taylor
no issue

B) **Sir Anthony** Edward Norman **Bellingham, 8th Baronet** (*24
Mar 1947 Stockport) suc. brother as Baronet 12 Jul 1999
=1 16 Feb 1990 Santa Barbara, California (dv.1998); **Denise**
Marie **Moity** (*22 Feb 1954 New Orleans, Louisiana) daughter
of Henry Moity & ...
=2 ... (dv.); **Namphon Buchar** (...)
issue of 1st (none by 2nd):

   1) **William** Alexander Noel Henry **Bellingham** (*19 Aug
1991) heir-apparent to Baronetcy

II) **Constance** Catherine Mary Pia **Bellingham** (21 Oct 1912 –
...)
=1 23 Apr 1935; **Brenden Russell** (... - 23 Jun 1956) son of
Charles Russell

=2 7 Jan 1963; Robert **Oswald** H. **Shaw-Hamilton** (1904
Suffolk - ...) son of Robert Shaw-Hamilton
issue of 1st (none by 2nd):
A) **Heber Russell** (*1936)
  = 1961; **Cora** Ann **Walsh** (…)
  1) **Nigel** Brenden Charles **Russell** (*1962)
  2) **Hilary** Elizabeth Ann **Russell** (*… 1965)
B) **Una Russell** (*1939) (twin)
  = 1965; **Patrick** Rory **White** (…)
  1) **Sharon** Ann **White** (*1966)
C) **Anne** M **Russell** (*1939) (twin)
  = 1967; **Charles** W **Fyson** (…)
  1) **Erik** Christopher **Fyson** (*1969)
D) **Patrick Russell** (*1942)
  = 1966; **Carol** Ann **Banbrook** (*1943) daughter of
  Henry Banbrook & Dorothy Potts
  1) **Brendan** Daniel **Russell** (*1967)
  2) **Nicholas** Damian **Russell** (*1968)
3. **Sister Edith** Horatia Emma Frances **Noel** (1849 - 22 Aug 1890
London)
4. **Sir Charles** William Francis **Noel, 3rd Earl of Gainsborough**
etc. (20 Oct 1850 Campden House, Chipping Camden,
Gloucestershire – 17 Apr 1926 Campden House) suc. father as
Earl 13 Aug 1881
=1 9 May 1876 Pershore, Hereford; **Augusta** Mary Catherine
Berkeley (18 Mar 1852 Spetchley, Worcestershire – 5 Nov 1877
Spetchley) daughter of Robert Berkeley & Lady Mary Brown
=2 2 Feb 1880 in Ireland; **Mary Elizabeth Dease** (1858 Turbotston,
Westmeath, Ireland – 17 Nov 1937) daughter of James Dease &
Charlotte Jerningham
issue of 1st:
a. **Lady Agnes** Mary Catherine **Noel** (9 Oct 1877 Spetchley – 1 Mar
1915 Oakham)
issue of 2nd:
b. **Lady Norah** Ida Emily **Noel** (4 Jan 1881 Campden House – 23
May 1939 Brighton)
= 8 Sep 1915 Exton; **Count Robert** Charles **Bentinck**[12] (5 Dec

---

[12] This branch of the Bentinck family was granted the title of Count by the Holy Roman Emperor in 1742. Queen Victoria granted the family permission to continue to carry the title in 1886 as British subjects.

1875 London – 12 Mar 1932 Ashwell, Hertfordshire) son of Count Henry Bentinck & Harriett McKerrel

I) **Countess Brydgytte** Blanche **Bentinck** (11 Nov 1916 Bristol – 5 Sep 2010 Haren, Netherlands)
= 2 Feb 1937 London; **Jonkheer**[13] **Adriaan** Hendrik Sibble **van der Wyck** (22 Jun 1906 The Hague – 4 Nov 1973 Haren) son of Jonkheer Evret vand der Wyck

A) **Caroline** Norah Frederique Adrienne **van der Wyck** (*1 Jun 1938)
   = May 1961; Karel Jan **André** Guyon, **Baron Collot d'Escury** (12 Jul 1933 Kloosterzande - 17 Jun 2008 Kloosterzande) son of Henrik, Baron Collot d'Escury & Juliette Vogelvanger
   1) **Guyon** Adolf Andre **Collot d'Escury** (*25 Apr 1962)
   2) **Juliette** Brygytte Blanche **Collot d'Escury** (*12 Aug 1963)
   3) **Marina** Caroline Norah **Collot d'Escury** (*30 Mar 1965)
      = 1992; **Christaan Bellaar Spruyt** (*1964)
      a) **Nora Bellaar Spruyt** (*1999)
      b) **Anneke Bellaar Spruyt** (*2001)
      c) **Andre Bellaar Spruyt** (*2002)
   4) Robert **Willem** Frederick **Collot d'Escury** (*1970)
      = ...; **Caroline Gockel** (...)

B) Brydgytte Agnes **Dawn van der Wyck** (*6 Jan 1940)
   = 2 Mar 1968 (dv.1990); **Paul** Heinz Maria Dirk **Vermeer** (*1935)
   1) **Robert** Paul Adriaan Henry Simon **Vermeer** (*14 Oct 1968)
      issue by **Mirielle Brasz** (...):
      a) **Romy Vermeer** (*2004)
      b) **Amy Vermeer** (*18 Mar 2006)
   2) **Fiona** Victoria Regina Brydgytte **Vermeer** (*1970)
   3) **Nadia** Norah Noel **Vermeer** (*1971)
      issue by **Bert-Jan Waanders** (*1967):
      a) **Joep Waanders** (*2002)
      b) **Norah Waanders** (*2007)

C) **Raina** Jeanne Woltera **van der Wyck** (*2 Dec 1942)
   = 1973; **Hendryk van Harrenfeld** (...)
   1) **Hugo** Johannes Hendrik **van Harrenfeld** (*1974)
   2) **Wendela** Blanche Catheriune **van Harrenfeld** (*1977)
   3) **Diederik** Godard Adriaan Roelant **van Harrenfeld** (*1980)

---

[13] Jonkheer is a Dutch style of nobility that does not have an English translation.

D) **Jonkheer Evert** Rein Robert Henry **van der Wyck** (*12 Aug 1945)
= 1967; **Tanja Wolff** (*1944)
  1) **Rhoderick** Wolter Arnold **van der Wyck** (*20 Apr 1968 Capetown, S.Africa)
    = 9 Nov 2002 Voorschoten, Netherlands (civil) & 9 Nov 2002 Braschaar, Belgium (rel); **Emily** Anna Hubertina Maria **Bremers** (*1970 Groesbeek, Belgium) daughter of Louis Bremers & Lisanne Rottier
    a) **Philip** Rein Lodewijk **van der Wyck** (*17 Jun 2003 The Hague)
    b) **Maurits** Rhoderick August **van der Wyck** (*5 Aug 2004 The Hague)
  2) **Arnaud van der Wyck** (*1969)
    = Jun 2004 Voorschoten; **Anouk ...** (...)
    issue ?
  3) **Alexander van der Wyck** (*... 1971)
    = 8 (civil) & 15 (rel) Dec 2001 Voorschoten; **Stephanie Carlier** (...)
    a) **Gwendolyn van der Wyck** (*20 Jul 2003 The Hague)
    b) **Felicia** Stephanie Elizabeth **van der Wyck** (*20 Oct 2004 The Hague)
E) **Jonkheer Douglas** Roderick Arthur Duncan **van der Wyck** (*9 May 1955)

II) **Henry** Noel **Bentinck, 11th Earl of Portland,** Viscount Woodstock, Baron Cirencester, **Count Bentinck** (2 Oct 1919 London – 30 Jan 1997 Litle Cudworthy, Devon) suc. cousin as Count Bentinck 4 Aug 1968; suc. the 9th Duke of Portland as Earl etc.31 Jul 1990
=1 13 Oct 1972 London; **Pauline Mellowes** (15 Oct 1921 London – 10 Jan 1967 Potten End, Hertfordshire) daughter of Frederick Mellowes & Doris Watts
=2 23 Feb 1974 Nettleden, Hertfordshire; **Jenifer Hopkins** (*13 May 1936 London) daughter of Reginald Hopkins & Nancy Page
issue of 1st (none by 2nd):
A) **Lady Sorrel** Deirdre **Bentinck**[14] (*22 Feb 1942 Selborne,

---

[14] Although entitled to by styled Count or Countess Bentinck, the children of the Earls of Portland have chosen to be known only by their British styles.

Hampshire) resumed maiden name 1990
= 24 Jun 1972 Nettleden (dv.1988); **Sir John** Philip **Lister-Kaye, 8th Baronet** (*8 May 1946 Wakefield, Yorkshire) son of Sir John Lister-Kaye, 7th Baronet & Audrey Carter; =2nd Lucinda Law; suc.father as Baronet 1982

1) John **Warwick** Noel **Lister-Kaye** (*10 Dec 1974 Inverness, Scotland) heir-apparent to Baronetcy

2) **Melanie** Helen **Lister-Kaye** (*12 Oct 1976 Inverness) (twin)
= 4 Nov 2000 Inverness; David **Ieuan** Picton **Evans** (*22 Mar 1975 Sawnsea, Wales) son of Alan Evans & Mary Harries
   a) **Harris** Ifan Picton **Evans** (*16 Dec 2008)
   b) due 2011

3) **Amelia** Helen **Lister-Kaye** (*12 Oct 1976 Inverness) (twin)
= 11 Oct 2008 Camabridge; **Andrew** Colin **Williamson** (*6 Mar 1970 London)
   a) **Arthur** Leonard Jupiter Lister **Williamson** (*8 Aug 2008 Cambridge)
   b) **Elisabeth** Lily Bo Sorrel **Williamson** (*9 Sep 2009 Cambridge)

B) **Lady Anna** Cecilia **Bentinck** (*18 May 1947 Selborne) retained her maiden name
=1 24 Jul 1965 Berkhamstead, Herfordshire (dv.1974); **Jasper** Hamilton **Holmes** (*14 Nov 1941 Hartford, Cheshire)
=2 19 Jul 1975 London (dv.1977); **Nicholas** George Spafford **Vester** (*30 Mar 1944 Cambridge)
no issue by marriages
issue by **Arnold** George Francis **Cragg** (*30 Sep 1943) son of Rt. Rev. Kenneth Cragg:

1) **Gulliver** Jack Bentinck **Cragg** (*1 Jul 1978 London)
2) **George** Finn Gareth Bentinck **Cragg** (*4 Oct 1980 London)
3) **Iris Cragg** (* & + 15 Jul 1986 London) (twin)
4) **Pierre Cragg** (* & + 15 Jul 1986 London) (twin)
5) **Charlotte-Sophie** Camden Bentinck **Cragg** (*29 Mar 1988 London)

C) **Timothy** Charles Robert Noel **Bentinck, 12th Earl of Portland** etc, **Count Bentinck** (*1 Jun 1953 in Tasmania) suc.father as Earl and Count 30 Jan 1997

= 8 Sep 1979 London; **Judith** Ann **Emerson** (*10 Oct 1952 Newcastle-under-Lyme) daughter of John Emerson & Mary Graham

> 1) **William** Jack Henry, **Viscount Woodstock** (*19 May 1984 London)
> 2) **Hon. Jasper** James Mellowes **Bentinck** (*12 Jun 1988 London)

c. **Sir Arthur** Edward Joseph **Noel, 4th Earl of Gainsborough** etc. (30 Jun 1884 Exton Park – 27 Aug 1927 Exton Park) suc. father as Earl 17 Apr 1926
= 10 Nov 1915; **Alice** Mary **Eyre** (17 Oct 1886 Lima, Peru – 11 Jun 1970 London) daughter of Edward Eyre & Elisa Ainsworth

> I) **Lady Maureen** Therese Josephine **Noel** (7 Mar 1917 London - 25 Nov 2009 Chipping Camden, Gloucestershire)
> =1 19 Feb 1944 London; **Sir Charles** Walter James **Dormer, 15th Baron Dormer, 15th Baronet** (20 Dec 1903 Malta – 27 Aug 1975 London) son of Sir Charles Dormer, 14th Baron Dormer & Caroline Clifford; suc.father as Baron 4 May 1922
> =2 22 Jul 1982; **Peregrine** Edward Lancelot **Fellowes** (8 Jul 1912 Calgary, Alberta – 15 Feb 1999 Chipping Camden) son of Henry Fellowes & Georgina Wrightson; =1st Olwen Stuart-Jones
> issue of 1st (none by 2nd):
> A) **Hon. Jane** Maureen Therese **Dormer** (*20 Nov 1945 London)
> =1 21 Jul 1966 London (dv.1978); Henry Alistair **Samuel Sandbach** (*1944) son of Ralph Sandbach
> =2 1980 London; **Geoffrey** Edward **Meek** (1921 - Mar 1984)
> =3 Jan 1988 London; **Robert** Nigel Forbes **Glennie** (…)
> issue of 1st (none by others):
> 1) **Emma** Pauline Jane **Sandbach** (*29 Jun 1967)
> = May 1993; **Graham** Anthony **Defries** (*1972) son of Nicholas Defries
> a) **Charles** Samuel Nicholas **Defries** (*Feb 1996 London)
> b) **Elisa** Jane Catherine **Defries** (*Apr 1999 London)
> c) **Lara** Betty Maureen **Defreis** (*May 2001 London)
> d) **Arthur** Joseph Graham **Defries** (*Nov 2004 London)
> 2) **James** Peter Charles **Sandbach** (*1969 London)
> B) **Hon. Catherine** Mary **Dormer** (*2 Apr 1950 London)
> =1 14 Feb 1973 London (dv.1989); **Christopher** John Godfrey **Bird** (*1946) son of Garth Bird & Elizabeth Vavasour

=2 May 1992; **Simon** Michael **Stone** (…)
issue of 2nd: (none by 1st):
1) **Raphael** Charles **Stone** (*Dec 1992 London)
II) **Sir Anthony** Edward Gerald **Noel, 5th Earl of Gainsborough**
etc.(24 Oct 1923 London – 29 Dec 2009 Exton Park) suc.father
as Earl 27 Aug 1927
= 23 Jul 1947; **Mary Stourton** (*24 Sep 1925) daughter of Hon.
John Stourton & Kathleen Gunther
A) **Lady Juliana** Mary Alice **Noel** (*27 Jan 1949 Barham Court,
   Rutland) has resumed maiden name
   = 29 Jan 1970 London (dv.2001); **Edward** Peter Bertram
   Savile **Foljambe, 5th Earl of Liverpool**, Viscount
   Hawkesbury, Baron Hawkesbury (*ph.14 Jan 1944) son of
   Peter Foljambe & Elizabeth Gibbs; suc.grand-uncle as Earl
   13 Mar 1969; =2nd Marie Michel de Pierredon; =3rd Georgina
   Rubin
   1) **Luke** Marmaduke Peter Savile, **Viscount Hawkesbury**
      (*25 Mar 1972)
   2) **Hon. Ralph** Edward Anthony Savile **Foljambe** (*24 Sep
      1974 London)
      = Oct 2003; **Rebecca Parker** (…) daughter of Gordon
      Parker
      a) **Jemima** Fleur **Foljambe** (*6 Mar 2005)
      b) **Arthur Foljambe** (*2006)
      c) **Hector** George Jocelyn Savile **Foljambe** (*22 Dec 2009)
B) **Anthony** Baptist **Noel, 6th Earl of Gainsborough** etc.
   (*16 Jan 1950 Barham Court) suc.father as Earl 29 Dec
   2009
   = 23 May 1972 London; **Sarah** Rose **Winnington** (*29
   Apr 1951 London) daughter of Thomas Winnington &
   Lady Betty Anson
   1) **Henry** Robert Anthony, **Viscount Campden** (*1 Jul
      1977)
      = Sep 2005 London; **Zara van Cutsem** (*Dec 1978)
      daughter of Geoffrey van Cutsem & Sally
      McCorquodale
      a) **Hon. Edward** Patrick Anthony **Noel** (*30 Apr
         2007)
      b) **Hon. Violet** Ruth **Noel** (*12 Nov 2009)
C) **Lady Maria Noel** (*3 Feb 1951 Barham Court)
   = 17 Apr 1971; **Robert D Pridden** (*1945 Exton,

Rutland) son of John Pridden & Ivy Ewin

1) **Benedict** John Anthony **Pridden** (*23 Sep 1973 London)
= May 2005; **Georgina** Rose Alianore **Lethbridge** (*1980) daughter of Sir Thomas Lethbridge, 7th Baronet & Susan Rock
   a) **Charlotte** Susan Mary **Pridden** (*8 Nov 2006 York)
   b) **Agatha** Maria Rachael **Pridden** (*4 Apr 2008 Scarborough)
   c) **Robert** Ralph Baptist **Pridden** (*29 Aug 2009 Scarborough)
2) **Lucy** Charlotte Ivy **Pridden** (*15 Jun 1976 London)
= 15 Jul 2006 Exton Park; **Piers** Mark **Woodnutt** (*28 Mar 1977 London) son of Martin Woodnutt & Susannah Harrison
   a) **Jack** Robert Mark **Woodnutt** (*31 Jan 2008 London)
   b) due 2011

D) **Lady Janet Noel** (* & + 23 Jan 1953 Barham Court)

E) **Lady Celestria** Magdalena Mary **Noel** (*27 Jan 1954 Exton Park, Rutland)
= 1 Mar 1990 London; **Timothy Hales** (*2 Apr 1933 London) son of William Hales & Katherine Johnston
1) **Catherine** Rose Mary **Hales** (*11 Jun 1990 London)

F) **Hon. Gerard** Edward Joseph **Noel** (*23 Jan 1955 Exton Park)
= 1985; **Charlotte Dugdale** (*15 May 1955) daughter of Sir William Dugdale, 2nd Baronet & Lady Belinda Peydell-Bouverie
1) **Belinda** Mary **Noel** (*Jul 1986)
2) Francis **Reginald Noel** (*Jul 1987)
3) **Lettice** Catherine **Noel** (*Dec 1989)

G) **Hon. Thomas Noel** (*9 Mar 1958 Exton Park)

H) **Hon. Edward** Andrew **Noel** (*22 Nov 1960 Exton Park)
=1 1990 (dv.1994); **Lavinia** Jane **Bingham** (…) daughter of George Bingham
=2 19 Jul 1997; **Sarah** Kate **Yeats-Brown** (*9 Jul 1961 London) daughter of David Yeats-Brown & Annesley Eden
issue of 2nd (none 1st):
1) **Joseph** David **Noel** (*20 Jan 2000)

153

III) **Hon. Gerard** Eyre Wriothesley **Noel** (*20 Nov 1926 London)

= 1 Feb 1958 London; **Adele** Julie Patricia **Were** (…) daughter of Bonville Were

A) **Philip** Arthur Nicholas **Noel** (*26 May 1959)

B) **Robert** John Baptist **Noel** (*15 Oct 1962)

C) **Elizabeth** Alice Mary **Noel** (*24 Sep 1967)

= 28 Sep 1996; **Henry** John **Pittman** (…) son of Hugh Pittman & Rosemary Dickinson[15]

1) **Luke** Nicholas **Pittman** (*6 Jan 1999)

2) **Marina Pittman** (*10 Sep 2001)

d. **Hon. Charles** Hubert Francis **Noel** (22 Oct 1885 Exton Park – 26 Apr 1947 Kinross, Scotland)

= 31 Jan 1912 London; **May Douglas-Dick** (Jul 1884 London– 1 Apr 1964 London) son of Archibald Douglas-Dick & Isabelle Parrott

I) **Jane** Isabelle Mary **Noel** (21 Nov 1912 London – 7 Mar 1952 Nunwick, Northumberland)

= 26 Sep 1942 London; **Guy** Hunter **Allgood** (4 Oct 1892 Alnwick, Northumberland – 1 Jun 1970 Nunwick) son of Robert Allgood & Isabel Clayton

A) Lancelot **Guy Allgood** (1 Feb 1944 Newcastle-upon-Tyne - Jan 1999 Hexham, Northumberland)

= Cirencester; **Veronica Pitman** (*20 Jan 1950 London) daughter of Stuart Pitman & Cynthia …

1) **Jane** Elizabeth **Allgood** (*3 Apr 1977 Hexham)

= 2008; **James** R **Lamb** (...) son of Robert Lamb

2) **George** Hunter **Allgood** (1 – 19 May 1979 Hexham)

3) **Alice** Louise **Allgood** (*14 Aug 1980 Hexham)

4) **Mary** Rosamund **Allgood** (*21 Feb 1983 Hexham)

= 2010/11; **Henry** H **Lobb** (*1982 Manchester) son of Edward Lobb

B) **Charles** Noel **Allgood** (*1 May 1945 Corbridge-on-Tyne, Northumberland)

C) **James** Major **Allgood** (27 Jun 1948 Nunwick – 15 Mar 1949 Nunwick)

II) **Archibald** Charles William **Noel** (5 Jan 1914 London – 8 Feb 1997)

---

[15] Rosemary Dickinson Pittman =2nd Andrew Parker-Bowles, the ex-husband of HRH The Duchess of Cornwall.

=1 30 Aug 1945; **Bridget** Mary **Fetherstonbaugh** (26 Dec 1918 – 3 Sep 1976) daughter of William Fetherstonbaugh & Adela Cayley

=2 22 Dec 1977; **Andrée** Marie **Duchen** (…) daughter of Pierre Duchen

issue of 1st (none by 2nd):

A) **Charles** William **Noel** (*4 Jul 1948 Crickhowell)

= 1985; **Diane** Margaret **de Freitas** (…) daughter of Gerald de Freitas

1) **Elizabeth** Bridgit Maggie **Noel** (*19 Nov 1986 London)

2) **Alexander** Charles FitzWilliam **Noel** (*19 Jan 1989 London)

B) **Edward** Albany **Noel** (*28 Sep 1956 Crickhowell)

III) **Carola** Mary **Noel** (3 Jun 1916 London – 19 Mar 1989 Aberfeldy, Scotland)

= 21 Apr 1936 Dundee; **Thomas Steuart Fothringham** (5 Apr 1907 Edinburgh – 9 Sep 1979 Edzell, Scotland) son of Walter Steuart Fothringham & Elizabeth Nicholson

A) **Robert** Scrymsoure **Steuart Fothringham of Pourie**(*5 Aug 1937 Boughton Hall)

= 16 Feb 1962; **Elizabeth** Mary Charlotte **Lawther** (19 Mar 1938 London - 15 Aug 1990 London) daughter of Thomas Lawther

1) **Mariana Steuart Fothringham** (*1966)

= 1 Apr 1989 Murthly, Perthshire; **Christopher** Berkeley **Pease** (27 Apr 1958 London)

a) **Edward** Robert **Pease** (*7 Jun 1991 London)

b) **Dorothea** Elizabeth **Pease** (*29 Oct 1992 London)

c) **Sybilla** Mary **Pease** (*2 Jul 1994 London)

d) **Carola** Rosemary **Pease** (*19 Feb 1996 London)

2) **Ilona Steuart Fothringham** (*3 Nov 1969)

= 30 May 1998 Murthly; **Christopher** Alexander David **Boyle** (…) son of Paul Boyle & Helen ...

a) **George** Alexander David Lindsay **Boyle** (*29 Dec 1999 London)

b) **Henry** Robert Alfred Lindsay **Boyle** (*1 Apr 2002 London)

c) **Elizabeth** Mary Agatha **Boyle** (*24 Sep 2008 Carlisle)

3) **Thomas Steuart Fothringham** (*20 Sep 1971)

= 7 Aug 1999 Murthly; Anna **Catherine Macdonald** (*11 Apr 1969 Melbourne, Australia) daughter of Allan

Macdonald & Anthea Poultney
- a) **Alexander** Donald **Steuart Fothringham** (*30 Sep 2001 Edinburgh)
- b) **James** Andrew **Steuart Fothringham** (*17 Nov 2005 Dundee)
4) **Lionel Steuart Fothringham** (*27 Apr 1973)
= 2005; **Elizabeth Waller** (…) daughter of David Waller
- a) **Charlotte** Rose **Steuart Fothringham** (*6 Dec 2009)
B) **Walter Steuart Fothringham** (26 Mar 1939 Edinburgh– 3 Jun 1989 Grantully Castle, Aberfeldy)
= 8 Jan 1972; **Patricia** Anne **Watherston** (…) daughter of Sir David Watherston
1) **Teresa** Catherine Frances **Steuart Fothringham** (*22 May 1975)
= 2005; **Warren Elsmore** (…) son of Malcolm Elsmore issue ?
2) **David** Frederick **Steuart Fothringham** (*2 Mar 1979)
C) **Henry Steuart Fothringham** (*15 Feb 1944 Edinburgh)
= 20 May 1972 Glencreran; **Cherry** Linnhe **Stewart** (25 Jun 1940 Singapore – 17 Dec 2001) daughter of Ian Stewart & Ursula Morley-Fletcher
1) **Patrick** Donald **Steuart Fothringham** (*23 Apr 1973 Perth, Scotland)
= 2005; **Suzanna Wilson** (…)
- a) **Hester** Mary **Steuart Fothringham** (*7 Dec 2008)
2) **Charles** Henry **Steuart Fothringham** (*6 Apr 1974 Perth)
= 11 Feb 2011 Grantully, Perthshire; **Sophia MacCarthy-Morrogh** (…) daughter of Alexander MacCarthy-Morrogh
3) **Ian** Archibald **Steuart Fothringham** (*13 Jan 1976 Perth)
IV) **David** Franics Douglas **Noel** (18 May 1919 London – 2 Jan 1974)
V) **Andrew** Mungo James **Noel** (27 Jul 1921 – 21 Oct 1972)
= 10 Jan 1950; Mary **Edina Walmesley** (16 Nov 1925 - 13 Jul 2008) daughter of Charles Walmesley & Dorothy Mayne no issue
VI) **Douglas** Robert George **Noel** (*16 Apr 1924 Dundee)
= 2 Jun 1949 London; **Eleanor** Susan Jane **Younghusband** (*11 Apr 1928 London) daughter of George Younghusband & Mary Foster
A) **James** Douglas George **Noel** (*14 Aug 1950 Crickhowell, Wales)

B) **William** Edward Douglas **Noel** (5 Aug 1953
Crickhowell – 3 Nov 2006)
=1 19 Jul 1975 London (dv.1982, ann.1984); **Victoria**
Mary **Younghusband**[16] (*14 Jul 1954 London) daughter
of George Younghusband & Sybil Stuart[17]
=2 1993; Juliet **Catherine Reade** (…) daughter of Arthur
Reade; =1st Henry Hayward
issue of 1st (none by 2nd):
  1) **Teresa** Sybil **Noel** (*6 Feb 1976 Oxford)
  2) **Arthur** Douglas **Noel** (*6 Oct 1977 London)
    = …; **Marie Bertin** (…)
    a) **Thomas Noel** (*18 Nov 2005)
  C) **Caroline** Mary Jane **Noel** (*6 Jun 1956)
  = 3 Oct 1987 London; **Charles** Anthony **Wentzel** (…)
  son of John Wentzel & Philippa …
    1) **Philippa** Mary **Wentzel** (*1991)
e. **Lady Clare** Mary Charlotte **Noel** (3 Mar 1882 Oakham – 11
Mar 1962)
= 2 Oct 1907 Oakham; **Charles** Mervyn **King** (1878 Clifton,
Gloucestershire – 25 Jan 1965 Bristol) son of Mervyn King &
Agnes Bright
  I) **Agnes** Celestria Mary **King** (1917 - Oct 2005)
f. **Hon. Robert** Edmund Thomas More **Noel** (10 Apr 1888 – 2
Feb 1918 Massassi, Zimbabwe) killed in action
5. **Hon. Edward Noel** (28 Apr 1852 Oakham – 9 Nov 1917)
= 7 Oct 1884 London; **Ruth Lucas** (1852 - Apr 1926)
a. **Edward** William Charles **Noel** (14 Apr 1886 – 10 Dec 1974)
=1 6 Apr 1923; **Katherine** Florence **Ross** (1896 – 6 Feb 1952)
daughter of Robert Ross
=2 1954; **Simone Corbiau** (22 Dec 1902 – 27 Oct 1974)
daughter of Jean Corbiau
issue of 1st:
  I) **Rev. Robert** Anthony **Noel** (26 Jan 1924 – 15 Aug 1966)
  II) **Denys** Edward **Noel** (23 Nov 1925 - 1978)
  = 13 Dec 1947; **Petronelle** Moore **Bostock** (…) daughter of
  Austin Bostock
    A) **Julian** Roden Bostock **Noel** (*5 Jun 1949)
    = 1982; **Susanne** Elisabeth **Dodd** (…) daughter of

---

[16] William & Victoria are 4th cousins
[17] Sybil is a direct descendant of the 1st Marquess of Bute

Benjamin Dodd
no issue

B) **Laura** Frances **Noel** (*6 Sep 1951)
= 1979; **Peter** Clement **Coe** (…)
1) **Toby** Richard **Coe** (*1983)
2) **Lucy** Josephine **Coe** (*1985)
3) **Jennifer** Mary **Coe** (*1988)

b. **Hubert** Lewis Clifford **Noel** (19 Oct 1888 Newton Abbott, Devonshire - 1954)
= 25 Aug 1934; **Mary** Maxwell **Currie** (1876 Newcastle-upon-Tyne - 1953) daughter of James Currie & ...; =1ˢᵗ Francis Russell
no issue

c. **John** Baptist Lucius **Noel** (26 Feb 1890 – 13 Mar 1989)
=1 1915; **Sybil Graham** (… - 1939)
=2 1941; **Mary Sullivan** (12 Jun 1908 - 1984)
issue of 2ⁿᵈ (none by 1ˢᵗ):
I) **Sandra** Ruth Catherine **Noel** (*15 Apr 1943)

B. **William** Harry **Hay, 19ᵗʰ Earl of Erroll** etc.(3 May 1823 Bushy Park – 3 Dec 1891 Slains Castle, near Cruden, Aberdeenshire) suc. father as Earl 19 Apr 1846
= 20 Sep 1848 Montreal; **Eliza** Amelia **Gore** (24 Feb 1829 Montreal – 11 Mar 1916 London) daughter of Hon. Sir Charles Gore & Lavina FitzRoy

1. **Charles** Gore, **Lord Kilmarnock** (10 – 12 Oct 1850 Slains Castle)

2. **Sir Charles** Gore **Hay KT, 20ᵗʰ Earl of Erroll** etc. (7 Feb 1852 Montreal – 8 Jul 1927) suc. father as Earl 3 Dec 1891; KT 1901
= 11 Aug 1875 Muncaster, Cumberland; **Mary** Caroline **L'Estrange** (May 1849 Tickhill Castle, Yorkshire - 12 Oct 1934) daughter of Edmund L'Estrange & Lady Henrietta Lumley

a. **Sir Victor** Alexander Gerald **Hay, 21ˢᵗ Earl of Erroll** etc. (17 Oct 1876 Slains Castle – 20 Feb 1928) suc. father as Earl 8 Jul 1927
= 22 May 1900 London; Mary **Lucy** Victoria **Mackenzie** (18 Jun 1875 Ness Bank, Inverness- 18 Jan 1957) daughter of Sir Allan Mackenzie, Baronet & Lucy Davidson

I) **Josslyn** Victor **Hay, 22ⁿᵈ Earl of Erroll** etc. (11 May 1901 London – 24 Jan 1941 near Nairobi, Kenya) murdered; suc. father as Earl 20 Feb 1928
=1 22 Sep 1923 (dv.1930); **Lady** Myra **Edina Sackville** (26 Feb

1893 – 5 Nov 1955) daughter of Gilbert Sackville, 8th Earl De La Warr & Lady Muriel Brassey; =1st David Wallace; =2nd Charles Gordon; =4th Donald Haldeman; =5th Vincent Soltau
=2 8 Feb 1930; Edith (**Molly**) Mildred Mary Agnes **Maude** (1893 London - 13 Oct 1939 Happy Valley, Kenya) daughter of Richard Maude; =1st Guy Hunter; =2nd Cyril Ramsay-Hill issue of 1st (none by 2nd):

A) **Diana** Denyse **Hay, (23rd) Countess of Erroll**, Lady Hay and Slains (5 Jan 1926 Nairobi – 17 May 1978 Oban, Argyll) suc. father as Countess 24 Jan 1941
=1 19 Dec 1946 London (dv.1964); **Sir** Robert **Iain** Kay **Moncreiffe of that Ilk, 11th Baronet** (9 Apr 1919 – 27 Feb 1985) son of Gerald Moncreiffe of that Ilk & Hilda de Miremont; suc. cousin as Baronet 17 Nov 1957; =2nd Hermoine Falkner
=2 27 Nov 1964 Lonmay; **Raymond** Alexander **Carnegie** (9 Jul 1920 – 6 Sep 1999) son of Hon. Alexander Carnegie & Susan Rodakowski; =1st Patricia Dawson; =3rd Maria Alexander
issue of 1st:

1) **Sir Merlin** Serald Victor Gilbert **Hay, 24th Earl of Erroll** etc[18], **12th Baronet** (*20 Apr 1948 Edinburgh) suc.mother as Earl 17 May 1978; suc.father as Baronet 27 Feb 1985
= 8 May 1982 Winchester, Hampshire; **Isabelle** Jacqueline Laline **Astell** (*22 Aug 1955 Brussels) daughter of Thomas Astell & Jacqueline de Jouffrou d'Abbans; =1st ... Hohler
   a) **Harry** Thomas William, **Lord Hay** (*8 Aug 1984 Basingstoke)
   b) **Lady Amelia** Diana Jacqueline **Hay** (*23 Sep 1987 Basingstoke)
   c) **Lady Laline** Lucy Clementine **Hay** (*21 Dec 1988 Basingstoke)
   d) **Hon. Richard** Merlin Ian **Hay** (*14 Dec 1990 Basingstoke)
2) **Hon. Peregrine** David Euan Malcolm **Moncreiffe of that Ilk** (*16 Feb 1951) recognized as Moncreiffe of that Ilk 11 Jan 2001

---

[18] The Earl of Erroll also serves as the Hereditary Lord High Constable of Scotland. This position gives him precedence before all hereditary Peers and after only the Royal Family in Scotland.

= 27 Jul 1988; **Miranda** Mary **Fox-Pitt** (*1968)
daughter of Mervyn Fox-Pitt & Janet Wedderburn
  a) **Ossian** Peregrine **Moncreiffe, Younger of that Ilk**
     (*3 Feb 1991)
  b) **India** Mary **Moncreiffe** (*3 Nov 1992)
  c) **Elizabeth** Miranda Zuri **Moncreiffe** (*2 Feb 1995)
  d) **Alexandra** Hutton Melville **Moncreiffe** (*19 Nov
     1996)
  e) **Lily Moncreiffe** (*6 Nov 1998)
  f) **Euan Moncreiffe** (*12 Sep 2000)
 3) **Lady Alexandra** Victoria Caroline Anne Hay
    Moncreiffe (*30 Jul 1955 Edinburgh)
    = 22 Feb 1989 Perth; **Jocelyn** Christopher Neill
    Connell (*16 May 1952 Perth) son of Christopher
    Connell & Daphne Wilson
    a) **Flora** Diana Catherine Ceclia **Connell** (*24 Feb 1990
       London)
    b) **Ciara** Edith Elizabeth **Connell** (*28 Mar 1994 London)
    issue by **Sir Michael** Iain **Wigan, 6ᵗʰ Baronet** (*3 Oct 1951
    London) son of Sir Alan Wigan, 5ᵗʰ Baronet & Robina
    Colquhoun; suc. father as Baronet 3 May 1996:
    c) **Ivar** Francis Grey de Miremont **Wigan** (*25 Mar 1979
       Perth)
  issue of 2ⁿᵈ:
 4) **Hon. Jocelyn** Jacek Alexander **Carnegie** (*21 Nov
    1966)
    = 1990; **Susie** Mhairi **Butler** (…) daughter of Thomas
    Butler
    a) **Merlin** Thomas Alexander Bannerman **Carnegie**
       (*25 Apr 1991)
    b) **Cecilia** Diana Catrina Pearl **Carnegie** (1993 - 1994)
    c) **Maximilian** Archibald Josslyn **Carnegie** (*21 Dec
       1995)
    d) **Finn** Kenneth Redvers **Carnegie** (*21 Oct 1997)
    e) **Frederica** Cecilia **Carnegie** (*6 Apr 2000)
    f) **Willa** Cecilia Susan **Carnegie** (*9 Sep 2001)
II) **Gilbert** Allan Rowland **Boyd, 6ᵗʰ Baron Kilmarnock** (15
    Jan 1903 - 15 May 1975 London) suc. brother (Earl of

Erroll) as Baron 24 Jan 1941[19] resuming the ancestral name Boyd

=1 12 Jul 1926 (dv.1955); **Hon. Rosemary** Sibell **Guest** (7 Mar 1906 – 21 Mar 1971) daughter of Ivor Guest, 1st Viscount Wimborne & Hon. Alice Grovesnor; =2nd John Berger

=2 17 May 1955; **Denise** Aubrey Doreen **Coker** (1930 - 1989) daughter of Lewis Coker & Doreen Chichester

issue of 1st:

A) **Alistair** Ivor Gilbert **Boyd, 7th Baron Kilmarnock** (11 May 1927 - 19 Mar 2009) suc. father as Baron 15 May 1975

=1 10 Sep 1954 (dv.1969); **Diana** Mary **Grant Gibson** (30 Sep 1924 – 30 Jun 1975) daughter of Donald Grant Gibson; she =1st ... Hawkins

=2 18 Feb 1977; **Hilary** Ann **Sidney** (1928 – 24 Jun 2010) daughter of Leonard Sidney & Marjery Bardwell; =1st (later Sir) Kingsley Amis; =2nd Shackleton Bailey

issue of 2nd (none by 1st):

1) **Hon. James** Charles Edward **Boyd** (*27 Jan 1972)[20]

B) **Hon. Laura** Alice **Boyd** (10 Jun 1934 London – 25 Feb 1999)

= 11 Jan 1962 London; Robert **Anthony Hyman** (*3 Apr 1928 London) son of Alexander Hyman & Fanny Rubinstein

1) **Anthony Hyman** (*27 May 1962 London)

= ...; **Suzanne Eaton** (...)

a) **Max Hyman** (*23 Dec 1997)

b) **Luke Hyman** (*22 Sep 1999)

2) **Fanny Hyman** (*19 Dec 1963 Kintyre)

= 26 Mar 1994; **Charles** Richard **Mills** (*26 Jan 1958) son of Kenneth Mills & Jane Pelly

a) **Samuel** Charles **Mills** (*17 Dec 1995)

b) **Silvia** Fanny **Mills** (*22 Jul 1997)

c) **Victor** George **Mills** (*22 May 2001)

3) **Merlin Hyman** (*10 Sep 1969 London)

---

[19] The Barony of Kilmarnock was created in he Peerage of the United Kingdom which generally does not permit succession by a female unless there is a special remainder included in the creation. In this case there was not, so while the Countess of Erroll was able to inheirt the Scottish titles, the UK title went to the next male.

[20] Being born before his parents' marriage, James is not entitled to inherit the Barony of Kilmarnock

= …; **Katy Vincent** (…)
   a) **Harry Hyman** (*4 Jan 2000)
   b) **Elizabeth** Laura May **Hyman** (*7 Dec 2001)
   c) **Florence Hyman** (*15 Jul 2003)
C) **Juliet Hay** (1 – 2 May 1937) (twin)
D) **Iris Hay** (* & + 1 May 1937) (twin)
E) **Hon. Caroline** Juliet **Boyd** (*31 Jul 1939)
   = 1969 London; **Alan** Thomas **Bloss** (*1938) son of
   Thomas Bloss & Jane Hodgson
   no issue
F) **Robin** Jordan **Boyd, 8th Baron Kilmarnock** (*6 Jun
   1941) suc. brother as Baron 19 Mar 2009
   =1 1977 (dv.1986); **Ruth** Christine **Fisher** (…) daughter
   of Michael Fisher
   =2 2000; **Hilary** Vivian **Cox** (…) daughter of Peter Cox
   issue of 1st:
   1) **Hon. Simon** John **Boyd** (*1979) heir-apparent to
      father
      = 2004; **Valeria** Beatriz **Matzkin** (...) daughter of
      Jorge Matzkin
      a) **Florence** Emilia **Boyd** (*2005)
      b) **Lucien** Michael **Boyd** (*2007)
   2) **Hon. Mark** Julia **Boyd** (*1981)
   issue by **Catherine Hoddell** (…):
   3) **Alice** Rowena **Boyd** (*1989)
issue of 2nd:
G) **Hon. Jonthan** Aubrey Lewis **Boyd** (*1 Oct 1956
   London)
   = 20 Mar 1982; **Annette** Madeleine **Constantine** (*1956
   London) daughter of Joseph Constantine & Mary Cotter
   1) **Edward** Gilbert **Boyd** (*14 Mar 1989 London)
   2) **Arthur** William **Boyd** (*11 Dec 1994 London)
H) **Hon. Timothy** Iain **Boyd** (*5 Apr 1959 London)
   = 1988; **Lucy** Teresa Emily **Gray** (…) daughter of
   Michael Gray
   1) **Daisy Boyd** (*1988)
III) **Lady Rosemary** Constance Ferelith **Hay** (15 May 1904 –
19 May 1944)
=1 29 May 1924 (dv.1935); **Rupert** Sumner **Ryan** (6 May
1884 Melbourne – 25 Aug 1952 Berwick, Victoria) son of
Sir Charles Ryan & Alice Sumner

=2 27 Jun 1935; **James** Frank **Gresham** (21 Dec 1909 -
1983 Aberconwy) son of Frank Gresham
issue of 1st (none by 2nd):
A) **Patrick** Victor Charles **Ryan** (5 May 1925 Koblenz,
 Germany – 15 Jul 1989 Melbourne, Australia)
 = 1949 South Yarra, Victoria, Australia; **Rosemary**
 Elizabeth **Chesterman** (10 Oct 1927 Hobart, Tasmania –
 19 Sep 1996 Victoria) daughter of Francis Chesterman &
 Thelma Foster
 1) **Dominic** Rupert Charles **Ryan** (*21 May 1956 London)
 2) **Siobhan** Ferelith Fionola **Ryan** (*25 Aug 1959Melbourne)
 = Mar 1994 South Yarra; **Mark Douglas** (…)
 a) **Hunter Ryan-Douglas** (*12 Mar 1990 Melbourne)
b. **Hon. Serald** Mordaunt Alan Josslyn **Hay** (Nov 1877 – 12 Nov
 1939)
 = 26 Apr 1915; **Violet Spiller** (…) daughter of Duncan Spiller
 no issue
c. **Hon. Ivan** Josslyn Lumley **Hay** (31 Oct 1884 Slains Castle – 6
 Sep 1936)
 = 8 Nov 1921; **Pamela Burroughes** (Apr 1895 Seal, Kent – 23
 Nov 1977) daughter of Francis Burroughes & Abbe Bourke
 I) **Alexandra** Cecilia Mary **Hay** (26 Sep 1922 – 29 Apr 1991
 London)
 II) **Elizabeth** Anne **Hay** (3 Feb 1925 - Dec 2005 Birmingham)
 = 20 Oct 1945 London (dv.1970); **Jeremy** Christopher
 Gurney (15 Oct 1925 - Oct 1991 London) son of Christopher
 Guerney & Joan Grenfell
 A) **Michael** Jeremy **Gurney** (*3 Nov 1946)
 = 14 Feb 1981 London (dv.1997); **Hon.** Diana **Miranda**
 Hovell-Thurlow-Cumming-Bruce (*6 Jul 1954)
 daughter of Francis Hovell-Thurlow-Cumming-Bruce, 8th
 Baron Thurlow & Yvonne Wilson; =2nd Vanya Boestoem
 1) **Rohan** Samphie Katherine **Gurney** (*1981)
 2) **Mungo** James Nicholas **Gurney** (*1982 London)
 B) **William** Ivan **Gurney** (*23 Mar 1948)
 = 10 Aug 1973; **Annette** Marie **Deutsch** (*6 Jan 1949
 Limerick) daughter of Robert Deutsch & Elizabeth …
 1) **Stella** Elizabeth **Gurney** (*1975 Birmingham)
 = Jul 2003 London; **Mark Griffiths** (...)
 2) **Luke Gurney** (* & +1977 Birmingham)
 3) **Leo** Robert Ivan **Gurney** (*1978 Birmingham)

163

= ...; **Kate** Rose **Hall** (*19 Oct 1978 London) daughter of
Dave Hall & Wendy ...
   a) **Rosa Guerney** (*11.4.2010 Newcastle)
  III) **Penelope** Constance Lumley **Hay** (*26 Mar 1930)
= 25 May 1957; **George** Harold Armine **Dare** (2 Nov
1918 - 13 Mar 2010) son of Harold Dare & Sibyl Morriss
  A) **Henry** James **Dare** (*3 Mar 1959)
  B) **Amelia** Alexandra Elizabeth **Dare** (*27 Nov 1961
    London)
3. **Hon. Arthur Hay** (16 Sep 1855 Slains Castle – 1 May 1932)
4. **Lady Florence** Alice **Hay** (28 May 1858 Slains Castle – 15 May
1859 Slains Castle)
5. **Lady Cecilia** Leila **Hay** (4 Mar 1860 – 7 Jan 1925)
= 31 Oct 1883 London; **George** Allan **Webbe** (15 Jan 1854
London – 19 Feb 1925 Ascot, Berkshire) son of Alexander
Webbe
no issue
6. **Hon. Francis Hay** (14 Aug 1864 Slains Castle – 24 Sep 1898
Queensland, Australia)
7. **Lady Florence** Agnes Adelaide **Hay** (31 May 1872 Slains
Castle – 16 Oct 1935)
= 9 May 1895 Chelsea; **Henry Wolrige-Gordon** (1 Jan 1863
London – 9 Oct 1923) son of Henry Wolridge & Anne Gordon
no issue
C. **Lady Agnes** Georgiana Elizabeth **Hay** (12 May 1829 London – 18
Dec 1869 London)
= 16 Mar 1846 Paris; **Sir James Duff KT, 5**[th] **Earl of Fife** Viscount
Macduff, Baron Braco, **1**[st] **Baron Skeene** (6 Jul 1814 Banffshire – 7
Aug 1879 Braemar, Aberdeenshire) son of Sir Alexander Duff &
Anne Stein; suc.uncle as Earl 9 Mar 1857; cr. Baron Skeene 2 Mar
1860; KT 1860
1. **Lady Anne** Elizabeth Clementina **Duff** (16 Aug 1847 Edinburgh-
31 Dec 1925)
= 17 Oct 1865 Brighton; **Sir John** Villiers Stuart **Townshend, 5**[th]
Marquess Townshend Viscount Raynham, Baron Townshend,
10th **Baronet** (10 Apr 1831 Brighton – 26 Oct 1899) son of Sir
John Townshend, 4th Marquess Townshend & Elizabeth Stuart;
suc. father as Marquess 10 Sep 1863
a. **Sir John** James Dudley Stuart **Townshend, 6**[th] **Marquess
Townshend** etc.(17 Oct 1866 London – 17 Nov 1921) suc.father
as Marquess 26 Oct 1899

= 9 Aug 1905; **Gwladys** Ethel Gwendolen Eugenie **Sutherst** (1885 – 10 Oct 1959) daughter of Thomas Sutherst; =2nd Bernard le Strange

I) **Sir George** John Patrick Dominic **Townshend, 7th Marquess Townshend** etc.(13 May 1916 – 27 Apr 2010) suc. father as Marquess 17 Nov 1921

=1 2 Sep 1939 (dv.1960); **Elizabeth** Pamela Audrey **Luby** (29 Sep 1915 - 1989) daughter of Thomas Luby; =2nd Sir James Gault

=2 22 Dec 1960; **Ann** Frances **Darlow** (29 Jan 1932 - 1988) daughter of Arthur Darlow

=3 7 May 2004 Fakenham, Norfolk; **Philippa** Sophia **Montgomerie** (*25 Apr 1935) daughter of George Kidston-Montgomerie of Southanan & Lydia Mason; =1st Humphrey Swire

issue of 1st:

A) **Lady Carolyn** Elizabeth Ann **Townshend** (*27 Sep 1940) resumed her maiden name

=1 13 Oct 1962 (dv.1968); **Antonio Capellini** (…) son of Vincenzo Capellini & Donna Anna Candeo Vanzetti Levida Zara

=2 Jan 1973 (ann.1974); **Edgar** Miles **Bronfman** (*20 Jun 1929) son of Samuel Bronfman & Saidye …; =1st Ann Loeb, he =3rd (married twice) Georgiana Webb, =4th Jan Aronson; issue of 1st (none by 2nd):

1) **Vincenzo** Charles **Capellini Townshend** (*1963)
= 1994; **Rachel Daniels** (…) daughter of Mark Daniels
a) **Luca** Charles **Capellini Townshend** (*Feb 1995 Ipswich)
b) **Sofia** Elizabeth **Capellini Townshend** (*Jul 1996 Ipswich)
c) **Luisa** Carolyn **Capellini Townsherd** (* Sep 1998 Ipswich)

B) **Lady Joanna** Agnes **Townshend** (*19 Aug 1943) resumed her maiden name

=1 27 Sep 1962 (dv.1968); **Jeremy** George Courtnay **Bradford** (…) son of George Bradford

=2 1 Jan 1978 (dv.1984); **James** Barry **Morrissey** (*... Boston)

=3 1991; **Christian** Marc **Boegner** (…) son of Etienne Boegner

issue of 1st (none of others):

1) **Francis** James Patrick **Bradford** (*28 Oct 1963)
C) **Charles** George **Townshend, 8th Marquess of Townshend** etc.(*26 Sep 1945)
=1 8 Oct 1975; **Hermoine Ponsonby** (23 Jan 1945 - 1985) killed in car crash; daughter of Robert Ponsonby & Dorothy Lane; =1st Anthony Evans
=2 1990; **Alison Combs** (…) daughter of Sir Willis Combs; she =1st … Marshall
issue 1st (none by 2nd):
  1) **Thomas** Charly, **Viscount Raynham** (*2 Nov 1977)
    = 2010/2011; **Octavia** Christina **Legge** (*1980 London) daughter of Christopher Legge & Sarah Marshall
  2) **Hon. Louise** Elizabeth **Townshend** (*23 Jul 1979)
    = 2006; **Edson da Paixao**(...)
issue of 2nd:
D) **Lord John** Patrick **Townshend** (*17 Jun 1962)
=1 12 Sep 1988 Wadour Castle, Tisbury, Wiltshire (dv.1991); **Rachel** Lucy **Chapple** (*1960) daughter of Sir John Chapple
=2 23 Sep 1999 London; **Helen Chin-Choy** (*17 Jun 1960 Bracknell) daughter of Larry Chin-Choy & Cathy Oatham; =1st William Burt
issue of 2nd (none by 1st):
  1) **Isobel** Ann **Townshend** (*27 Jul 2001 London)
  2) **George** Ivan **Townshend** (*Nov 2003 London)
E) **Lady Katherine** Anne **Townshend** (*29 Sep 1963)
=1 Apr 1991 (dv.2000); **Piers W Dent** (*1963) son of Robin Dent & Diana Delap; =2nd Katherine Steel
=2 Aug 2001; **Guy** Langford **Bayley** (*1964)
issue of 1st
  1) **Lucia Dent** (*1992)
  2) **Mollie** Elsa **Dent** (*Oct 1995 Gloucester)
issue of 2nd:
  3) **Inca** Nell **Bayley** (*15 Feb 2001 Bristol)
  4) **Skye** Georgina **Bayley** (*24 Oct 2002)
II) **Lady Elizabeth** Mary Gladys **Townshend** (16 Oct 1917 – 31 Dec 1950)
=1 20 Oct 1939 (dv.1947); **Sir** Eric **Richard** Meadows **White, 2nd Baronet** (29 Jun 1910 – 26 Apr 1972) son of Sir Robert White, 1st Baronet & Rose Pearce-Senocold; =2nd Ann Eccles

=2 15 Mar 1949; **John** Clifford **Roberts** (…) son of John
Roberts
issue of 1st (none 2nd):
A) **Sir Christopher** Robert Meadows **White, 3rd Baronet** (*26
Aug 1940) suc.father as Baronet 26 Apr 1972
=1 14 Apr 1962 (dv.1967); **Anne** Marie Ghislaine **Brown** (…)
daughter of Thomas Brown
=2 1968 (dv.1972); **Dinah** Mary **Sutton** (…)
=3 1976; **Ingrid** Carolyn **Jowett** (*1947) daughter of Eric
Jowett & Madaline Jeary
no issue
  b. **Lady Agnes** Elizabeth Audrey **Townshend** (12 Dec 1870
  London – 15 Mar 1955)
  = 2 Sep 1903; **James** Andrew **Cunninghame-Durham** (8 Aug
  1879 – 30 Sep 1954) son of James Durham & Anne Duke
  I) **Nicholas** James Redvers Johan Townshend **Cunninghame-
  Durham** (13 Jan 1905 London – 17 Mar 1943 Mareth) killed in
  action
  = 26 Mar 1934; **Joyce** Wynyard **DuPre** (9 Feb 1912 London –
  …) daughter of William DuPre & Youri Wight
  no issue
  II) **Victoria** Townshend **Cunninghame-Durham** (9 Apr
  1908 London – 7 Dec 2002)
2. **Lady Ida** Louise Alice **Duff** (10 Dec 1848 Duff House – 29 May
  1918)
=1 3 Jun 1867 Garendon Park, Leicestershire (dv.1873); **Adrian**
Elias **Hope** (8 Apr 1845 – 18 Nov 1914) son of John Hope &
Countess Mathilde Rapp; =2nd Mildred Scott
=2 20 Sep 1880 London (dv.); **William Wilson** (1844 – 16 Feb
1905 Derby)
issue of 1st (none by 2nd):
  a. **Agnes** Henrietta Ida May **Hope** (1868 London – 15 Jul 1920
  London)
  = 28 Aug 1889 Garendon Park; **Edwin** Joseph Lisel **March
  Phillipps de Lisle** (13 Jun 1852 – 5 May 1920) son of
  Ambrose de Lisle & Laura Clifford
  I) **Mary** Agnes Adeodata **March Phillipps de Lisle** (13 Jun 1890
  London - Oct 1944)
  = 22 Apr 1914; **Dino, Count Spetia di Radione** (14 Jan 1882
  Fossombrone - 20 Nov 1958 San Remo) son of Alessandro,
  Count Spetia di Radione & Antonietta Dona; =2nd Gladys

McConnell

A) **Paganello dei conti Spetia** (1 Apr 1917 Ferrara - 1995)

II) **John** Adrian Frederick **March Phillipps de Lisle** (27 Sep 1891 London – 4 Nov 1961)

= 12 Jul 1924; **Elizabeth** Muriel Sarah Smythe **Guinness** (20 Jan 1892 – 30 Mar 1974) daughter of Robert Guinness & Lydia Smythe

A) **Alathea** Henriette Mary **March Phillipps de Lisle** (14 May 1925 – 11 Nov 2008 Lamastre Ardech, France)

= 25 Jul 1953; **George** Hamilton **Boyle** (15 Sep 1928 – 27 Apr 2007) son of Edmund Boyle & Maida Evans-Freke

1) **Robert** Edmund John **Boyle** (*28 Sep 1954)

= 1985; **Gabrielle** Georgiana **Smollet** (*7 Jul 1960) daughter of Patrick Smollet

a) **Albinia** Mary **Boyle** (*1988)

b) **Patrick** Gordon Tobias **Boyle** (*1991)

2) **Richard** William **Boyle** (*8 Jan 1959)

= 1990; **Suzanne** Jean **Bingham** (*1963) daughter of Charles Bingham

a) **Clementine** Pamela **Boyle** (*1997)

b) **Jonathan** Charles **Boyle** (*2001)

3) **Rupert** Lancelot Cavendish **Boyle** (*19 Sep 1960)

= 1986; **Sarah** Daphne **Berry** (*1963) daughter of Simon Berry

a) **Angus** Hugo Edmund **Boyle** (*1989)

b) **Christopher** Simon Hamilton **Boyle** (*1992)

c) **Jocelyn** William Rupert **Boyle** (*6 Apr 1998)

B) **Elizabeth** Catherine Denise **March Phillipps de Lisle** (*19 Aug 1927)

= 24 Jan 1951; **Jeremy** Anthony **White** (*13 Jan 1926) son of Anthony White & Flora Scott

1) **Philippa** Elizabeth **White** (*12 Jun 1952)

2) **Juliet** Anne **White** (*15 Feb 1955)

= 7 May 1983; **Peter** Anthony **Fenton** (*1955) son of Mark Fenton

a) **Emily** Victoria **Fenton** (*26 Jan 1986)

b) **Christopher** Belmont **Fenton** (*8 Jul 1888)

3) **Anthony** John **White** (*8 Jan 1958)

= 18 Oct 1982; **Tessa** Marion **Hugo** (*1960) daughter of Sir John Hugo

a) **Zara** Elizabeth Hugo **White** (*21 Dec 1987)

b) **Charlotte** Antonia **White** (*24 May 1989)

c) **Serena** Isabel **White** (*16 Jun 1992)

4) **Annabel** Mary **White** (*1 Jan 1962)

= 28 Aug 1990; Hugh **Edward** John **Montgomery** (*1960) son of Hugh Montgomery

a) **Alexander** Charles **Montgomery** (*4 Jul 1993)

b) **James** Anthony **Montgomery** (*29 Oct 1995)

c) **Nicholas** Rollo **Montgomery** (*8 Oct 1999)

C) **Everard** John Robert **March Phillipps de Lisle** (8 Jun 1930 Snitterfield, Warwickshire– 30 Apr 2003 Stanion, Northampton) killed in a car crash

= 2 Apr 1959 London; **Hon. Mary** Rose **Peake** (*23 Apr 1940 Welwyn, Hertfordshire) daughter of Osbert Peake, 1st Viscount Ingleby & Lady Joan Capell

1) **Charles** Andrew Everard **March Phillipps de Lisle** (*18 Aug 1960 London)

= Sept 2003 Leicester; **Sharon** Rachel **Davis** (*1969) daughter of Eric Davis; =1st ... Abelman

a) **Charlotte** India Rose **March Phillipps de Lisle** (*26 Nov 2006)

2) **Timothy** John **March Phillipps de Lisle** (*25 Jun 1962 London)

= 4 May 1991 Compton, Berkshire; **Amanda** Helen **Barford** (*1964 London) daughter of Clive Barford & Helen Foster

a) **Daniel** Barford **March Phillipps de Lisle** (*24 Jan 1994 London)

b) **Laura** Jane **March Phillipps de Lisle** (*20 Apr 1998 London)

3) Mary **Rosanna March Phillipps de Lisle** (*18 May 1968 London)

has issue:

a) **Arthur** Rowan Luke **de Lisle** (*26 Aug 2010 London)

D) **Julian** Peter Alexander **March Phillipps de Lisle** (2 Feb 1936 Snitterfield, Warwickshire - 19 Dec 1993 Medbourne, Leicestershire)

=1 1968 London (dv.1970); **Judith A Howard** (...)

=2 21 Apr 1971 London; **Diana** Barbara **Welchman** (*14 Mar 1944 Minehead, Somerset) daughter of John Welchman & Valerie Riley

issue of 2nd:

1) **Alexandra** Elizabeth Hope **March Phillipps de Lisle** (*12

169

Jul 1972 London)

= 24 Oct 2009 Medbourne; **Shamus** Diarmid **Ogilvy** (*24 Jan 1966 London) son of Hon. James Ogilvy & June Ducas

 a) **Angus** Julian Frederick **Ogilvy** (*21 Aug 2010)

 2) **Clare** Catherine Alice **March Philipps de Lisle** (*29 Jan 1975 London)

 3) **John** Julian Edward **March Phillipps de Lisle** (*14 Aug 1977 London)

= 11 Jul 2009 Anglesey, Wales; **Flor Gruffudd Jones** (...) daughter of Dafydd Grufford Jones

 a) **Zinnia** Alice Victoria **March Phillipps de Lisle** (*8 Jan 2011)

III) **Rudolph** Henry Edward **March Phillipps de Lisle** (11 Nov 1892 – 17 Aug 1943)

IV) **Sister Bertha** Mary Henriette **March Phillipps de Lisle** (6 Nov 1893 Garendon Park - 1973 London)

V) **Ambrose** Paul Jordan **March Phillipps de Lisle** (15 Nov 1894 Garendon Park – 8 Sep 1963)

= 2 Dec 1939; **Christiane de Conchy** (1908 - 10 May 2001) daughter of ..., Baron de Conchy

A) **Gerard March Phillipps de Lisle** (*20 Sep 1940)

= 1965; **Edith Karup** (*1938)

 1) **Frederick March Phillipps de Lisle** (*1957)

= 1986; **Hon. Aubyn** Cecilia **Hovell-Thurlow-Cumming-Bruce**[21] (*1958) daugher of Francis Hovell-Thurlow-Cumming-Bruce, 8th Baron Thurlow & Yvonne Wilson

 a) **James** Gerard **March Phillipps de Lisle** (*1987)

 b) **Ralph** Francis **March Phillipps de Lisle** (*1989)

 c) **Rosalie** Yvonne **March Phillipps de Lisle** (*1991)

 2) **Peter** Andrew Paul **March Phillipps de Lisle** (*1959)

= 1984; **Leanda Dormer** (*1959)

 a) **Rupert** Gerard Xavier **March Phillipps de Lisle** (*1986 London)

 b) **Christian** Michael Frederick **March Phillipps de Lisle** (*1988 London)

 c) **Dominic** Robert Peter **March Phillipps de Lisle** (*1990 London)

B) Ambrose Bertram (**Bertie**) **March Phillipps de Lisle** (*8

---

[21] Aubyn is the sister of Miranda who married Michael Gurney

Jul 1945)
= 1972; **Catherine Renardier** (*1947)
1) **Alexia March Phillipps de Lisle** (*1973)
2) **Edward** Ambrose **March Phillipps de Lisle** (*1976
   London)
   = 2006; **Sarah Rawstron** (*1977)
   a) **Zac March Phillipps de Lisle** (*2008)
   b) a child (*2009)
3) **Jasmine** Mary **March Phillipps de Lisle** (*1982
   London)
   = 2009; **Michael Jardine** (*1981)
   no issue
C) **Hubert March Phillipps de Lisle** (*15 Aug 1946)
   = 1976 Paris; **Marie-Dominique Quentin** (*1946)
   1) **Geraldine** Marie **March Phillipps de Lisle** (*1978)
      = 15 Sep 2007 La Roche-Posay, France; **John** Patrick
      Arbuthnott (*1977) son of James Arbuthnott & Hon.
      Louisa Hughes-Young
      a) due Jul 2011
   2) **Thomas March Phillipps de Lisle** (*24 Oct 1979 in
      Germany)
      = 14 Jun 2008 Hindon, Wilts; **Caroline Budge** (*7 Mar 1981
      London) daughter of David Budge & Sarah McClintock
      a) **Maximilian** Lancelot Hubert **March Phillipps de Lisle**
         (*8 Nov 2009 London)
D) **Edwin** Rudolph Joseph **March Phillipps de Lisle** (*2
   Feb 1948)
   = 1979 Tur Langton; **Caroline** Astrid **Rowley** (*28 Jun 1955)
   daughter of Sir Charles Rowley, 8th Baronet & Astrid Massey
   1) **Alexander** Edwin **March Phillipps de Lisle** (*9 Dec
      1983 Kettering)
      = 9 Oct 2010 Long Clawson; **Hannah Day** (*8 May 1980
      Nottingham) daughter of Charles Day & Pamela ...
      a) **Hugo** Charles **March Phillipps de Lisle** (*16 Jun 2009
         Singapore)
   2) **Nicholas** Charles **March Phillipps de Lisle** (*24 May 1991
      London)
VI) **Lancelot** Joseph Everard **March Phillipps de Lisle** (22
   Nov 1895 Garendon Park – 25 Sep 1928)
VII) **Alexander** Charles Nicholas **March Phillipps de Lisle** (6
   Dec 1896 Garendon Park – 20 Nov 1917) killed in action

VIII) **Sister Philomena** Edwina Dolores **March Phillipps de Lisle** (13 Feb 1903 Garendon Park – 1969 London)

b. **Mildred** Louisa Annie **Hope** (15 Jun 1869 London - 1957)
= 24 Jun 1909 London; **Robert** Astley **Smith** (1865 Brampton Ash, Northamptonshire - 1913) son of Rev. Sydney Smith & Hon. Frances Scarlett
no issue

c. **Ethel** Alexina Agnes **Hope** (1871 London - 1967 London)
= 21 Apr 1903 London (dv.); **John** Percy **Lockhart Mummery** (14 Feb 1875 Northolt – 24 Apr 1957 Hove); =2nd Georgette Maier
no issue

3. **Sir Alexander** William George **Duff, KG, KT, GCVO, 1st Duke of Fife** Marquess of Macduff, Earl of Macduff, **6th Earl of Fife** etc, **2nd Baron Skeene**[22] (10 Nov 1849 Edinburgh – 29 Jan 1912 Aswan, Egypt) suc.father as Earl of Fife, etc.7 Aug 1879; cr. Duke of Fife and Marquess of Macduff 29 Jul1889; cr. Earl of Macduff 16 Oct 1889[23]; KT1881, GCVO 1901, KG 1911
= 27 Jul 1889 Buckingham Palace; **HRH Princess Louise** Victoria Alexandra Dagmar **of Great Britain and Ireland, The Princess Royal** Princess of Saxe-Coburg and Gotha, Duchess of Saxony (20 Feb 1867 London – 4 Jan 1931 London) daughter of Edward VII, King of the United Kingdom & Princess Alexandra of Denmark; usage of the Saxon titles was discontinued 17 Jul 1917

a. a son (stillborn 16 Jun 1890 Richmond)

b. **HH Princess Alexandra** Victoria Alberta Edwina Louise **of Fife, (2nd) Duchess of Fife** Countess of Macduff (17 May 1891 Richmond – 26 Feb 1959 London) nee Lady Alexandra Duff, cr. Princess 9 Nov 1905 by grandfather; suc.father as Duchess 29 Jan 1912
= 15 Oct 1913 London; **Prince Arthur** Frederick Patrick Albert **of Connaught, Prince of Geat Britain and Ireland** (and Prince of Saxe-Coburg and Gotha, Duke of Saxony until 17 Jul 1917) (13 Jan 1883 Windsor – 12 Nov 1938 London) son of Prince Arthur, 1st Duke of Connaught and Stathearn & Princess Luise Margarete of Prussia

I) **Alastair** Arthur **Windsor**[24], **2nd Duke of Connaught and**

---

[22] Upon the death of the 1st Duke of Fife, all of his titles except the Dukedom of Fife and the Earldom of Macduff became extinct.
[23] The Dukedom of Fife and Earldom of Macduff were recreated in 1900 to include the daughters of the 1st Duke.

Strathearn, Earl of Sussex (9 Jul 1914 London – 26 April 1943 Ottawa, Canada) suc.grandfather as Duke 12 Sep 1938 and was heir-apparent to the Dukedom of Fife at the time of his death

c. **HH Princess Maud** Alexandra Georgina Bertha **of Fife** (3 Apr 1893 Richmond – 14 Dec 1945 London) née Lady Maud Duff, cr. Princess 9 Nov 1905 by grandfather

= 12 Nov 1923 London; **Charles** Alexander **Carnegie,**[25] **11ᵗʰ Earl of Southesk**, Lord Carnegie, Baron Balinhard (23 Sep 1893 Edinburgh – 16 Feb 1992 Kinnaird Castle) son of Charles Carnegie, 10ᵗʰ Earl of Southesk & Ethel Bannerman

I) **James** George Alexander Bannerman **Carnegie, 3ʳᵈ Duke of Fife**, Earl of Macduff, **12ᵗʰ Earl of Southesk** etc.(*23 Sep 1929 London) suc.aunt as Duke 26 Feb 1959; suc.father as Earl of Southesk 14 Feb 1992

= 11 Sep 1954 Perth (dv.1966); **Hon. Caroline** Cecily **Dewar** (*12 Feb 1934 Milngavie) daughter of Alexander Dewar, 3ʳᵈ Baron Forteviot & Cynthia Starkie

A) a son (stillborn 4 Apr 1958)

B) **Lady Alexandra** Clare **Carnegie** (*20 Jun 1959)

= 11 May 2001 London; **Mark** Fleming **Etherington** (*10 Dec 1952 Newmarket, Ontario) son of Donald Etherington & Mary Mercer

1) **Amelia** Mary Carnegie **Etherington** (*24 Dec 2001 London)

C) **David** Charles, **Earl of Southesk** (*3 Mar 1961 London)

= 16 Jul 1987 London; **Caroline** Anne **Bunting** (*13 Nov 1961 Windsor) daughter of Martin Bunting & Veronica Cope

1) **Charles** Duff, **Lord Carnegie** (*1 Jul 1989 Edinburgh)

2) **Hon. Georg** William **Carnegie** (*23 Mar 1991 Edinburgh)

3) **Hon. Hugh** Alexander **Carnegie** (*6 Oct 1993 Dundee)

4. **Lady Agnes** Cecil Emmeline **Duff** (18 May 1852 London – 11 Jan 1925 Cimiez, France)

=1 4 Oct 1871 (dv.1876); **George** Robert, **Viscount Dupplin** (27 May 1849 London – 10 Mar 1886 Perthshire) son of George Hay-Drummond, 12ᵗʰ Earl of Kinnoull & Lady Emily Somerset; heir-

---

[24] Titled Prince of Great Britain, Prince of Saxe-Coburg and Gotha, Duke of Saxony until 1917 when Royal Decrees were issued discontinuing the use of the German titles and then restricting the royal titles to children and grandchildren of a Sovereign. Alistair was a great-grandson of Queen Victoria and there for was not longer styled Prince.

[25] The 11ᵗʰ Earl of Southesk was the uncle of Raymond Carnegie who married Diana, Countess of Erroll

apparent to father at time of his death

=2 5 Aug 1876 London; **Herbert Flower** (1851 Bath – 30 Dec 1880 London) son of Philip Flower & Mary Flower

=3 4 Jul 1882 London; **Sir Alfred Cooper, Kt.** (1838 Norwich – 3 Mar 1908) son of William Cooper & Anna Marsh; Kt. 1902

issue of 1st:

a. **Hon. Agnes** Blanche Marie **Hay-Drummond** (6 Dec 1873 London – 13 Dec 1938)

   = 21 Feb 1903 Rome; **Herbert von Beneckendorff und Hindenburg** (1 Apr 1872 Berlin – 31 Jul 1956 Burg Bassenheim, Germany) son of Konrad von Beneckendorff und Hindenburg & Countess Sophie zu Münster

   I) **Marie von Beneckendorff und Hindenburg** (* & + 25 Dec 1903)

issue of 3rd (none by 2nd):

b. **Stephanie** Agnes **Cooper** (5 Sep 1883 London – 9 Dec 1918)

   =1 19 Dec 1903 London; **Arthur** Francis **Levita** (15 Feb 1865 Manchester - 18 Nov 1910) son of Emile Levita & Catherine Rée

   =2 10 Oct 1916; **Maurice** ffolliot Rhys **Wingfield** (8 Sep 1879 Stow on Wold, Gloucestershire – 9 Apr 1941) son of Edward Wingfield & Edith Wood; =1st Lydia Rudge; = 3rd Muriel Dunsmuir

issue of 1st (none by 2nd):

I) **Violet** Frances **Levita** (10 Sep 1904 London – 1999 London)

   =1 9 Nov 1926 London (dv.1933); **Richard** Barrow **Hirsch** (1899 London – 11 May 1947) son of Leopold Hirsch & Mathilde ...

   =2 24 Dec 1937 Mumbai, India (dv.); **Ronald Critchley** (Aug 1905 - ...) son of Edward Critchley & Elizabeth Critchley; =2nd Contance Byass

   issue of 1st (none by 2nd):

   A) **Nicholas** F **Hirsch** (1930 London – 3 Oct 1983 Dunning Perthshire)

      = 3 Jun 1965; **Barbara Peacocke** (... – 22 May 1976) killed in a car crash

      no issue

II) **Enid** Agnes Maud **Levita** (10 Feb 1908 London - 1993)

   =1 17 Dec 1930 (dv.); **Euan** Donald **Cameron** (1906 - 1958) son of Ewen Cameron & Rachel Granger; =2nd

Marielen von Meiss-Teuffem

=2 1961; **Hon. Robert** Fraser **Watson** (1901 - 1975) son of
Joseph Watson, 1st Baron Manton & Claire Nickols
issue of 1st (none by 2nd):

A) **Ian** Donald **Cameron** (1 Oct 1932 Blairmore House,
Huntly, Aberdeen – 8 Sep 2010 Toulon)
= 20 Oct 1962; **Mary** Fleur **Mount** (*22 Oct 1934)
daughter of Sir William Mount, 2nd Baronet & Elizabeth
Llewellyn

1) **Allan** Alexander **Cameron** (*27 Aug 1963 London)
= 19 May 1990 London; **Sarah** Louise **Fearnley-
Whittingstall** (*23 Jul 1963) daughter of William
Fearnley-Whittingstall & Daphne Shortt

a) **Imogen** Clare **Cameron** (*3 Oct 1992 London)

b) **Angus Cameron** (*8 Oct 1994 London)

2) **Tania** Rachel **Cameron** (*7 Mar 1965 London)
= 9 Sep 1995 Peasemore, Berkshire; **Carl** I O **Brookes**
(...)

a) **Oliver** Aiden **Brookes** (* May 2002 London)

3) **Rt.Hon. David** William Donald **Cameron** (*9 Oct
1966 London) Prime Minister since 2010
= 1 Jun 1996 East Hendred, Oxfordshire; **Samantha**
Gwendolen **Sheffield** (*1971 London) daughter of Sir
Reginald Sheffield, 8th Baronet & Annabel Jones[26]

a) **Ivan** Reginald Ian **Cameron** (8 Apr 2002 London – 25
Feb 2009 London)

b) **Nancy** Gwendoline **Cameron** (*19 Jan 2004 London)

c) **Arthur** Elwen **Cameron** (*14 Feb 2006 London)

d) **Florence** Rose Endelion **Cameron** (*24.10.2010 Truro,
Cornwall)

4) **Clare** Louise **Cameron** (*1971 London)
= 24 Apr 2010 Peasemore; **Jeremy Fawcus** (...) son of
Graham Fawcus & Diana Spencer-Philips

a) **Molly Fawcus** (*23 Dec 2010)

c. **Hermione** Mary Louise **Cooper** (11 May 1885 London - Nov
1923 Wiesbaden, Germany)
= 1904 London; **Neil Duff Arnott** (1870 London - 16 Jun
1929 London) son of ...; =1st Evelyn Hewlett

---

[26] Annabel Jones later married the 4th Viscount Astor, half brother of Hon. Emily Astor
(another William IV descendant).

I) **Ian** Neil **Duff Arnott** (1905 London - 1950 London)
= 1930 London; **Phyllis** Mary S **Innes** (1908 Plymouth,
Devonshire - 1956 Birmingham)
 A) **Portia Duff Arnott** (1 Jan 1931 London - 2009 Cyprus)
  = ..; **James Lord** (...)
  1) **Simon** M D **Lord** (*1959 Portsmouth)
   = Dec 1986; **Sarah** A **Pyne** (*1959)
   a) **Victoria** Catherine **Lord** (*Feb 1988 London)
   b) **Alice** Elizabeth **Lord** (*May 1991)
   c) **Olivia** Charlotte **Lord** (*Oct 1993)
  2) **Alexandra Lord** (*1962)
   = Jul 1997; **Miguel Buceta San Martin** (*...) son of
   Luis San martin
   a) a daughter (...)
   b) a son (...)
 B) **Tancred Duff Arnott** (* & + 1934 Birmingham)
d. **Sybil** Mary **Cooper** (26 Nov 1886 London – 3 Jan 1927
London)
= 19 Jan 1904 London; **Richard** Vaughan **Hart-Davis** (1 May
1878 Farnham, Surrey – 26 Aug 1964 London) son of Henry
Hart-Davis & Anne Whittingham
 I) **Sir Rupert** Charles **Hart-Davis, Kt**[27] (28 Aug 1907
 London – 8 Dec 1999 Northallerton, Yorkshire) knighted
 1967
 =1 23 Dec 1929 London (dv.1933); Edith Margaret (**Peggy**)
 Ashcroft (later Dame Peggy, DBE) (22 Oct 1907 Croydon
 – 14 Jun 1991 London) daughter of William Ashcroft; DBE
 1956; =2nd Theodore Komisarjevsky; =3rd Jeremy
 Hutchinson, Baron Hutchinson of Lullington
 =2 25 Nov 1933 London (dv.1964); Catherine **Comfort**
 Borden-Turner (15 Aug 1910 – Aug 1970) daughter of
 George Turner & Mary Borden
 =3 19 Oct 1964 London; Winifred **Ruth Ware** (... - 31 Jan
 1967 Edinburgh) =1st Oliver Simon
 =4 13 Jun 1968 Richmond; **June Clifford** (*1924) daughter
 of Arthur Clifford & Edith Bowell; =1st David Williams
 issue of 2nd (none by others):
 A) **Bridget** Min **Hart-Davis** (*13 Jan 1935 London)

---

[27] Although Richard Hart-Davis was Rupert's legal father, Rupert himself always intimated
that his biological father was one Gervase Beckett.

= 1963 London; **Sir David** Malcolm **Trustram Eve, 2ⁿᵈ Baron Silsoe**, 2ⁿᵈ Baronet (2 May 1930– 31 Dec 2005 Reading) son of Sir Malcolm Trustram Eve, 1ˢᵗ Baron Silsoe & Marguerite Nanton; suc.father as Baron Dec 1976

    1) **Hon. Amy** Comfort **Trustram Eve** (*13 Jun 1964 London)

    2) **Sir Simon** Rupert **Trustram Eve, 3ʳᵈ Baron Silsoe** etc.(*17 Apr 1966 London) suc.father as Baron 31 Dec 2005

B) Peter **Duff Hart-Davis** (*3 Jun 1936 London)

= 22 Apr 1961 Builth Wells, Powys, Wales; Diana **Phyllida Barstow** (*30 Sep 1937 London) daughter of John Barstow & Diana Yarnton; =1ˢᵗ ... Mills

    1) **Alice Hart-Davis** (*27 May 1963 Builth Wells)

    = 19 Aug 1989; **Matthew** William **Hindhaugh** (*23 Aug 1958 Saltburn, Yorkshire) son of William Hindlaugh & Jenneth ...

    b) **Felicity** Mary **Hindhaugh** (*24 Feb 1995 London)

    c) **Elizabeth** Rose **Hindhaugh** (*9 Dec 1996 London)

    d) Robert **John Hindhaugh** (*4 Aug 1999 London)

    2) **Guy** Edward Peter **Hart-Davis** (*28 Nov 1964 Henley-on-Thames, Oxfordshire)

    =1 1991 Las Vegas; **Michele** C **Batcabe** (19 May 1965 - 8 Jan 1998)

    =2 2000; **Rhonda Holmes** (...)

    issue of 2ⁿᵈ (none by 1ˢᵗ):

    a) **Edward Hart-Davis** (*5 Sep 2000)

C) **Adam** John **Hart-Davis** (*4 Jul 1943 Henley-on-Thames)

=1 21 Dec 1965 Oxford (dv.1995); **Adrienne Alpin** (17 Aug 1944 West Yorkshire - Jan 2005 Oxford) daughter of Joseph Alpin & Dorrien Heys

=2 19 Jun 2010; **Susan Blackmore** (*29 Jul 1951)

issue of 1ˢᵗ (none by 2ⁿᵈ):

    1) **Damon Hart-Davis** (*18 Aug 1967 Fulford, York)

    = ...; **Jean Ryder** (...)

    a) **Eloise Hart-Davis** (*14 Dec 2005)

    2) **Jason Hart-Davis** (*27 Aug 1971 Oxford)

    = 1996; **Michele Gunn** (...)

    a) **Louis** Sewavi Rupert **Hart-Davis** (*30 Dec 1997)

II) **Dierdre** Phyllis Ulrica **Hart-Davis** (5 Jul 1909 – 23 Nov

1998)

=1 24 Apr 1930 London; **Ronald** Egerton **Balfour** (1896 –
17 Apr 1941) killed in a car crash

=2 1946 London (dv.); **David Wolfers** (*1911 London) son
of Samuel Wolfers & Sarah Delmonte

=3 35 Jul 1950 London; **Anthony** John **Bland** (1904 - Jan
1993) son of Jack Bland

=4 1978; **William Inman** (…)

issue of 1st:

A) **Susan** Mary **Balfour** (*30 Mar 1931 London)

B) **Annabel** Clare **Balfour** (*20 Oct 1935 London)
   = 15 Apr 1961 London; **Charles** Benedict **Rathbone** (...)
   1) **Paul B Rathbone** (*1962)
   2) **Oliver A Rathbone** (*1965)
      = May 1997 London; **Rachel Andrew** (...)
      a) **Alice** Eleanor **Rathbone** (*Jun 1998 London)
      b) **Marcus** Benedict **Rathbone** (*Sep 2000 London)
   3) **Benjamin** Charles **Rathbone** (*1967) (twin)
      = Jun 2001; **Lynn** Elaine **Huggins** (*1967 London)
      daughter of Michael Huggins & Peggy Balch
      a) **Willow** Eve **Rathbone** (*Nov 2004 Brighton)
   4) **Polly** Leonore **Rathbone** (*1967) (twin)
   issue of 3rd (none by others):
   C) Henrietta **Lucy Bland** (*1952 London)

e. **Sir** Alfred **Duff Cooper GCMG, 1st Viscount Norwich** (22
   Feb 1890 London – 1 Jan 1954 at sea off coast of Vigo, Spain)
   cr. Viscount 5 Jul 1952
   = 2 Jun 1919 London; **Lady Diana** Olivia Winifred Mard
   Manners[28] (29 Aug 1892 Uckfield, Sussex – 16 Jun 1986
   London) daughter of Henry Manners, 8th Duke of Rutland &
   Violet Lindsay
   I) **John Julius Cooper, 2nd Viscount Norwich** (*15 Sep 1929
      London) suc.father as Viscount 1 Jan 1954
      =1 5 Aug 1952 Guildford, Surrey (dv.1985); **Anne** Frances May
      Clifford (*5 Jan 1929) daughter of Hon. Sir Bede Clifford &
      Alice Gundry
      =2 14 Jun 1989 London; **Hon. Mary Makins** (*11 Jul 1935)

---

[28] Lady Diana chose not to be known as Viscountess Norwich and retained the
style Lady Diana Cooper after her husband's elevation to the peerage.

daughter of Roger Makins, 1ˢᵗ Baron Sherfield & Alice Davis; she =1ˢᵗ Hon. Hugo Philipps (later 3ʳᵈ Baron Milford) issue of 1ˢᵗ (none by 2ⁿᵈ):

A) **Hon.** Alice Clare Antonia Opportune (**Artemis**) **Cooper** (*22 Apr 1953 London[29]) she has retained her maiden name
= 1 Feb 1986; **Anthony** James **Beevor** (*1946 London) son of John Beevor
  1) **Eleanor** Allegra **Beevor** (*19 Jan 1990 London)
  2) **Adam** John Cosmo **Beevor** (*10 Feb 1993 London)
B) **Hon. Jason** Charles Duff Bede **Cooper** (*29 Oct 1959 Beirut, Lebanon) heir-apparent to Viscountcy

issue by **Enrica Soma** (May 1929 - Jan 1969) killed in a car crash; wife of John Huston:

C) **Allegra Huston** (*26 Aug 1964 London)
issue by Francisco (**Cisco**) Antonio Miguel Niño de Ortíz Ladrón **de Guevara** (*24 Apr 1952 Las Alamos, New Mexico) son of Francisco Guevara & Emilia Luz Garcia Nuñez:
  1) **Rafael** Patrick Geronimo Niño de Ortíz Ladrón
     de Guervara (*30 Sep 2001 Taos, New Mexico)

issue by **Susan** Mary **Jay** (19 Jun 1918 Rome - 18 Aug 2004 Washington DC) daughter of Peter Jay & Susan Alexander; wife of William Patten, Sr.; =2ⁿᵈ Joseph Alsop:

II) **William** Samuel **Patten Jr.** (*4 Jul 1948 Paris)
=1 Sep 1970 Cambridge, Massachusetts; **Katharine Bacon** (...) daughter of Robert Bacon & Katharine Jay[30]
=2 24 Nov 1999 Lancester, Massachusetts; **Sydney Camp** (*... Worcester, Massachusetts) daughter of ...; =1ˢᵗ ...
Hayes
issue of 1ˢᵗ:

A) William **Samuel Patten** III (*1971 Washington, DC)
  = 1998; ...
  1) **Max Patten** (*29 Mar 1999 Camden)
B) **Elizabeth** Anne **Patten** (*11 Apr 1974 Charlestown, Massachusetts)

---

[29] Artemis Cooper was born at the stroke of midnight between the 22ⁿᵈ and 23ʳᵈ. Her parents opted to register the birth as the 22ⁿᵈ to avoid their daughter having to share her brithday with the Queen.

[30] William and Kate are 2ⁿᵈ cousins, their grandfathers, Peter and Delancy Jay, were brothers.

= Aug 2002 Brooklyn, Maine; **Obediah Ostergard** (...)
    1) **Sophie** Morgan **Patten-Ostergard** (*2004)
    2) **Cyrus Patten-Ostergard** (...)
   C) **Sybil** Alexandra **Patten** (*26 Oct 1978 Camden, Maine)
  5. **Lady Alexina Duff** (1851 – 30 Apr 1882 London)
    = 22 Jul 1870 Severn Stoke, Worcestershire; **Henry** Aubrey
    Coventry (10 Oct 1846 Windsor – 13 May 1909) son of Hon.
    Henry Coventry & Caroline Dundas; =2nd Mary Miles
    no issue
 D. **Lady Alice** Mary Emily **Hay** (7 Jul 1835 – 7 Jun 1881)
   = 16 May 1874; **Charles** Edward Louis Philip Casimir **Stuart**[31]
   (1824 – 24 Dec 1880) son of Charles Allen & Anna Beresford
   no issue
VII. **Lord Adolphus FitzClarence** (18 Feb 1802 Bushy Park – 17 May
  1856 Easingwold, Yorkshire)
VIII. **Lady Augusta FitzClarence** (17 Nov 1803 Bushy Park – 8 Dec
  1865)
=1 5 Jul 1827 Bushy Park; **Hon. John Kennedy-Erskine** (4 Jun 1802
Dun House, Montrose – 6 Mar 1831) son of Archibald Kennedy, 1st
Marquess of Ailsa & Margaret Erskine
=2 24 Aug 1836 Windsor Castle; **Lord John** Frederick **Gordon** (15
Aug 1799 – 29 Sep 1878 Kettins, Forfarshire) son of George Gordon,
9th Marquess of Huntley & Catherine Cope
issue of 1st (none by 2nd):
A. **William** Henry **Kennedy-Erskine** (1 Jul 1828 Dun House – 15 Dec
  1870)
  = 18 Nov 1862; **Catherine Jones** (1840 – 13 Feb 1914) daughter of
  William Jones
  1. **Violet** Augusta Mary Frederica **Kennedy-Erskine** (1 Sep 1863 –
    9 Sep 1946)
    = 27 Oct 1894; **Arthur** Otway **Jacob** (28 Aug 1867 Laoighis,
    Ireland - 1936) son of David Jacob & Sarah Fishbourne
    a. **Arthur** Henry Augustus **Jacob** (1895 – 16 Jul 1916 Calais,
      France) killed in action
  2. **Augustus** John William Henry **Kennedy-Erskine** (12 Apr 1866 –
    2 Feb 1908)

---

[31] Both he and his father called themselves Count of Albany, based on a
fantastical claim they were legitimately descended from King James II in the male
line. Charles' birth was registered with the name Stuart but his father was legally
names Allen. The senior Charles pretended to the name Stuart.

= 3 Nov 1896 London; **Alice** Marjorie Cunningham **Foote** (… - 3 Jul 1947)

    a. **Violet** Marjorie Augusta **Kennedy-Erskine** (1897 – 25 Dec 1934 London)

    b. **Millicent** Alison Augusta **Kennedy-Erskine** (1899 - 1980 Montrose, Aberdeen)
    = 17 Jul 1943; **Thomas** Maitland **Lovett** (29 May 1893 - 1946) son of Hubert Lovett & Lina Howard Brookes; =1st Millisainte …; =2nd Morah Brunskill
    no issue

    c. **Augustus** John **Kennedy-Erskine** (14 Nov 1900 - +young) (twin)

    d. **William** Henry **Kennedy-Erskine** (14 Nov 1900 – 21 May 1963) (twin)
    = 1944; Beatrice **Doreen Plews** (1907 - May 1992 London); she =1st … Croall; =2nd Gerard van de Linde
    no issue

  3. **Millicent** Augusta Vivian **Kennedy-Erskine** (12 Aug 1867 – 2 Nov 1883)

B. **Wilhelmina Kennedy-Erskine** (27 Jun 1830 Dun – 9 Oct 1906 Brighton)
= 1855; (her first cousin) **William FitzClarence, 2nd Earl of Munster** (1824 – 1901)
see above

C. Augusta **Millicent** Anne Mary **Kennedy-Erksine** (11 May 1831 Windsor - 11 Feb 1895)
= 17 May 1855 Wemyss Castle, Fife; **James** Hay **Erskine-Wemyss** (29 Aug 1829 Wemyss Castle – 29 Mar 1864) son of James Eskine-Wemyss & Lady Emma Hay[32]

  1. **Dora** Mina **Erskine-Wemyss** (6 Feb 1856 Wemyss Castle – 24 Dec 1894 Chester)
  = 21 Apr 1887 Wemyss Castle; **Lord Henry** George **Grosvenor** (23 Jun 1861 London – 27 Dec 1914) son of Sir Hugh Grosvenor, 1st Duke of Westminster & Lady Constance Leveson-Gower

    a. **Millicent** Constance **Grosvenor** (14 Jan 1889 – 24 Aug 1944)
    =1 15 Nov 1909 London (dv.1919); **William** Molyneux **Clarke** (28 Sep 1869 London - …)
    =2 Aug 1919; **Frank Billinge** (1886 - 28 Dec 1928)

---

[32] Lady Emma was a sister of the 18th Earl of Erroll who married Lady Elizabeth FitzClarence

=3 6 Aug 1932; **John** Finlay **Dew** (1893 - …) son of Rev. Edward Dew

issue by 1st (none by others)

I) a son (* & + 1912)

b. **Lady Dorothy** Alice Margaret Augusta **Grosvenor** (22 Aug 1890 – 11 Jan 1966)

=1 15 Apr 1909 London (dv.1919); **Albert** Edward Harry Mayer Archibald, **Lord Dalmeny** (later **KT, 6th Earl of Rosebery**) (8 Jan 1882 – 30 May 1974) son of Archibald Primrose, 7th Earl of Rosebery & Hannah de Rothschild; suc.as Earl 21 May 1929; KT 1947; =2nd Hon. Eva Bruce

=2 16 Mar 1920 (dv.1927); **Robert** Bingham **Brassey** (18 Nov 1875 – 14 Nov 1946) son of Albert Brassey & Hon. Matilda Bingham; =1st Violet Lowry-Corry; =3rd Constance Britten

=3 26 May 1929 (dv.1938); **Chetwode** Charles Hamilton **Hilton-Green** (1895 - 31 Dec 1963) son of Francis Hilton-Green

=4 7 Feb 1938; **Richard** Herbert **Mack** (1886 in Norfolk - 6 Dec 1967) son of Philip Mack

issue of 1st (none by others):

I) **Archibald** Ronald, **Lord Dalmeny** (1 Aug 1910 – 11 Nov 1931)

II) **Lady Helen** Dorothy **Primrose** (1913 – 16 Oct 1998)

= 26 Jun 1933; **Hon. Hugh** Adeane Vivian **Smith** (25 Apr 1910 – 20 Mar 1978) son of Vivian Smith, 1st Baron Bicester & Lady Sybil McDonnell

A) **George** Harry Vivian **Smith** (*13 Jul 1934)

=1 31 Jan 1962 (dv.1965); **June** Rose Jager **Foster-Towne** (…) daughter of Basil Foster-Towne & Diana Beatrice

=2 16 Feb 1966; **Susan** Mary **Goodfellow** (…) daughter of Frank Goodfellow

issue of 1st:

1) **Charles** James **Smith** (*7 Sep 1963)

issue of 2nd:

2) **Sarah** Helen **Smith** (6 Nov 1968 – 27 Feb 1995)

3) **Amanda** Mary **Smith** (*1 Sep 1972)

B) **Elizabeth** Vivian **Smith** (*30 Mar 1939)

= 26 Apr 1960; Alexander **James Macdonald-Buchanan** (*1931) son of Sir Reginald Macdonald Buchanan & Hon. Catherine Buchanan

1) **Hugh** James **Macdonald-Buchanan** (*10 Sep 1961)

= 2003; **Emma Wakefield** (…) daughter of John Wakefield

a) **Hector** Hugh John **Macdonald-Buchanan** (*2 Sep 2004)
b) **Matilda** Jessica Helen **Macdnald-Buchanan** (*18 May 2006)
2) **James** Iain Harry **Macdonald-Buchanan** (*4 Feb 1963)
= 1996; **Julia Crossley** (*1960) daughter of Anthony Crossley & Jean Russell
a) **Angus** Anthony **Macdonald-Buchanan** (*1997)
b) **Flora** Ione **Macdonald-Buchanan** (*1999)
3) **Nicholas** Mark **Macdonald-Buchanan** (*26 Apr 1967)
= 1996; **Vanessa Bates** (…) daughter of William Bates
a) **Archie** Nicholas **Macdonald-Buchanan** (*1998)
b) **Orlando Macdonald-Buchanan** (*2000)
4) Charles **Alexander Macdonald-Buchanan** (*1970) engaged (announced Oct 2010) to **Poppy** Augusta **Fraser** (*1979) daughter of Hon. Hugh Fraser & Drusilla Montgomerie

c. **William Grosvenor, 3rd Duke of Westminster**, etc.(23 Dec 1894 Chester – 22 Feb 1963) suc.cousin as Duke 19 Jul 1953

2. **Mary** Frances **Erskine-Wemyss** (30 Jun 1857 Edinburgh - 1923 Oakham, Rutland)
= 28 Feb 1882 London; **Cecil** Stratford **Paget** (25 Sep 1856 London – 26 Feb 1936) son of Lord George Paget & Agnes Paget
a. **Agnes** Millicent Augusta Dorothy Canning **Paget** (28 Mar 1883 London – 2 Jan 1935)
b. **Henry** Forbridge **Paget** (17 Aug – 28 Nov 1886 London)
c. **Louis** George **Paget** (26 Feb 1891 London - 13 Sep 1943 New Hampshire, USA)
= 29 Mar 1934 New York City; **Harriett Bullock** (…) daughter of George Bullock & …; =1st … Burton
no issue

3. **Randolph** Gordon **Erskine-Wemyss of Wemyss** (11 Jul 1858 – 17 Jul 1908)
=1 18 Jul 1884 London (dv.1898); **Lady Lilian** Mary **Paulett** (26 Jul 1859 – 11 Nov 1952) daughter of John Paulett, 14th Marquess of Winchester & Hon. Mary Montagu
=2 23 Nov 1898 London; **Lady Eva** Cecilia Margaret **Wellesley** (… - 4 Mar 1948) daughter of William Wellesley, 2nd Earl Cowley & Emily Williams
issue of 1st (none by 2nd):
a. **Mary** Millicent **Erskine-Wemyss** (15 May 1885 London - …)
= 30 Apr 1917; **Ernest** Casell **Long** (…)

no issue
b. **Michael** John **Wemyss of that Ilk** (8 Mar 1888 London - 1982)
recognized as Head of the Wemyss Clan 1910
= 25 Nov 1918; **Lady Victoria** Alexandrina Violet **Cavendish-
Bentinck** (27 Feb 1890 London – 8 May 1994 Wemyss Castle[33])
daughter of William Cavendish-Bentinck, 6th Duke of Portland &
Winifred Dallas-Yorke
I) **David Wemyss of that Ilk** (11 Feb 1920 – 26 Jan 2005
Invermay, Perth) suc. father as Head of the Wemyss Clan 1982
= 21 Jul 1945; **Lady Jean** Christian **Bruce** (*12 Jan 1923)
daughter of Edward Bruce, 14th Earl of Elgin and Kincardine &
Hon. Katherine Cochrane
A) **Michael** James **Wemyss of that Ilk** (*10 Nov 1947) suc.
father as Head of the Wemyss Clan 26 Jan 2005
= 1975; **Charlotte** Mary **Bristowe** (…) daughter of Royle
Bristowe
1) **Hermione** Mary **Wemyss** (*1982)
= 2006; **Thomas** Richard **Bell** (…) son of Peter Bell
2) **Leonora** Anne **Wemyss** (*1986)
= 14 Aug 2010; **Steven L Wendt** (...) son of Henry Wendt
B) **Charles** John **Wemyss** (*26 Jul 1952 Forteviot, Perth)
= 21 Oct 1978 Sternfield, Suffolk; **Fiona** Elizabeth **Penn** (*12
Sep 1956 London) daughter of Sir Eric Penn & Prudence
Stwart-Wilson
1) **Mary** Victoria **Wemyss** (*20 Nov 1981 London)
2) **Elizabeth** Katherine **Wemyss** (*8 Nov 1985 Edinburgh)
3) **James** Michael **Wemyss** (*25 Jun 1987 Edinburgh)
II) **Andrew** Michael John **Wemyss** (*3 Oct 1925)
= 8 Feb 1967; **Janet** Alethea **Scott** (19 May 1932 - 12 Feb 2006
London) daughter of John Scott & Althea Smith
A) **Isabella** Althea **Wemyss** (*22 Feb 1968)
B) **William** John **Wemyss** (*8 Oct 1970)
= 3 May 2002; **Katherine Piper** (*6 Sep 1970) daughter of
David Piper & Elizabeth Michell
1) **Olivia Wemyss** (*6 Aug 2004) (twin)
2) **Jonathan Wemyss** (*6 Aug 2004) (twin)
4. Hugo Erskine-Wemyss (31 May 1861 London – 12 Mar 1933)
5. **Sir Rosslyn** Erskine **Erskine-Wemyss GCB, 1st Baron**

---

[33] Having lived to the age of 104, Lady Victoria Wemyss was the last living godchild of
Queen Victoria.

Wester Wemyss (12 Apr 1864 Wemyss Caslte – 24 May 1933 Cannes) cr. Baron 18 Nov 1919[34]; GCB 1919
= 21 Dec 1903; **Victoria Morier** (… - 22 Apr 1945) daughter of Rt.Hon. Sir Robert Morier & Alice Peel
  a. **Hon. Alice** Elizabeth Millicent **Erskine-Wemyss** (1906 – 31 Dec 1994)
    = 11 Feb 1953; **Francis** Henry **Cunnack** (1899 in Cornwall – 5 Jan 1974)
    no issue
IX. **Rev. Lord Augustus FitzClarence** (1 Mar 1805 Bushy Park – 14 Jun 1854)
= 2 Jan 1845 London; **Sarah** Elizabeth Catherine **Gordon** (1827 – 23 Mar 1901 London) daughter of Lord Henry Gordon & Louisa Payne
  A. **Dorothea FitzClarence** (27 Oct 1845 London – 15 May 1870)
  = 17 Mar 1863; **Thomas** William **Goff** (6 Jul 1829 Oakport, co. Roscommon, Ireland – 3 Jun 1876) son of Thomas Goff & Anne Caulfield
    1. **Ethel** Anne **Goff** (12 Jan 1864 Roscommon, Ireland – 1 Mar 1928 London)
      =1 23 Dec 1885; **Henry** de Courcy **Agnew** (1 Nov 1851 – 6 Mar 1910) son of Sir Andrew Agnew, 8th Baronet & Lady Louisa Noel
      =2 27 Jul 1911 London; **Edmund Charrington** (1861 - May 1943) son of Thomas Charrington
      issue of 1st (none by 2nd):
      a. **Dorothea** Alma **Agnew** (1887 – 27 Feb 1969)
        = 14 May 1907 London; **Harold Swann** (29 Jan 1880 – 7 Nov 1953) son of Sir Charles Swann, 1st Baronet & Elizabeth Duncan
        I) **Helen Swann** (6 Oct – 8 Dec 1911)
        II) **Charles** Brian **Swann** (21 Jul 1913 – 7 Jan 1960)
          =1 9 Sep 1939 (dv.1955); **Vanessa** Fiaschi Dalrymple **Tennant** (23 Aug 1919 - 1995) daughter of Ernest Tennant & Leonora Fiaschi
          =2 8 Aug 1955; **Anne** Corben **Harrison** (…) daughter of Cyril Harrison; =1st John MacKinnon
          issue of 1st (none by 2nd):
          A) Julia **Vanessa Swann** (*30 Aug 1940)
            = 22 Oct 1960 (dv.); **Blyth** Metcalf **Thompson** (…)
            1) **Vanessa** Eirene **Thompson** (*17 Sep 1961)

---

[34] Lord Wester Wemyss' peerage became extinct upon his death.

2) **William** Rowland **Thompson** (*14 Nov 1962)
3) **Moya** Ann **Thompson** (*16 Oct 1965)
4) **Hannah** Yvonne **Thompson** (*5 Jul 1967)
5) **Sonya** Suzanne **Thompson** (*5 Jun 1969)
6) **Denys** Martin Blythe **Thompson** (*1972)
B) **Karin** Clarissa **Swann** (*8 Jun 1942)
= 1977 London; **Michael** M **Grime** (*1941) son of Thomas
Grime & Edith Pegler
issue ?
C) **Virginia** Caroline **Swann** (*31 Oct 1948)
=1 28 Apr 1971 (dv.); **David** Winkfield **Hughes** (…)
=2 …; **Edward** Willis **Fleming** (…)
=3 …; **Michael Cann** (…)
issue of 1st (none by others):
1) **Harriet** Elfreda **Hughes** (*1972)
= Sep 1998 London; **Blake Shorthouse** (…)
a) **Coredelia** Holly **Shorthouse** (*1999)
b) **Violet** Miranda **Shorthouse** (*2001)
2) **Thomas** Percy Winkfield **Hughes** (*1974)
b. Louisa **Hazel Agnew** (… - 15 Apr 1949)
= 30 Oct 1913 London (dv.1926); **Sir Francis** Lynch
Wellington **Stapleton-Cotton, 4th Viscount Combermere**,
Baron Combermere, **9th Baronet** (29 Jun 1887 – 8 Feb 1969)
son of Sir Robert Stapleton-Cotton, 3rd Viscount Combermere,
etc.& Charlotte Fletcher; suc.father as Viscount 20 Feb 1898;
he =2nd Constance Drummond
no issue
2. **Muriel** Helen **Goff** (20 Nov 1866 Dublin – 17 Jan 1951 Windley,
Derbyshire)
3. **Thomas** Clarence Edward **Goff** (28 May 1867 London – 13 Mar
1949)
= 15 Apr 1896 London; **Lady Cecilie Heathcote-Drummond-Willoughby** (24 Jun 1874 – 27 Jul 1960) daughter of Gilbert
Heathcote-Drummond-Willoughby, 1st Earl of Ancaster & Lady
Elizabeth Gordon[35]
a. **Elizabeth** Moyra **Goff** (30 May 1897 - Jan 1990 London)
b. **Thomas** Robert Charles **Goff** (16 Jul 1898 London – 18 Mar
1975)

---

[35] Lady Elizabeth was a first cousin to Sarah Gordon who married Lord Augustus
FitzClarence

B. **Eva FitzClarence** (1 Jan 1847 Mapledurham, Oxfordshire – 2 Mar 1918 London) (twin)

C. **Beatrix FitzClarence** (1 Jan 1847 Mapledurham – 18 Mar 1909 Hastings, Sussex) (twin)

D. **Augustus FitzClarence** (13 Feb 1849 Mapledurham – 16 Oct 1861)

E. **Henry** Edward **FitzClarence** (19 Jan 1853 Mapledurham – 19 Feb 1930 London)

= 11 Jun 1879; **Mary** Isobel Templer **Parsons** (1861 – 17 Jul 1932 London) daughter of John Parsons

  1. **Augustus** Arthur Cornwallis **FitzClarence** (16 Mar 1880 – 28 Jun 1915) killed in action

    = 7 Apr 1910; **Lady Susan Yorke** (7 May 1881 – 21 Aug 1965) daughter of John Yorke, 7th Earl of Hardwicke & Edith Oswald; she =2nd Wyndham Birch

    no issue

  2. **Cynthia** Adela Victoria **FitzClarence** (7 Feb 1887 London – 8 Feb 1970 Windsor)

    = 11 Jun 1908 London; **Roland** George **Orred** (1887 – 20 Jun 1963 Sunninghill, Berkshire) son of John Orred

    a. **Diana** Susan **Orred** (4 May 1909 – 5 Dec 1932)

    b. **Angela Orred** (*21 Mar 1915)

      = 11 Jul 1939 London (dv.1951); Lionel **Thomas** Caswall **Rolt** (11 Feb 1910 Chester - 9 May 1974 Stanley Pontlarge) son of Lionel Rolt; =2nd Sonia South

      no issue

F. **Mary FitzClarence** (Sep 1854 London – 14 Mar 1858 London)

X. **Lady Amelia FitzClarence** (21 Mar 1807 Bushy Park – 2 Jul 1858 Hutton Rudby, N. Yorkshire)

= 27 Dec 1830 Brighton; **Sir Lucius** Bentinck **Cary GCH, 10th Viscount Falkland, Lord Cary, 1st Baron Hunson** (5 Nov 1803 – 12 Mar 1884 Montpellier) son of Charles Cary, 9th Viscount Falkland, etc. & Christiana Anton; suc.father as Viscount 28 Feb 1809; cr. Baron Hunson 15 May 1832; =2nd Elizabeth Gubbins

A. **Lucius** William Charles Augustus Frederick, **Master of Falkland** (24 Nov 1831 London – 6 Aug 1871 Tonbridge, Kent)

  = 11 May 1858 London; **Sarah** Christiana **Keighly** (14 Jun 1832 Madras - 4 Oct 1902 Kingsclere, Hampshire) daughter of Henry Keighly & Emma Huet; =2nd Boyle Vandeleur

  no issue

issue of marriage:

XI. **HRH Princess Charlotte** Augusta Louise **of Clarence**, Princess of
Great Britain and Ireland, Princess of Hanover, Duchess of Brunswick-
Lüneburg (* & + 21 Mar 1819 Hanover, Germany)

XII. **HRH Princess Elizabeth** Georgiana Adelaide **of Clarence**, etc.(10
Dec 1820 London – 4 Mar 1821 London)

Selected Bibliography

Burke's Peerage Ltd. *Burke's Genealogical and Heraldic History of the Landed Gentry*. London: 1886-1972

Burke's Peerage Ltd. *Burke's Peerage and Baronetage*. London: 1840-1999

Cokayne, George. (ed. Vicary Gibbs) *The Complete Peerage, 2nd Edition*. London: 1910

Cooper, Artemis. *A Durable Fire; The Letters of Duff and Diana Cooper 1913-1950*. New York: 1984

Debrett's Peerage Ltd. *Debrett's Peerage and Baronetage*. London: 1899-2003

Dixon, Douglas. *The King's Sailing Master*. London: 1948.

Fox, James. *White Mischief: The Murder of Lord Erroll*. New York: 1982

Hart-Davis, Rupert. *The Arms of Time: A Memoir*. London: 1979

Hart-Davis, Rupert. *The Hart-Davis Lyttleton Letters*. 6 vols. London: 1978-1981

Munster, (Wilhelmina) Countess of. *My Memories*. London: 1904

Norwich, John Julius. *Trying to Please*. Mount Jackson: 2010

Patten, Willia S. *My Three Fathers and the Elegant Deceptions of my Mother, Susan Mary Alsop*. New York: 2008.

Tomalin, Claire. *Mrs. Jordan's Profession, The Actress and the Prince*. New York: 1995

Ziegler, Philip. *King William IV, The First English King in America*. New York: 1971

Ziegler, Philip. *Rupert Hart-Davis, Man of Letters*. London: 2004

INDEX

191

192

193

194

196

198

199

200

201

203

207

208

209

CPSIA information can be obtained at www.ICGtesting.com
Printed in the USA
LVOW041613240412

278951LV00014B/135/P

9 781460 964798